'The opening is a truly stunning account of ship torpedoed during the Second World War. Gordon McInnes survives the attack, and years later his grandson is a teenage lifeguard on a beach in Germany when two children die on his watch. The novel concerns three turning points that change the course of three lives for ever'
Bookseller

'With lively dialogue and descriptive passages, this is an absorbing and emotional tale that spans two generations'   *STAR* magazine

'A thought-provoking literary page-turner'
Sydney Morning Herald

'Stunning . . . It is a wonderful story about fate and the small important details that make us who we are'   *We Love This Book*

Kenneth Macleod was born in Glasgow in 1972. He began working as a newspaper reporter at the age of seventeen then worked in the Scottish media for twelve years, before completing a Masters in Creative Writing at the University of East Anglia. He divides his time between Glasgow and Berlin, where he works as a tour guide. *The Incident* is his first novel.

the
Incident

KENNETH
MACLEOD

PHOENIX

A PHOENIX PAPERBACK

First published in Great Britain in 2012
by Weidenfeld & Nicolson
This paperback edition published in 2013
by Phoenix,
an imprint of Orion Books Ltd,
Orion House, 5 Upper St Martin's Lane,
London WC2H 9EA

An Hachette UK company

1 3 5 7 9 10 8 6 4 2

A CIP catalogue record for this book
is available from the British Library.

ISBN 978-1-7802-2104-5

Typeset by Input Data Services Ltd, Bridgwater, Somerset

Printed and bound in Great Britain by Clays Ltd, St Ives plc

The Orion Publishing Group's policy is to use papers
that are natural, renewable and recyclable products and
made from wood grown in sustainable forests. The logging
and manufacturing processes are expected to conform to
the environmental regulations of the country of origin.

www.orionbooks.co.uk

The Incident

On the north coast of Germany, where the green bright land is caught and held by the heavy waters of the Baltic Sea, there is a narrow strip of sand that runs unbroken for eighty miles. The conditions here are just right for the local sports of sailing and kite flying and windsurfing, for even on the hottest days there is usually enough of a breeze that you can plant your feet on a board, arch back from the sail, and go slapping across the water like a piece of coloured shale thrown by god's own hand.

The beach itself is white and hot to walk on. In most places just ten or twelve strides will take you from the slopping foam to the sloping dunes, tough with grass, which hide the flat fields and woods beyond.

Atop the dune line – at intervals of half a mile or so – dark lifeguard towers rise up on stilts against the sun. The wooden faces of these towers are dry and cracked from seasons of reflected light, and if you climb the metal steps of one and go inside the first thing you'll notice is the smell: a pungent musk of faded sweat, suntan lotion and spilled beer. Coils of rope and sailing equipment clutter against the walls here, and the single long window sill is littered with the shrunken husks of flies and wasps, which spill over onto the slatted floor with its fine carpet of sand.

To English ears, the Germans call a tower like this a 'tomb', and that is exactly what it can feel like if you work in one for the summer, listening to the calls of families on the beach and the flutter of wind in sails, while inside the pine box, as the sun melts the leeward side of the tar roof, the sweat trickles down your neck and the blood flows like mud in your veins.

Certainly there are ghosts in these towers. For me they are the ghosts of two children. And even now – ten years later and seven hundred miles away – I still wake most nights with the muffled

1

echo of their cries in my ears and the weight of their deaths on my conscience.

I don't know, really, how I can lay the ghosts of those children to rest. I only know that if I ever stood alone in my old tower again it would not be long before the memories came rushing in on me – jeering and damning and brutal – chasing me back out onto the top step to leave me clutching at the metal handrail and blinking in the wind.

Tower number six was my tower, and there were wasps in it. Either they'd been blown there or else they'd taken shelter from the breeze. Once inside they settled on every surface, crawling, tasting, pulsing. They were big wasps, long and thin, and when they were still their hairy bodies throbbed while their heads moved from side to side and their gritty feelers probed. I used to watch them – once I counted twelve on the big front window alone – and I discovered that the weakness of a wasp is in its neck. If you take, say, the edge of a pair of binoculars, or the calloused wedge of your hand, and bring it down across the centre of the insect's body, its insides bulge and the pressure bursts out at the neck. A flattened wasp, its head half off, will continue to twitch after it is dead, its body labouring to move and its feelers waving feebly.

No one in the tower was stung while I was there – I was never stung – but sometimes one of the children from the beach, crying or even screaming, would be shepherded up the steps to have a sting needled out and vinegar dabbed on to soothe the venom.

Often we lifeguards would set traps for the wasps. Glasses of a sugary drink or half-empty bottles of beer would be left on the window sill and in the corners. The wasps would hum in the air above these traps, crawl over the outside surface, crouch busily on the rim. They always seemed cautious, although their feelers went wild as they sensed the sugar. I think they could sense there was danger too. Many times they would start down the inside of the glass or bottle only to abort and rise upwards, hovering. But they always went back. They always went back, despite the danger, for the sweet bait. And they always drowned. It must have been in their nature, I think.

My story is coming. We'll get to it soon enough.

But none of it would have happened – none of it – if it hadn't been for my grandfather, and an incident that took place during the war . . .

Part One
War Story

It was my grandfather who taught me to swim. He began teaching me at such a young age, in fact, that I no longer remember the experience of my first lessons. The mechanics of swimming are now so ingrained in me that I sometimes feel like the offspring of one of those 'progressive' mothers whose idea of a 'natural' birth is to expel the baby directly into the lukewarm water of an inflatable birthing pool. Unlike those babies though – who instinctively hold their breath and begin, using reflexes from some forgotten aquatic phase of our evolution, to swim under-water – I have often felt as if I was never subsequently plucked out and towelled dry. At the very least, I can remember no significant period in my life when I wasn't taking part in swimming lessons or, later, training three or four times a week.

In the same way that I have always known how to swim, I have always known the reasons my grandfather had for wanting to teach me. He had very good reasons, and these were so well known in my family that, like swimming itself, I no longer remember when I first acquired the knowledge of them, or first heard the story of how they came about. That particular story of my grandfather's was a hard one to hear, especially if you knew him, but to me, as a child, it was just another fact of family life, like the not-quite-realistic glass eye my other grand-father wore, or the notorious absentmindedness of my Aunt Jean, who once realised in the middle of taking a shower that she was still wearing her socks and shoes. Unlike these and other family idiosyncrasies, however, my grandfather's unusually serious attitude to swimming was never joked about, and it was always accepted that he would teach all of his grandchildren to swim – not just me – in the same way he'd taught his own children, and indeed, generations of other people's children in the classes he ran at the council baths in the town of Helensburgh, near Glasgow, where I grew up.

My grandfather's story was a war story, of course. Just as my mother's father came back from fighting the fascists in Spain with a gaping, empty socket where his left eye had been, my father's father returned from East Africa after the Second World War with the conviction that everyone should be able to swim. Both men, in their different wars, had been wounded, but my paternal grandfather's injury wasn't a physical one. Physically, he emerged from the war unscathed. Mentally, however, he suffered for the rest of his life from a bigger blind spot than my other grandfather, with his glass eye, ever did.

The reason my grandfather, Gordon McInnes, felt that everyone should learn to swim was because at the start of the war he was unable to. At that time he was a qualified merchant seaman, and for a poorly schooled young man from a working-class Glasgow family he considered himself, prior to 1939, fortunate in his job. It was secure and well paid and it showed him people and places he would never otherwise have seen. He already had a wife and two young children, with a third baby (my father) on the way, and marriage being what it was in those days perhaps he also felt relief at being absent from his family responsibilities for the long duration of the voyages – for he was still only in his mid-twenties. So it was for a mixture of reasons, probably, that he thought of himself as very lucky. But it wasn't until some months after war broke out that he began to realise he would *need* to be very lucky – very lucky indeed – if he wanted to come out of that same job at the end of the war alive and more or less in one piece.

For at a time when hazardous jobs were becoming commonplace, my grandfather now found himself, largely by accident, in one that was more hazardous than most. Shortly after the outbreak of hostilities the British government had passed an emergency shipping law, and as a result my grandfather's ship was converted from a cargo vessel to a tanker and pressed into service in the Middle East, where it was employed in transporting back fuel from Britain's colonial oil fields. Makeshift tankers like these, of course, were prime targets for the German navy, whose U-boats, by the end of 1940, were sinking up to one million tonnes of British shipping per month. Thus my grandfather – exempt from conscription because of his occupation, and without ever having volunteered for military service – suddenly found that his civilian job was, statistically, very nearly as dangerous as that of being a fighter pilot during the Battle of Britain.

In defiance of both paper statistics and tangible danger, however, my grandfather's luck, and that of his ship, held for a full two years. During this time his vessel made five return trips to the Persian Gulf. It so happened that my grandfather missed one of these sailings when he was hospitalised with appendicitis, but on the other four voyages he had ample opportunity to see what happened when a ship's luck (and the luck of its crew) finally ran out. For although tankers like my grandfather's always sailed in convoy, and although the convoys were escorted by Royal Navy cruisers, the submariners of the German *Kriegsmarine* proved themselves, time and again, to be formidably good hunters.

As a consequence, British maritime losses along the Middle East routes were even worse, proportionally, than those in the North Atlantic. Yet despite the awful toll extracted by the U-boats, and despite all the sinkings he'd seen, my grandfather never once worried during that time about the possibility of death by drowning. Even when the sinkings were at their worst, he always said, the prospect of such a death never occurred to him. Instead, like many of the men who worked the tankers, he was preoccupied, to the point of distraction at times, by the image of what seemed to him to be a much more likely fate. For after twenty-four months of sailing to and from the Persian Gulf, my grandfather had become convinced that at some point in the near future he was going to be roasted alive.

As fears go, he knew this one to be extremely well-founded. Each fuel tanker, on a fully laden return journey, carried tens of thousands of gallons of refined oil in its hold. This oil was highly flammable, and during the nine weeks or so it took to make the voyage home the threat of fire was omnipresent. No one on those ships was allowed to forget, even for a moment, that a single stray spark could ignite a blaze that would burn with such intensity it would melt steel.

Not that my grandfather, or any of the men he sailed with, was likely to forget such a thing. For they had already seen with their own eyes – on every voyage – exactly how the cargoes of convoy ships could burn like that. They burned like that when the ships were torpedoed. And the sight of such raging, roiling infernos, which could consume a vessel like their own in a matter of ten or fifteen minutes, was not a sight that any of those men would easily forget. Most would remember for the rest of their lives the way the heat, even at a distance of half a mile or more, had singed their hair and burned their skin badly enough to raise blisters. And they would remember too the incredible noise of the flames, which had forced them to shout their oaths to one another as they stood in line at the rails to watch their colleagues die. And when, at the height of such fires, even shouting had become impossible, they would never forget the way the scalding heat, conducted by the metal hull of the burning ship, had made the sea around the sinking vessel boil and bubble and steam, even as the thick, black, greasy smoke gushed upwards to block out the sun.

After seeing such fires four or five or six times, none of the tanker crews had any illusions about what to expect if their ship was hit: some of them, when morale was low, even talked of their plan to jump down into the hottest part of the blaze, in the hope of ending the horror sooner.

So despite all the sinkings my grandfather had seen, and the even more numerous deaths of British merchant seamen, the fact that he was unable to swim was never a source of worry for him. Instead, after four trips to and from the Middle East, the only form of death that concerned my grandfather – that kept him awake through the long, stifling nights in his cramped shared cabin – was the awful prospect of death by immolation. Drowning, had it ever occurred to him, would surely have seemed like a merciful luxury in comparison.

My grandfather's luck never quite deserted him, but the luck of his ship finally ran out a few minutes after 9 p.m. on the evening of 15 May, 1942. The vessel was sixty-two miles off the coast of East Africa and the event, when it came, was no great surprise to any of the twenty-eight sailors on board. All of them, from the captain down to the cook, had been waiting for something to happen since the middle of the previous morning, when it had first become apparent that there was a serious problem with the ship's engine. In the following hours, as the mechanics and engineers struggled to fix what turned out to be a cracked casing around the main propeller drive shaft, the fifteen other ships in the convoy reduced speed to match that of their struggling sister vessel. But when it became clear that the tanker would have to come to a complete halt in order to finish the repairs, there was no question of the rest of the convoy halting along with it. Standing orders required the other ships and their navy escort to continue on towards Suez. And so by mid-afternoon my grandfather and his colleagues found themselves stranded, alone and in dangerous waters, a full three days from the coast of Egypt. They were armed only with a handful of bolt-action rifles and the fast-fading hope of being able to make their repairs quickly enough to catch up with the convoy before it sailed completely out of range.

If my grandfather's ship had been a sailing schooner instead of a tanker she would still have been dead in the water that day, for there was no wind at all. The sea was a bright, blue mirror and the air above the ship's scorching metal foredecks was blurred with heat. It was around the edges of these decks that the men who weren't working in the engine room slowly began to gather, sweating silently and straining their eyes against the harsh white light that glared off the sea. One in every three of them had been issued with a rifle, on the theory that if they could somehow spot a U-boat periscope and shoot out its lens the enemy would be rendered blind and unable to fire. Every time they blinked the sweat from their eyes it must have seemed to those men that they saw the trail of a torpedo rushing towards the ship. There were three false alarms that first day, five on the second.

There was no alarm given before the one attack that proved real, however. The arrival of evening on the second day brought with it some relief from the heat, and this, together with the prospect of safety that darkness would bring, had caused the tension on board to ease somewhat. The mood among the men improved further a few minutes before eight o'clock, when word went around that the repairs to the engine were almost complete. The tanker would be underway before midnight, the captain had confirmed, and on hearing this news some of the crew, celebrating prematurely, had set up a table with a makeshift awning and commenced a loud and enthusiastic game of cards. Five sailors remained on official submarine watch, but it may have been that they, like the rest of the off-duty men, were paying more attention to the spectacular sunset that evening than they were to their jobs. Since the tanker was stationary in the water, however, there was no real action that could have been taken even if the alarm had been given.

My grandfather used to say that that sunset was the most beautiful he'd ever seen. Quite possibly his appreciation of it was sharpened by fear, for although he wasn't normally a superstitious man he found himself, in those circumstances, regarding the sky's fiery colours as something of an omen.

But however spectacular the view might have been from the ship that evening, the view through the periscope of the U-boat three-quarters of a mile to starboard must have seemed, to the commander of that vessel, even more beautiful. For the moment he turned his mirrors westwards the German captain would have seen the distinctive profile of my grandfather's tanker silhouetted against the flaming sky, and he would have recognised the outline instantly for what it was: a prime target, disabled and helpless before him. It may even, conceivably, have troubled his conscience to have to attack such a vulnerable vessel, but if that were the case he didn't let his feelings interfere with his duty. He ordered his submarine onto a course that aimed it directly amidships, brought it up to a depth of fifteen feet and gave the order to fire.

Luck is a curious thing. It would be more than a decade before my grandfather found out, almost by accident, the circumstances that combined to save his life that evening. Not until 1955, in a dockside pub in Hamburg, would he finally hear the story of his tanker's destruction from the point of view of one of the U-boat crew that sank it. At the time, as he watched the setting of the sun from his vantage point by the portside rail, he had no idea that an enemy torpedo was streaking towards the far side of his ship, and he couldn't possibly have known that the submarine which had fired it was itself in a bad way, her fuel and power reserves dangerously low and her torpedo supply all but exhausted.

'And it's just as well,' Bernward Dombach would tell my grandfather, somewhat drunkenly, halfway through their third litre of beer in that Hamburg *Stammtisch* eleven years later. 'Because otherwise you wouldn't be here now. And too many good seamen died in that damned war.'

Whereupon the two of them raised their glasses and drank a toast: to their friendship and good fortune, and to the memory of colleagues less lucky than they.

But that came later. In May 1942, my grandfather knew only that he'd been lucky to survive for as long as he had. He didn't know that in the next thirty seconds he and his colleagues would be luckier than most men are in their lives.

Because although the torpedo hit the ship, it failed to detonate.

Faulty wiring, a leaky percussion cap, an act of sabotage by a slave worker in the munitions factory – there was never any way of telling. Not that it mattered to my grandfather. It would be enough for him to know, in later life, that instead of being blown apart in some initial oil-fuelled explosion, or roasted to death in the hellish inferno that would surely have followed, the only immediate effect the torpedo strike had on him was to send a series of vibrations through his hands and arms, transmitted via his grip on the metal rail.

In the wake of the impact there was a period of confusion on both vessels. On the ship itself, it was several minutes before the crew could confirm exactly what had happened and discover that a large amount of oil was leaking from a hole below the starboard waterline. Once this news had reached the bridge, however, it only took the captain a few seconds to review the options before him. He now knew for certain that he was being stalked by an enemy submarine and could therefore expect a follow-up attack at any moment. It wasn't clear as yet whether the damage sustained by his ship would prove serious enough to sink her, but with the engine out of commission he had no way of operating the bilges, much less of taking evasive action. Without power there was nothing, realistically, that could be done for the vessel. The captain was neither a hero nor a fool. He immediately gave the order to launch the lifeboats and abandon ship.

Three quarters of a mile to the east there was a similar period of consternation aboard the U-boat. The German commander, studying the tanker's silhouette through his periscope, didn't know if his strike had been successful or not. He'd been expecting to observe some sort of explosion when the torpedo hit its target. In the past he'd seen similar ships literally crack in two from the awesome force of the combusting cargo. This time, however, the lack of any visible detonation left him with a dilemma. Under normal circumstances he would simply have assumed that the weapon had missed and ordered the launch of a second strike, but as the U-boat's *kapitan* he was very much aware that the circumstances were not normal and that his submarine, after seven gruelling weeks at sea, had only a single torpedo left in its armoury. With several more weeks of sailing ahead of him before he could reach a safe harbour, he was anxious to keep this weapon in reserve if he possibly could.

At the same time as he was wrestling with this concern, the German was also confronted with the problem of what, if anything, had gone wrong with the torpedo that had just been fired. The shot had been an easy one, he knew, and it seemed inconceivable to him that it could have gone wide. U-boat strikes weren't always accurate, but misses were usually due to rough weather or evasive action on the part of the target ship. Yet surface conditions here were perfect, while the tanker itself was stationary in the water and well within range. Besides, the *kapitan* thought, he'd studied the torpedo's wake as it was fired and been quite sure that it had streaked towards the ship on a true heading. So the question remained: why no explosion?

For a brief moment he allowed himself to consider the possibility that the tanker in front of him might be empty. If that were the case, the detonation from the torpedo alone wouldn't have been large enough to observe from that distance. But almost as soon as this theory occurred to him he abandoned it, for even a brief glance through the periscope was enough to show that the British ship was riding low in the water – so low that she had to be heavily loaded. If not with oil, at least with something. Another cargo then? Not fuel, but something else for the war effort. Something non-explosive. Rubber perhaps, or even cloth. In such a circumstance the ship could be sinking by degrees even as he watched.

But then that still wouldn't explain the lack of smoke. For whatever cargo the ship was carrying should certainly be burning, and although he might not be able to see the actual fire he would still expect to see the smoke. Lots of it. And there was no smoke coming from the tanker's silhouette.

So however unlikely it might seem, it looked as though the torpedo must have missed. And there was only one reason the German could think of why a torpedo fired on the correct course on a calm evening might somehow miss a large, stationary ship less than a mile away. It was just conceivable that the depth-setting on the torpedo's guidance mechanism had malfunctioned. Such a thing was rare but had been known to happen. In which case the torpedo could have sunk to a depth where it had passed *underneath* the ship, exploding harmlessly some distance beyond. And if that had happened it was certainly his duty to fire a second torpedo, regardless of whether or not it was his last.

This, after some thought, was the U-boat captain's reluctant conclusion. He spent several minutes discussing the situation with his second-in-command, who agreed that a failure with the depth-control mechanism was the most likely explanation for the lack of any explosion. The possibility that the first torpedo might have struck the ship but failed to detonate didn't occur to either man – and wouldn't have made any difference even if it had.

By the time the German commander grudgingly gave the order to fire his second and final torpedo my grandfather had already taken his place in the lifeboat he'd been assigned to. The tanker had two lifeboats, one on either side of the ship. Both had space for fifteen men each. My grandfather was in the port lifeboat, on the far side of the ship from the submarine. There were fourteen other men with him. The thirteen remaining crew members, including the captain, the chief engineer and the senior radio operator, were all in the starboard lifeboat, which was being lowered into the thick, fuel-slick water on the other side of the ship.

About half the men in my grandfather's boat were already wearing life-vests. Those who weren't, including my grandfather, were issued ones from the boat's store once it was in the water. Four large oars were then produced and slotted into place, and two crew members assigned to each oar. At a word from the bo'sun these men began pulling in tandem, stroking the lifeboat away from the tanker. My grandfather was up near the bow, squeezed between two colleagues. There wasn't enough room for him to put on the bulky life-vest sitting down. The lifeboat was 300 yards away from the tanker and he was just standing up to put on the vest when the second torpedo struck the ship.

To my grandfather and the other men in the boat, the explosion was incredible. The tanker seemed to erupt from within with a searing white light and heave itself momentarily clear of the water, like something alive. An instant later the blast hit the lifeboat with all the force of a tidal wave hitting a sandcastle. My grandfather, standing in the bow, was hurled forty feet through the air, the life-vest torn from his hand. At the same moment as he was slammed backwards he saw, through the darkening tunnel of his vision, the lifeboat rise up stern first and flip over lengthwise, flinging rowers and crew in all directions. Then he hit the water with a force that knocked the breath from his body and left him stunned. He didn't see, thirty feet away, the upturned hull of the wooden boat spontaneously bursting into flames from the intense heat of the blazing ship.

Miraculously, given the size of the detonation, only four men from my grandfather's lifeboat were killed outright. The rest landed in the sea alive, where they at least had a fighting chance. On the far side of the tanker, however, where the captain's boat had been moving clear of the spilled fuel, the handful of men who'd been unlucky enough to survive the initial explosion were parboiled to death within a minute.

My grandfather, of course, knew nothing of this. Partially blinded by the light of the explosion, deafened by the noise of it, and concussed by the shockwave, he was never able to recall the next few minutes with any clarity. Probably this was a good thing, for without his life-jacket he must have been panicking, flailing about as he started to drown. He may even have gone under once or twice. But at some point his groping hand must have knocked against something substantial – something solid, something float-ing – and this, it seems, he grabbed hold of with all the mindless, animal instinct for survival; at first clinging to it, then gathering

16

his strength to haul himself half on top of it – getting it under his arms so that most of his torso was out of the water. But almost as soon as he'd pulled himself up he felt the scorching, unbearable heat of the flames on his skin, forcing him back down behind the floating mass he was clinging to. From there, largely submerged and sheltering his face as much as possible, he began kicking away from the tanker as best he could.

Three quarters of a mile to the east, the U-boat captain was studying the blaze with satisfaction. After a minute or two he stepped back from the viewfinder and ordered the periscope to be retracted. He took a brief moment to collect his thoughts before picking up the microphone that allowed him to address his crew over the intercom. He told them, quietly but sincerely, that they'd done a fine job on a hard voyage and had just capped their efforts with another trophy – a British tanker – and were now returning to base. He added that he was proud of the professionalism and fortitude they'd shown over the last seven weeks, and hoped that they were looking forward to a well-deserved period of shore leave.

His announcement was greeted with cheers throughout the vessel. Down in the engine room, an eighteen-year-old conscript by the name of Bernward Dombach was cheering as loudly as anyone. In that first, flushed moment of triumph, mixed with relief at having come through the voyage unscathed and without shame, the young German could never have guessed that one of the crew from the ship he'd just helped destroy – a man who at that moment was desperately struggling to survive in the water a mile away – would in little more than a decade become one of his greatest friends. And he could never have guessed that more than forty years after that, following almost half a century of friendship, the grandson of that same British sailor would travel to Germany to work for him, for several summers, on the shore of a very different sea.

In such curious ways does our past determine our future, and those who are spared to their later years always find something to marvel at in the course their lives have taken.

As yet ignorant of these events, the young Dombach continued to celebrate with his crewmates as the U-boat carried on its way.

Above on the surface, time passed. In the warm saltwater, in his pain and confusion, my grandfather was no longer aware of its passing, or of darkness falling. The tanker was still blazing so brightly that he couldn't look at it directly, and if he raised his head he could still feel the heat of it scorching his face. But eventually, after minutes or hours, he found that he'd kicked his way to a place where the flames didn't pain him too badly, and when his body realised this it gave up the kicking of its own accord, exhausted.

My grandfather, at this point, was in a bad way. He was still shocked and concussed from the blast, and his grasp of the situation was poor. There was blood running from both of his nostrils and he felt sick to his stomach. He'd sustained third-degree burns on his arms, chest and face. He was having difficulty focusing his vision, and apart from a painful ringing in his ears he'd been rendered temporarily deaf by the noise of the explosion.

It was some minutes before he could fully understand where he was and what had happened. It took him a minute or two more to realise what it was he was holding onto – the floating thing that had saved his life. It was the corpse of one of his colleagues. One of the crew members who'd been wearing a life-vest. That vest was now keeping both of them – one dead, one alive – afloat.

Even if my grandfather had wanted to, he wouldn't have been able to identify the man. The corpse was badly burned and something – some jagged piece of flying metal from the tanker – had sheared off half its head in the explosion. Only the chin, mouth and part of the nose remained. As for the life-vest itself, the intense heat appeared to have fused the fabric to the dead man's skin. The flotation panels were still intact, but the whole thing was firmly glued to the corpse's charred and blistered torso. My grandfather, injured and exhausted as he was, was unable to tear it free. On the other hand, he knew that if he let go of the body he would drown.

In the end he compromised as best he could. After a number of failed attempts, he finally managed to gather enough strength to haul himself back on top of the corpse. He was now lying sideways across it, with his own chest and belly clear of the water. In this position the mass of the body was largely submerged, and my grandfather was more comfortable and able to rest a little. He

18

tried his best to think of the thing beneath him as an object rather than a person, and he avoided looking at the destroyed face. He was thankful then for his injured nose, thick with blood, because it prevented him from smelling the bacon reek of the cooked flesh.

In this way, my grandfather watched his ship burn in the night.

The ship burned for a long time. An unusually long time for a tanker: it was fifty minutes before she finally sank. As the oil was consumed the inferno diminished to something approaching a normal fire, and as it did so my grandfather, still dazed, gradually became aware that his hearing was returning. At first all he could hear was the intense roar of the flames in front of him, but as that lessened and his senses improved he began to distinguish other noises: moans and groans and high, panicked voices emerging from the watery darkness behind him. It is a measure of how shocked he still was that it took some time before he associated these noises as having anything to do with him – as coming from his colleagues. Once this became clear, however, he realised that a lot of the crew were alive in the water nearby. Of the voices he could discern, several were moaning in pain, one was swearing viciously and continuously, and a number of others seemed to be calling back and forth, apparently trying to meet up in the darkness behind him. It sounded as if most of the survivors had managed to get further away from the tanker than he had, although he could see at least one corpse – in addition to the body he was resting on – floating amongst the surface detritus in front of him.

My grandfather made no effort to call out to the other men or make his way towards the sound of their voices. It seemed to him, in his dazed state, pointless. The ship was burning, after all, and without it they were all dead anyway. Sooner or later. So what did it matter? And as it turned out, there was no need for my grandfather to make such an effort. For as the flames engulfing the ship slowly diminished, and the circle of light cast by those flames slowly shrank, the other survivors came to him. One by one, out of the darkness, they kicked and struggled and splashed their way towards the dying fire and the single living person nearest it, seeking the light and the warmth of companionship.

As they arrived, in their dribs and drabs, my grandfather ignored them. He made no reply to their greetings or questions, their oaths or complaints. It was as if, still stunned by the enormity of what had happened, he was physically incapable of responding. He felt numb and sick, and the effort of acknowledging their empty, panicky chatter seemed both pointless and beyond him. So he watched the burning tanker silently while they collected in a loose circle around him, eight or nine men bobbing awkwardly in their life-vests while he floated a little above them on his corpse. And for the next half hour he held his tongue as they talked amongst themselves: irrelevancies mostly, or outright nonsense – for they were to a greater or lesser extent in the same shocked state as my grandfather, who, for his part, barely listened.

As the flames sank lower, however, this strange, disconnected conversation gradually diminished, until eventually only the groans or curses of the injured punctuated the silence. Amongst those men with superficial wounds all eyes were fixed on the tanker, now hardly recognisable as such. Most of the vessel's superstructure had gone, melted or collapsed in on itself, and the 12,000 tonnes of her hull had been reduced to a great, glowing hulk of malformed metal, almost shapeless. The damage was so complete that none of the survivors could understand what strange property might be keeping her afloat, for most ships would have gone to the bottom long before. And so they watched for a time with something like awe until, at last, the final few flames on the warped deck flickered and died away, and the only light now came from the dull, glowing red of the metal hull. And as the more seriously injured in the circle noticed the fading of this light even they quietened, until the only noise carrying over that silent sea was the agonised sobbing of a man somewhere behind them, fifty metres or so away in the outer darkness, too badly hurt or too far gone to swim the distance to his fellows.

And then at last, almost an hour after she was first hit, the ship began to sink. Slowly, slowly, she started to twist and roll in the water, lolling cumbersomely onto her back, and as she did so a great groaning noise came from the wrenching metal of her innards, a desolate sound, almost mammalian, that seemed to those men to echo the growing sense of hopelessness they could feel now rising in their chests. And as the different sections of the red-hot hull touched the water, the noise emitted by the sudden, gigantic, hissing clouds of steam drowned out even the moans of the dying man behind them, and as these clouds billowed up and the ship rolled over and slipped, finally, beneath the water, the light came now from under the surface – a glowing circle of greenish orange steaming light that shrank slowly as the ship sank – and the men, all the men there, watched that shrinking light in horror, because every one of them was with that dead ship as it sank deeper and deeper, ever deeper, and my grandfather and those around him realised properly for the first time, as the glow of the ship faded slowly from sight, just how enormously deep the water beneath them was, two thousand fathoms or more, and in that moment the reality of their situation was clear to all, and the force of that reality left each of them with a physical sensation very much akin to the urge to vomit.

Then the glow went out and they were left in total darkness.

It was some time before anyone spoke. Eventually, though, a hoarse Glaswegian voice broke the silence.

'Hey, Sandy,' the voice said accusingly. 'How many times have we telt ye, son, no tae play wi' matches.'

A few weak chuckles greeted this remark, but Sandy, the nineteen-year-old engineer's apprentice, was having none of it.

'Away tae fuck, Cookie,' the boy replied with spirit. 'We all of us ken that fire got started 'cause ye went and left the stove on once tae often. Mind you,' he continued. 'If it spares us any mair of that dog shite ye used tae serve up as food then Ah for one reckon it'll be a blessin' in disguise.'

And all at once, in the burst of guffaws that followed, the awful tension of the last hour seemed to dissolve in a babble of chatter and relieved hilarity.

'Ah don't know about youse boys,' someone else said. 'But if no one's got a better idea Ah vote we splash oot an' take a taxi back the night.'

'Strewth,' a cockney voice shot back. 'We must be right in the old Tom Tit if that's a jock offerin' to pay for a taxi out the goodness of 'is bleedin' heart!'

'It's no him should be havin' tae pay for it,' someone else interjected. 'Send the bill tae that bastard Churchill. The fat auld fucker owes us that much at least. Mind?'

And suddenly the prime minister's plummy, bulldog growl went echoing out over the water.

'Never ... in the field of human conflict ... have so many ... owed so much ... to so few.'

In the darkness the impression sounded uncannily accurate, and there was another round of laughter.

It was my grandfather who put a stop to the hilarity.

'Does anybody ken ...' he said, raising his voice above the hubbub. 'Does anybody ken if Greenwood got a call out afore we launched the boats?'

The laughter stopped abruptly. Greenwood had been the radio operator.

Nobody spoke for a moment or two, then Cookie's gruff voice came rasping back.

'Wud it make any difference if he hud?'

'Naw,' my grandfather replied. 'Right enough. It wouldn't.'

And there was silence again.

They floated there for hours, mostly not talking. At one point someone asked my grandfather what it was he was lying on.

'Well,' he replied, through gritted teeth. 'It could be McPartland or it could be Williams, but it's sort o' hard tae tell without his fuckin' heid, ken?'

No one asked him any more questions after that.

The sharks arrived about midnight. One of the injured had bled to death some time before and they listened to the thrashing sounds in the dark as his body was torn apart and eaten twenty feet from them. After a while they heard similar disturbances, further away, as the corpses of their other colleagues were devoured one by one. They waited, expecting to be attacked at any moment, but for some reason it never happened, and eventually the noises stopped, as if the fish had lost interest or perhaps just eaten their fill. They never came back.

Everybody wanted a cigarette.

Nobody knew what time it was when the singing started. By then time no longer mattered. It was Sandy, the apprentice, who started the singing off, in a shaky but surprisingly deep and mellow bass.

> Amazing Grace,
> How sweet thou art,
> That saved a wretch like me.

And one by one the others joined in:

> I once was lost,
> But now I'm found,
> Was blind, but now I see.

They did all six verses. And once they'd started singing they didn't want to stop. The sound of the words swelled in the darkness and for a brief time banished their fear. They were helpless, floating in the middle of the Persian Gulf, in thousands of square miles of ocean, with no real hope of rescue. So they sang.

They sang all the hymns they could think of. They sang 'Onward Christian Soldiers' and 'All Things Bright and Beautiful'. They sang 'My Eyes Have Seen the Glory of the Coming of the Lord', and 'Nearer My Saviour to Thee'. They even sang 'Away in a Manger'. And when they ran out of hymns they started on the other songs: 'It's a Long Way to Tipperary'; 'Pack Up Your Troubles in Your Old Kit Bag'; 'I Know A Lassie, A Bonny, Bonny Lassie'. They sang a song that began: 'The first time I saw her she was naked and tied to a tree' and another one entitled 'I Said I'd Be Home By Ten O'Clock, But Hitler Started A War'.

They sang themselves hoarse, everyone except my grandfather, and then they stopped.

The whole time the others were singing my grandfather remained silent, clinging to the corpse he was floating on. Perhaps he was suffering from a delayed reaction to the events of the evening, or perhaps it was some symptom of fever triggered by his wounds, but the longer he lay there, the more convinced he became that he was about to lose his grip on that body and slip off into the water and drown. He was terrified of the prospect: of sinking helplessly, endlessly, into the great abyss below. As long as he remained conscious it wasn't likely to happen, but in the prison of his own mind that night he was beyond logic, and as the hours dragged slowly by he came to feel as if the smallest movement, the slightest breath, would be enough to dislodge him from his awful perch and send him, struggling heavily, down towards a deep, dark, lonely death he'd come to fear more than anything he'd ever known or been able to imagine.

For the whole of that long night, while the others dozed in their life-vests, my grandfather thought only of those 2000 fathoms yawning beneath him, waiting.

As an old man he never talked about the terror of those hours – not because he couldn't bear to remember it (he remembered every day) – but because he didn't have the words to describe it.

Somehow, dawn came. My grandfather was certain it would be the last he'd see. He was surprised, not by how much he wanted to live, but by how much he wished he'd died in the fire. He knew it would have been so much quicker.

There has never been a world war. The 'Second World War' was, in reality, a First World war – a war of the developed industrial nations. Between 1939 and 1945, in the Third World, a significant proportion of the population didn't even know there was a war going on. In those five years, more than 50 million people, half of them Slavs, were killed; and 300 million South American peasants – for example – knew next to nothing about it.

The sailors on the Egyptian dhow that saved my grandfather knew there was a war going on, but it wasn't something that touched their lives in any real way. For the whole of 'The Duration' they'd been plying their trade between Egypt and India in the same manner their forefathers had for 700 years; following the same currents, using the same winds and the same kind of wooden sailing ships. The only difference between the Egyptian trading dhows of the twelfth century and the dhow that saved my grandfather was that *this* dhow had recently been equipped with a petrol engine, to be used whenever the wind died away for extended periods, as it tended to do in those waters at that time of year. Fortunately for my grandfather and his colleagues the Egyptian sailors were unfamiliar with the workings of this engine, and some ill-advised tampering with the fuel-intake regulator caused it, temporarily, to stop functioning; at which point the startled crew heard the faint yelling of my grandfather and his colleagues drifting over the becalmed water. They would never have been rescued otherwise.

My grandfather survived, then, thanks to a double failure of twentieth-century technology. First of all a torpedo, and then a petrol engine. Despite this, or perhaps because of it, he distrusted technology for the rest of his life; even refused, for fifteen years, to learn to drive a car. Instead, the first thing he did when he returned to Britain at the end of the war was to take up a different course of lessons entirely – swimming lessons – and then go on to get the qualifications he needed to make sure that other people learned to swim as well. He was quietly obsessive about it, and in time he became one of the best swimming coaches in the country. He taught me to swim.

And I suppose, indirectly, he taught me what real fear was.

Part Two
Summer Job

I still remember waking up that morning. In fact I've often wondered, looking back on it all, if the first few minutes of that day aren't somehow to blame for everything that happened afterwards. I think perhaps I was more affected by that early episode than I realised, so that hours later, on the beach, I remained off-balance and disoriented (or even just tired), which meant that when the fatal scene presented itself to me, in the dying moments of the afternoon, I was unable to draw the necessary connections, to see clearly enough into the future to recognise tragedy. And I wonder too if – when we had to act, Holger and I – the edge of my will wasn't blunted, dulled maybe by those earlier fears, so that I failed to move decisively and thus wasted the precious seconds we needed in order to pull those children out alive.

For it wasn't exactly normal, the way I woke up that particular morning. It wasn't normal at all. For a start there was nothing gradual about it, no slow gathering of the senses into a single strand of consciousness. Instead, the transition between deepest sleep and full, wide awake cognition was brutal and instant. For the longest time I had been nothing – empty, a void – and then I was jerking upright, eyes staring, the breath trapped ballooning in my chest and my heart pummelling away within. It seemed as though I was suffocating, although mind and logic told me that I wasn't, and along with that realisation came too the knowledge that someday I would die, and I felt then in every nerve and cell and synapse the fact of my own mortality.

I lay as I'd woken, half-propped up on one arm in the tiny caravan, motionless with fright. Gradually, over minutes, the terror and sheer certainty that had overwhelmed me began to lessen. My breathing, after an initial choking pause, started again: at first fast and shallow and then deeper and longer. My heart shrank and

29

slowed. At length, because my body could not sustain them, the panic and fear receded, and after a while I had calmed enough to take note of my surroundings.

The caravan was hot and cramped and stuffy. My body was slick with sweat and the sheets were damp and twisted about me. The zipless sleeping bag that served in place of a duvet had slipped to the floor. I was naked, male, exposed. Twisting my neck slightly, I saw from the small travel clock on the window sill that it was 7.45 a.m. I'd overslept.

The understanding came as a relief, as something to place me in my life. I followed the logic gratefully, like a man caught in a flood pulling himself to shore on a rope that's been thrown to him: I'd overslept because I was supposed to get up at 7.30 a.m.; I was supposed to get up then because that's when breakfast was served; I was supposed to eat breakfast because I had to go to work; I had to go to work because that was the way the world was, and I was in the world.

I was in the world.

I moved to the edge of the bed and planted my feet on the floor. I could feel grains of sand on the linoleum, and this too helped root me in the reality of my existence. I ran a hand through my hair and took several deliberate, deep breaths. I began to feel steadier.

For some time I stayed like that, thinking.

I'd experienced similar episodes previously, earlier in the summer, although they'd never been quite so disturbing. I knew that they passed quickly, as this one was passing. I could never remember any dream or nightmare that might have prefigured them, and I was loath in my own mind to give them the title of panic attacks. My gut feeling, on the whole, was to put the phenomenon down to too much sun and a late-night forgetfulness when it came to opening the caravan's skylight for ventilation. Having to speak German all the time probably didn't help either.

At length a noise from outside roused me from these thoughts. I could hear the slap of flip-flops on concrete, coming nearer, and the low sound of a man humming to himself. The noise stopped by my curtained window and in the next moment the walls shook with the force of a fist hammering on the caravan's door.

30

'Craig!' my boss shouted. '*Du faules Schwein! Schlaffst du denn den ganzen Tag, oder was?*'

I straightened up, sighing. The fist banged once more.

'Craig!'

'Yes, Bernward,' I replied loudly in German. 'I hear you. I'm coming.'

'Ha! About time too, by god!'

The flip-flops receded around the corner and I found myself smiling, cheered by the human contact. I stood up, yawning and scratching myself, then slipped into a pair of neon-yellow shorts and put on my sunglasses. I grabbed my shaving bag and keys and went outside.

I stepped down into bright sunlight. My caravan was in a relatively isolated corner of the summer camp, in an L-shaped nook formed by the rear wall of the generator building. The children that made up the bulk of the camp's guests weren't allowed in this area, and I was grateful for the peace. A light breeze ruffled the leaves of the overhanging trees and I could hear the movements of birds behind me, in the hedge bordering the quiet road. I plucked a beach towel from my washing line and, slinging it over my shoulder, set off for the staff washrooms.

Fifteen minutes later I emerged, smelling of a mixture of shower gel and shaving foam. I was whistling. The fear seemed to have left me completely. I remembered it now as I would remember an experience related to me by someone else. In a quest for something to eat I followed the back path that ran past the laundry building and the camp's handful of private rooms. As I approached the kitchens I could hear the commotion coming from the canteen beyond. It was something I'd never been able to get used to – the sound of four hundred children eating breakfast. Or lunch or dinner, come to that.

Just as I reached the door, Edith appeared with a bucket of slops. She was in her mid-fifties, short and stout and happy, with a face like a smiling bulldog's and dyed-red hair cut like an army sergeant's. In profile, she looked like Mussolini. Her son, Holger, was my colleague on the beach.

'Morning, Edith!' I called.

When she saw me, Edith grimaced in mock horror and made as if to flee.

'Ohhh no! No you don't. You keep away from me, young man! I know your kind. Only after one thing.'

'Edith!' I grinned. 'Edith, my love! But you're the light of my life!'

Edith laughed, wagging a finger at me.

'Look at you,' she scolded. 'You're still drunk, I bet. You've been out half the night with that no-good son of mine, drinking and dancing and chasing young ladies. Well,' she sniffed. 'Don't think you can charm some breakfast out of me. We should put you in one of the tents with the kids. Wouldn't oversleep then, would you?'

'Any chance of a pot of coffee?'

'Ha!' Edith folded her arms and stuck her chin in the air, looking every inch, even in her white working clothes, like a 1930s photograph of *Il Duce*.

'Cheek!' she snorted. 'Bare-faced cheek.' She regarded me for another moment, then gave a long-suffering sigh.

'Oh all right then. But this is the last time, understand?'

She disappeared into the kitchen, returning two minutes later with a large plastic *kanne* of coffee and two *brotchen* filled with salami.

'Thanks, Edith, you're a gem.' I took a bite out of one of the rolls. 'Seen Holger anywhere this morning?'

She shrugged.

'Dead drunk in a ditch, if I know him. He's even worse than you are. But I can't stand here chatting all day. And as for you, you should get yourself to work, or you'll be late for that as well.'

I left Edith to the slops and retraced my steps to the caravan, polishing off the first salami roll on the way. I replaced my shaving kit and put on a white T-shirt and sandals, then fished out a knapsack into which I dropped my flask of coffee and the second roll. I added my beach towel and the book I was reading – a paperback copy of *Moby Dick* – then slung the knapsack over my back and stepped outside, locking the door behind me. Ducking around one side, I hauled out the ramshackle bicycle which – like the caravan and the three square meals a day – came with my summer job. As I mounted the bike I heard a distant, rising hubbub which meant that breakfast was over and the children had been let out. I swore, knowing I was running late, then rolled around the corner and out through the camp's rear gate, picking up speed as I joined the smooth black tarmac of the road that led to the beach.

I chained the bike to one of the wooden posts that fenced off the dunes. From the crest of the path I could see down onto Lenste Strand, a thin, straight ribbon of sand five kilometres long. The dark form of our lifeguard tower rose up from the dune line fifty metres to my left, and behind it, in the distance, I could just make out the stone sea wall of the 'cheap' harbour, where the locals moored their boats. Far to my right, the beach vanished around a curving coastline which hid the town of Gromitz: a tourist resort of designer boutiques, restaurants and luxury hotels, and boasting a marina that bulged with motor cruisers and teak-finished yachts.

It was still early enough for the beach to be empty, although the sand was scuffed with the tracks of late-night drinking parties and dawn dog-walkers. The darkness had left behind a thick line of weed along the shore, and there was a haze in the air above the calm sea which had yet to be burned off by the sun. It was going to be hot.

I closed my eyes and raised my face towards the sky. The offshore breeze was warm and weak against my cheeks, and I wondered how it would develop over the day. With luck it would be just right for the children to practise their windsurfing, but there'd be no point in taking my own rig out, as I well knew. At that time of year, at the height of the season, only the sort of winds raised by a sudden summer rainstorm could get me excited enough to haul down the battered Hi-Fly Racer I'd reserved for myself. And even then the chances were that the water would be crowded with *profis* – university students from Hamburg, mainly – who followed the weather forecasts in convoys of Volkswagens and Dormobiles, the sails of their rigs battened for speed and their boards customised for kicks.

I took off my sandals and stepped onto the beach, digging my toes into the sand. Under the surface it was still cold from the night before. I crossed to the shoreline, covering the distance in ten easy strides, and squinted out over the Baltic Sea.

A negligent swell sighed through the water, leaving the surface unbroken. About eighty metres out, between the dark shadings of the second and third sandbanks, a flock of gulls floated quietly. There were no swans out there, as there were some mornings. Beyond the gulls a line of white buoys, at intervals of twenty-five metres, ran parallel to the beach, marking the outer limit of the bathing area. I turned northwards and made for the tower.

As I approached I saw that everything appeared to be in order. Below the tower, on the sand, four rowing boats lay chained to each other, upturned, presenting their keels to the world. Next to them, in two tall metal frames, a collection of plastic kayaks rested, stacked according to colour. Red then green then yellow. Beyond the kayak stands similar structures held our windsurfing boards, and a final stand at the end contained our four Optis – small, toy-like boats used for teaching the children to sail.

It was always an anxious moment, checking the equipment. Although everything was secure against theft, there was nothing to prevent casual damage. Bernward's attitude was that if the stuff stood up to what the kids put it through, vandals couldn't make much of a difference. But it didn't always work out that way. One morning the previous summer I'd arrived to find jagged holes smashed into the hulls of two of the rowing boats, and a few days later the tower had been sprayed with graffiti: a giant FUCK YOU in spindly green letters. It had taken me an entire afternoon, using turpentine and a wire brush, to scrub the obscenity off.

That morning the tower was unmarked, however, and as far as I could tell there was nothing wrong with the equipment either. I began unlocking the frames, removing the padlocks and standing on tiptoe to slide out the securing rods. I fastened each lock and rod to the top wire of the dune fence so they wouldn't get lost in the sand. When it came to the rowing boats, I found that I couldn't fit the key into the padlock because there was sand in it. I had to lie down on the beach to blow it clean. When I finally hauled the chain away, its links rattled roughly through the wooden loops of the prows. I wrapped it around one of the fence posts and left it there.

34

The tower itself was on a patch of flattened ground on the crest of the dunes. It was squat and dark and square, and stood solidly on thick, round legs about four feet high. The space between these legs was fenced off with wire grilling, forming a cage where we stored the kayak paddles, boat oars, and several large plastic barrels containing wetsuits and buoyancy aids for the kids. We kept most of our heavy tools under there as well – things like shovels and pliers and baling wire – and over the years the remaining space had filled up with toys which had been lost or forgotten by day-trippers. As a result, we now had an impressive collection of buckets and spades, inflatable rings, beach balls and frisbees.

I ignored the cage for the moment and jogged up the metal stairs to the door. The bannisters shook from my movements. There was a trick to opening the door because the jamb had been warped by the sea air. I had to twist the key extra hard in the lock and push my knee against the wood until it gave.

With the shutters still closed, the interior of the tower was dark and cool. I took off my sunglasses and waited a moment until my eyes adjusted to the gloom. It was surprisingly bare and deceptively large inside, with enough room for about eight people to stand in. The only furniture consisted of two large sea chests with padded lids that stood against the back wall, and two white plastic garden chairs. These had been tipped forward on their front legs so that they rested against the single long window sill, which was broad enough to use as a desk. Against the far wall a full-size stretcher lay on its side on the floor, and above it were the two shelves where we kept our first-aid kit, an emergency-waveband walkie-talkie, the small-tools box, the spares box and the binoculars. In the corner to my left was a large broom for sweeping out the tower and, tucked half out of sight behind it, a wooden baseball bat that we liked to keep handy in case of trouble.

I dropped my rucksack and sandals inside the doorway and checked my watch. It was already twenty to nine. I was ten minutes late, yet there was still no sign of Holger or Bernward. I cursed them both, wondering where they'd got to. The beach would probably remain quiet enough for me to manage alone for another hour or two, but I still had to prop open the tower's heavy wooden

35

shutters, and I knew from experience that it was really a two-man job.

In the event I put it off for as long as I could, hoping that Holger would arrive to help. There were plenty of other duties that I could busy myself with instead. First, I checked the battery and reception of the walkie-talkie, making sure that it was working properly by exchanging a few clipped phrases with the coastguard's duty officer. Next I took the broom and swept out the tower, brushing down the steps afterwards for good measure. When I reached the bottom of the steps I ducked underneath the tower and squatted on my haunches to unlock the door of the cage. I swung it open and began sorting through the tangles of plastic and wooden paddles until I found the two that went with our racing kayaks, the ones we used for patrolling the water. I slid these out, leaning them against the back wall of the tower where they could be reached easily. Finally I extracted a bucket and a pair of work gloves, then made my way down to the beach to scour the sand for litter. Ten minutes later I dumped a jumble of crushed beer cans, cigarette packets and sweet wrappers into the metal bins at the end of the dune path.

I returned to the tower, chucking the gloves and bucket back into the cage. At the top of the stairs I paused, turning to look back down the beach towards Gromitz. The sand was still empty of people, but in the distance I could see the familiar orange-and-black shapes of the council's rubbish trucks making their way along the shoreline. It was something they did every morning, scooping up the ragged row of seaweed and dead jellyfish before it began to smell. The breeze carried a faint rumble of the trucks' diesel engines to my ears. I turned my back on the sound and re-entered the tower.

Having to raise the two shutters alone would be heavy and painful work, but it was after 9 a.m. now and there was no longer any avoiding it. I opened the windows with a sigh, swinging them inwards to gain access to the shutter panels. These were hinged at the top and bolted shut at the bottom, which meant that I first had to unscrew the butterfly nuts securing the bolts on the inside, then curl my hand down through the gap and pull the bolts out backwards from the outside, being careful not to let them drop and get lost in the dunes. Each time I drew my hand back in, the rough wood scraped the skin along the inside of my wrists and left tiny splinters in the flesh, and at one point as I worked on the final bolt the breeze caught the shutter and slammed it shut on my fingers. I hopped about the tower, wringing my hand and swearing.

When all the bolts had been removed I went over to the sea chests and hauled out four steel props, each about four feet long. I chose one at random and inserted the top of it through the left-hand bolt hole in the first shutter. Taking a deep breath and bracing myself I pushed the prop forwards, forcing the shutter out and upwards until it stretched horizontally above the window. The strain made my arms shake and my face flush. With the shutter held precariously upright I then had to wedge the bottom of the prop carefully into place against the outside of the window frame, so that the hole through the metal was aligned with a bolt hole through the wooden frame. When I eventually managed this I slid a bolt back through the two holes, spinning a butterfly nut on tight to make sure the prop couldn't be knocked out accidentally. If the shutter came down on my head before I'd braced the other side, my skull would be cracked.

The second prop was tricky in a different way, because the shutter was already open, sagging a little on the side that was still unsupported. Holding the prop in both hands, my belly wedged against the sill, I had to lean out of the window as far as I could and try to push it up into the right-hand bolt hole. It took six or seven attempts before I managed it, and when it was done I had to start the whole process over again with the second shutter.

When I finally finished I was sweating freely and my lower back and arms ached. Spots of blood welled from my right wrist. I sucked at the flesh and bit down, extracting the tiny splinters with my teeth and spitting them out. The whole job, with short rests between each prop, had taken me quarter of an hour, whereas with someone to help me it would have been over in less than two minutes. I was determined to give Holger a big dose of aggro when he eventually showed up, but at least now the tower commanded a view over our hundred-metre stretch of beach and the expanse of water beyond, while the lid-like shutters would counteract the inevitable glare from the sun later in the day.

Glad to have finished the job at last, I fished my towel out of my knapsack and used it to wipe the sweat off my face. Then I took hold of the nearest chair and dragged it out onto the broad top step. As I emerged into the sunlight the sudden revving noise of an engine startled me. Looking up, I saw that the rubbish trucks were much nearer now, barely eighty metres away, and I settled back in the chair, propping my feet up on one of the railings to watch them work.

There were three trucks: one with a big front shovel for scooping up seaweed, one with a great tipping bin into which the seaweed was dumped, and a third vehicle that followed along behind, dragging a giant rake over the sand. Four men in overalls walked beside the trucks, tidying up any litter that had been left on the beach. The group progressed surprisingly quickly, leaving behind them a scraped-clean shoreline and smoothed-over sand. For some reason, perhaps owing to the way I'd woken up that morning, I found myself falling now into a philosophical mood, and as I studied the trucks over the next few minutes I couldn't help reflecting that their daily labour, in attempting to impose a human order on the beach, was ultimately a waste of effort. Watching them at their task, I was reminded first of the story of King Canute and his vain attempt to command the sea; but then gradually another image, a stronger one, began to form in my mind. It was an image of Sisyphus and his rock, and the parallel, now it had occurred to me, was obvious. For even before the trucks had passed a spot – even as the great shovel, full of seaweed, was being lifted from the ground – the very next wave that swept ashore brought with it new strands of dying debris. And where the rake had smoothed the golden sand, gulls swooped and pecked, leaving their mark on the surface as they squawked and squabbled and fought each other for any uncovered scraps. The work of the trucks was work that had no end, or would have been, except that the beach – this beach that was so carefully and conscientiously swept clean each morning – was itself being swept away, I knew. It was vanishing slowly, grain by grain, the currents sifting out the sand and washing it further along the coast in a process noticeable to man only in terms of decades, but noticeable nonetheless.

Within minutes the trucks had arrived on the sand in front of the tower, and two of the overalled workers raised their hands towards me in acknowledgement. I waved back and watched them move forward until they passed out of sight. Gradually the noise of the engines faded away, and I was left listening to the sigh of the sea, the occasional cry of a gull, and the whispering of the breeze in the dune grass. The water sparkled and the newly cleaned beach was still and beautiful. The sun was pleasant on my skin, and its warmth soothed my aches.

In the peace of that moment I think I could have fallen asleep. And if only I had: just let the front legs of the chair drop gently down and allowed myself to drift off. For who knows? Maybe half an hour's doze – perhaps even twenty minutes – would have been enough to refresh me, to dispel the faint mist of foreboding that had remained in my mind since I'd woken up that morning; so that later, when it mattered, my head would have been clear enough, and my senses sharp enough, for me to have known instinctively what needed to be done, and to have done it.

But I didn't go to sleep. Instead I leaned over sideways in the chair and, my tongue protruding slightly from my mouth in lazy effort, stretched out my left arm for my knapsack. I took out the flask of coffee Edith had given me. It was the sort with a lid that doubles as a cup. The coffee was hot and black and steam rose as I poured it. I put the cup on the ground before reaching again into my knapsack and pulling out my copy of *Moby Dick* and the second salami roll. Settling back in my chair, munching at my breakfast and occasionally reaching for a sip of coffee, I opened the book to the point – about three quarters of the way through – where I'd last left off, and began to read.

I'd started *Moby Dick* nearly six weeks before, when I'd first arrived at the camp, and had expected to finish it within a fortnight at the most. But it turned out that I had less spare time than I'd hoped, while much of the reading that I ended up doing had been concerned with improving my German. Then, too, on those occasions when I *had* got around to looking at *Moby Dick* I'd found myself struggling with certain sections. The copy that I'd brought with me was the complete and unabridged version of the novel, and I was beginning to understand why the publishers might originally have felt the need to cut it. Some of the chapters seemed exhaustively detailed, particularly those dealing with the history and mechanics of whaling, the processes by which the whale's body was broken down, and the uses that whale products could be put to – the real nuts and bolts of the job, as it were. Although I thought I understood the reasons behind this – I told myself that the careful and accurate depiction of mundane reality contrasted with, and thus emphasised, the story's allegorical nature, while providing a backdrop against which the author could examine more abstract questions of religion and philosophy – I nonetheless found my attention beginning to wander. It was only the knowledge that Melville was writing with complete authenticity, from his own experiences, that stopped me skipping over the sections in the way that, the previous autumn, I had skipped, in total, about one sixth of *Ulysses*.

Still, despite the slowness with which I was getting through the book, I was nonetheless enjoying it, and indeed I even found myself laughing out loud at the humour in some places. I read now for half an hour or so, and, undisturbed as I was, would probably have continued to read, if I hadn't come across a passage which had a most unsettling effect on me, echoing, as it somehow did, the deep and nameless fear that had possessed me earlier that morning.

The excerpt that struck me so forcefully came towards the end of chapter ninety-three, which was entitled 'The Castaway'. It was only a few paragraphs long, but it had more of an impact on me than the previous four hundred pages put together. It deals with the fate of Pip, the *Pequod*'s black ship-keeper, who is seconded to one of the long boats as a replacement for an injured oarsman, and who jumps overboard from fright while the boat is being dragged by a harpooned whale. He is left alone in the middle of the Pacific Ocean, and goes mad. Melville describes the experience so:

> *Now in calm weather, to swim in the open ocean is as easy to the practised swimmer as to ride in a spring-carriage ashore. But the awful lonesomeness is intolerable. The intense concentration of self in the middle of such heartless immensity, my god! Who can tell it? ... By the merest chance the ship itself rescued him;*

but from that hour the little negro went about the deck an idiot;
such at least they said he was. The sea had jeeringly kept his
finite body up, but drowned the infinite of his soul ... He saw
god's foot upon the treadle of the loom, and spoke it; and therefore
his shipmates called him mad. So man's insanity is heaven's
sense; and wandering from all mortal reason, man comes at
last to that celestial thought, which, to reason, is absurd and
frantic; and weal or woe, feels then uncompromised, indifferent
as his god.

Reading this, the terrible fear and nausea I'd experienced earlier that morning welled up within me once more. For with one sentence Melville had summed up the feeling – the knowledge, rather – that I'd woken with but been unable to define: *The intense concentration of self in the middle of such heartless immensity*. That was precisely how I'd felt in that panic-stricken moment as I'd started upright in bed less than two hours before. Why or how I'd come to feel that way I didn't know, but now, as I read the passage over and over, my heart thumping wildly, the message that I gleaned from it was not so much that I feared the inevitability of my own death, but rather that I was recoiling from the true and indifferent nature of life.

I make this realisation sound logical, perhaps, but if that is the case I don't mean to. For it occurred to me first on a level below conscious thought. The words stirred a physical reaction within me, a start of recognition, and it was only after some moments, ten or fifteen seconds maybe, that I calmed to an extent where I was able to piece together their meaning and begin to understand why they so disturbed me. And it wasn't until several minutes after that, when the adrenaline of recognition had receded still further, that I was able to put away my own feelings and start considering, tentatively and from a more rational standpoint, how it might actually feel to be lost in the middle of the ocean, alone, and – unlike Pip – without any hope of rescue. There was something both compelling and awful about that image, something to do with the way it seemed such a perfect physical representation of my own existential fear.

I mulled this over for some time, brooding on it, but before

I could come to any conclusions I was roused from my thoughts by the sudden loud and rapid barking of a dog. Looking up, I saw that there was indeed an animal on the beach. It was running madly between the dune path and the shoreline, pausing each time to bark at the water before racing back. The barking, although deep and loud, wasn't particularly vicious. Rather, it was an expression of confident, joyous power, and looking closer I saw with a sinking heart that the dog was a young, unmuzzled Pit bull.

The dog's owners weren't far behind. I saw heads bobbing above the high sides of the dune path and a moment later four figures emerged onto the sand. A family. They paused for a moment, seemingly to decide which direction to go in, and I held my breath, hoping they would start walking towards Gromitz. But I knew how, on an otherwise empty beach, the presence of the tower and the brightly coloured boats on the sand could act as a magnet, and I wasn't surprised when they began to make their way in my direction.

As they approached, the dog continued to scamper in front of them, dashing up and down the shoreline. I watched them from my vantage point, and even from a distance of fifty metres or so, even without the binoculars, I knew they were going to be trouble.

It wasn't the children who gave that impression, of course. They were two young boys aged about eight and ten, very similar-looking and with haircuts that made their short, blond hair stand up from their scalps. They had their arms around each other's shoulders as they walked, their heads wedged together, and for one startled instant I thought they were kissing, until I realised that they were merely play-wrestling, trying to trip each other up.

The woman who walked beside them was tall and slim with long, dyed-blonde hair. She wore a pair of tight jeans with a tucked-in T-shirt, and had a full, good-looking figure – so good that I found myself doubting whether she was the children's natural mother. Yet despite her undeniable attractiveness, it was the man who drew my attention, who made me grit my teeth and swear under my breath.

The first thing I noticed about him, incongruously enough, was his swimming trunks. These looked like tight-fitting black boxer shorts and were probably designer-made, for they sported a white belt around the waist in the sort of 1950s retro-style made popular in magazines. As for the man himself, he wasn't particularly tall – his wife, or girlfriend, was slightly taller – but he was strongly built and obviously took pains to keep himself in shape, for his arm and chest muscles were large and well-defined. Yet he didn't have the ugly, unnatural physique of an obsessive body-builder, and he didn't walk with any of the stiff, passive narcissism those pumped-up men invariably display. Instead, I was alarmed to see, there was a glowering, rolling menace to his gait, which projected the unmistakable threat of violence. This impression was so pronounced that, watching him approach – taking in his shaven head, the gold chains around his neck, and his sullen, aggressive features – I couldn't help but think of him in much the same terms as I thought of the Pit bull he owned: an animal trained for intimidation, confident in his power. I might have taken him for a soldier, but the presence of the family, the dog, and the open beer can in his left hand somehow combined to belie that. Instead, I found myself assuming that he was some kind of criminal, and I felt thankful for the nearby presence of the baseball bat, knowing, as I did, that I would almost certainly have to confront him in the next few minutes.

Any hopes I had that the family might pass by and continue along the beach were soon dashed. As they came abreast of the tower the children ran to the kayaks, looking over them eagerly and beginning an argument about which ones to take. The man and woman crossed to the rowing boats and, although they must have seen me as they approached, they began spreading their towels and other belongings over the white hulls without even a glance towards the tower. At one point the man even jumped up on top of the boats, making a pretence of shading his eyes and looking out to sea.

While he was standing there the woman turned towards me and took off her T-shirt. She wore no bra underneath. Holding the T-shirt in one hand, she looked down at herself for a moment before lightly and deliberately brushing at one of her large brown nipples, as if there was sand on it. Then she unzipped her jeans and pulled them down, wriggling slightly, before stepping out of them. Underneath she wore a tight black G-string. She picked up

43

her jeans and turned her back to me, bending over to put the clothes in her bag. Her legs were slightly apart and as she bent over she gave me a clear, unhurried view both of the mound of her sex and of a colourful butterfly tattoo on one perfect buttock. Although she gave no sign that she was aware of me I was quite sure she knew I was watching. There was something – some edge – to this performance that I instinctively resented, but despite myself I could feel the first slow swelling of an erection against my thigh.

I didn't like the man standing on our boats. I wanted to call out to him, to order him down, but I didn't want to give the woman the satisfaction of hearing the hoarse catch of desire in my throat. Before I had a chance to cough it away the man jumped off anyway. With a quick word over his shoulder to the woman he started up the path towards me.

I'd assumed from the moment he and his family began walking up the beach that I was going to get into an argument with him, but despite his intimidating appearance I wasn't unduly worried. I got into similar arguments four or five times a day and had long before, with advice from Bernward and Holger, worked out the best way to handle these *spinners*, as we called them. The speech I used on these occasions was so polished that even my grammar was perfect, despite the fact that I delivered it using the formal *sie*, which I almost never used otherwise. The rule of thumb we had in the tower for people like these – people who ignored or flaunted our rules – was to stay as friendly and helpful as possible, without giving them any leeway whatsoever.

Then I saw the man's knife, and my complacency vanished.

Lots of working-class German men carry small knives. It's usually some kind of penknife, often kept in a sort of small leather pouch threaded onto a belt. This man's knife was small as well, only three or four inches long, and he wore it on the unusual plastic belt of his swimming trunks. But the blade of this knife, judging by its sheath, was triangular, and the handle of it was in the form of a small brass ring. It wasn't the sort of knife that might be used for slicing up a salami, or for opening the battery panel of a bicycle lamp. Instead, I realised with a start that it was a knife that was meant to be slipped over a finger, to project from the outside of a clenched fist. It was a knife made for punching

44

somebody with – in the cheek or the stomach or the throat – and looking at it I felt the cold, coppery taste of anxiety pervade my mouth.

I sat up straighter in my chair, but without taking my feet down from the railing. *Relaxed and friendly*, I told myself. The man breasted the path and I fixed a wide smile on my face. Instead of halting at the bottom of the steps he kept coming, climbing the stairs until he reached the step below mine. He stood there, looming over me, staring at me without saying anything. My smile faltered.

'*Guten Tag,*' I said to him, hearing my voice catch in a sort of nervous glottal stop. 'McInnes.'

He blinked at my accent and the sound of my surname, and the trace of a sneer appeared at the corner of his mouth. It was easy to see what he thought of foreigners. I was glad now that I was wearing my sunglasses, because I could feel that my eyes were round and wide, reflecting my nervousness, and I hated myself for it. I was taller than this man, and I was strong and fit, but I knew in my bones that I'd never stand a chance against him. I'd never be angry enough. The thought of raising the baseball bat against him made me shiver.

He didn't return my greeting or offer his own name.

'What's it cost?' he said gruffly.

'I'm sorry?'

'The canoes there,' he growled. 'How much does it cost to rent them out?'

'Oh! I see. The kayaks. Ah ...' I shifted uneasily in my seat. 'Didn't you see the sign? At the top of the dune path there?' I waved my hand in the direction the family had come from.

The man just looked at me. I knew of course that he *had* seen the sign, because there was no way he could have missed it. It stood at the entrance to the dunes, right next to another sign which showed the silhouette of a poodle overlaid with a red line, with the words *Hunde Verboten!* written underneath. He'd ignored that one as well.

'It's just that if you'd read the sign you'd know that this is a private beach,' I told him. 'And we're a private watersports centre.

I'm afraid this equipment is reserved for the sole use of guests from our summer camp.'

The man continued to stare down at me. Then he turned his head and studied the expanse of empty beach. Then he turned back to me.

'What fucking guests?' he said.

I gave a short laugh.

'Well, as you can see, there aren't any at the moment. But I'm expecting some to turn up soon. About a hundred and fifty of them, in fact.'

'Is that right?'

'Yes,' I said. 'In fact I'm not sure what's keeping them. They should have been here already.'

'Well,' he said. 'If they ever turn up we'll bring the canoes back for them. I want three for an hour. What'll that cost?'

I shrugged apologetically.

'I don't think you understand, sir. It doesn't cost anything to rent the kayaks, but they're only for the use of our guests. Our insurance cover doesn't extend to members of the public, I'm afraid. And besides, you normally have to have a morning's training before you can go out without an instructor.'

This last claim was an outright lie. Apart from the two professional kayaks we used for our patrols, the rest were plastic, unsinkable toys. Even when they were full of water they stayed afloat and upright. And on a day as calm as that day was, a five-year-old could have steered them.

I could see that the man was about to start arguing, so I pressed ahead quickly in an attempt to forestall him. I was going to have to bring up the subject of the dog soon enough.

'You see, sir,' I went on, 'we rent this stretch of beach from Gromitz town council, and we have to observe certain safety procedures or else they'll withdraw our licence and take the beach away from us. Unfortunately one of those rules is that there are no dogs allowed on the beach. None at all. It doesn't matter whether it's a Dachshund or a Corgi, or a Pit bull like the fine-looking one you have there. A real pure-bred, by the looks of it. How old is it, by the way?'

The man didn't answer, but his expression had darkened.

46

'Don't get me wrong,' I went on quickly. 'Members of the public are still welcome on our beach. Very welcome. But I'm afraid that you won't be able to use the kayaks, and the dog really does have to go. I'm sorry. There's a stretch of beach just beyond the harbour where dogs are allowed.'

The man shook his head.

'The dog's fine here,' he said slowly. 'He's not doing any harm. And we won't let him take a shit on your precious fucking beach.'

I gave another small laugh.

'Of course not. I can see you wouldn't. But the thing is, sir, we can't have any dogs on the beach. At all.'

Despite my sunglasses, I found it hard to meet his eye. I glanced away, towards the beach. The two boys were still standing by the kayaks, looking up at the tower expectantly. The dog had stopped running and had begun to dig a hole near the shoreline. Sand flew frantically in all directions as it sought to expend some of its mindless, pent-up vitality.

'Tell me,' the man said. 'Where're you from? What country?'

The change of subject took me by surprise.

'Me? Er, I'm from Great Britain.'

He nodded to himself as though I'd confirmed his suspicions. Then he leaned over me, bringing his face to within three or four inches of mine, and when he spoke his voice was low and vicious.

'Well, *Britischer*, in case you haven't noticed, this fucking country here is Germany. And this fucking land here, right here where we're standing, this land is fucking German land. And the fucking beach down there, that you seem to think you're fucking king of, that's German too. And all the people who live round here? They're Germans. *I'm* a fucking German. And we Germans don't like fucking foreigners coming to our country and taking our jobs, and we sure as fuck don't like them telling us where we can or can't walk our fucking dogs. Understand?'

In the silence that followed I could hear the faint buzz of some insect inside the tower. Eventually I found my voice.

'The rules are set by the council,' I said hoarsely. 'It's not up to us.'

'Fuck the fucking council,' the man said deliberately. 'And fuck you too. The dog's staying. Hear me? He's staying.'

I shrugged. The next words caught in my throat and I had to squeeze them out.

'Don't make me call the police.'

'What?'

I swallowed and tried again.

'I said: Don't make me call the police.'

The man's face flushed in anger and disbelief.

'The police?' he snarled. 'You want to call the fucking police?'

'If you make me,' I said hoarsely. 'I'll have to.'

The man brought his fist up under my nose, shaking it.

'Go ahead and call the police, if that's what you want. Let's see you try it, *Britischer*.'

He drew his fist back a little, and although I didn't believe he was actually going to hit me, I never found out whether he meant to or not, because at that moment a sudden bellow from behind him made us both freeze.

'HEY!'

The man, still staring at me, slowly lowered his arm until his fist hung by his side. Then he straightened up and turned to see who had shouted. I followed his gaze and felt relief flow through me like cool water.

I'd never been so glad to see Holger in all my life.

He was standing on the flat patch of ground beside the tower, about four feet from the steps, giving himself plenty of space. His legs were slightly apart, his feet planted firmly, and he looked ready for anything. His knapsack was on the ground beside him.

'Is there a problem here, Craig?' he asked, and although he didn't shout this time there was a deep and sure confidence in his voice.

I sat up in the chair, running a hand through my hair and puffing out my cheeks.

'Ermmm . . . I was just explaining to this gentleman that he'll have to remove his dog from the beach.'

'That's right,' Holger said, nodding his head but not looking at me. His gaze was fixed on the man's face.

'That's right,' he repeated. 'There's no way we can let a fighting dog just run around our strand. That's the way children get their faces ripped off. And I must ask you to step down from the tower, sir. Members of the public aren't allowed up here unless it's for medical attention. Please return to the beach.'

The man was ignoring me completely now, I realised. He had his back to me.

'Who the fuck are you?' he asked Holger.

'This is my colleague,' I said, but the man didn't even glance over his shoulder.

'That's right,' Holger confirmed. 'I work here.'

In fact, directly translated, what Holger said was '*Ich wache hier*' – I guard here – a phrase which, while it could indeed be applied to us because of our jobs as lifeguards, also carried strong overtones of warning, for the words '*Ich wache hier*' are often seen on the front gates of German houses, next to a picture of an Alsatian or a Dobermann. '*Ich wache hier*' is the German equivalent of 'Beware of the dog'.

The irony wasn't lost on me, but I didn't have much time to think about it, because in the next moment the man bundled down the steps. I saw Holger shifting his stance in readiness.

Without thinking, I got off my seat and went into the tower.

Holger was twenty-nine, nine years older than me, and I'd come to think of him as a sort of elder brother. He was short – like the man, about five feet nine or ten – but whereas the man was lean and muscular, Holger was much bulkier. In the last few years he'd begun to inherit his mother's weight problem and his nickname on the beach now was 'Sausage', because of the way he looked whenever he squeezed into a wetsuit. Yet despite this growing layer of fat he was still extremely strong and very fit, I knew, and he'd spent two years of national service as a *Kampftaucher* – a sort of scuba-diving commando – with the German navy. I had no doubt that Holger could handle himself; but so, obviously, could the man he was confronting. And then there were the added factors of the knife and the Pit bull to consider.

All this went through my mind during the few seconds I was in the tower.

From outside I heard the man say loudly, 'Come on then!', and I suddenly felt sick.

When I came back out onto the steps I had the walkie-talkie in my left hand and the baseball bat in my right. Holger and the man were squaring up to each other. To get their attention, I hit the baseball bat against the metal bannister as hard as I could. The noise of it rang out, reverberating across the dunes.

They both backed off slightly and turned to look up. I pointed at the man and then gestured towards the harbour.

'Right,' I told him, and the strength in my voice surprised me. 'This is the way it is, and this is what's going to happen ... *sir*. This beach is our beach, and we don't want you here. So you and your dog are going to walk over there, towards the harbour, for sixty or seventy metres. *At least* sixty or seventy metres. Once you get there, you can do what you like as far as I'm concerned, because you're no longer our problem. You'll be the council's headache, not ours.'

I paused for a moment to let this sink in, and when I spoke again I tried to put a fierceness into my words that I didn't feel.

'If you come back onto our beach,' I continued, 'I'll call the police. If your dog comes back onto our beach, I'll call the police. If I see you in our water, I'll call the police. And if you set a single foot up *here* again, by this tower, I won't even *bother* with the police. I won't even bother asking questions.' I lifted the baseball bat. 'I'll just use this. Now. Do *you* understand?'

For several seconds after I'd spoken, nobody moved. The man just glared at me. Then he turned his head to look at Holger, and then he looked back at me again.

'Fuck you,' he said at last. 'Fuck you both.'

He spat on the ground. Then, after another threatening look at each of us, he turned and started walking back down the path. His swagger was even more pronounced than before.

I watched him descend, and my gaze went beyond him to the woman. She was looking directly at me, I saw, and the expression on her face was a mixture of hatred and contempt. If I hadn't been wearing my sunglasses I knew I would've looked away.

Holger joined me on the steps. To my astonishment, he had a wide grin on his face.

'Nice one,' he said, clapping me on the shoulder.

It was only when I felt the weight of his hand resting on me that I realised I was trembling a little. My knees felt hollow.

'Did you see that fucking knife he had?' I asked.

'Oh yeah,' Holger said, nodding his head emphatically. 'I certainly did. Our friend there is bad news. Very bad news indeed.'

'He's a fucking scumbag,' I said with feeling. 'What do you think? Should we call the police anyway?'

Holger was silent for a moment. He sucked in his cheeks, considering.

'I don't think so,' he said at last. 'Let's wait and see if he does what you told him. I mean, he's not done anything they could arrest him for, has he? All they could do is fine him over the dog, maybe, and move him on – and that would piss him off even more probably, in which case I wouldn't put it past him to come back at night and burn this tower to the ground.'

He shrugged.

'We're better off leaving it for the moment, I reckon.'

The man had reached the beach now. He was talking angrily to the woman, gesturing violently and looking back over his shoulder at us. I turned and went inside, but continued to watch from the window. They wouldn't be able to see me there, I knew, because I was in shadow. Even inside the tower, I could hear occasional snatches of the man's swearing.

Holger joined me, sitting down on one of the sea chests.

'That was well done, Craig.'

I looked at him askance and he added: 'Seriously.'

'No it wasn't,' I sighed. 'I was terrified the whole time. That guy really scared me.'

'Of course he did,' Holger said. 'And no wonder, man. He's a scary guy. An animal. I was worried too.' He paused, then nodded firmly. 'You did well.'

I wanted to believe him, but my heart was still pounding.

'Ach,' I said. 'If I'd kept my head it wouldn't have gone that far in the first place. And if you hadn't shown up, well ...' I let my voice trail off. I didn't want to think about what might have happened if Holger hadn't shown up.

I looked down at the boats again. The couple had finished gathering up their belongings, and the woman and children had taken the first few steps along the beach. The children had gone very quiet and I felt momentarily sad for them. The man was lingering behind to call to the dog, which seemed reluctant to abandon the hole it had dug. He was shouting its name furiously, taking his anger out on the animal, I realised, and I wondered briefly what he'd do if the dog ever followed its nature and retaliated. Maybe that was why he carried the knife.

I could hear the man's shouts plainly.

'*Kalel! Kalel!* Come here! *Kalel!*'

It was a strange name for a dog, I thought. I didn't think I'd heard it used before, and I was sure it wasn't German. Yet there was something about it that seemed vaguely familiar.

'Holger,' I said. 'Where does that name come from? Kalel? How do I know it?'

Holger thought for a moment, then grinned.

'Isn't that Superman's name?' he said. 'His real one? His Krypton name?'

I thought back to the comics I'd read as a kid – Holger was right.

I shook my head slowly in amazement.

'I don't believe it. He went and named his dog after Superman.'

Holger was shaking his head too, chuckling slightly.

'Oh well,' he said at last, rolling his eyes. 'At least it makes a change from Rambo.'

We looked at each other for a moment, and then we both burst out laughing.

We stopped laughing soon enough. As soon as it became clear that the man wasn't leaving the beach.

He followed his family in the direction of the harbour for a short distance, but after just fifty metres or so they all stopped. I watched through binoculars as they spread out their towels next to the dune fence.

'Fuck,' I said over my shoulder to Holger, once I was sure. 'They're definitely sticking around.'

The binoculars were very powerful. From close range, I saw the man reach into one of the bags and pull out a dog lead. He fastened it to the animal's collar, then looped the lead around one of the fence posts and knotted it. When he was finished he turned around, staring back towards the tower, and for a moment he seemed to look directly into my eyes. I flinched, jerking my head back from the binoculars, before remembering he was probably too far away to see me.

Holger came to the window.

'Let's have a look.'

I handed over the binoculars. He stared through them for some time.

'He's trying to prove a point,' I said. 'Trying to show us that we can't push him around. The guy's an idiot.'

'Well,' Holger said. 'We know *that*.'

'So what do we do?'

He was silent for a while longer, studying the family.

'Nothing,' he said at last.

'Nothing?'

Holger sighed, lowering the binoculars and gesturing with one hand.

'Look, Craig, I know what you're thinking. But it's not worth the hassle, man. It really isn't. I mean, think about it. The guy knows the score now – he knows we mean business. He's gone far enough away so we're able to ignore him, and he's tied up the dog. As long as he doesn't let it run loose again, we won't have a problem.' He raised his eyebrows. 'So maybe we should just leave it at that, eh?'

'You reckon?' I asked doubtfully.

'Yeah,' Holger said. 'I reckon. I don't feel like starting a war this morning, and besides . . .' He grinned, raising the binoculars and refocusing them slightly. 'That woman's got a great pair of tits.'

I snorted, shaking my head.

'It's a shame you didn't see the show she put on earlier, then,' I told him. 'But she's as bad as he is, believe me.'

Holger shrugged. 'With a body like that, who gives a fuck about her personality?'

He went back to looking through the binoculars, but I'd had my fill of voyeurism for one morning. I turned away and went over to the sea chests. I lay down on them with my hands behind my head, staring up at the wooden slats of the ceiling. I took several deep breaths and sighed heavily. I suddenly felt exhausted.

It was my habit to wear my watch on the inside of my wrist.

Now, as I turned my head slightly, my glance fell on it.

Immediately I sat up again, swinging my feet around.

'Hey, Holger!' I said accusingly. 'What time do you call this anyway? It's after ten o'clock! Where the fuck have you *been*? And where's Bernward? Where are the kids, for that matter?'

'Didn't Bernward tell you?' Holger asked in surprise.

'Tell me what?'

'Jesus,' Holger said, shaking his head. 'I was wondering why you left camp so early. So Bernward never told you we've got the day off?'

'The day off? What do you mean, the day off?'

On the beach, at the height of the season, we usually worked seven days a week.

Holger shrugged.

'They've taken the kids to that amusement park near Neustadt,' he said. 'Hansa Land, or whatever it's called. They left straight after breakfast. Won't be back till late tonight.'

'What?' I asked incredulously. 'They took all of them? All four hundred kids?'

Holger nodded.

'Yep. Some kind of discount deal or something. There's a couple of small groups left. Maybe thirty or so. But they've told Bernward they'll be in the camp all day.' He smiled. 'So we've got the day off, if there's something else you want to do.'

'Fuck,' I said, throwing up my hands. 'It's a bit late now, isn't it? And when exactly was all this decided?'

'Yesterday morning.'

'Yesterday morning! And no one told me?'

Holger frowned.

'Well,' he said slowly. 'I just assumed that Bernward was going to.'

'You're kidding, aren't you?' I cried bitterly. 'Not only did he not *tell* me, the old bastard actually came hammering on my door this morning, shouting about how late I was!'

I shook my head in disgust. I couldn't help thinking about everything I'd been through in the last few hours. It had all been a waste of time and effort, I realised now: the terrible fear and panic I'd experienced waking up; my rush to get to work and

54

my anxiety at being late; the painful struggle with the window shutters; the confrontation with the Pit bull owner. It had all been completely pointless. For if I'd known in advance that I had the day off, I'd have stayed out the night before and continued to drink, then slept right through until lunchtime. Instead of sitting in the tower now – shaken by the events of the morning – I could still have been in bed. Oblivious.

I felt a sudden wave of anger and frustration surge over me. I thumped my fist down as hard as I could on the lid of the sea chest.

'Christ,' I swore bitterly. 'I mean, FOR FUCK'S SAKE!'

In the confines of the tower, my shout was magnified several fold.

'Steady on, Craig,' Holger said, and I could hear the concern in his voice. 'Calm down, man. What's got into you this morning anyway?'

I looked at the floor and shook my head without replying.

'I mean,' he went on. 'It's no big deal, is it? So you got up an hour or two earlier than you needed to. Jesus. It's not the end of the world, man.'

I barely heard him. I was overwhelmed by the strength of my feelings. I wanted to punch the walls; to kick, to tear, to destroy. The need was so powerful that if the Pit bull owner had appeared at the door in that moment, I might have hit him. I had to do something, so I bit down sharply on my tongue, welcoming the sudden pain that flooded my mouth. I kept biting until my eyes began to water and I tasted the warm saltiness of blood. Gradually, the urge to violence subsided.

'Ah Christ, Holger,' I said at last, when my feelings were back under control. I held up a hand in apology. 'I know, I know. I'm sorry. It's nothing. Really. I'm just having a bad day, that's all. It's just … it's just …'

Words failed me.

'Man. It's just that there's all this *shit* happening!'

Holger gave a loud snort and raised his eyebrows.

'Well,' he said. 'That's life, isn't it?'

I looked away from him, staring out of the door at the dunes.

'I guess so,' I said at last, quietly. 'I fucking guess so.'

The anger seeped out of me slowly. In its wake, my body and limbs felt strangely weak. It took a conscious effort of will to stand up and cross to the doorway. I leaned heavily against the jamb, looking out at the world. The light breeze brushed my face, reviving me a little, and feeling the coolness of it I suddenly realised that my forehead was beaded with sweat.

I wiped the perspiration away with the back of my hand, continuing to gaze down at the beach. There were more signs of life now. About halfway towards Gromitz a handful of people had appeared on the sand. They'd already laid down blankets and were in the process of setting up a volleyball net. Beyond them I could see other figures dotted about the beach, walking along the shoreline or sitting on towels. The strand would start to fill up quickly now, I knew, and by mid-afternoon it would probably be crowded. As far as I could tell, no one had ventured into the sea yet, but out in deeper water, beyond the buoys, I could see the first of the motor cruisers from the marina making its expensive way in our direction. It was following a course that ran parallel to the beach and would anchor somewhere out beyond our water, I was sure. For a moment I allowed myself to imagine how the owners would let the day trickle quietly away, fishing or drinking or sunbathing – or maybe just sitting in their big air-conditioned cabin watching satellite TV. Whatever they did though, I thought, you couldn't call it sailing. There'd be lots of other boats like it gathering out there in the next few hours.

'You know what your problem is?' Holger said from behind me.

'Go on then,' I said, 'enlighten me.'

'Two things. First, you think too much. And second,' there was the sound of clinking glass. 'You don't drink enough.'

Holger had opened the knapsack next to him on the window sill and had pulled out two bottles of beer. I shook my head tiredly at him and he smiled. He stretched out an arm and hauled the first-aid kit off its shelf. Clicking open the plastic case, he studied the inside of the lid for a moment before he found what he was looking for. With a sudden flourish he plucked out a combined corkscrew and bottle-opener. 'Does Bernward know you keep that there?' I asked him.

'It was Bernward who put it there,' he replied, winking. 'Don't worry, man, it's out of sight.'

He closed the kit and replaced it, then popped open the two beers. The lids came off with a sharp fizz. He put the bottle-opener down and held out a beer to me.

'Here,' he told me. 'Just what the doctor ordered.'

I looked at the squat brown bottle, hesitating.

'Oh come on, for god's sake. The beer's cold enough, even for you.'

'It wasn't the temperature I was thinking about,' I said. 'It's a bit early, isn't it?'

'Give me a break, man. We're not on duty now. We're just like everybody else. We're on holiday!'

Holger's grin was open and happy, and I didn't want to disappoint him. I reached across and took the bottle from his hand.

'Ah well,' I shrugged. 'Why not?'

'That's the spirit.' He picked up his own bottle and we clashed the two together.

'*Prost!*'

'*Prost!*'

We tipped our heads back and drank.

Holger wiped a trace of foam from his mouth with the back of his hand.

'Man oh man,' he said, smacking his lips. 'That tastes good. Cold and good.'

We drank in silence for a while. Holger sat on the window sill, swinging his legs and toying with one of the bottle tops.

'Where did you get to last night, anyway?' he asked at last. 'You disappeared pretty sharpish.'

'It wasn't that early,' I said defensively. 'It was after one. But I was tired. And I had some reading to do.'

Holger laughed.

'Like I said, Craig. You think too much.' He paused for a moment. 'It's just that one minute you were there, and the next minute you were gone. What happened? I thought you were getting on well with that blonde. What's her name again?'

'Katarina?'

'That's the one. Pretty lady.'

I shrugged, taking another swallow of beer.

'Yeah sure. But like I said, I was tired.'

Holger shook his head.

'You know, man, a lot of the time I think I don't understand you. And the rest of the time, I *know* I don't understand you. She really liked you, I reckon.'

I nodded but didn't say anything. I knew he wanted me to ask how things had gone with his girl, but I didn't feel like talking. We finished the beers in silence. I could feel the alcohol mixing with the coffee I'd drunk earlier. It relaxed me and lifted my mood a little. I still felt alert, but my head seemed to float.

Holger put his empty beer to one side and pulled out another two bottles.

'Hey,' I protested, holding up a hand. 'It really is too early.'

'Nonsense!' Holger said. 'It's never too early.'

'But it's not even lunchtime. How's it going to look if we go back to the camp pissed?'

'We're not going back,' Holger said simply. 'No point. The kitchen's closed for the afternoon because the kids are away.'

'You're kidding!' I exclaimed in dismay. 'But what the hell are we supposed to do for something to eat then?'

Holger laughed.

'Don't worry,' he replied. 'My mum's coming to the beach for her afternoon off. She'll bring us some sandwiches.'

'Sandwiches?' I said grudgingly. 'Well . . . Just as long as they're not salami. She gave me that for breakfast.'

Holger rolled his eyes.

'Jesus Christ,' he said, exasperated. 'Look. Never mind that. The question at the moment isn't food. It's drink. So what do you say? Do you want this beer or don't you?'

I considered it. I was certainly tempted, but something made me hold back. I found myself taking a decision that I hoped would lift my mood.

'No thanks,' I told him. 'Maybe later. Right now I think I want to go for a swim. Do some training.'

I stood up, stretching.

'Oh come *on*, man,' Holger moaned. 'The only reason I came

down here on my day off was to drink a few beers with you! You can't run out on me now.'

'No?' I said, smiling. 'Watch me.'

I opened one of the sea chests and rummaged through the mound of wetsuits until I found my Speedo trunks and goggles. As I changed into them Holger continued to protest.

'Honestly, Craig,' he said. 'I don't believe you sometimes. We get our first day off in three weeks and what do you want to do? Go training! I swear to god, I think you're losing your mind.' He shook his head sorrowfully.

'It's not as if you don't train enough the rest of the time,' he went on. 'Christ. Anyone would think you had gills instead of lungs. And didn't anyone tell you this water's safe? What the fuck are you training for, for god's sake?'

He raised his hand with the beer bottle in it and pointed his forefinger at me.

'When was the last time this tower had to carry out a rescue? Eh? Tell me that.'

I shrugged.

'Come on,' he taunted. 'When was it?'

'There was that windsurfer last year,' I reminded him.

Holger snorted.

'I mean an emergency. A real emergency. You know as well as I do ... if that guy could've been bothered to dismantle his sail he could have paddled back in. I mean a proper rescue.'

I shrugged again. 'How would I know?'

'I'll tell you,' Holger said. 'Nineteen seventy-six! That was the last time this tower saw any real action. And even then it was just some old grandpa who had a heart attack while he was playing on the beach with his grandkids.'

'Yeah?' I was intrigued. I hadn't heard the story, but I wondered if Holger was having me on. He'd fooled me before.

'Yeah,' Holger said, nodding. 'So. Maybe you can tell me why it is you need to go training four times a week, when we both know you could pass the fitness test here standing on your head.'

I didn't answer immediately. I looked down, pulling the draw-string of my Speedos tight and knotting it. Then I grinned at him.

'That's an easy one, Sausage,' I said. 'It's so I don't get fat like you.'

Holger eyed me for a moment, then laughed and took a swig of his beer.

'Just for that, pal,' he said, 'I'm going to drink all the booze I brought along for you.' Then he sighed, resigning himself. 'Ah well. How long do you think you'll be?'

I looked at my watch. It was quarter past ten.

'About an hour, probably,' I said. 'Maybe a bit less. Depends how I feel. Want to come with me?'

'No fear. Anyway, someone's got to stay here. You never know. That woman might sunburn her breasts, and someone should be around to rub ointment on for her.'

I laughed.

'Never mind her breasts, you pervert. Do the back of my shoulders instead, will you?'

Despite my tan, I knew that my shoulder blades and the back of my neck would burn if I wasn't careful. Holger rubbed on a thick layer of water-resistant cream. When he'd finished he slapped my back so hard it stung.

'Go on. Piss off then.' He shook his head. 'Honestly, sometimes I think you must be shagging a mermaid, you're that keen to get out there.'

I picked up my goggles and left the tower. Behind me I heard Holger come outside and settle into the chair. As I walked onto the beach I knew that he was watching me, beer in hand, and I had a feeling he was still shaking his head.

The water wasn't as cold as I'd expected initially. In the paddling area before the first sandbank it was almost tepid. I waded out, the sea rising to a level just above my knees and then falling away again. By the time I stood on the first sandbank it barely covered my ankles. I swung my arms, cocking my head to one side and then the other to stretch my neck muscles. I put on my goggles, making sure they were secure, then took a bearing on a buoy, a hundred metres out, that I wanted to aim for first. I started to run, my feet spattering through the shallow water. As it deepened I lifted my knees higher and higher, then just as my momentum was about to falter I threw myself forwards in a shallow dive.

The water out here was colder, and the shock of full immersion drove the breath from my body. I gave several hard dolphin kicks and broke up through the surface, gasping from the chill. My right arm was already arching above me and I drew it down and back, focusing the pull through my shoulders as I started to kick. I felt my body surge forwards, cleaving the water, and I lowered my head, staring blindly at the sea bed, as I surrendered myself to the strong, clean sensation of front crawl.

I knew that my movement would soon warm me, so I tried to forget about the cold and concentrate on the rhythm of my swimming. I passed through one of the waving lines of seagrass that ran parallel to the sandbanks. The dark, slimy tendrils enfolded me, caressing my body, but I was long since used to the sensation and it didn't break the rhythm I was building. As soon as I'd passed through the seagrass the water began to grow shallower again as the second sandbank approached. When one of my hands touched bottom, stirring up a swirling cloud of sand, I lunged to my feet and sprinted the ten metres I needed to cover before it grew deep enough for me to dive again.

The running broke my concentration and made my breathing ragged, so it took me a few moments of swimming to recover my rhythm. This time, though, I knew that it wouldn't be broken again, and I was able to relax into it fully.

The sandbanks were a nuisance when it came to serious swimming, I found, but they were undoubtedly the feature that made this particular stretch of coast so perfect for family holidays. For Holger had been quite right: our water was remarkably safe. Compared to the beaches further west, our section of strand was about as dangerous as a paddling pool. Just fifty miles away, on the coastline that gave onto the North Sea, there were around twenty drowning incidents each year, yet only one or two people died in the Baltic. This difference was largely due to the fact that the Baltic was non-tidal: there was no strong ebb tide to sweep the unsuspecting out to sea. Yet even amongst the Baltic beaches our stretch of coast was the safest of all, and this was precisely because of the unusual formation of the sandbanks. Their existence ensured that everyone – even non-swimmers and children – could bathe safely up to a distance of sixty metres offshore, while full-grown adults could be certain of finding their feet up to ninety metres out, on the final sandbank before the buoys. Consequently, although we continued to practise drills, no one in the tower – or no one that I knew – had ever been exposed to any sort of serious incident, whether a rescue or a fatality. Instead the job of lifeguard focused mainly on instruction, on teaching the children how to kayak and windsurf, while ensuring that they didn't hurt themselves or allow their rigs to drift too far out (for a strong offshore breeze was a real danger to inexperienced windsurfers, if not to swimmers). No one had ever been seriously injured on our beach or in our water, and the first aid that we carried out was generally limited to the treatment of sunburn, minor cuts, and wasp stings.

That was why, as I fought to regain my breath and swimming rhythm after sprinting across the second sandbank, I was glad of its presence rather than irritated. For it was thanks to the sandbanks that the tower hadn't had to deal with a fatality for more than twenty years.

It took me another full minute of front crawl before I reached the line of buoys. On the way, as I passed over the final sandbank – this time with a good two feet of water between my outstretched fingertips and the sand – the temperature dropped noticeably once again. I was leaving behind the sun-warmed shallows and entering the open sea. Out here, where the currents met and mixed, the warmer water was pushed to the surface, and from that point on, as I followed through on every stroke, I could feel my hands and forearms brushing momentarily against a deeper chill.

Visibility was excellent. The water was unusually clear, diffused with a dark, green light, and from behind my goggles I could see about fifteen metres in every direction. Below me the sea bed sloped gently downwards, before levelling off, temporarily, at a depth of ten feet. Stones and rocks were strewn across the bottom, and clumps of weed waved back and forth in the slight swell.

Because of the noise and movement of my swimming there was no sign of any fish, but as usual there were a fair number of jellyfish around. These floated at various depths: strange, translucent aliens trailing wisps of milky tendrils. They were very beautiful, but in less favourable conditions they could be difficult to spot, and it was normal, once or twice in a training session, to collide with one head on. Fortunately their stings were mild, and I usually suffered nothing worse than a slight jerk of surprise at the sudden contact, followed by a fleeting pang of regret, as I continued on my way, at having perhaps caused the creature some harm.

That morning, however, the water was so clear I could see the jellyfish coming and swim around them. I didn't even have to raise my head to get a fix on the buoy I was making for. Moments after I'd crossed the last sandbank I saw its anchor chain, twelve metres in front of me and to my right. I corrected my course slightly and put on a brief burst of speed as I approached.

The buoy was big, about the size of an inflatable beach ball, and made from hard white plastic. Its top half was stained from the weather and crusted with dried seagull droppings. When I came abreast of it I turned southwards, towards Gromitz, and as I did so my left shoulder bumped against the bobbing float and pushed it aside.

I continued swimming for the next thirty minutes, travelling along the ragged line of buoys. It was easy-going. The light current and swell were both with me, bearing me forwards, and I moved quickly. Most of the time I kept my eyes fixed on the sea bed, turning my head to breathe once every six strokes. Twice I had to look up briefly in order to check on the position of the next buoy and confirm that I was holding my line, but generally I was able to navigate from sightings of the anchor chains underwater. No sooner had one chain gone by than the next appeared out of the gloom in front of me.

It was a strange, cold world out there. The sea bed alternated between barren patches of pebbled sand and dark beds of weed. Several times I saw the fronds of these beds writhe and jerk with the thick lashing passing of eels. And always, as I moved above this eerie, silent landscape, I was aware of deeper, blacker, colder regions nearby, just beyond my vision, where the bottom started to shelve again and the real depths began.

Yet paradoxically, in all that water – in that hostile ocean environment – I felt sheltered and safe as I swam. It was a feeling that grew stronger in me the further I travelled from the tower. It was as if I was somehow cut off from the world, cocooned in my own sound and movement. All I could hear was the soft rushing splash of my stroke, the regular rasp of my breath, and the rumbling of bubbles when I exhaled. These noises enveloped me, and together with the rhythmic motion of the swell they had a comforting, hypnotic quality. I could feel the tension of the morning slowly dissipating, expended through the hard, flowing pull of front crawl, and the further I swam the more the effort of it soothed me.

In this way, as I continued southwards, I gave myself up to the athlete's mantra of movement. My body, conditioned by long years of training, gradually displaced my mind, until I was no longer conscious of the dull ache in my arms, the labouring of my lungs, or the heavy pumping of my heart. The more buoys I passed, the more the events of the previous hours shed their relevance, and the anxiety that had been with me when I entered the water now washed quietly away in the waves.

After a while I dreamed, awake.

* * *

As I've already narrated, my grandfather was a man who'd suffered the terrible despair of being lost and shipwrecked in the middle of a foreign sea. It was an experience that scarred his soul, and in the following decades of his long life he never forgot that it was only luck – or a benign and merciful providence – that saved him from drowning in the Persian Gulf in 1942. Indeed, I think it's possible he even felt that some part of him, an important part, *had* died. Yet he survived. For eventually, some hours after sunrise the next morning, he'd been roused from his exhaustion by the frantic cries of his colleagues and, raising his face from the headless corpse beneath him, he saw, with stunned and disbelieving eyes, salvation in the form of an Egyptian dhow less than half a mile away.

I can barely begin to imagine the feelings that must have burst within him then. Surely, though, relief and gratitude would have been foremost amongst them. And yet in the sixty years that followed, no one in my family ever heard my grandfather express such gratitude, nor utter a single kind word in regard to the

Egyptian sailors who'd saved him. Quite the opposite.

For having been delivered from one terrible ordeal at sea, he and his colleagues were soon betrayed – for what my grandfather regarded as the most venal of reasons – into a second and very different ordeal on land.

Before continuing, I should perhaps note that at the time my grandfather was shipwrecked, in 1942, the situation in North Africa between the warring colonial powers was remarkably fluid. Neither side had yet managed to build up a decisive advantage, and with armoured vehicles roaming at long range in large numbers across the desert, the frontline between territories was prone, at times, to change dramatically. During an offensive it was not unusual for zones of control to shift, in some places, by several hundred miles in the course of a single week.

I think it's possible then that my grandfather and his colleagues weren't deliberately betrayed by the Egyptians who rescued them. Perhaps, having been absent from their own country for several months, the dhow's crew honestly believed they were about to enter a harbour still controlled by British forces. Who knows? What is certain is that two nights after the shipwrecked survivors were hauled from the water – and in turn had helped the Egyptians to fix their broken engine – the wooden vessel puttered out of the darkness into a small fishing harbour on the south-west tip of the Sinai Peninsula. And quarter of an hour after that, while the dhow's rescued human cargo were still sleeping, entirely unawares, in the hold, the Egyptian captain sold them to the commander of the German garrison there for the price of a handshake, twelve ampoules of penicillin and a fistful of local currency to share out amongst his crew.

My grandfather and his shipmates, still exhausted from their ordeal at sea (and half-drugged, too, by the blanket of heat trapped below decks and the overwhelming scent of spices emanating from the hessian sacks they slept upon) were shocked into bleary consciousness by the hard kicks and shouts of a large Bavarian sergeant wielding a Mauser.

Blinded and confused by the harsh light of electric torches, and the even harsher phrases being shouted at them by German soldiers, the British were led, stumbling, on deck at rifle point with their hands in the air. From there they were herded across a gangplank onto the harbourside, before being lined up with their backs to the water. They stood with their heads down and hands up, squinting against the lights of the two German army trucks which had now arrived and parked opposite them.

Because of the stifling heat in the dhow's hold, my grandfather and most of his colleagues had stripped to their underpants before lying down to sleep. So they were kept there dressed only in those, looking defeated and skinny and fearful – their torsos and legs milky white and their forearms and faces mahogany brown – while the German soldiers lounged around in shirtsleeves or stood in groups, smoking and laughing at their prisoners' expense.

My grandfather and his colleagues had to stand there for a long time.

Eventually, after ninety minutes or so, a dusty open-topped staff car drew to a halt on the packed earth next to the pier, and a major dressed in the uniform of the *Abwehr* – German military intelligence – opened the door and climbed down from the back seat. He looked over the prisoners briefly and conferred with the garrison commander. In stilted English he asked the British seamen how they came to be there and when he received no answer he tilted back his head to study the stars for some moments and then gave a loud and heartfelt sigh. He nodded at the garrison commander and one by one the men were grabbed and brought forward, then taken around to the rear of the trucks and bundled inside.

Five days later my grandfather began thirty long months of prison-camp internment.

Although it certainly didn't feel like it to my grandfather and his colleagues at the time, in the course of being captured they turned out to be lucky on several counts. Firstly that they fell into the hands of the *Abwehr* rather than the *Gestapo*, who might well have had them all shot as spies. Secondly, that the *Abwehr* interrogators accepted, fairly quickly, that they were indeed the merchant sailors they claimed to be, and were therefore entitled to be treated as enemy civilians rather than enlisted British navy personnel. Thirdly, that the German officer in charge of their case decided, for god-knows-what reason, that this particular batch of civilian prisoners should be kept in Africa, and sent to an internment camp in the German colony of Namibia. Incredibly, the *Wehrmacht* even flew them there by transport plane.

It was a decision that seemed to make no logical sense whatsoever.

The vast territories of Africa were largely untouched by World War Two. Most white colonials of European descent who wanted to see real fighting had to volunteer for it and then travel overseas. But of course there were some battles in the very north, in Algeria and Tunisia and Egypt, and the lives of some European settlers living elsewhere on the continent were badly disrupted as a consequence of the conflict.

In the German-run colony of Namibia, most British nationals had already left for friendlier territory before the war broke out. The remainder were immediately rounded up and interned by the authorities the moment hostilities were announced in 1939.

Fortunately for my grandfather, the camp that he and his colleagues arrived at in 1942 had been built for prisoners who were all British males or white male colonials, and therefore racially acceptable in the eyes of the third-rate *Wehrmacht* soldiers and German colonial teenagers who guarded them. Indeed, according to my grandfather many of the British prisoners, when discussing the subject of the native populations, sounded every bit as racist as their guards.

Millions had already died in German-run camps in Europe, but at my grandfather's KZ in Namibia the inmates remained happily ignorant of such horrors. The Geneva Convention was adhered to and the prisoners found their treatment acceptable – at times even lax. The camp's food was bland, but they received enough of it to keep them healthy and avoid hunger. Work tasks were voluntary and sports encouraged, and the prisoners had plenty of freedom to arrange entertainment within the camp, provided they didn't cause their captors any trouble and lined up twice a day to be counted.

Given these relatively good conditions, and the sheer size of Namibia itself, the few escape attempts that took place seemed to be prompted more by boredom than any serious hope of getting across 1200 miles of plain and bush to the nearest heavily guarded border.

Internment was certainly a hardship, but for the 800 or so men locked behind the wire fences there was only one real *danger* – the mosquito season that followed hard on the heels of the yearly rains.

My grandfather spent two-and-a-half years in that PoW camp in Namibia. He later said that only three things of note occurred to him while he was there:

Unlike two of his less fortunate colleagues he managed to survive a raging bout of malaria.

He learned, through daily fraternisation with the guards, to speak German fluently.

And while he never thought much of the three or four dyed-in-the-wool Nazis among the camp's personnel – *dummkopfs*, he always called them with contempt – he marched out at the end of the war with a genuine liking for most of the other Germans he'd come into contact with there.

Two-and-a-half years passed very slowly, but eventually the war was declared over and he walked through the camp's barbed-wire gates a free man.

At the repatriation centre he was offered a sea passage back to Britain leaving within six weeks. But his dreams were still haunted by the flaming fate of his oil tanker and he refused point blank to put to sea again, while the British government, for its part, made it clear he wasn't going to be offered the luxury of flying home.

From the little he'd seen of Africa in his few days of freedom, my grandfather had decided that he liked it, and the fact of his having a wife and young family back in Scotland proved, for whatever reason, insufficient to offset the lure of the great continent before him. So instead of trying to return to Britain, he collected some of his back pay and embarked on a six-month period of travel, revelling in Africa's vast horizons after his long imprisonment.

At last he arrived in Kenya, where – almost by accident – he found employment as the pilot of a river ferry. He rented a large wooden house with a big veranda and two native servants and finally sent for my grandmother and their three children, one of whom (my father) he'd not yet laid eyes on.

The little family stayed there together, fairly happily, for four years. Then they held on – uncertainly – for another three, as the country's Mau-Mau rebellion descended into savagery on both sides.

My grandfather was making plans to get his family out in the spring of 1953, as the British and colonial forces finished building internment camps and began to round up hundreds of thousands of native men, women and children. He'd already told my grandmother to pack when rumours started to percolate amongst the white population: rumours of torture and disease and killing in those camps – of genital mutilation of male prisoners, and of petrol being poured over victims and then set alight.

I think, given my grandfather's fear of immolation from his tanker days, that this last rumour may have been the final straw. Certainly he never seemed to doubt that it was happening. And when, two decades later, my own father asked him why he'd been so sure the rumours were true, my grandfather clenched his fists so hard his knuckles turned white and replied:

'Because I drank with some of the cunts that were doing it, and not only were they fuckin' boasting aboot it, their uniforms still stank o' the fuckin' petrol.'

And so, choking on the bloody dust rising up from the collapse of the British Empire, my grandfather and his little family left the searing sun of Kenya and returned to the grey slate skies and blustery rain which so often characterise the West Coast of Scotland in June.

Of course my grandfather needed a job. He hadn't been home in twelve years, but he was stocky and strong and muscular, he knew ships and boats, and he could speak German fluently.

He still suffered nightmares, though, and because of that he knew he would never go back on the open sea. Nor was there much demand in Scotland for river boat pilots.

On his fifth morning back, he sat down in the cramped little kitchen with a piece of paper to write down all the possibilities he could think of. Two days later he still only had:

Tug-boat pilot.

Manual labourer.

The town they'd come back to, Helensburgh, had a smallish harbour for fishing boats and pleasure yachts, but it was no commercial port, and anyway he would have needed years of training and a certificate to become a tug-boat pilot. He couldn't think what his German might be useful for.

A few nights later he was in one of the town's pubs, and as well as his usual beers he was laying into the whisky. He was with a group of people – acquaintances – he knew from his younger days, and as the drinks went down he started to hold forth, loudly, regarding the problem of his job prospects, and then, sometime later, on what he'd heard was taking place in the camps in Kenya.

'Tae fuck wi' them!' one man interrupted vehemently. 'Thir only blackies anyway. Smelly fuckin' animals, the lot o' them. Monkeys jist, but mair vicious.'

My grandfather was rising from his stool, fists clenched, when he felt a restraining hand on his shoulder. He looked up to see a stranger, a broad-faced man in his late forties or early fifties, standing over him.

'Yir name's McInnes, right?' the other said now. 'Ah heard ye sayin' ye were lookin' fir a job. Well ma name's McPherson. Ah knew yir feyther thirty years ago, an it jist so huppens Ah work fir some people that could mebbey use a man wi yir skills.'

My grandfather's utter surprise robbed him of his anger. After a moment of confusion, at the older man's suggestion he picked up his drinks and together they crossed to a little table in a corner nook.

Twenty minutes later my grandfather shook the man's hand and stood up, smiling. He'd just landed himself an unusual but lucrative job.

The Berlin Wall wasn't built until August 1961. Prior to that, East Germans could travel to the West whenever they felt like it. All they had to do was journey to East Berlin and then walk across the streets into West Berlin. And from West Berlin they could travel out to Western Europe.

Between the end of the war in 1945 and the Wall going up in 1961, more than two and a half million East Germans moved to Western Europe, permanently.

Thousands of them were seamen.

My grandfather got lucky that evening, and it was a stroke of luck that would give him financial security for the rest of his life. To take advantage of it, though, he had to abandon certain working-class principles of solidarity which he'd grown up with and espoused all his adult life. He appears to have shed them without a second thought.

In the mid-1950s the Western world was experiencing a trading boom in consumer goods. Merchant sailors were much in demand – not to mention unionised – and as a result were becoming increasingly demanding in their turn. To the annoyance of shipping line owners and shareholders these merchant sailors wanted more pay, more time on shore between voyages and bigger pension contributions.

In that same period there was a steady stream of experienced seamen coming out of East Germany, all of them used to working for about a tenth of the pay of their western counterparts. These new arrivals were keen to embrace the opportunities of capitalism, but as yet had no job and often no place to live. Most were willing – even desperate – to sign a contract that would keep them sailing, perhaps constantly, for two, three, or sometimes even five years.

My grandfather could speak German almost fluently. He knew all about ships and the skills that were needed to keep them running. And after two-and-a-half years in a prisoner of war camp, he could tell the difference between men who were reliable and those who weren't.

In November 1954 he moved the family to Hamburg and became a black-leg recruiter for a number of merchant shipping lines.

Most of the time he met prospective applicants in pubs near the Hamburg docks, an arrangement which suited him fine. He received a handsome monthly retainer plus a bonus for each man he signed; the bonus increasing in line with the length of contract the new employee agreed to. My grandfather quickly proved himself to be both persuasive and an excellent judge of character, and he came to be regarded by the shipping lines as a valuable asset in his own right.

Quite early in his stay in Hamburg it occurred to my grandfather to try to research the circumstances around the sinking of his tanker ten years earlier. He visited the naval archives in the city, only to be told that the U-boat records were kept in Kiel, where the old Submarine Academy still stood.

Kiel was just an hour-and-a-half away by train and he made the journey two weeks later.

> *May 15th 1942. Persian Gulf. Target sunk: British Oil Tanker*
> *That was what my grandfather wrote on the information form he handed to the archivist – the date his tanker went down, the region in which it sank, and the type of ship it was. The archivist took the piece of paper away and brought the answer back in less than five minutes:*
> *U-Boat 577, departed port St Le Tourve, South of France, 2nd April 1942. Captain Arne Fromm in command of 49 crewmen. Five enemy vessels destroyed during voyage. Returned safely to port July 28th.*

My grandfather rubbed at the stubble on his chin, feeling his heartbeat quicken with a mixture of emotions. He asked to see the entire record file for U-boat number 577. The archivist grimaced but retreated again.

This time almost fifteen minutes passed before the man finally returned holding a large black ring folder. A white sticker on the front told my grandfather everything he needed to know:

Summary Record of Service for U-Boat #577.

Type IX long-range reconnaissance and attack submarine. Commissioned 8th January 1939. Sea trials completed and vessel launched 15th March 1940.

Vessel attacked and sunk on active duty in the North Atlantic on 10th March 1944. Approximate location 54 degrees 56 mins North, 35 degrees 18 mins West. Sinking confirmed.
Captain Arne Fromm and all 49 hands on board lost.

So that was that. The German submarine and crew that had destroyed his ship had in turn been destroyed a little less than two years later.

His nightmares had begun to subside by then. He still dreamed about the burning tanker and the charred corpse that had kept him afloat, but no more than once a week; perhaps twice, in a bad week.

And now, on those nights when he woke at 3 a.m., gasping with panic, to lie there rigid next to his sleeping wife – waiting as his fear subsided and his sweat cooled and the pounding of his heart gradually slowed to normal – he had a different image to contrast with that of his own memories:

The image of ice-cold jets of water bursting, catastrophically, into the cramped metal confines of a submarine; blasting through bulkheads, smashing helpless men against machinery and door-frames; the entire vessel filling with water in just one or two fatal minutes, twisting and sinking as it does so – sinking end first into the endless empty depths below, while the few poor wretches still alive in the pitch-black freezing air pockets gasp and sob with the agonising cold and the blind, helpless wait for death . . .

Picturing the vessel as it falls, slowly, down and down and down into the unimaginable, vast blackness.

Until eventually it implodes, crushed like a tin can by the pressure.

No survivors.

It was seven months since his visit to the archives in Kiel.

The East German sitting across from him in the pub booth was a young man in his late twenties, pale-faced and dark-haired and tired-looking.

Outside in the late afternoon twilight it was snowing, although it wasn't quite cold enough yet for the snow to lie. Inside the pub it was warm – almost uncomfortably so – and bright with yellow light from the bar. Christmas music was playing on the radio although the day itself was still several weeks away.

My grandfather had been sitting in the pub for three hours, during which time he'd interviewed five prospective employees and hired two of them. He'd taken off his woollen jumper and had one arm up resting across the back of the booth, his face slightly flushed from a combination of beer and heat.

The young man opposite him was his last interview of the day and had only just arrived. The snow was still melting on his navy-blue donkey jacket as he unbuttoned it, and when he pulled off his knitted black wool hat his hair stood up in clumps.

His name was Bernward Dombach, and he said he'd only left East Germany two months ago. He got my grandfather's telephone number from someone he met in a bar in West Berlin – a fellow seaman – and he'd travelled up to Hamburg the day before, hitchhiking, as soon as his Western papers were issued to him. He'd worked at sea since leaving school during the war. Firstly in the U-boat service and then, after things settled down in the late 1940s, on East German ships doing the Baltic run to St Petersburg. He'd had two years more of the Baltic than he wanted and no sign of promotion because he'd got on the wrong side of the first mate, who happened to be the boat's Stasi informer and number one arsehole. So he'd left East Germany and that life behind him for good in order to travel the Western oceans and see what the free world had to offer.

My grandfather asked a series of questions about the work the young man did on his ship, but he'd felt an instinctive liking for the lad as soon as he'd come through the door and had already made up his mind to hire him.

He got the kid to write down all his details on a form and explained to him the job on offer and exactly what it entailed.

The *Ossi* was keen to sign the contract and once he did so my grandfather shook his hand and called for the barman to bring over two beers. They drank a toast and settled back into the padded seats, relaxing, and started to chat. My grandfather had no one else to interview that day and when the beers were finished he called for another two.

They were halfway through those when my grandfather enquired, idly, which routes the boy had worked when he was in the U-boat service. He was only making conversation and expected to hear about Wolf Pack duty in the middle of the North Atlantic.

'Well,' the *Ossi* said, 'she was a type nine sub – long distance – and we did reconnaissance twice along the East Coast of America, shadowing freighter convoys heading for Britain trying to run our Wolf Packs. And before that, my first time out, we did a sixteen-week run to the Persian Gulf and back, targeting fuel tankers.'

My grandfather froze in the act of raising the beer to his mouth. From his research in Kiel he knew that only two U-boats were ever active in the Gulf.

He lowered his glass slowly, frowning and focusing on the table, gripping the edge of it tightly.

'It wasn't U-577, was it?' he asked, deadpan. 'Under Captain Fromm?'

The *Ossi* stared at him in astonishment.

This was all the answer my grandfather needed. He sniffed and nodded slowly as he took it in.

'So how come you weren't on board when she sank?' he asked at last.

The lad collected himself with an effort, shifting uneasily.

'There was a bombing raid on Kiel two nights before we were due to sail. I got an eight-inch splinter of glass in my right arse cheek and had to spend the next two months in a hospital bed, lying on my stomach. Turned out it saved my life though. But tell me ... How the hell do you know so much about my old tin cigar?'

'Ah,' my grandfather said, drinking down his beer and wiping his mouth. He smiled, a little sadly, and nodded to the barman who was already bringing over another two full glasses.

'Ah,' he said again. He leaned forward and clinked his glass against the young man's.

'Now *that's* a story.'

* * *

I don't know if I thought about any of this as I swam. Like a dream you forget the instant the alarm clock rings, whatever had filled my mind as I followed the buoys south vanished completely the moment I came back to myself and my surroundings. This I did, abruptly, when I arrived at the black-and-yellow buoy marking the beginning of the yacht club's water. Recognising where I was, I felt a start of surprise at realising how far my body had taken me without my being aware of it. I'd travelled the best part of two kilometres – more than enough for the first leg – and I coasted to a halt beside the buoy and straightened up.

My goggles had fogged over from the heat of my exertions and I pulled them off to wash them. After the cool green gloom of underwater the bright sunlight made me squint. I shaded my eyes, moving my legs a little faster to compensate for my raised arm, and studied the beach. The strand here was private, owned by the club, and the sunloungers in front of the terrace were largely unoccupied. The only activity was at the water's edge, where a small group of tourists, decked out in orange life-jackets, was receiving rigging instruction around a large, beached catamaran. There were perhaps eight or ten pupils in the group, and knowing what the course involved I couldn't help wondering, with professional arrogance, if any of them would stick at it long enough to get their licence.

Beyond the beach, on top of the grass dyke that ran behind the yacht club and the dunes, I could see the point where the promenade began. Out here, this far from the town, it was nothing more than a wide concrete path, but a kilometre or so further on it turned into a row of cafes and shops that marked the start of Gromitz proper. As far as I could tell from my position in the water, the main stretch was fairly crowded. The town's beaches seemed busy as well, although the endless ranks of brightly coloured *korbs* – twin wickerwork seats that could be rented out by the day or the week – made it difficult to be sure.

Like the stretch of water I'd just come to the end of, the sea in front of the town was officially reserved for bathing. In order to get there, however, I would have to cross five hundred metres of yacht club water, and swimming there was forbidden. The club generated a high volume of sailing traffic, and the risk of a swimmer being struck by a boat was too great. At that moment it happened to be quiet, but I knew that if I started across there was a fair chance I'd be seen by one of the coastguard spotters, and a high-speed rubber dinghy would be dispatched to haul me unceremoniously back to shore. It wasn't worth the hassle, and besides, I'd come far enough. The tower was a tiny black speck behind me, and I imagined that Holger would be waiting impatiently. So I fitted my newly cleared goggles back into place, took a deep breath, and began swimming back the way I'd come.

The return leg wasn't so easy. In this direction the current was against me, and although it was relatively light the difference was noticeable. I was having to pull harder and kick faster in order to maintain the same pace as before. Also, because I preferred to breathe on my right side when swimming freestyle I was now turning my face, every six strokes, directly into the incoming swell. To avoid inhaling a mouthful of saltwater I had to concentrate on my timing, synchronising my own movements with that of the waves.

After a while though I settled into a reasonably steady rhythm, and although it was interrupted occasionally by an unexpected wave, or the need to crane my neck to spot the next buoy against the sun, I nonetheless managed to slip back – partially, at least – into that automatic, meditative state of physical exertion which endurance athletes know so well.

Endurance is all about rhythm. If the rhythm is broken, the body's movements don't flow, and the mind is recalled from its dreaming to concentrate on the matter in hand. By the time I was three-quarters of the way back – after almost four kilometres of front crawl – I was beginning to tire. My arms felt heavy, and my neck ached from holding up my head, away from the slap of the back swell. I was trying not to fight the water, to move with it instead, but even though I knew from experience that I still had energy in reserve it was nonetheless hard work. It was work that I welcomed, however, given that every move seemed to be cleansing me of the bad feelings of the morning.

Indeed, now that the emotions of the last few hours had been banished by exercise I found myself able to reflect quite dispassionately on them. As I moved into the final section of my swim I began to examine, more objectively, the nature of the experience I'd had in the caravan earlier that morning, and the possible causes of it.

Certainly the fear I'd felt then – the *dread* – hadn't been normal. It had shaken me badly and I didn't know why. There seemed, at least on the surface of things, to be no good reason for it. But now as I continued swimming I began to wonder if that was really the case. Might there not be, I asked myself, a simple, even mundane explanation for it all? Not only for what I'd gone through on waking up in the caravan, but also for what I'd felt while reading about Pip's predicament in *Moby Dick*, and then too, later, for the surge of anger and frustration I'd experienced while talking with Holger in the tower. Couldn't those reactions, extreme as they were, have perhaps been caused by something more ordinary, more everyday, than first appeared? After all, I reminded myself, I was living in a foreign country and learning a foreign language. And having to speak German all the time, having to concentrate and struggle with it all day, every day, was exhausting. True, I'd almost reached university standard as far as reading and writing were concerned, but conversation still held pitfalls for me, especially when talking to strangers with thick accents or dialects, which I had to do all the time on the beach. And the fact that I was often arguing with those people only added to the stress I was under, even as I fumbled my way through the complex grammar and slang.

Then, too, in addition to the effort I was making with the language, I was also training hard. Holger's complaints in the tower about the amount of time I was putting into my sport had more than a ring of truth to them. I was doing a ten-kilometre road run twice a week, and swimming three kilometres a day on top of that. Add to that the physical requirements of the job itself – all the kayaking, rowing, and heavy lifting involved in getting the equipment in and out of the water – and you had a lot of physical stress to go with the mental stress of the language.

And as if all that wasn't enough, there was also the burden of responsibility the work entailed. To be employed as a windsurfing instructor and lifeguard seemed like a great idea back in Scotland, a dream summer job, but I'd soon discovered it was neither as simple nor as fun as it sounded. At the height of the season we could have four hundred children on the beach and in the water, in kayaks, rubber tyres, sailing boats and windsurfing rigs, with a hundred and fifty non-guests, say, running around on top of that. Trying to keep track of them all, to stop them from going too far out or from running a kayak into the side of some swimmer's head, wasn't easy. And the whole time, as I ran about trying to do seven different things at once, at the back of my mind there was always the knowledge that a single lapse in concentration could lead to tragedy. One mistake and a child could drown.

It wasn't something that seemed to bother Bernward or Holger, or indeed any of the other members of the Hamburg swimming club who came to the beach for a week or ten days every summer to work as lifeguards and instructors. They never seemed concerned at all. And why should they be? There had never been a serious incident on the beach. Yet for some reason I found it difficult to share their sangfroid. Possibly because I was the youngest, or perhaps because I always felt like an outsider, a foreigner, for me the fear loitered permanently around the fringes of my consciousness, like a burglar preparing to rob a house.

And of course that was why I trained. That would have been the real answer to Holger's question in the tower an hour before: 'What the hell are you training *for*, for Christ's sake?'

'I'm training for the off chance,' would have been the honest reply. 'I'm training just in case something does go wrong.'

I trained as hard as I did because – however unlikely it was – someone might drown on my watch. If that happened, I wanted to be sure in my own mind that the fault wasn't mine; that the child hadn't died because I'd been too lazy to keep myself in shape. That was why I trained so hard, because I wasn't sure I could live with that guilt.

Given all that, I asked myself now – given all the various pressures the job entailed – was it any wonder that I'd woken up that morning in fear, with that terrible intimation of mortality?

And having grown up the way I had, having always known the story of my grandfather's wartime experiences in the Persian Gulf, was it really any wonder that Pip's predicament in *Moby Dick* had struck a chord with me that morning?

No, I thought as I swam, it wasn't.

*

By the time I was two hundred metres from the end of my swim I'd had enough. My arms felt like lead and my stroke had lost all its form, its efficiency. My body was telling me that it wanted to rest, but instead, for the final eight buoys, I pushed myself harder than ever.

All athletes have mind games, their own ways of tapping into aggression and reserves of energy. In the case of professionals, sports psychologists work with them to help refine these techniques, getting them to visualise in every detail the perfect gold-medal performance, or the crushing of their competitors. My own tricks were nothing like as refined, but they were good enough for my purposes. I tended to rely on violent or sexual urges to release adrenaline, and an altruistic fantasy to prolong endurance.

That training session I didn't have to dig far into my subconsciousness to come up with a hate figure. Simply allowing myself to recall my confrontation with the Pit bull owner was enough to feel all the anger of the morning come roaring back. The frustration and rage I'd experienced earlier in the tower swept through me once again, but this time I welcomed it, channelling the feelings into the pull of my arms and the kick of my legs. I imagined myself swinging the baseball bat into the side of the man's head, smashing his skull to bits like a melon, and the sheer joy I felt in my mind at this was mirrored by the physical reaction of my body, as the fatigue and aches receded and new strength came back to my limbs.

The benefits of such visualisations are powerful but short-lived. Within fifty seconds or so the adrenaline had faded, leaving my muscles burning and my lungs gasping for air as my body tried frantically to catch up. I had no lust left for a fight now, the image of the Pit bull owner receded, and I engaged another fantasy in an effort to counteract the pain and fatigue I was feeling.

It was my usual fantasy when I was training in the water and I'd been using it for almost three years – ever since the day my grandfather had explained that he'd arranged a summer job for me, if I wanted it, with his old friend Bernward Dombach, who ran a watersports centre on a beach in Germany. It was this fantasy that had helped me through the hundreds of miles of front crawl I'd done in training sessions since then, giving me the motivation to get out of bed at 6 a.m. four times a week during the cold, wet Scottish winters.

I pretended that a child was drowning, and I was swimming to save him.

It was a boy, about ten years old, with fair hair, called Max. He could swim well, but had got into difficulties and would be dead in a few minutes if I didn't reach him. There was no one else in the water apart from the two of us, and to get there in time I'd have to push myself to the very limits. If I didn't, Max would die.

My arms felt like they were melting. My lungs were bursting. I was sobbing for air every time I turned my head to breathe but I still wasn't taking in anything like enough oxygen. I was in danger of vomiting, and felt as if I might lose control of my bowels. But none of that mattered. The only thing that mattered was putting everything I had – all my strength, all my speed, all my will – into moving through the water as fast as I could. To get to little Max before he drowned.

I didn't make it. If Max had been real he'd have been dead by the time I got to him. I'd misjudged the distance and my own reserves of strength. I'd gone for broke too soon, and instead it broke me. The last forty metres I was a mess, arms flailing, legs dragging, my rhythm gone to hell – jerking my head up to breathe every two or three strokes instead of every six. My eyes were open but I saw nothing.

I floundered my way to the last buoy and stopped, writhing in pain as my exhausted muscles spasmed. I could feel the heat radiating from my face and when I lifted my head out of the water the sweat began swelling from my pores and streaming down my brow and cheeks. It was all I could do to float there on the surface, gasping for air as I fought to get my breathing back under control.

It's the recovery that proves your fitness, though, and I was very fit. Within twenty seconds or so the cramps eased and my breathing became deeper and more controlled. My runaway heart slowed and steadied, and although my arms felt like liquid the pain receded quickly. I lay on my back, looking up at the blue sky, and since I was in the open sea instead of a swimming pool

I surrendered to the insistence of my bladder and allowed myself to pee a warm stream of urine into the surrounding water. The relief of that mirrored the relief of remembered pain.

Apart from leaden arms and a stiff neck, within a minute or so I was back to normal. I let myself float for a while, spreadeagled, listening to the pulse beat slowly in my head and staring up at the sky until I felt like I was falling into the blue. Eventually my stomach lurched and I straightened up, pulling my goggles onto my forehead. Holding the buoy's anchor chain with one hand, I shaded my eyes with the other and squinted seawards, looking for evidence of the motor cruiser I'd spotted earlier from the tower. But I was very low in the water and the sunlight glinting off the waves dazzled me. After a moment or two I gave up and twisted around, facing back towards the beach. In this direction, with the sun behind me, there was no glare, and I allowed my gaze to linger for some time on the postcard view: bright shallows, warm yellow sand, and the tower, dark and solid against the summer sky. I could make out the small splashes of colour that were the kayaks in their frames, and, above them, the white blur of the plastic chair on the tower's top step. There was no sign of Holger, and I assumed he'd retreated back inside to finish his beer in the shade.

I wasn't ready to go back to the beach, and with the endorphins running through me from the exercise I felt flushed with good feeling. I decided that before returning to shore I wanted to enjoy at least some of the sensation of freedom that being in the ocean can give you. I wanted to play. So I pulled my goggles back down over my eyes, took several deep breaths, and disappeared below the surface in a duck-dive.

Gripping the anchor chain, slimy with weed, I pulled myself down the twelve feet or so to the sea bed, releasing air bubbles as I went to reduce my buoyancy. Descending, I passed through two distinct layers of colder water, one about a foot and a half under the surface, and a second layer about five feet from the bottom. I could feel the goose pimples rising on my skin.

The concrete breeze block that anchored the buoy was hollow, and as I arrived on the bottom I saw a pale, fragile-looking crab, about the size of a small child's hand, scuttle back into its makeshift home there. I let my legs sink back underneath me, folding them around the chain so that I was floating cross-legged just above the breeze block, and looked around.

The sea bed was mostly sand, with clumps of gently waving weed dotted here and there, but at that moment there was nothing else in sight, not even a jellyfish. Tipping my head back on a whim, I opened my mouth to release a single bubble of air that rushed upwards, silvery, like something alive. My eyes followed its translucent ascent until I lost it against the sharp flashes of sunlight fragmenting on the surface.

My pulse was slow and steady and I felt comfortable apart from the chill. I hung there, weightless but heavy, making a conscious effort to relax and stay completely still, to try – however briefly – to become part of this strange, quiet world. My heart beat to the rhythm of the passing seconds, and as it did so I could feel a sense of peace and isolation spreading through me; a sense, almost, of something profound. Like no other place I'd ever come across, the ocean gave me the feeling that there might really be a Whole, a Purpose – an Understanding to be gained. It was the closest thing I had to a church.

I couldn't stay long to pray. With my body still recovering from the swim, about fifty seconds was the longest I could manage. By then the need to breathe was too insistent to ignore. I dug my fingers and toes into the sand of the sea bed, lingering for a brief moment over the sensation of it against my skin, then straightened and pushed with my legs, rising swiftly upwards in that familiar rushing, weightless feeling. As always, it was accompanied by a mild regret that I couldn't stay for longer.

I broke the surface in a shower of spray, gasping for breath. I filled my lungs deeply – once, twice, a third time – planning to dive again. And I was bobbing up and down, about to do so, when I happened to look up as I filled my lungs for a final time and saw something that pulled me up short, banishing all thoughts of further diving for the moment.

There was a large crowd of people walking up the beach, heading for the tower.

I cursed, pulling my goggles off in order to see better. Yes. A group of children, thirty or forty of them, accompanied by a handful of adult *Betreuer* – student volunteers. Striding up the beach about twenty metres in front of them was the tall, unmistakable figure of Gerd, the head *Betreuer* of a group of ten to eighteen year olds from Kiel. As he started up the path to the tower I saw the stocky shape of Holger emerge from the doorway and start down the steps to meet him. The two figures came together in the shadow of the tower and conferred for a moment, before moving back down the path to the beach, heading for the equipment stands. I didn't need to wait to see Holger bending to unlock the frames. I swore again, pulled my goggles down over my eyes, and began swimming back towards the beach.

By the time I got there four kayaks were already sitting at the water's edge and Holger and Gerd were carrying a fifth across the sand, Holger at the front and Gerd at the back, each slightly lopsided from the weight. As I jogged up onto the sand Holger lifted his head and grinned at me.

'Hey, Gerd,' he called back over his shoulder as he walked. 'Remind me to order in another foreigner for cheap labour, will you? This one here's a dud. Only ever shows up once he knows we've done most of the work!'

Gerd laughed heartily and I shot him a look.

'Don't laugh, Gerd, for god's sake,' I said. 'You'll only encourage him.'

Holger plunked the prow of the kayak down beside my feet. Gerd lowered his end and moved forward to shake my hand, smiling. He was a big man in his late thirties, well over six feet tall, with bushy black hair and a handsome, large-boned face that radiated friendliness and good humour. A history teacher by profession, he'd been bringing groups of kids to the camp every summer for the last five or six years. We didn't always have an easy relationship with the *Betreuer* leaders – Bernward in particular was quick to take offence if he thought they were trying to interfere too much – but everybody liked Gerd, and the kids in his group adored him. Although he pretended, especially with the teenagers, to have nothing but mildly amused disinterest in what they got up to, in reality he was both dedicated and good at his job. The groups he brought were always polite and well-behaved, never hurt each other or caused serious trouble, and at the end of their two weeks we were always sorry to see them go.

'Don't pay any attention, Craig,' Gerd grinned now, his big paw engulfing my hand. 'The only person lazier than Holger is me. How're you doing anyway? Good swim?'

'Great thanks,' I said, nodding my head and slicking my wet hair back from my forehead. 'But what about your lot? Weren't you all supposed to be going off to that amusement park today?'

'Supposed to be,' Gerd said, shrugging. 'Till the bloody bus broke down, that is. Fan belt, believe it or not. Looked like it was going to take a couple of hours to fix the thing so we said sod it – let's go to the beach today and leave the roller coasters for next week. I hope you don't mind?'

'Hell no.'

'You sure?' Gerd looked doubtful. 'Aren't we ruining your day off?'

'Day off? They didn't even bother telling me I had one until an hour ago. And anyway, what was I going to do with it?' I waved a dismissive hand in Holger's direction. 'Sit here listening to this alcoholic insulting me all day?'

Holger opened his mouth to reply, but his rejoinder was lost in the sudden commotion of the children arriving. The keenest of them had dumped their stuff on the sand and were running over to inspect the kayaks, obviously wanting to bag the ones they liked best. I'd never been able to work out on which criteria it was they based these decisions, unless it was by colour.

'Back! Back!' Gerd commanded as the first of them rushed up, squealing and greedy. 'Let's do this properly, okay? No chaos this time.' He turned to me, raising his voice above the noise. 'I've got about ten or twelve of them wanting a windsurfing lesson and Holger said they were yours. Do you mind? There'll be a few shots of tequila in it for you tonight, if you want.'

'Yeah sure,' I said. 'No problem. They know most of the basics already anyway.'

Holger went off to get a couple of the teenage boys to help him with the rest of the kayaks. Gerd cupped his hands around his mouth and shouted over the sand: 'WINDSURFERS! Where are the windsurfers? I want the windsurfers over here on the double! Move it, you lot!'

Leaving Gerd to round up my pupils, I headed up the path to the tower, a rag-tag group of noisy kids following in my wake. Squatting at the entrance to the cage, I began to slide out the kayak paddles one by one and pass them back. I could feel eager hands snatching at them even before I'd pulled them clear of the slings, and one boy was in such a hurry to return to the beach that he whacked me on the shin with the blade as he turned. I swore loudly in English, provoking laughter and jeers from his friends, but he was already scampering back down the path and didn't hear me.

Rubbing at the pain, I passed out the last of the paddles and crawled further inside the cage to get to the pile of thick black rubber rings at the back. There were five of these – inflated car tyre inner tubes – and I started tossing them over my shoulder, turning my head to avoid the spray of dried sand that flew off as I did so. When the last one had been hauled away I turned and peered out at the ten or so remaining kids.

'No more kayaks or tyres,' I told them. 'We've spades, volley-balls, beachballs and frisbees. What do you guys want?'

'Spades.'

'Spades?' I looked at their silhouettes against the sun. 'What, all of you?'

There was a chorus of nods.

'Going to dig to China or something?'

'Gerd said there'd be a prize for the biggest hole.'

I laughed. 'And you believed him?'

They just shrugged, so I turned back and started passing out the spades. A few were plastic, but most were the real thing – work tools that we used for resetting fence posts. They had sharp metal blades and long wooden handles that were too big for these ten and eleven year olds to use properly.

'Watch out for these things,' I told them. 'If you're not careful you'll end up slicing off your toes. Take care, okay?'

'Okay.'

'And don't leave them lying about!' I shouted at their retreating backs. 'Bring them here when you're finished.'

One of the girls in the group paused for a moment and waved in acknowledgement, but I knew at the end of the day I'd probably have to go along the beach gathering up the tools just the same.

With the last of the children gone, I turned my attention to the two plastic barrels tucked away on the right-hand side of the cage. They had different coloured lids – one white and one orange – and I manhandled the one with the orange lid closer to me, tipping it on its side and rolling it to the entrance. Outside, I prised off its lid to reveal a jumble of black neoprene wetsuit jackets. Ducking into the cage again, I hauled out four windsurfing sail booms, before going back up the stairs into the tower to get my keys.

Looking down I could see that Gerd had assembled the wind-surfers and was waiting patiently. I came out onto the top step and waved.

'It's okay, Gerd! Send them up!'

As the group started across the sand I made my way back down the steps and around to my right, where yet another metal frame squatted in shadow at the rear of the tower. This one contained a collection of long, pink plastic pipes lying horizontally in four rows of four. Selecting a key, I sprang open the padlock and pulled on the steel rod that held the lids of the top row of pipes in place. Then each lid came off with a resonant *plop*. I reached into the first pipe and slid out a two-and-a-half metre metal mast with a plastic sail wrapped tightly around it. My pupils arrived a moment later and I handed it to one of them.

'It's three to a rig today,' I told them. 'Someone else grab a boom. Take them down to the sand and rig them up – you remember how?'

They nodded.

'Good. When you've finished, come and get yourselves a jacket. I'll sort out the boards for you and check the sails, okay?'

'Okay, Craig.'

When the final mast had been carried away I went back up into the gloom of the tower. Opening the first of the sea chests, I pushed aside more wetsuits to reveal a collection of skegs and daggerboards lying on the bottom. I picked out four of each to go with the boards I was planning to use, then moved over to the tool box to extract the screwdriver I'd need to fix the skegs in place.

Back on the beach the children were already in the process of rigging up their sails. I dumped the skegs and daggerboards in a pile next to them, and together with Gerd crossed to the first of the frames that held our windsurfing boards. These were broad, stable Hi-Flys, perfect for the children to learn on.

'You made quite an impression last night,' Gerd said as I worked.

'Eh?' I glanced up at him. 'How do you mean?'

'Katarina.'

I was silent for a moment, my fingers fumbling to clip the padlock that secured the boards back to its chain.

'That so?' I said at last, as it clicked into place.

'That was the general consensus, anyway.' He paused for a moment, watching as I stood up and wiped the sand from my knees.

'As a matter of fact, I think she was hoping you would stick around a little longer.'

'Like I told Holger,' I said. 'I had some reading to do.'

'Let me guess. *Penthouse* magazine?'

I laughed.

'Not exactly. More like homework. Trying to brush up on my German.'

'There are better ways to do that than reading,' Gerd said with a wink. 'Katarina's a nice girl, but I bet she could teach you vocabulary you won't find in any dictionary.'

I ignored this, reaching up instead to slide the bow of the topmost surfboard out of the frame. Gerd put a hand on the stern to help.

'What's it to you anyway?' I asked him. 'You pimping for her or something?'

Gerd smiled.

'Not guilty, your honour. But she's a sweet girl and she really does seem to like you. And you like her, don't you?'

'Sure,' I said. 'She's terrific.'

'And very good-looking.'

'That too.'

'Well then,' Gerd shrugged. 'I just wanted to say that it looks like the opportunity's there for you, if you want to take it.'

'Thanks for your concern,' I said dryly. 'I'll think about it.'

'You do that,' Gerd retorted, raising his eyes to look beyond me. 'But if I were you I'd do it quickly. That's her coming now.'

Startled, I twisted my neck to follow the direction of his gaze. Sure enough, Katarina was moving up from the shoreline towards us. She wore a loose, shapeless T-shirt over her bathing suit, but her long tanned legs and blond ponytail were enough to draw stares from the group of teenage boys nearby.

'Hey, Katarina,' Gerd said loudly as she arrived. 'I was just telling Craig here that you want to try your hand at windsurfing. And guess what? He says he'll give you a lesson.'

Katarina raised her eyebrows at me.

'Really, Craig? That would be great!' Then she frowned slightly. 'I mean, as long as it's no trouble. I know you're busy.'

'Don't worry,' I said quickly. 'I'd be happy to, really. But, um . . . I'll need about twenty minutes to get the kids sorted out first. That all right?'

'Sure.' She smiled brightly. 'No problem. I'll look forward to it.'

'Great.'

There was an awkward pause. Katarina tucked a stray strand of hair behind her ear.

'Well then,' she said at last. 'I just wanted to check it was going to be okay. Let me know when you're ready, will you?'

I nodded.

'Speak to you later, Gerd.'

'Bye, Katarina.'

With a final smile she turned and walked away. A moment later I felt the surfboard judder, and I turned to see Gerd shaking with silent laughter.

'Son of a bitch,' I said, grinning.

Gerd shook his head.

'Puppy love. It's so sweet.'

'You're just jealous.'

'Not me,' he said, tapping his wedding ring. 'I'm a happily married man. But let me tell you . . . If I was ten years younger you wouldn't have a chance. I'd be all over her like a gallon of honey.'

I laughed.

'Ten gallons, Gerd, the way you pour it on.'

'Why not? That's the way they like it.'

I shook my head, then slapped the board decisively, suddenly feeling cheerful.

'Come on. We can't hang around here all day. Better get these handed out, before your damn kids start bashing each other to death with the masts.'

'Christ.' Gerd rolled his eyes. 'Let them, as far as I'm concerned. At least that way there'd be a few less of the little sods to worry about.'

We were still laughing at that on the way back to the second board.

By the time all four of the boards were laid out, upside down, on the beach, my pupils had finished rigging their sails. I sent them up to get wetsuit jackets while I turned my attention to fitting the skegs. These were small plastic fins, similar in shape to a shark fin, which had to be inserted in a shallow slit at the rear underside of the boards to help with steering. Each skeg had a small vertical hole through its bottom edge with a screw in it, and these screws had flat, square washers on the ends. To fit the skegs in place, I first had to unscrew the washers and insert them into the slits, then slide the skeg in carefully afterwards, lining it up in such a way that the screw was directly over the hole in the washer.

Once the skegs were in place I started on the daggerboards: thick plastic foils, the length of my arm, that went through the slits in the middle of the boards to prevent sideways movement when the rig was in the water. I pulled the first Hi-Fly onto its side and straddled it, using my knees to hold it up while I pushed a daggerboard through, pivoting the foil so it lay flush against the underside of the hull. Out on the water, beyond the second sandbank, the children would be able to extend it without it hitting the sea bed.

With the surfboards finally ready I turned my attention to the sails, examining the kids' work. They seemed to have remembered most of what I'd taught them, but one sail was a little slack and I had to make adjustments – sitting down on the sand to loosen the tack knots, then putting my foot against the base of the mast and pulling the cord through as far as I could, increasing the downhaul in order to give the sail more tension against the wind. Afterwards I stood back to let the children fit the masts to the boards, before making a final check to see that everything was secure.

The kids were impatient to get into the water, but instead of letting them go I quietened the group and made them sit down in a semi-circle around me. As they plonked themselves onto the sand I saw that some were already grinning, knowing what was coming.

'Right, guys,' I said at last, once they'd settled down. 'Let's see how well trained you really are. You remember the golden rules?'

There were nods, and more giggles from the girls.

'Think so, eh? Well let's see.'

I composed my features, paused a moment for effect, then started into the litany.

'Earnest Pupils. What is the first golden rule of windsurfing?'

The response was loud and immediate.

'TO DO IT SAFELY, HOLY MASTER!'

I nodded wisely.

'Indeed. Earnest Pupils, what is the second golden rule of windsurfing?'

'TO DO EVERYTHING YOU TELL US, HOLY MASTER!'

'Quite right, and don't forget it. Earnest Pupils, what is the third golden rule of windsurfing?'

'TO DO EVERYTHING YOU TELL US WHILE WIND-SURFING SAFELY, HOLY MASTER!'

'Excellent.' I smiled. 'And tell me, Earnest Pupils, what do you do if you drift too far out and can't get back to shore?'

'ALWAYS WAIT FOR RESCUE, NEVER TRY TO SWIM!'

I nodded in approval, satisfied. 'Earnest Pupils, you are truly earnest.' I stood up. 'Right then, you noisy lot. Off you go. I'll be out with you in a minute.'

They scrambled for the rigs. I waited around just long enough to make sure they were carrying them in correctly – one child at each end of the board and a third holding the sail by the boom – then grabbed the screwdriver and jogged back up the path to the tower. Holger was waiting for me.

'Everything all right?' he asked as I arrived.

'Fine.' I leaned past him through the doorway, tossing my screwdriver and keys onto the window sill. There were five open beer bottles lined up there already, I saw, a half inch of liquid at the bottom of each.

'You sure you want to leave those lying about?' I asked him, nodding at the bottles.

'Wasp traps,' he said. 'I killed four of the buggers while you were away swimming.'

'Really? Shit.' I shook my head. 'I thought I heard something buzzing about in there earlier. Think it means we'll get another plague of them?'

'Who knows?' Holger said. 'But there must be a nest in the dunes somewhere. The council guys dump driftwood there in the spring. Big pieces. Big enough to hold a nest, some of them. I'll ask Bernward to have a look and smoke it out.'

I grunted agreement. Wasps were a nuisance at the best of times, but they also posed a real danger, the potential for causing something more serious than the usual localised swelling and half an hour of pain. Every year there were stories in the newspapers about people who'd suffered allergic reactions, falling into severe shock within a few minutes of being stung. In some cases, if the patients weren't transported to hospital in time, it could prove fatal. Anaphylaxis, the medics called it.

'By the way,' Holger went on, suddenly changing the subject. 'I meant to say to you. Fred came by while you were gone. Told me to say hi. Said he'd stop off again on his way back down the beach this afternoon.'

'Fred? Let me guess. Another constitutional?'

'Looked like he was all set to walk to Hamburg.'

I smiled. Fred was the closest thing we had on the strand to a beach bum. He was a Belgian in his late fifties, a kind, quiet man who'd retired from his job as a university librarian after receiving a small inheritance. For most of the year he lived in Florida, in a condominium near Coco Beach, but for three months every summer he stayed in a large caravan parked in a field not far from the camp. He spent his days sitting in a deckchair reading, or going for endless walks along the beach, stopping occasionally to muse over a few chapters on religion or philosophy, or to stare at the ocean. Fred was the most consistently serious reader I'd ever met, and he'd once described himself to me as a man who liked to think about things without coming to any conclusions. Occasionally he lent me books in English.

'Cool,' I said. 'Did you happen to see which book he had with him today?'

Holger looked at me incredulously and I raised my palms in mock surrender.

'Okay, okay. Forget I asked.'

I dropped my hands and turned around, leaning my elbows on the rails to survey our beach and water. The contrast with the peace and solitude of earlier couldn't have been more marked. The sea beyond the second sandbank was a busy and colourful sight now, the reds, greens and yellows of the kayaks and the orange sails of the surf rigs standing out against the deeper blue. Closer in, children splashed through the ankle-deep water of the first sandbank, or ran across the beach, dodging half-dug holes and the occasional group of sprawled teenagers, who broke off from smoking semi-surreptitious cigarettes to swear briefly before settling back on their towels to talk, flirt, and listen to the inevitable ghetto blasters in their midst. I could see a group of *Betreuer* sitting near the rowing boats chatting, Katarina among them.

I studied the scene, paying particular attention to the water. Holger seemed to read my thoughts.

'Sixteen kayaks,' he said. 'Five rubber tubes. And your four surf rigs, of course.'

I nodded, committing this to memory. The numbers were important. Every ten minutes or so you counted the equipment in the water, making sure it was all still there, where it was supposed to be. If the kids took something too far out or paddled too far along the coast in either direction, you had to get in one of the racing kayaks and fetch them back.

'Some of the older ones wanted to take out the rowing boats,' Holger continued. 'But I managed to stall them. Told them to wait until later this afternoon. With any luck they'll forget about it.'

'Nice one,' I replied. The rowing boats were heavy to shift, and the teenagers would probably get bored with them after twenty minutes.

I straightened up. 'I'd better go out with my surfers for a bit. You okay to look after things here?'

'Sure.' Holger pulled over the chair, settling himself into it comfortably and gesturing at the view in front of us. 'It's not like there's much to do.'

I nodded, putting a hand on his shoulder and squeezing past him into the tower. Inside, I opened the first of the sea chests and rummaged around for my wetsuit jacket. I pulled it on and zipped up the front, more to prevent sunburn than because I was concerned about keeping warm. When I came back out I saw that Holger had propped his feet on the lower bannister rail.

'I'll be back in fifteen minutes,' I called as I stepped over his legs and started down the stairs.

'No hurry,' Holger replied. He stretched his arms above his head and sighed contentedly. 'We're on holiday, remember? What could happen?'

'Nothing at all,' I said, waving a hand at him and heading for the beach.

It felt good to be back in the water. I waded out to my pupils, stopping for a moment just before the second sandbank in order to lie down and let my jacket fill. The thin layer of liquid, trapped by the neoprene, would warm quickly from my body heat and I'd be able to stay in the water all afternoon if I wanted to.

My pupils didn't look as though they needed much help. With the breeze freshening from off-shore they were taking it in turns to sail a beam-reach course, parallel to the beach, before tacking and sailing back to their original starting point. For some reason – perhaps because, in general, they tended to pay more attention during the lessons – the girls were proving more proficient at tacking than the boys, and there were squeals of delight and derision whenever one of the latter failed to turn his board and instead fell into the water.

I was happy to see that everyone seemed to be waiting their turn patiently. Sharing a board between three or four kids wasn't the most efficient way for them to learn, but it was a useful system from our point of view. It cut down on the work we had to do on the beach, and it was also safer. If the pupils knew that someone was waiting for them to return the rig they were necessarily limited in how far they could sail, and therefore less likely to get into trouble. And even if something did happen, we were secure in the knowledge that the others would be quick to raise the alarm.

I spent a few minutes watching to see how they were handling the rigs, occasionally shouting encouragement or advice, but the rest of the time I just messed about, larking around with the kids who were waiting. They were all aged between ten and twelve, and even the tallest of them, a dark-haired, pale-faced girl called Insa, was light enough for me to pick up and throw. The favourite game – theirs and mine – was what Holger and I had dubbed 'The Moon Launch', and this is what we played now. Moving out to chest-deep water, I'd reach back over my shoulder to take a child's hands in mine, starting a countdown from five to zero and bouncing up and down as I did so. When the countdown ran out I submerged myself, allowing the child to step onto my shoulders and steady themselves by pulling on my hands. I'd wait until he or she was settled, then burst upwards out of the water with all the force I could muster. At the same time the child would straighten their legs and propel themselves backwards, letting go of my hands as they did so. With good timing and practice the lightest of them could fly five or six feet before hitting the water with an almighty splash. The other children awarded each launch with points for style, technique and water displacement. The winner was usually a boy called Torsten, who'd perfected the game to the point where he could manage a back somersault in mid-air and still hit the water with his feet together, holding his nose with one hand and saluting, NASA-style, with the other.

We'd been playing for about ten minutes and I was starting to grow tired when I spotted Katarina, standing waist-deep in the water of the second sandbank, watching me. I smiled and raised a hand in greeting, then turned back to the waiting kids.

'Right,' I told them. 'Game's over for today. I need to do some work. You guys keep surfing. Okay?'

There were groans of disappointment.

'I'm serious,' I said. 'There's other stuff I need to sort out. But you're all doing well. If you've any problems come and see me. I'll be just over there.' I pointed vaguely in the direction of the beach. 'All right?'

They weren't happy but there wasn't much they could do about it. I left them to their grumbling and swam over to Katarina, my front-crawl clumsy because of the jacket I was wearing.

'Hi.'

'Hey.'

I stood up, running a hand through my hair, squeezing the water out. She had taken off her T-shirt and was wearing a black one-piece bathing costume. She looked stunning, and something in her stance told me that she knew it.

'Sorry,' I said. 'I didn't mean to keep you waiting. I guess I got carried away.'

She smiled, absolving me.

'I saw you from the beach,' she said. 'It looked like fun. I thought I might come and join in.'

'What, Moon Launching?' I shrugged. 'We were just mucking about. Keeps them from getting bored while they're waiting.'

'Well, they seemed to be enjoying themselves. You're great with the kids, Craig. They really like you.'

I felt my face flush at the compliment.

'We just have fun. All I do is order them about, really. It's the surfing they love.'

'That too, of course,' she said. 'But it's more than that – it's you and Holger, the way you both go about things. They all think you're great.'

'Honestly,' I protested, shaking my head and laughing to cover my embarrassment. 'We have it easy. It's easy for us to keep the kids happy. Especially the boys. Trip them up on the beach and rub their head in the sand and you've made their day.'

Katarina smiled.

'Don't get me wrong,' I added hastily. 'Obviously we don't

96

hurt anybody. But that kind of messing about, they love it. And it's a lot of fun for us, too. Five and a half hours a day and then it's over – the rest of our time's our own. Not like you guys. You've got to spend about twenty hours a day with the little monsters.'

'It can get a bit tiring after a while,' she admitted.

'I couldn't do it. Two days of that and I'd be hanging myself by my jockstrap from the roof of the tent.'

Katarina laughed.

'It's not *that* bad. Besides, we get a few hours off now and again. Like last night, for example. Typical. I'd just got talking to someone interesting and then he disappeared.' She reached out and touched my arm. 'What happened anyway? Where did you go?'

'Yeah. Sorry about that. I had some stuff to do for university.'

'What? Immediately?'

'Well . . .'

'Uh huh.' She lay back in the water, still looking at me. I tried not to stare at her long, slim body.

'I suppose you think that's some kind of excuse?' she continued. 'I mean you've got, what? Another five or six weeks before you go back.'

'I've a tendency to leave things to the last minute. It's a habit I'm trying to get out of.'

'Still. It wasn't fair of you to run off and leave me like that.'

'I didn't exactly *run*!'

'You might as well have.' She straightened up again, her smile broadening. 'Honestly, Craig. Anyone would think you were scared of something.'

I shook my head. 'I'm not scared,' I told her.

'No?'

'No.'

She studied my face, and there was a warmth in her look that made my heart beat faster.

'Good,' she said quietly.

We stood there in silence, looking at each other.

'So,' I said at last, hoarsely. 'You want to try windsurfing then?'

Katarina threw back her head at this, laughing in delight.

'What's so funny?'

She shook her head, smiling to herself.

'No seriously. What's the joke?'

'Well no, actually,' she said. 'I don't want to try windsurfing.'

'You don't? But I thought you told Gerd . . .'

'I never told Gerd any such thing.'

'You didn't?'

'Oh, Craig.' She reached out and squeezed my forearm. 'You're so sweet.'

'Then why did he . . .'

'Gerd was just having some fun,' she said. 'He was just trying to help.'

'Oh,' I said, suddenly feeling foolish. 'So . . . You don't want to go windsurfing then?'

'No.'

'Right.' I pursed my lips, taking this in. 'So what *do* you want to do?'

'Well,' she said brightly. 'How about we just mess around for a bit?'

'Sure,' I said. Then I looked her up and down, grinning. 'But I've got to tell you, you're a bit big for Moon Launching.'

She laughed.

'Is that a diplomatic way of saying I'm fat?'

'No, no,' I said hastily. 'You're not fat. Obese, maybe. But definitely not fat.'

'Obese!' she squealed, slapping her hand on the surface of the water so it splashed in my face.

'Well . . . Maybe "gargantuan" would be more diplomatic.'

'You think so, do you?'

'You did ask.'

'And I suppose you think that big, flabby bum of yours actually looks attractive?'

I shrugged, turning my head and glancing down over my shoulder. 'I haven't had any complaints.'

'Ha! That's because it's so huge you can't sit near enough to anyone to hear them complaining! Honestly, Craig. You're *so* out of shape.'

'Yeah?' I said, grinning.

'Yeah!'

'Prove it then.'

'Okay. I will.'

She put her hands on her hips, looking out over the water. After a moment she pointed.

'Right. I'll race you to that buoy over there.'

'In your dreams, Katarina.'

'In *your* dreams, you mean.'

'You don't have a chance,' I said, 'I'll . . .'

But I never got round to saying what I'd do, because at that moment she stepped neatly forward, hooked an ankle round my legs, and pushed me backwards into the water.

'Tough guy, huh?' she said as I splashed down helplessly. She pressed her hand against my forehead. 'It's morons like you . . .'

But the rest was lost to me as I sank beneath the surface in a froth of foam, laughing helplessly.

By the time I emerged she was already three or four metres away. I shook myself and started after her. I was handicapped by the jacket I was wearing, but she was handicapped too, by laughter. Or perhaps she just wanted to be caught, because by the time we reached the water over the third sandbank I was able to get hold of her, my hand reaching out to grab her ankle firmly, bringing her to an abrupt halt. She let out a squeal but my grip was good and I wasn't about to let go, despite the water she was kicking in my face.

'You'll have to do better than that,' I said, putting a hand below her knee and pulling her closer. She twisted around, and I let go of her leg, grabbing her arms and pinning them behind her back.

'You lose,' I said, smiling. I pulled one hand away from hers, loosening my grip, ready to release her.

'You all right?' I asked, my voice softening. 'I didn't hurt you, did I?'

She shook her head, then shifted her weight, trying to find a better footing on the sea bed, and as she did so the whole length of her body leaned into mine. The sudden warmth of her went through me and my blood jumped.

'So,' she said quietly, her face a few inches from my own. 'You've caught me. Now what?'

I released her, then reached out and stroked her cheek.

'Guess you think I'm pretty stupid, huh?'

'No.'

I held her gaze for a moment, then bent my head and kissed her slowly on the lips. She didn't respond and I pulled back, eyes questioning.

'Okay?'

She nodded, and this time she reached a hand behind my neck and pulled me to her. Her mouth opened and I tasted the salt on her tongue, smelled the scent of her skin and her sweet breath. I could feel my heart beating as she slipped a leg between mine, pressing against me. After a while she pulled back a little.

'About time too,' she said quietly.

'Sorry it took so long.' I put an arm round her waist. 'But we only got talking last night.'

'And whose fault was that? I've been waiting for you to make a move for the last six days.'

'Hey,' I smiled. 'I can't help it if I'm shy.'

'I think it's sweet. Besides . . .' She took my chin and pulled me down to her. 'I can always help you out.'

This time, after a minute or so, it was my turn to pull away.

'Listen,' I said, glancing behind me. 'Don't get me wrong. This is great. But are we sure we want to be doing this here? People can probably see us.'

She shrugged. 'It doesn't bother me if it doesn't bother you.'

'It's just . . . It makes me a bit uncomfortable. You know? The thing about this place is that everybody knows everybody else's business, Katarina. I can't sneeze in my caravan without people talking about it at breakfast. And it can get me down sometimes. It *is* getting me down. Or something is. And this . . . This is nobody's business but ours, yeah?'

She tilted her head slightly.

'Are you saying you don't want to do this?'

'Of course I want to. You know that.' I looked into her eyes, pressing against her.

'Uh huh.' She pressed back. 'Feels good.'

I stroked her hair. 'But the camp's a small place, you know? We're living in each others' laps here. There's no privacy. Or not enough anyway.'

'So what are you saying?'

'I'm saying ... I'm saying this is great. And I want more of it. I want more of *you*. But I'm also saying I'm sick of people knowing about every little thing I do. Even Holger and Gerd, and I really *like* Holger and Gerd.' I frowned. 'Seriously, Katarina. As far as we're concerned, you and me, I want you all to myself, without all the gossip and stuff that goes on at the camp.'

'I know what you mean,' she said huskily. 'I want that too, Craig.'

'Then I'm a lucky guy.'

She laughed. 'I didn't know you could be so charming.'

We kissed again.

'So,' she said at last, nuzzling my ear. 'What exactly did you have in mind?'

'Well.' I took a deep breath. 'I want more of this, obviously. But I don't want it to be like last night, with everybody watching us. People placing *bets*, for god's sake. Just you and me, alone. How does that sound?'

'Sounds good.'

'Well, how about tonight then?'

She considered a moment. 'It should be okay,' she said slowly. 'I think Anja will cover for me. But I'll have to check. And even if she can, it'll probably be all round the camp by tomorrow morning.'

'But they won't know for sure,' I said. 'Tell them we're going to Gromitz or something. The point is, I want to get away from them for a while. I want some time alone. For us. For *me*.'

'Shhhhh,' Katarina said, stroking me. 'Don't get upset.'

'I'm not upset.'

'You need to relax, Craig. Really. You're too uptight. Too serious. I think you need a massage. A special one. I've got some oils with me.'

'Sounds terrific.'

'Good.' She kissed me again. 'So the question is, where and when?'

I thought for a moment. 'How soon can you get away?'

'Not before midnight.'

I nodded slowly. 'And how long will you have?'

'Four hours, maybe. Five at the most.'

'I'd invite you to the caravan. But . . .'

'But?'

'It's not private. Not really. Anyone walking past would know.'

'So where?'

I jerked my head over my shoulder, towards the beach.

'There.'

'There? What, the *dunes*?'

'Not exactly. The tower.'

She pulled back, her eyes widening.

'No really,' I said quickly. 'We have parties there, sometimes. There's candles, blankets, and . . .'

'And?'

'Well . . .' I shrugged awkwardly. 'We've an air mattress in one of the sea chests. A double one, with a foot pump. It's very comfortable.'

She studied my face so intently that I had to look away.

'You're full of surprises,' she said dryly.

'I've been coming here for a few years. The other lifeguards know about it too.'

'I see. And what are the rules? No smoking in bed for a start, I imagine.'

I laughed.

'Something like that.'

She stared across at the beach, considering.

'Okay,' she said at last. 'If that's what you want. It sounds like fun. Different anyway.'

'I'll get there a little earlier, set up the candles, stuff like that.'

'And you're sure we won't be disturbed? No drunks running around the strand or anything?'

'Not very likely,' I said. 'Not at that time of night. It should be okay.'

'Good.' She smiled up at me. 'Why not? I'll look forward to it, Craig.'

'Me too.'

We kissed for a final time and then she pulled away, giving me a warm, steady look full of promise. I watched for a moment as she started her swim back, then lay down in the water, looking up at the sky, and it seemed as though I lay there for a long, long time.

'It's *my* turn!'

'No it's not! It's mine!'

'Craig, tell her it's mine! It's *my* turn.'

I sighed. I wasn't even back at the first sandbank yet and already I'd been roped into a fight between two nine year olds.

'Let go! I told you, it's mine!'

'Girls. Girls.' I held my hands out pleadingly. 'Don't you know that Marx believed that all property is theft?'

They stopped for a second and looked at me, eyes narrowed suspiciously at this strange interruption, before resuming their tug-of-war over the kayak paddle. I had the distinct impression that the argument was about to turn vicious.

'It's *my* turn!'

I reached forward and grasped the paddle in the middle. After a moment, reluctantly, they both let go.

'Craig. Tell her it's *mine*.'

'Actually,' I said. 'Regardless of whether you analyse it from a communist viewpoint, or Adam Smith's standard take on capitalism, this kayak and its paddle undoubtedly belong to the people of Hamburg.'

The petulant, sulky looks that were turned on me struck me as being very adult.

'If, however,' I continued, 'we take the two opposing philosophies – the thesis and the antithesis, as it were – and merge them, according to Hegel a synthesis is bound to ensue.' I slapped the kayak enthusiastically. 'In other words, guys, both of you get in.'

They looked at each other doubtfully.

'Come on,' I said cheerfully. 'Get in and we'll play motorboats.'

They'd played the game before and I knew that they liked it. I held the plastic vessel steady while they reluctantly climbed in.

'Okay,' I said, once they had settled. 'How fast do you want to go?'

'Slow,' the first one said, still uneasy about the turn events had taken.

So I started slowly, pushing through the water and making engine noises from my throat, occasionally lifting the stern a little and bouncing it up and down. But within a few minutes I was running at full speed, roaring as loudly as possible and heaving and shaking the kayak as much as I could without the pair of them falling out. They were shrieking with delight, the earlier argument forgotten, but the noise attracted the attention of the other kids, who all wanted to play as well. It was another quarter of an hour before I finally got back to the beach, out of breath and with my arms and legs aching.

I trudged up to the tower, calf muscles protesting. As I reached the top of the steps I saw that Holger and Gerd were both inside, standing with their backs to the doorway. I was about to greet them, but they both turned suddenly, breaking into a cheer and stepping forward to spray me with the contents of two shaken-up beer bottles. I flinched, putting my arms up to protect myself, but they grabbed hold of me and poured the rest of the alcohol over my head.

'Congratulations,' Holger said as I wiped the beer from my face. He clapped me on the shoulder. 'That was quite a show you two lovebirds put on there.'

My heart sank. Gerd was grinning too, and I noticed that the binoculars were hanging around his neck.

'Nicely done, Craig,' he told me. 'Even if it did take you a few days to get around to it.'

I stepped past them without replying, pulling off my wetsuit jacket and dropping it on the floor. Holger's beach towel was hanging from a hook on the far wall. I took it and began to dry myself.

'Man, I thought she was going to suck your face off,' Holger continued. 'You should have seen the fight I had with Gerd over the binoculars. He almost had a go at me with the baseball bat!'

'I probably should have,' Gerd said, laughing.

I finished drying myself, scrunched up the towel and threw it lightly at Holger's face. 'Give it a rest, will you?' I told him. 'You're not funny.'

Holger caught the towel neatly with his free hand. He turned and looked at Gerd with raised eyebrows.

'Ohhhh,' he said in a high falsetto. 'Touchy, eh? Must be love.'

Gerd was studying me, frowning slightly.

'Come on, Craig. What's the problem? You should be happy, man. You just got lucky, and what's more it was with the best-looking girl in the camp.' He pointed at Holger. 'Not like the charity cases poor Sausage here always ends up with.'

Holger laughed.

'I don't know about that, Gerd. I wouldn't say your wife was exactly a charity case.'

Gerd reached out and punched him lightly on the shoulder. I shook my head at the pair of them.

'You know who you guys remind me of?' I said bitterly. 'Laurel and fucking Hardy, that's who.'

Holger and Gerd exchanged looks.

'What's up with him anyway?' Gerd asked, genuinely puzzled.

'Don't worry about it, Gerd.' Holger waved a hand dismissively. 'Craig's been acting weird all day. I think he got out of bed on the wrong side this morning.'

'Something like that,' I muttered.

I began wiping at a part of my cheek that was still sticky, ignoring the uncomfortable atmosphere that had settled over us. Gerd leaned over and reached for his rucksack, pulling out three more beer bottles. He held them up, clutched in his big hand.

'Another drink, anyone?'

'God. Absolutely,' Holger said.

'That'll be your fifth this morning. No wonder you're acting like a kid.'

'For Christ's sake, Craig!' Holger snapped. 'Loosen up, will you? We're supposed to have the day off, in case you've forgotten.'

'Yeah?' I said, pointing at the window. 'Doesn't look like it out there.'

'Gentlemen, gentlemen,' Gerd interrupted. 'Let's not argue. I guess I should apologise. It's my fault for bringing the kids back and messing up your free day. But let me make amends.' He popped the lids off the bottles with a series of deft movements. 'Here. Have a beer on me.'

Holger took his gladly, but Gerd caught the look on my face and hesitated.

'Seriously, Craig,' he said. 'I'm sorry if we've ruined your day off. It's my fault, I suppose. But it was just one of those things. And I'm sorry we sprayed you with beer. It was meant to be a bit of fun.' He leaned across, offering the second bottle to me. 'No hard feelings, eh?'

I looked at his outstretched hand, feeling the weight of Holger's gaze on me. After a moment I sighed and took the beer from him.

'Okay,' I said. 'Fuck it then.'

'Good man,' Gerd replied, lifting his own and tilting it at me. 'Cheers.'

'Cheers.'

All three of us tipped back our heads and drank. Holger and Gerd lowered their bottles after a second or two, smacking their lips, but I kept going, swallowing the whole lot down in seven or eight gulps. I looked across at them as I finished, smiling at the surprise on their faces, then opened my mouth to release a long, loud, rumbling burp. Holger snorted with laughter and Gerd rapped his bottle on the window sill in approval.

'That's more like it,' he said. 'Want another one?'

'Sure,' I replied, suppressing a second burp. 'Why not?'

He reached for the rucksack, pulling out another bottle and popping it open. I sipped at it, leaning back comfortably against the wall.

'Man,' I said. 'I feel better after that.' And I meant it.

'So,' Holger said as I took another swig. 'Tell us. Did she let you fuck her, or what?'

I jerked forward, spluttering and coughing as the beer bubbles frothed up my nose.

'You prick,' I said, grinning at Holger as I wiped the runnels of alcohol from my chin. 'You timed that perfectly, you bastard.'

'He's got back his sense of humour, anyway,' Gerd said.

'Yeah,' Holger replied. 'Isn't it amazing what a quick beer can do for you?'

'You should know,' I told him.

106

'Honestly, Craig,' he said. 'You're so ungrateful.'

'Ungrateful!' I exclaimed. 'You mean you expect me to thank you for pouring beer all over me?'

'I'm not talking about that.' He turned to Gerd. 'Craig has a very short memory. I don't suppose he mentioned anything about the fact that I stopped him from being beaten up this morning?'

'No,' Gerd replied, taken aback. 'What's that all about then?'

'Like I said,' Holger answered. 'I stopped him from being beaten up this morning. Seriously. Ask him, if you don't believe me.'

'Hold on a minute,' I said loudly. 'I saved you, if I remember rightly. That guy was about to tear into you when I came out waving the baseball bat.'

Holger snorted.

'You'd have been trying to swing that bat with two broken arms if I hadn't turned up when I did.'

'Wait a minute,' Gerd interrupted. 'You're not seriously saying that Craig had to use that baseball bat on somebody this morning, are you?'

'Well,' Holger said. 'He didn't actually *hit* the fucker with it, if that's what you mean. But he did threaten the guy. And to be fair to him, it was probably the right thing to do. I was pretty impressed. He handled the situation well.'

'But how come?' Gerd asked. 'I mean, what the hell did the guy do?'

'Well,' I said, not quite sure where to begin. 'For a start he had a knife.'

'A *knife*?'

'And a dog,' I continued. 'A Pit bull.'

'A *Pit bull*?'

'And a wife with great tits,' Holger added, taking a swig from his bottle.

'Got another one, by any chance?' I asked him, draining my own. 'I've a bit of catching up to do, by the looks of things.'

Gerd nodded and reached into his rucksack again.

'It's true,' Holger continued. 'The guy was trouble, man. No doubt about it.'

'He was a fucking arsehole,' I said with feeling, reaching out for the new bottle. 'Cheers, Gerd.'

'Cheers,' Gerd replied, distracted. 'So what happened?'

'Just another moron on the beach,' Holger said. 'We get them sometimes. The guy went ballistic when Craig here wouldn't let him use our kayaks. I turned up in the middle of the argument and warned him off, but he wouldn't back down, so Craig came out swinging the baseball bat. That was enough.' He nodded in my direction. 'He didn't actually have to use the thing, thank god.'

'But still,' Gerd puffed out his cheeks. 'Jesus.'

'Yes,' I said. 'That was pretty much my reaction too.'

'And what happened to this bloke?' Gerd asked. 'Did he just go home, or what?'

I sat up. 'Good question.' I looked at Holger, who shrugged.

'As far as I know he's still up the beach with his family.'

I hopped off the sea chest and moved across to the left hand window. A moment later Holger and Gerd joined me. We stared out across the sand in the direction of the harbour.

'See?' Holger said. 'He's still there.'

Gerd lifted the binoculars to his face.

'God,' he said after a moment. 'You weren't joking, were you? He does look like trouble.'

'Wait till you see the knife he's got on his belt,' I said. 'The guy's an idiot. One hundred percent dickhead, take it from me.'

Gerd continued to study the scene through the binoculars.

'I see what you mean about her tits, Holger,' he said at last. 'Not to mention that arse. She's something else.'

'Lap-dancer.' Holger said with conviction. 'Fifty marks says she works in one of the Reeperbahn clubs. As for the bloke, he's got "gangster" written all over him.'

'Hang on a second,' I interrupted. 'Gerd. Let me have those for a moment, will you?'

Gerd removed the cord from around his neck and handed them to me. I adjusted the focus, watching as the two figures came sharply into view. The man was sprawled on his back, sunbathing. The woman lay on her front, propped up on her elbows reading a magazine, her bare breasts brushing the towel she was lying on and the butterfly tattoo a dark smudge of colour on one buttock.

'There's no sign of the kids,' I told Holger. 'And where's the dog?'

'The dog's not there?' Holger asked worriedly. 'You sure? What about the sea?'

I turned the binoculars on the water. There were a few figures further up, towards the harbour, but none of them were children.

'No,' I said, shaking my head. ''Fraid not.'

'Gone to get an ice cream?' Gerd suggested.

'Could be,' I conceded. 'But on the other hand ... Hang on a second.' I squeezed in front of Gerd, moving to the right until my hip was jammed up against the window sill, craning my neck in order to see as far down into the dunes as I could. After a moment I spotted some movement, and I raised the binoculars again, confirming my fears.

'Yeah,' I said, groaning slightly. 'They're in the dunes. Playing with the dog in the dunes.'

'Fucking brilliant,' Holger said. 'Just what we need.'

'What's up?' Gerd asked. 'I don't get it.'

'The dunes are out of bounds,' Holger said. 'And it's our job to make sure no one goes in there, unfortunately.'

'Well I know they're out of bounds,' Gerd replied. 'But so what? What's the big deal if a couple of kids happen to be running about in there?'

'Because it's dangerous,' I told him. 'Mildly so, anyway.'

Holger nodded.

'There's all sorts of shit in there,' he said. 'Broken glass. Ripped cans. Pretty much any piece of crap you can think of. Some of it gets dumped there by tourists in the summer. Other stuff washes up in the winter – you wouldn't believe how hard a winter storm can hit here, sometimes. That's why they built the dyke, to stop the land on the other side from flooding. And the council can barely find the money to keep the *beach* clean during the summer.' He nodded towards the dunes. 'There's forty years of washed-up garbage in those sandhills that they can't afford to clean up, and a five-year lawsuit just waiting to happen if one of those little morons slices open an artery or something.'

Gerd nodded thoughtfully.

'I can see what you're saying,' he said. 'But there are signs up all over the place telling people not to go in there.'

Holger snorted, shaking his head.

'I didn't say they'd *win* the lawsuit, did I? The point is, the council's insurers would have to pay for any case that's brought, and that means the premiums would go up. We're talking five, maybe even six figures here, yeah? So in order to cover their arses the council makes us responsible for making sure that no one goes in. You see?'

Gerd nodded. 'I suppose . . .'

'Shit always falls downwards,' Holger said. 'And in this case, it's about to land right on our heads.'

'On your head, you mean,' I said quickly. 'I'm staying well away from that guy. I've had enough of him for one lifetime.'

'Enough of who, exactly?' a stern voice said behind us.

All three of us turned to see a familiar figure standing in the doorway.

'Bernward!' Holger said, moving forward. 'Morning, boss. Didn't hear you come up. Wasn't expecting you for another hour or so.'

Bernward sniffed, looking around at the interior of the tower with a mixture of irritation and disgust. His gaze took in the crumpled beach towel lying on the sea chest, Gerd's rucksack and my wetsuit jacket on the floor, the footprints of wet sand I'd tracked in over the morning.

'Obviously,' he said, moving inside. 'This place is a damned pigsty. And what the hell are those doing here?' He pointed at the beer bottles lining the window sill.

'Wasp traps,' Holger said, with remarkable conviction.

Bernward looked at him, eyebrows glowering under his shock of white hair.

'Alcoholics, are they?' he asked.

Holger and I exchanged glances.

'Get rid of them,' Bernward growled. 'I don't pay you two to sit here drinking beer all day. And while we're at it I think we'll get rid of these as well.' He crossed the floor and took the bottles from our hands. 'You two have had enough for today, by the looks of things.'

He went out onto the top step, leaned over the railings and poured the contents onto the ground.

'Indigestion,' Holger whispered. 'You can always tell.'

I started to snicker, but Bernward came back in, so I composed my face and reached for the broom in order to make a start on sweeping the floor. Holger picked up Gerd's rucksack and my wetsuit jacket, then busied himself with the empty bottles.

Bernward sat down on one of the sea chests, watching us closely. He was dressed in his habitual summer outfit – baggy full-length jogging bottoms and a thick grey sweatshirt – but despite the unseasonable clothes and a small pot-belly he still looked a decade younger than his sixty-eight years. His tanned features and tough wiry body projected an unmistakable impression of physical energy, and from behind his glasses his eyes seemed to regard the world with a wry humour very much at odds with the disciplinarian manner he tended to adopt whenever he was on the beach. At that moment he was clearly enjoying our discomfort, but was trying to hide the fact by wiping vigorously at his nose and sniffing.

'I suppose it was you who gave them those beers?' he asked Gerd.

''Fraid so,' Gerd admitted. 'Sorry. I was just trying to make up for the fact that their day off's been ruined.'

Bernward tutted.

'A waste of good beer, giving it to them,' he said. 'There are other people who're more deserving, wouldn't you say?'

It took Gerd a few moments to get the point.

'Actually, Bernward,' he said hurriedly. 'I was about to ask you. There's still one left. Would you like it?'

'Why, Gerd!' Bernward replied with mock surprise. 'How very thoughtful of you. A cold one would go down nicely, thanks.'

Gerd fetched the final beer and they clinked their bottles together.

'Cheers,' Bernward said. He nodded in our direction. 'Here's to a productive afternoon.'

'Absolutely,' Gerd chuckled. 'I'll drink to that.'

'And it was going to be such a nice day, too,' Holger said loudly.

'Ach!' Bernward exclaimed, slapping his hand against the sea

111

chest. 'Did you hear that, Gerd? Insubordination! *Insubordination*! Quite unacceptable!'

'I wouldn't stand for it if I were you, Bernward,' Gerd said solemnly.

'I don't plan to!' Bernward replied, raising his fist in the air. 'I will. Not. Stand. For. It! You hear me?' He lowered his arm, laughing heartily as Gerd joined in the joke.

'I take it that's not your first beer today then either?' Holger asked pointedly.

Bernward sniffed again, a tell-tale sign that he'd had at least three.

'It's not for the workers to question their superior. Besides, I'm an old man enjoying his retirement. You two are the donkeys here.'

'Eee-orr,' Holger brayed sarcastically.

I finished sweeping out the last of the sand, brushing it off the top step and propping the broom back in its place beside the doorway.

'Donkey is the operative word,' Bernward went on. 'Stubborn, stupid and needing to be controlled with a large stick.'

Gerd threw back his head at this, laughing in delight.

'Well what can you expect?' Bernward asked. 'You just can't get the help these days.'

'Try paying decent wages then,' Holger told him.

'I would,' Bernward said reasonably. 'But I wouldn't want to price you two out of the market.'

'Hey, Bernward,' I said suddenly. 'How come you banged on my door this morning, telling me I was late? Holger says we were supposed to have the day off.'

'The day off!' he exclaimed, turning to the others. 'Did you hear that? The day off! That's the British for you. How they ever managed to get themselves an empire is beyond me.'

'You could at least've told me, though,' I persisted, ignoring the laughter of the other two.

Bernward shook his head.

'Craig, Craig,' he said sorrowfully. 'We both know that if I hadn't come by this morning you'd still be lying in your bed right now. In fact, if it wasn't for me you'd have slept away some of the

112

best years of your life. And what kind of an existence would that be, eh?'

'A happy one,' Holger replied.

'Ach!' Bernward appealed to Gerd again. 'You see what I have to deal with? What am I supposed to do with two lazy idiots like these?'

Gerd opened his mouth to reply but Bernward cut him off.

'Anyway,' he continued. 'Enough of this nonsense. If I'd wanted to listen to moans and complaints I would still be at home with my wife. What I really want to know, Craig, is what you were talking about when I came in. Who is it that you've had enough of for one lifetime, eh?'

The sudden change of subject took me by surprise.

'Well, the thing is, Bernward,' I told him. 'We had a bit of trouble this morning.'

'Trouble?' he asked sharply. 'What kind of trouble?'

'Nothing serious,' Holger broke in quickly. 'Just a nuisance really, Bernward. Some guy turned up earlier and gave Craig a bit of hassle because we wouldn't let his kids use the kayaks. We had to send him away. No big deal.'

'Oh really?' Bernward asked sceptically. 'So if it's no big deal how come you were both getting so excited about it when I came in?'

I shifted uneasily, folding my arms.

'It's just that when we checked a few minutes ago the guy's kids were playing in the dunes.'

'In the dunes!' Bernward exclaimed, sitting up straight. 'But what the hell are you waiting for then? Go and get them out!'

'I would,' I told him. 'It's just ...'

'Just what, for god's sake?'

Holger coughed.

'Actually, Bernward,' he said. 'The guy was pretty aggressive, you know? Pretty threatening.'

'So?'

'So,' Holger said patiently. 'We were just working out the best way to deal with it, that's all.'

Bernward thumped his fist down on the lid of the sea chest. 'Honestly!' he barked. 'It's always the same with you two. If I want

113

something done around here I have to do it myself.'

He stood up, glowering.

'So where the hell are these people?'

'I'll show you,' I said quickly, moving away from the wall and crossing to the left-hand window. Bernward followed.

'They're just over there,' I said. 'About forty metres ...'

But even as I was raising a hand to point, my voice died away in dismay. Looking down from our vantage point I could see that the oldest child and the dog were now back on the beach, while the younger boy was in the process of scrambling back through the wire strands of the fence to join them. Whatever game it was they'd been playing in the dunes they appeared to have grown bored with it.

'What?' Bernward asked, incredulously. 'You mean that's them? That's what you two were making all the fuss about?'

'Well ... yeah,' I said defensively. 'I mean, they were messing around in the dunes a few minutes ago. And there's the dog too.'

'Oh, for heaven's sake,' Bernward muttered, turning to look at us both. 'What's the matter with you two?'

We didn't answer. Gerd was studying his feet, embarrassed.

'A pair of idiots,' Bernward continued. 'Honestly. It amazes me sometimes that either of you have the sense to remember to breathe.'

'The problem wasn't with the kids,' Holger started to say. 'It was the father ...'

'I don't want to hear it, Holger,' Bernward snapped. 'I'm starting to get tired of all the excuses I keep hearing around here.'

'But if you'd only listen a minute ...'

'That's enough!' Bernward told him sharply. 'I'm telling you, Holger – and you too, Craig – I'm sick of this nonsense. You're not taking the job seriously enough, either of you. It's high time you both started living up to your responsibilities, you hear me?'

'Yes, Bernward,' Holger replied sullenly. 'I hear you.'

'Good,' Bernward said, slightly mollified. He put his hands on his hips. 'Just so we're all quite clear on this. Craig, I'm making you responsible for keeping those kids on the beach from now on. Understand? That's your job. If they start messing about in the dunes again I want you over there dealing with it. And Holger . . .'

'What?' Holger asked, still scowling.

Bernward waved a hand in exasperation. 'Just use your common sense, both of you. Assuming you've got some. Okay?'

Holger's face flushed at this so I changed the subject quickly.

'By the way, Bernward,' I said. 'There was something else we wanted to mention to you.'

'What's that then?'

'The wasp nest,' I told him, turning to Holger. 'Remember?'

'Ah that.' Holger cleared his throat reluctantly. 'Well, yeah, I did mean to say something to you, Bernward. It's just that I've noticed we seem to have been having a problem with wasps around here over the last few days. I've killed a couple already this morning and we were starting to think that there might be a nest in the dunes again.'

'Really?' Bernward looked around the interior of the tower. 'Are you sure? It doesn't seem like much of a problem to me.'

'Not at the moment, maybe,' Holger conceded. 'They sort of come and go. But there's been more about than usual, believe me. I was beginning to worry that we might get another plague of them, you know? Like last year.'

'Well,' Bernward said slowly. 'We wouldn't want to go through that again. But it was pretty unusual, after all. And the weather's different this summer. I wouldn't have thought it'd happen again. Especially this late in the season.'

Holger shrugged. 'We thought you should know, just in case.'

'Of course.' Bernward stroked his chin for a moment, considering. 'Okay. I tell you what. I'll go into the dunes this afternoon and have a look around. All right?'

'We'd be grateful,' Holger said.

'Right then,' Bernward looked at us both sternly. 'So tell me. Can I actually trust the two of you to look after things here while I cycle over to the shops and pick up a newspaper? I mean, you won't let anybody steal the tower out from under you or anything, will you?'

'I'm sure we'll be fine,' I said.

115

'I'll believe that when I see it,' Bernward muttered. 'I'll be back in half an hour. Anyone want anything?'

'A six pack of Flensburger,' Holger said, deadpan.

Bernward smiled sourly.

'Nice try.'

'We could probably do with a couple of bottles of water,' I told him.

He nodded. 'Anything else?'

'Oh, and what's happening about lunch?' I asked. 'Holger said Edith was bringing over some sandwiches.'

'Trust you to be thinking about your stomach, Craig,' Bernward said, looking down at his watch. 'But yes, she should be here any time now.'

He turned to Gerd.

'I'm not sure what's happening about your lot, though. Have you got anything arranged?'

'The same thing, Bernward,' Gerd replied. 'The kitchen staff are going to make up some lunch for us and bring it over. As long as that's not a problem for you? You don't mind if we stay on the beach over lunchtime?'

'It's a free world,' Bernward told him. 'One thing though. Watch out for the sun. It's hotter than you think out there, despite the breeze. Make sure they've all got cream on.'

'No problem. We'll be careful.'

'Good. I'll see you in half an hour then.'

He gave a final wave and ducked out. We watched in silence as he walked down the path to the beach.

It was Holger who spoke first.

'What's the bet that's the last we'll see of him for the next three hours?' he asked bitterly.

'I don't care what odds you're giving,' I said. 'I'm not putting money on that.'

Gerd's forehead creased in a frown. 'Why didn't you tell him the truth about that guy on the beach?' he asked. 'I mean, if he's as bad as you say?'

'You don't think Bernward really cares, do you?' Holger said scornfully. 'I mean, you just saw what he's like. He walks in here a quarter of an hour before lunchtime, throws his weight around for five minutes, then makes some excuse and pisses off back to the camp for another six beers with his cronies. Let's face it, the last thing he wants is for us to start disturbing his routine.'

'His retirement routine,' I added.

'Exactly,' Holger nodded. 'His retirement routine. You see, Gerd,' he continued. 'What you've got to remember is that this beach is what Bernward received instead of a gold-plated carriage clock. It's his retirement gift. He worked for the council for thirty years, and because of his contacts and his work with the swimming club he managed to wrangle this cushy little number as a reward. So now he's got four months here every summer courtesy of the Hamburg taxpayer, not to mention a nice little supplement to his pension. There are enough odd jobs to keep him busy, and whenever he gets tired of drinking beer at the camp he can come down here and tell us what to do. Makes him feel like he's still useful.'

Gerd nodded slowly, taking this in.

'Sounds ideal,' he grinned.

'Absolutely,' Holger grunted. 'In fact I wouldn't mind doing the same thing when I retire.'

'He's not that bad, really,' I added, feeling a little guilty about talking like this behind Bernward's back. 'He's basically a good bloke. And he's been very kind to me.'

'Yeah,' Gerd said, his interest piqued. 'What's the score there, again? He knows your family or something?'

'My grandfather,' I told him. 'He knows my grandfather from way back.'

'Wasn't there some kind of story behind that?' Gerd asked. 'Some coincidence or other?'

'Kind of,' I said, but before I could continue a voice came floating up from outside.

'Hello? Is it all right if we come up?'

Holger twisted around in the doorway, looking over his shoulder.

'Of course,' he called down. 'No problem.'

'Lucky bastard,' he hissed at me. 'Seems like she can't keep away from you.'

I moved forward to look past him. Katarina was coming up the

117

steps, her arm around the shoulder of a young boy in swimming trunks who was limping badly.

'Oh,' I said. 'Hi again.'

She looked up, smiling at me.

'Rolf here stood on a shell or a sharp stone or something,' she told us.

Holger and I moved aside as the kid hobbled in.

'I'm not sure how bad it is,' Katarina went on, patting the boy reassuringly on the back. 'I hope he doesn't need stitches.'

'Well no,' I said. 'Let's hope not.'

I pulled over one of the plastic chairs and motioned the boy to sit down.

'Does it hurt?' I asked him.

He shrugged. 'A bit, I suppose.'

I let him settle into the chair, then moved over to the shelf to get down the first-aid box.

'Hey, Holger,' Gerd said abruptly. 'Could you help me out on the beach for a minute?'

Holger looked up, puzzled.

'What for?'

Katarina was in the process of helping Rolf get comfortable and missed Gerd rolling his eyes.

'Because there's some stuff I need help with,' he told him, jerking his head towards the door.

'Oh,' Holger said, comprehension dawning. 'Some stuff, eh? Well we'd better get that *stuff* done right away.'

He looked over at me.

'You don't mind if I leave you with your hands full, Craig?' he asked, leering.

'Not at all,' I said calmly, pulling the second chair over and sitting opposite Rolf. 'In fact I'd be grateful if you'd check on my surfers.'

'Right.' Holger gave me a big stage wink and a thumbs up and walked out. Gerd followed him, grinning.

As they bustled down the stairs Katarina looked across at me, smiling and shaking her head.

'I see what you mean about those two.'

'If you think that was bad you should try working with him.'

'No thanks,' she replied. 'I'll leave that to the professionals.'

I grinned, then turned my attention to the wound in front of me.

'Okay,' I said, opening the first-aid kit. 'Let's see what we've got here. I think the first thing I should do is clean it up a bit. Eh, Rolf?'

'Don't ask me,' the boy replied. 'You're the lifeguard.'

Katarina giggled. 'He's a bit of a handful, this one,' she said.

I scratched my chin ruefully. 'Well, Rolf, let's see how sarcastic you are once the disinfectant goes on.'

I began to clean the sand and blood from around the cut. It was less than two inches long but quite deep.

'As far as I can tell there's nothing in there,' I told them. 'It should heal up in a few days without stitches. I'll just patch it over for the moment, and you can let the doctor have a look at it tonight when he drops by the camp, okay?'

'Okay,' Rolf said quietly.

Katarina came around to my side to have a look at the cut. She leaned in over my shoulder, her right hand resting lightly on the back of my neck and her cheek touching mine.

'It does look quite deep,' she said. 'You're lucky it wasn't worse, Rolf.'

The boy grunted in reply and I made an effort to ignore her touch and concentrate on what I was doing. She stayed like that while I disinfected the wound – Rolf flinching a little as the iodine went on – then began sorting through the kit for the correct size of gauze pad and a bandage to keep it in place.

Rolf watched us both seriously from under his fringe of blond hair.

'Is that your boyfriend, Katarina?' he asked at last.

Katarina laughed, then straightened up and patted me on the shoulder.

'Maybe you shouldn't ask me,' she said. 'Maybe you should ask Craig here.'

I changed the subject hurriedly.

'What about you, Rolf? Have you got a girlfriend?'

Rolf looked at me disdainfully. 'I've got three,' he told me.

I nodded wisely.

'Three girlfriends, eh?' I said. 'That sounds like hard work, if you ask me.'

'Not really,' Rolf replied. 'I only see them one at a time.'

'Ah. That's clever of you. I wouldn't have thought of that.'

I finished tying the bandage and leaned back to survey my handiwork. It was quite a neat job, for me.

'I don't suppose you've brought his sock, by any chance,' I asked Katarina.

'Of course.' She held up a white cotton sports sock in her left hand. 'We came prepared.'

'Good. It'll help keep the bandage clean while he's on the beach.'

I put it on for him and then pushed back my chair.

'What do you think? Can you walk okay, Rolf?'

The boy stood and tested his weight on the foot. He nodded.

'Can I go back down now?' he asked Katarina.

'As long as you make sure you don't get it wet,' she told him. 'And Rolf . . .'

He paused for a moment in the doorway, looking back over his shoulder.

'Huh?'

'What do you say to Craig?'

'Oh,' his eyes flickered briefly to my face, not really seeing me. 'Thanks.'

'My pleasure,' I said, but he was already moving down the steps. We watched as he reached the bottom and scampered down the dune path, the only sign of injury the white sock on his left foot.

'He's something else, that one,' Katarina said, shaking her head.

'I don't believe you,' I told her, standing up. 'They're all like that, if you ask me.'

I put the first-aid kit on the window sill and began to pack away the contents. Katarina moved to my side, watching. After a minute she leaned in, slipping an arm through mine, then tilted her head up and bit my earlobe, pulling and sucking on it gently, and for a moment I forgot who I was.

When I came back to myself she'd pulled away slightly and was giving me a frank, evaluating look.

'Did you like that?' she asked.

I nodded, not trusting myself to reply.

'Good.' She smiled and kissed me on the shoulder. 'There's lots more where that came from. See you later.'

'Yeah,' I said hoarsely. 'Later.'

She started down the steps, ponytail bouncing along with her movements.

I leaned back heavily against the window sill, watching her go.

Bloody hell, I thought. And was startled to realise a moment later that I'd actually said it aloud.

Outside on the top step it was hot. The breeze had shifted slightly, and standing there in the lee of the tower I was temporarily sheltered from it. My eyes followed Katarina as she walked across the sand to her group of *betreuer*. Once she'd settled beside them I turned my gaze to the water, counting up the rigs and kayaks and other equipment. Everything seemed to be in order, so I dragged one of the chairs back out and settled into it, propping my feet up on the railings. It was almost one o'clock, the sun was at its height, and it wasn't long before I began to feel drops of sweat trickling from my armpits and running down the inside of my arms. Bernward had been right about the need for cream, I knew, and just as a precaution I smeared on some more as I studied the scene.

I could see Holger out in the water with my windsurfing pupils, standing waist-deep on the second sandbank, shouting instructions. It looked like the shifting wind was starting to give a few of them problems, and I was sure they'd be happy to break off for lunch when the time came. Two of the boys seemed to have done so already; having detached themselves from the group around Holger, they'd taken off their wetsuit jackets and were using them as weapons in a sort of whipping game that was churning up a lot of foam and would probably end with one or other – or possibly both of them – in tears.

About twenty metres to the left of the windsurfers a small group of kayaks floated together in a multi-coloured herd, but the rest of the vessels had already been beached, abandoned haphazardly along the waterline, prows on the sand and sterns in the water.

Most had their paddles balanced at right angles across the top, the way the kids had been told to leave them, but one paddle had fallen into the shallows and was floating slowly down the coast towards Gromitz. It was only moving a few inches a minute and I wasn't going to stir myself for it specially, but I made a mental note to make sure that I fished it out later, or – better still – got Holger to do it for me when he waded back to shore.

The beach itself was a mess now. The sand was churned up everywhere, pock-marked with half-dug holes and littered with abandoned spades, tyre rings and wet towels. And of course there were the people – mostly our own groups from the camp, but also two families I'd never seen before who'd staked out territory next to the kayak stands, propping up big sun umbrellas against the dune fence and laying out inflatable mattresses and large plastic drinks coolers. One of the fathers, his pale beer belly hanging over a skimpy pair of green-and-purple swimming trunks, was playing catch with his son and daughter in the shallows, leaving his equally large wife on the sand, basting herself in the sun.

Sitting in my chair, gazing down at this scene, I felt a sudden and irrational resentment at what all these people had done to the beach – my beach. I wished all of them gone – even Katarina – so that the beach would be clean and calm and peaceful again, and for me alone. The problem with this world, I found myself thinking irritably, is other people. And it always has been, for everybody. Even as this feeling flushed through me I knew it was a petty emotion, prompted perhaps by tiredness or stress from the morning, and I shook my head to dismiss it, despairing – not for the first time – of my own misanthropy.

But it had made me restless nonetheless. Without thinking I got to my feet, stretching my arms and turning my back on the strand. Pushing the chair to one side I crossed to the back railings, looking out over the dune grass at the sloping dyke in front of me and the trees that rose beyond. I could see an older couple strolling arm in arm along the path in the direction of the cheap harbour, and as I watched they separated briefly to allow a cyclist to pass the other way. Behind them, out of sight in the playpark that lay between the dyke and the woods, someone was flying a kite. The bright yellow diamond hung in the sky, long tail flickering, swaying and swooping like a snake being charmed by the wind. From the other side of the dyke I could hear a dog barking excitedly at it.

Leaning there, watching the movement of the kite, it wasn't long before my thoughts began to wander. I found myself thinking back to Bernward's brief appearance in the tower, and reflecting on his usual high-handed manner. But it wasn't something you could really blame him for, I told myself now. After all, he was getting older, the beach could be a lot of work, and everybody – including Holger and myself – made demands on him. It wasn't surprising that he'd want a quiet life at his age. And then, too, our failure to intervene with a family who were clearly breaking the rules must have seemed, from his point of view, a matter of sheer laziness. For despite all the moaning Holger and I indulged in, we were both well aware that Bernward's responsibilities meant he needed people in the tower he could rely on, and I found myself making a weak sort of resolution there and then to try to become more like the kind of person he needed – more decisive, more willing to take decisions on my own account, rather than worrying my colleagues with doubts and insecurities largely caused (I told myself, wanting to believe it) by the fact that I was living and working in a foreign country.

Such resolves are easy to make and harder to carry out, but nonetheless I felt a satisfaction at making this one. It was as though I'd sealed some sort of bargain with myself, and I raised my arms above my head and stretched lazily again, trying to loosen the muscles in my shoulders and neck. As the tension in them eased, my thoughts turned to the progress I'd made that morning with Katarina. I realised I was smiling, and a second or two later I found myself humming a popular tune which was fast becoming one of that summer's unofficial anthems. Standing there, my arms up in the air, fingers laced together, grinning and singing to myself as I wiggled my hips and jerked my head to one side and then the other to work my neck muscles, I must have presented an interesting sight to Edith and her two colleagues as they crested the dyke on their way to delivering everybody's lunch to the beach.

It took me a moment to notice their appearance on the path twenty-five metres in front of me. When their waves of greeting finally registered I dropped my arms abruptly, fumbling for a few seconds as I tried to stuff my hands casually into the pockets of my shorts, before realising that I was wearing only my swimming trunks. I put one foot up on the lower rung of the back railings, leaned my shoulder against the tower and waved back as coolly as I could. They exchanged a few words with each other, shaking their heads and laughing, then started down the steps on the near-side of the dyke. Their progress was slow, made awkward by the bulging plastic bags they carried in each hand and the heavy-looking knapsacks on their backs.

I loitered self-consciously on the top step as they disappeared from sight and reappeared a minute later on the sand. It took some time before they reached Katarina's group, but eventually greetings were exchanged and the plastic bags set down. After a few moments Edith detached herself from her colleagues, picked up her bags and headed towards the tower. She was obviously finding the unaccustomed exercise hard going, and as she approached I grabbed a chair and carried it down the steps, setting it on the flattened patch of ground next to the tower.

'Here, Edith,' I said as she arrived. 'Have a seat and catch your breath back.'

Edith paused, her face red and chest heaving. She opened her mouth, about to speak, but obviously thought better of it. I hurried forward and helped her take off the knapsack. The weight of it surprised me, and there was a dull sound of clinking glass as I put it on the ground.

'Oh my,' Edith gasped, settling her considerable bulk into the chair and fanning her face with her hand. 'I'm glad I don't have to do that every day.'

'I don't blame you,' I said. 'It must be a good half mile from the camp.'

Edith started in surprise. 'We didn't walk the whole way, for god's sake!' she exclaimed breathlessly. 'I mean, we're not idiots. Ernst gave us a lift in his car. Dropped us on the other side of that bloody dyke.'

'Oh,' I said, taken aback. 'Well ... I suppose that's the only sensible way to do it.'

'If we'd trekked the entire distance on foot it would have killed me,' Edith continued. 'It almost killed me just getting over that dyke, I can tell you. But we're here now, and for once I get to spend an afternoon on the beach.' She took a deep, shaky breath and gestured at the view. 'Isn't it lovely!'

'Yes, I suppose it is.'

Edith looked up at me out of the corner of her eye.

'It's just a shame such a nice place has to be spoiled with the likes of you and my idiot son posing about here every day,' she told me. 'Drowned any children yet this morning?'

'Not yet,' I replied, suppressing a grin. 'We had one in our sights earlier on, but there were too many witnesses. Besides, we knew you were coming so we thought we'd better save our strength. Holger reckons it'll be quite a job, dragging you out there and holding you under.'

Edith chuckled.

'I'd like to see you try it,' she said, raising a hammy fist and waving it under my nose. 'It's been a long time since I gave that son of mine a proper hiding. He's forgotten how hard I can hit. And speaking of Holger, where is the idle crotch-scratcher, anyway?'

I laughed and pointed to where he was standing on the second sandbank.

'Out there, keeping an eye on my windsurfing pupils.'

Edith leaned forward in the chair, squinting against the sunlight. After a moment she snorted in derision.

'I don't believe it!' she cried. 'He's actually working for once! First time in ten years. You'd better call an ambulance, Craig. He'll collapse.'

'We've radioed the helicopter,' I said. 'It's coming in for an airlift.'

Edith roared with laughter.

'Anyway,' she continued, 'I've brought you both some lunch, not that either of you deserve it.'

She indicated the plastic bags at her feet and the knapsack.

'There's a few beers for you in there too,' she added. 'If you want them, that is. Where's Bernward? We've brought some things for him as well.'

'Bernward?' I scratched my head. 'Well he dropped by about

twenty minutes ago, then buggered off again. I'm surprised you didn't pass him on his way back to the camp.'

Edith shrugged.

'Can't say I noticed him. But there's extra sandwiches in there if he bothers turning up again. And he'd better, since I went to the trouble of making his lunch for him.'

'Don't worry about that,' I told her. 'If he's not back in the next hour I'll eat them myself.'

'Don't you dare!' She leaned over the arm of her chair and cuffed me on the leg. 'There's plenty there for you already. Double portion, in fact. I don't know where you put it, I really don't. Bottomless pit, you are.'

'Ow,' I said, rubbing my thigh in pain. 'That really hurt, Edith.'

'Yes?' There was a distinct lack of sympathy in her voice. 'It'll be your head that's hurting if you don't get those bags inside double-quick. The sandwiches'll go soggy if they're left out in the sun.'

Still rubbing my thigh, I gathered the bags and knapsack and took them inside.

'We've got a sun umbrella around somewhere,' I called down. 'Want me to dig it out for you?'

Edith looked up at me and shook her head.

'No thanks, Craig. I spend most of my time working indoors, so I want to enjoy the sun while I can. If I get too hot I can always sit in the tower for a bit.'

Shrugging, I made my way back down the steps.

'Anyway,' I told her. 'You don't mind if I go and help Holger get my pupils sorted out? There's nothing you need?'

She waved a hand, dismissing me.

'Don't worry, I'm fine.'

I turned to go.

'You know,' she called after me, 'you're a good boy really, Craig. It's just a shame you're so damn ugly. God knows what happens when you go in the sea. You must scare all the fish away.'

I left Edith chuckling to herself and walked onto the beach. Holger must have noticed the arrival of lunch and was already moving towards the shore with the kids and their rigs. I waded out to meet them.

126

'Hey!' I called, pointing to the swiftly developing bruise Edith had given me. 'Your mum's got a really vicious right jab.'

'That's nothing,' he replied. 'Wait till she hits you with one of her upper-cuts. It'll knock your head into the middle of next week!'

I laughed ruefully and moved past him to help one of my group tow their rig back. The kids seemed happy enough, talking about how well they were doing with the latest manoeuvres and arguing cheerfully over who was best at them. We lifted the rigs onto the shore, laying the sails flat on the sand and turning the boards over so their skegs wouldn't break.

I sent the kids off to get their sandwiches, warning them not to misplace their wetsuit jackets and promising them another session in the afternoon if they wanted. As they scampered away, Holger went back out to bring in the kayakers and I walked down the beach to fetch the paddle that I'd noticed floating in the shallows earlier. Making my way back, I absentmindedly spun the long, double-bladed object over the back of my hand, like some New York cop from the 1930s spinning his night stick.

'Show off!' Holger jeered as I approached. 'I suppose you stood in front of the mirror for hours practising that move.'

''Fraid not,' I replied, grinning. 'I spent hours in front of the mirror practising *this* move. HA YA!'

I reversed the paddle's direction, delivering a series of kung-fu-style strikes that stopped just short of his head.

Holger didn't flinch.

'You've been spouting that Holy Master Sensei Surfer shit to the kids for so long you're starting to believe it,' he told me. 'What you seem to have forgotten is that in real life you couldn't beat up a teddy bear.'

I laughed, tapping the tip of one of the blades against his chest.

'Your weak insults are no match for Holy Master, oh fat dumb one. Beware the sting of my flashing staff as it cracks against your thick skull.'

'I think my skull can take it,' Holger replied calmly, and before I could respond he'd batted the paddle aside, darted forward and grabbed me tightly around my waist. All of a sudden I found myself in a painful bear hug.

'Owf,' I moaned, as Holger squeezed my stomach tightly. 'Christ man, that hurts.'

Holger's muffled voice rose up from somewhere around my navel.

'What use are your oriental fighting skills now, oh over-confident one?'

'I don't know,' I replied. 'But if you don't stop soon you'll have a foreigner's puke all down your back.'

Holger released me quickly and stepped away. His face was flushed and I was sure mine was too. I rubbed my stomach and the tight ache around my ribs. It hurt to breathe.

'Good grief, Holger,' I gasped plaintively. 'Has anyone ever told you how just like your mother you are?'

'Every day,' he replied, grinning again. He reached out and clapped me on the shoulder.

'All right, Craig? No harm done?'

I shook my head, still clutching my stomach.

'Don't think so. Nothing that a few organ transplants and a blood transfusion wouldn't cure.'

Holger laughed.

'I don't know about a blood transfusion,' he said. 'But I'm willing to bet my mum's brought us a couple of beers to have with our lunch. That'll sort you out.'

I reached down to pick up the paddle again, wincing at the stabbing pain from my ribs, then chucked it towards the kayak where it belonged.

Holger was busy surveying the crowded length of beach.

'So much for our day off,' I said, gesturing at the scene.

Holger continued to watch for a moment, taking in the milling groups of kids, teenagers, and messy clutters of equipment.

'You know something, Craig?' he said finally.

'What's that then?'

He turned his head, meeting my eye.

'I don't care what Bernward thinks. As far as I'm concerned, we do a damn fine job.'

I nodded at this, considering.

'Yes, I suppose we do, really.'

'You bet we do.' He punched me lightly on the shoulder. 'So

how about some lunch then? I think we've earned it.'

'Well, when you put it like that, Holger, I guess we have.'

And together, side by side, we made our way back across the soft, warm sand, heading for the path that led up to the tower.

Edith had made us enough food to last a week. Unpacking the bags and opening the tinfoil packages we found portions of salad, boiled eggs, baguettes filled with ham and cheese and cheese and tomato, and a ridiculous amount of jam sandwiches. But as much as Holger liked the food, his real delight came when he opened his mother's knapsack.

'Beer!' he crowed, reaching a hand in deep to feel the bottles. 'And they're cold! Straight from the fridge.' He pulled one out and squinted at the label. 'Flensburger. You beauty.'

'Thanks, Mum,' he called, leaning out of the doorway. 'You're a gem.'

Edith waved up at him from her chair.

'Just don't eat it all,' she warned him. 'The food's to do me and Bernward as well.'

'Yeah yeah,' Holger mumbled.

I leaned back against the window sill, and hopped up into a sitting position.

'Here,' Holger said. 'Catch.'

He tossed me the bottle of Flensburger and burrowed back into the knapsack to get one for himself.

'Hang on, there's something else in here.' There was a rustling sound as he drew out a newspaper from the bottom of the bag.

'Ah,' he said, holding aloft a copy of *BILD Zeitung*. 'Something to read through the long afternoon. Great.'

'Christ,' I said, looking at the tabloid disdainfully. 'Don't you ever get tired of looking at women's breasts, Holger?'

'No,' he replied simply. 'And neither do you. The difference is that you won't admit it.'

He tossed the paper onto the window sill. I knew that he'd go through it later, paying particular attention to the usual five or six photographs of half-naked women. I knew I would too.

'Right then,' he held up his bottle of beer, thumb pressed

against the metal opening mechanism. '*Prost*, Craig.'

'*Prost*.'

I raised my own in reply and the two plopped open simultaneously. Holger took a swallow and smacked his lips, sighing contentedly.

'Ahhh,' he said. 'And it tastes even better knowing how pissed off Bernward'll be if he sees us drinking it.'

'Yeah,' I said. 'But we should go easy this afternoon, eh? Have this one and save the rest for when we've got everything packed away at the end of the day.'

Holger took another swig, then shook his head at me despairingly.

'Honestly, Craig, sometimes I wonder what you're doing here. This is Germany, for god's sake. Even the *police* are allowed to drink beer on duty.'

'Only if they're eating, though,' I pointed out. 'And only a couple.'

Holger opened his arms, gesturing at the packages heaped up on the sea chests.

'It's not like we're going to be drinking on empty stomachs, is it? What do you want first? Cheese and tomato?'

'Sounds good.'

He picked out a baguette and threw it across to me. I was about to take a bite when a thought struck me.

'Hey, Holger.'

'What?'

'If we're going to be sharing the tower this afternoon do you think you could do me a favour? It's very important. Crucial, in fact.'

He stopped and looked across at me, a sandwich in one hand, its tinfoil wrapping in the other.

'Actually,' I went on. 'I'd go as far as to say that it could even be a matter of life and death.'

'Well?' he asked impatiently. 'What is it then?'

'If we're going to be sharing the tower this afternoon, can you please … please … *please* not eat any of those boiled eggs your mother's cooked for us?'

Holger regarded me impassively for a moment, then scrunched

130

up the tinfoil in his left hand. He raised his arm and I flinched, sniggering, as the silver missile ricocheted off my shoulder and landed on the floor.

'Should've kept your mouth shut,' Holger told me. 'Just for that I'm going to eat all of them.'

I smacked the palm of my hand against my forehead.

'Oh no,' I moaned. 'Death by suffocation. What a terrible way to go.'

I was just tucking into a second baguette when there was a clattering on the metal stairs outside and Gerd appeared in the doorway.

'*Mahlzeit*,' he said, giving the traditional German greeting for mealtimes.

'*Mahlzeit*,' Holger responded, beckoning him in. 'Want something to eat?'

Gerd shook his head and patted his stomach.

'No thanks. I've just had three.'

Holger reached a hand into the knapsack.

'How about a beer instead then?'

Gerd's eyes lit up. 'Ah,' he said. 'Now you're talking.'

Holger passed him a bottle and Gerd popped it open. He leaned against the window sill, sipping at it, and looked around the tower absently. Eventually his gaze came to rest on the newspaper lying beside him.

'Hello,' he said, picking it up and waving it in front of him. 'Is this piece of crap what you two call a newspaper?'

'Don't look at me,' I told him. 'Holger's the one who wanted to read it.'

'Hey!' Holger protested. 'That's Germany's most popular newspaper, that is.'

'Just because it's popular doesn't mean it's good,' Gerd said, putting down his beer down and unfolding the paper.

'Yeah, right,' Holger sneered. 'But you're still going to check out the girls in it, aren't you?'

Gerd shook his head, smiling.

'Not at all. But one thing about being on holiday here is that you do tend to lose track of what's going on in the rest of the world. No harm in seeing what the headlines are, is there?'

'Just make sure you don't drool on the topless models,' Holger warned him. 'I hate it when other people get saliva on my newspaper.'

'I'll try to control myself.'

He held the newspaper up, studying the front page.

'Oh that's right,' he muttered. 'Bloody Ronald Reagan's visiting Berlin. I'd forgotten he was coming. What's the bet he lobbed a couple of hand grenades over the Wall, just for fun?'

He turned the paper around so we could see a photo of Reagan making a speech in front of the Berlin Wall, the famous Brandenburg Gate rising behind it.

'Oh,' I said, taken aback. 'So what did he say, then?'

'Um ...' Gerd turned the newspaper around and read the headline. '*Mr Gorbachev, tear down this wall.* Apparently.'

I snorted. 'What with? His letter-opener? And isn't it East Germany's wall anyway? Isn't it up to Honecker to tear it down? Honecker's not exactly in love with Gorbachev's reforms, is he?'

'Christ,' Holger complained. 'Listen to you two. A pair of bloody Communists, the way you go on. If you hate Reagan so much go and live in the East, why don't you?'

Gerd grimaced.

'Thanks for the offer, Holger,' he said. 'But I almost died getting out of the East in the first place, and I have to say I've no particular wish to go back. The regime and I didn't exactly part on the best of terms. But that doesn't mean I have to admire Reagan's foreign policy, does it? Not with all the shit his government's pulled in Central America.'

I'd been slouching against the window frame, eating my sandwich, but now I sat bolt upright, my mouth falling open in amazement.

'Wait a second,' I said. 'Did you just say you *escaped*, Gerd? You mean you escaped from East Germany? Across the Berlin Wall?'

Gerd shrugged.

'Sort of,' he said casually. 'Actually it's complicated. But basically – in essence – yes.'

Holger was looking as stunned as I was.

'You mean you're an *Ossi*?' he cried, using the West German slang for their Eastern brethren.

'Used to be.'

Holger gazed at him for another few moments, then shook his head.

'I don't believe it. No way. You're having us on. I'd know if you were from the East. I'd be able to tell.'

'I've been in the West a long time,' Gerd said. 'It's been nearly twenty years since I came through the Wall. Time enough for the differences to be papered over, I suppose.'

Holger shook his head stubbornly.

'No way,' he repeated. 'You're winding us up.'

Gerd sighed at this, and for a moment I saw how he must look in the classroom: a patient man.

'I promise you, Holger. I'm not kidding. It's the truth. And I'd be happy to tell you the whole story. I don't mind getting into it all, but I don't want to bore you either. Because frankly it would take a while, and I'm not sure you guys want to spend your time that way. I mean, do you really want to sit here listening to me talking for the next forty minutes?'

I nodded emphatically.

'We've got enough time,' I said. 'It's our lunch break. Right, Holger?'

Holger gazed back steadily.

'Well hell,' he said at last. 'Forty minutes isn't much out of my life, and I suppose I might even learn something. Although I've got to say, Gerd, I'm still finding it hard to believe you.'

Gerd smiled thinly.

'Okay,' he said. 'I'll be happy to give you the full story. But you're right about one thing, it *is* hard to believe. Even I find it hard to believe sometimes, and it happened to me. But that's the kind of place East Germany is – some crazy stuff goes on there. Just don't blame me for it, okay? It's not my fault. That's the way things were.'

'No problem,' I replied quickly. 'We're just interested.'

'Okay then,' Gerd said, taking a swig of his beer and a moment or two to collect his thoughts.

And then he cleared his throat and began to tell us the story of his life. He spoke well – it was the teacher in him, perhaps – starting with his childhood and holding nothing back, his deep, rich voice casting a powerful spell. And we listened, increasingly fascinated, for it was indeed a remarkable tale. Occasionally, every five minutes or so, Holger would rise and cross to the window, looking out to check that everything was in order. But I sat there mostly unmoving, my beer and food quickly forgotten, while the immediate world around us – the beach and the low lapping surf on the shore and the faint shrill calls of the children – began to fade from my consciousness, as I found myself, almost against my will, being drawn deeper and deeper into his story.

Part Three
Gerd's Story

Gerd Volker Hagen was just seventeen years old – still a boy really – when he took the astounding decision to risk everything and try to escape to the West. He was unusually strong for a lad of seventeen, it's true, stronger in fact than many adult men can ever hope to be; tall and thick-shouldered and already, even at that young age, shaving twice a day, with a burly seaman's build and a slightly rolling seaman's gait, and clear blue seaman's eyes under a thickish mop of sandy windblown hair – all of which he'd inherited like a birthright, for the sea was in his family's blood, and probably had been for centuries.

Gerd grew up in East Germany in the 1950s, under Communism, and he was certainly no city boy: not for him some pale-faced childhood roaming the empty, furtive streets of East Berlin, with its drab urban backcloth of power cuts, shopping queues, and choking clouds of blue smoke billowing from the exhaust pipes of Trabant cars. Instead he was born and raised in a small seaside town on the north coast, only thirty miles by fishing boat from the Iron Curtain border with West Germany. He spent his early years roaming the open fields and sloping dykes of the patchwork coastal countryside, with the salt air of the Baltic filling his lungs and the endless cawing of gulls ringing in his ears, as he worked up an impressive appetite for the raw salted herring or steaming fish soup that his mother liked to have waiting for him when he returned home in the evenings.

It was a mostly happy childhood, he would assure us later: certainly there was nothing in those early years that made him later want to flee the country he called home. Indeed, by DDR standards his upbringing was relatively privileged. He was an only child – the offspring of a strong-willed mother and a quiet but drunken father who'd walked out for the last time when Gerd was seven (probably, he thought now, sent packing by his mother). But while he'd recognised early on, with a child's instincts, that his father was a sad and frustrated man, a malcontent in a society which did not permit people to be malcontented, his uncle – his mother's brother – was very different. For Uncle Jens was a bigwig in the party, a man with real political clout, and he seemed happy to act, albeit occasionally, as a substitute father to Gerd, perhaps because he himself had never married or had children. This uncle made sure to visit them at their seaside home every second or third weekend, and he invariably brought with him presents and luxuries from the city. The rest of the time he somehow contrived to look after them from a distance, wielding his power from behind the formidable redoubt of his office desk, which was hidden behind the thick stone façade of the party's monolithic headquarters in East Berlin.

It was surely thanks to this uncle's quiet influence that Gerd was blessed with such an easy and comfortable upbringing – smiled upon by his teachers and the local party hacks, and hazily aware of being singled out for better treatment and better opportunities than most of his friends.

And so whenever he thought back to his childhood, Gerd told us now, what he remembered wasn't the dull, endless repetition of the indoctrination lessons in school, or the party slogans posted on the walls, or the banners strung above the cobbled streets on special party days. Such things he simply took for granted, as children do – for what does a child know of politics? It was never these things that stood out in his memory, but rather the long summer days he spent playing on the beach in the holidays, or running through the woods with his friends in the autumn, hunting for mushrooms or berries, or trekking out in the cold, harsh light of winter to skate on the hardened lakes of shallow water that formed in the fields behind the dykes. These were the things he remembered. And he could recall too that afterwards, in the gathering darkness, he would run or cycle home with his cheeks pinched and his red nose running, to sit down to a welcome bowl of hot soup or heavy German stew, before snuggling up beside his mother in front of the fire (no shortage of meat for Gerd, and no cramped concrete box of a city apartment either), with his mother's favourite classical music playing on the radio and perhaps even the rare and special treat of a banana or an orange to eat, if his uncle had been to visit that week.

These were the things that Gerd remembered most about his childhood, from the years when he was eight or nine or ten.

And as he grew older, and the subsequent seasons added inches to his height and muscle to his chest, Gerd also progressed, without ever questioning the process, from the childish games of the Young Pioneers to the older and more political Free German Youth; not because he particularly desired to do so but because that was simply what you did – especially if your uncle was high up in the party. And he wore the uniforms of those organisations without ever thinking very much about it, and marched in the parades and listened to the speeches, again without thinking very much about it, because that was also what you did.

It would not be true, however, to say that there was *nothing* about these party activities that interested him. For, in common with many of his friends, there was one aspect of the duties that aroused his interest greatly – excited him even – and that was the numerous opportunities they offered for pursuing his favourite hobbies: girls and sport. Because as he'd grown into his teenage years, the young Gerd had discovered that he had something of a talent for both these things, and he was now able to indulge himself in each with more than reasonable success. The girls by night, and the sport – particularly swimming, rowing and kayaking – by day. And while he might never have won medals for his success with girls, except perhaps in his own head, he won medals for the other things, particularly the rowing and the swimming, and he put these medals and trophies up on the shelves in his bedroom, proudly on display, while further down the road (and well out of his sight) another page or two was added to the substantial cardboard file with his name on it that was kept under lock and key in his school, and a copy of which was passed, every year and also without him knowing, to a liaison officer in the ugly grey building near the centre of the city of Rostock, in which the *Staats Sicherheits Dienst* – the STASI – had their regional headquarters.

So it was that by the time he reached the age of sixteen, young Gerd Hagen was already big and strong and fit, popular with his teachers and sports coaches, and particularly popular with girls, even very pretty girls four or five years older than himself.

Yet looking back at it, Gerd told us later, he had to admit that in many other respects he was still more of a child than a man, immature in various ways – largely, perhaps, as a result of his privileged upbringing. And there was one area in particular where his attitude had been too childish for his own good, he felt. Indeed, with hindsight, he would go so far as to say that when it came to understanding the nature of the State in which he lived, and the character of the regime that ran it, his younger self had been quite simply naïve.

This, then, was roughly how things stood just after Gerd's sixteenth birthday, when he came home from school one day and learned from a stranger that his mother lay sprawled on the kitchen floor, stone cold dead with a knife through her throat.

Fortunately it wasn't Gerd who found her body. Although it didn't feel like much of a blessing at the time, he was never allowed to see her corpse. Not only was he spared by officials from having to view the body on some cold metal tray in the morgue, he wasn't even permitted to look down on her as she lay in her coffin at the funeral, because at the insistence of the State she was eventually cremated in a closed-casket ceremony, following the usual well-attended but drab, secular function the party did so well.

'It's better this way,' the various bureaucrats assured him, at first gently, but later, when he persisted in his requests, with increasing irritation.

Presumably they were right; that given the nature of her injuries it *was* better that he should never see her – but the unfortunate corollary for Gerd was that it left him unable to accept that his mother was really, truly, dead. He just couldn't bring himself to believe it, and the horror of the event retained a dreamlike unreality for him, so that subsequently there was never a time when he was able to feel any of the emotions appropriate to grieving. And for a year or more afterwards he would sometimes lie awake at night and berate himself for this strange fact.

What he was left to feel instead – in the weeks and months that followed – was mostly numb, and disbelieving.

It had happened on a school day. His mother had a part-time job three days a week, which was the least the State expected of a woman, but that morning had been free, so she'd taken the time to feed him breakfast and see him off at the door, waving and calling endearments as he walked down the street, much to his embarrassment and her amusement. At school he'd had to suffer slowly through two hours of mathematics, an hour of German grammar, and an hour of Marxist Political History on the subject of the Chronic Exploitation of the Proletariat by the Fascist–Capitalist System. Eventually, and much to his relief, the bell rang for lunch, followed – for those like him with special talent – by a full afternoon given over to sport: fifty minutes of swimming followed by two hours of rowing practice, rounded off with a ten-minute lecture on the patriotic need for military service by fit male Socialist Citizens.

So it wasn't surprising that he was feeling more than a little tired as he trudged his way up the hill towards his home at about 6 p.m. that evening. The showers in the changing room had been out of action, an annoying but not unusual occurrence, and his scalp and neck were rapidly chilling as leftover beads of sweat dried in the wind. It was September, the weather already brisk on the coast, and above the dark and choppy water the sky was shaping up for what looked to be a beautiful sunset. But all the young Gerd was thinking of was the prospect of a hot meal and a scalding bath, followed by the nine o'clock date he'd arranged with Winfred Gehlen in the sand dunes behind the boathouse. Winfred was his regular squeeze during the week, when he found himself largely confined to the town, although at weekends he liked to take out his racing bike – another present from Uncle Jens – and explore the possibilities further afield.

It was with such pleasant and idle concerns in his mind that he rounded the corner at the lower end of his street. His head was down and his eyes were fixed on the ground, so that from a distance he must have looked like any bored schoolboy scuffing his slow way home. But there were other eyes waiting for him on that road, looking out for him, and when he appeared there was a sudden low stirring amongst the small crowd of people gathered at the top of the street. He sensed this rather than saw it, but it brought him to a standstill nonetheless and caused him to lift his gaze.

The central feature of the sight that now struck him was the square bulk of an ambulance, parked ominously in the road outside his house. Around this, like piglets round a sow, were several dull-grey box-like cars and an indeterminate number of men wearing military-style uniforms of the same ugly shade. This was the distinctive colour reserved for the VoPo – the *Volkspolizei*, or People's Police. Between Gerd and the VoPo officers was a small crowd of onlookers, most of whom he recognised as neighbours. But even as he looked he could see several of these folk gesturing with their hands in his direction, at the same time turning their faces and apparently addressing someone behind them. After a moment these people moved aside, opening up a narrow space through which a man emerged, stepping with care. This man was of medium height, Gerd saw, barrel-chested and solidly built; even from a distance his body looked as though it was mostly slabs of muscle. He was wearing civilian clothes: grey slacks and a lightly checked grey jacket, white shirt, grey tie, black shoes, and a somewhat surprising grey homburg hat which even in that place and at that time must have been ten years out of fashion. Despite this get-up, however, any East German over the age of eight would have known at a glance that this was a person who had the full authority of the party and the State behind him.

For a moment the man stood still, hands by his sides, watching Gerd – almost, it seemed, measuring him up. And then, with deliberate, measured strides, he began to walk down the road towards the teenager. It seemed to take him a long time and the whole way, Gerd couldn't help but notice, the man's gaze never left Gerd's face.

The boy stood there and waited, heart pounding horribly in his chest, because there was nothing else to do.

In fairness to the investigating officials, it didn't seem as if they'd deliberately set out to tell a sixteen-year-old schoolboy that someone had plunged a knife through his mother's throat. Although it was hardly a consolation, that particular detail appeared to slip out by accident – and not until later. At first the grey man with the granite face had merely confirmed Gerd's identity, asking for his papers and flicking through them with a practised thumb and eye. Handing them back, he'd said in a deep and solemn voice:

'It's my sad duty to inform you, comrade, that your mother – Anja Celeste Hagen – is dead. You have my sympathies, and the sympathies of the State. She was a loyal Communist and a true worker. We are investigating her death. That means there are certain matters we must pursue and certain questions we must ask. Of many people. But also of you.'

He paused for a moment, perhaps looking for a reaction, then added: 'Do you understand this?'

Gerd's world had slipped on its axis during this clipped speech, and it took him a second to realise that something was expected of him, some reply. The best he could manage was a strangled noise in his throat and an otherwise dumb nod.

'Good,' the man said, apparently satisfied. 'Now, before we come to these matters, is there anybody else you would wish to be informed? Friends or relatives, perhaps, that you would like us to get in touch with?'

Gerd started to speak, stopped, cleared his throat, then tried again.

'You should tell my Uncle Jens,' he managed, hoarsely.

This was greeted with a brisk, almost approving nod.

'We are aware of your mother's family connection with Party Comrade Hagen,' the man said. 'He's being informed at this moment.'

Gerd nodded dumbly again. But he must have looked very lost, for the man suddenly reached out and clapped him awkwardly on the shoulder.

'Come,' he said, trying to soften his voice a little. 'You should come with us now. There are questions we have to ask. And of course we'll look after you. You'll be okay. You are a good boy, yes?'

And Gerd, a very young man with no real father present in his life, had nodded miserably in reply: *Yes.*

143

At this the officer turned slightly and raised his hand in what must have been some sort of prearranged signal, for one of the VoPo cars immediately started up and nosed its way through the crowd, rolling slowly down the street in order to pick them up.

There were no clocks on any of the walls in the labyrinthine building, and Gerd had long ago lost count of the hours that he'd spent amongst the various offices and hallways within it. At around 6.30 p.m., while he was still in an unthinking daze, he'd been driven out of his home town at speed and taken somewhere, probably Rostock, although he wasn't quite sure and hadn't yet got around to asking. At that moment he found himself alone in a strange office, surrounded on three sides by frosted-glass walls, with the door to the corridor a little ajar. He was exhausted, had a headache from the harsh overhead striplight, and he felt more than a little sick. He still hadn't had a chance to shower, and every time he shifted on the hard, upright wooden chair he caught a whiff of his own body odour that was strong enough to make him grimace. He knew only that his mother was dead, somebody was supposed to be telling his uncle about it, and nobody had asked him any real questions since he'd arrived in this miserable place, with its green institutional walls and its too-bright lighting. He'd been told there were details surrounding his mother's demise which had to be looked into, but that was something which he frankly hadn't been able to take in, and in truth all he wanted to do was get the hell out of there and go home, so he could have a warm bath and lie down in his own bed. In wishing for this, it must be said, it never occurred to him that he might be confronted with the sight of several pints of his mother's blood sprayed all over the kitchen.

Eventually from somewhere down the empty corridor he heard footsteps. As the steps came nearer he could make out shadows on the wall beyond the frosted glass, together with low mumblings that echoed weirdly in the corridor's strange acoustics. He realised that the voices belonged to two different men.

'. . . husband?' one of the voices seemed to be saying now.

'Looks like it,' the other replied, more distinctly, as the footsteps approached.

144

'H'd sh' die?' the first voice said, closer this time. Although this sounded indistinct, the next word suddenly snapped into focus: '*Knife?*'

'Uh huh,' the reply came. 'Straight through the windpipe. Bastard left it stuck in there, up to the hilt.'

There was a low whistle.

'Shit. What a fucking animal! They sending you the pictures?'

'Yes. I'll let you have a look. But ssshh now. Here we are.'

The murmuring ended, and a few moments later the shadows coalesced into solid, human shapes behind the glass. A hand grasped the open edge of the door. From the hazy but unmistakably squat outline it was attached to, Gerd recognised the official who'd approached him in the street – the grey man. This man had sat beside him in the back of the VoPo car, and also spent some time with Gerd since they'd arrived, coming in and out of the various rooms the teenager had been taken to. The man had his back to the door, and as he tugged it towards him now, lingering a little, Gerd caught a glimpse of the colleague he'd been speaking to. The eyes of this second man stared straight back at Gerd and there was a greedy curiosity in his gaze which was simply obscene.

'Later,' the grey man said impatiently, shifting his weight a little as if to block his colleague's stare.

'Yeah, later,' the other replied reluctantly. He managed to wrench his eyes away from Gerd and move off down the corridor.

The grey man was carrying two objects in his free hand, and after a moment Gerd realised with dull surprise that they were coffee mugs.

'Here,' the man said to Gerd with a brief, impersonal smile. 'Thought you might like something to drink.'

Gerd took the mug, and as the officer sat down opposite him he raised it automatically to his lips and gulped back a few lukewarm, milky mouthfuls.

The man wasn't wearing his homburg hat anymore. His head was as bald as a baby's arse and he rubbed his hand over it heavily.

'So,' he said at last. 'This might seem like a strange question, but I have to ask you, Gerd. I know that your father walked out

145

on you years ago, but what I really need to know now is whether or not he's been back to visit you recently?'

He paused for a moment, as if to let this sink in, then leaned forward.

'Think carefully, Gerd. Have you seen him at all, your father? Not necessarily at the house . . . maybe just on the streets. Hanging around, perhaps? Watching?'

In the silence that followed Gerd stared at the man. And then he vomited the coffee back up, violently, all over his knees.

The trial, a mere three months later, was not held in public and Gerd was permitted to attend only for a brief twenty minutes, and then only as a witness to testify about his parents' relationship. Although he was given to understand that his father was on trial for murder he was shocked to discover that there was no sign of him – or any defendant – in the courtroom. But it was explained to him by an officer that his father, suffering from alcoholic dementia, had refused point-blank to leave his prison cell to attend the proceedings and was therefore being tried *in absentia*. It never occurred to the teenager to ask to see or speak to him. He hadn't seen the man for almost ten years, and the attitude both of the party lawyers and the VoPo officer who accompanied him to and from the court building seemed tacitly to forbid it. Gerd wouldn't have known what to say to him anyway.

Nor was his father the only person conspicuous by his absence. Gerd's Uncle Jens wasn't around either, and indeed hadn't been since the murder. Gerd had been informed that this was because, on hearing the news, his uncle had collapsed on the spot with serious breathing difficulties and was now being treated in hospital for nervous exhaustion. Although he was receiving the very best treatment (as the VoPo officer repeatedly assured Gerd), his recovery was likely to be a slow one, and to achieve it his doctors had decreed that the respected party comrade must have complete rest. Almost as if in confirmation of this, a few days before a verdict was handed down by the judges, Gerd received a handwritten card from his uncle. The message was short, but the teenager recognised the handwriting immediately, although he was somewhat dismayed at the uncharacteristic, spidery weakness of the lettering. His uncle took the opportunity to offer his condolences and share in his nephew's terrible loss, and also to apologise that he couldn't be by Gerd's side at such a difficult time. He added, however, that he was untroubled by worries regarding Gerd's future, as he had every confidence in the party's ability to do the right thing by him, and could only urge his nephew in the strongest terms to put all his faith in the party's advice, and in particular to follow the suggestions of its representative in this matter. His uncle even singled out this representative by name – one Emile Koch – and after some reflection Gerd decided that this name probably referred to the bald man in the grey clothes who'd first given him the news of his mother's death.

In this assumption he was – to some extent, at least – correct.

The grey man who called himself Emile Koch finally returned to visit Gerd on 26th February 1969 – the day the teenager learned that his father had been sentenced to twenty-two years hard labour for the brutal murder of his mother.

'Although if you ask me he'll be lucky to survive *two* years, never mind twenty-two,' Koch told him grimly. 'The booze really took its toll on your old man, you know? Still, I've got to say that he deserves it, as I'm sure you'll agree.'

Gerd hadn't really known what to say to that, so he'd let it slide.

This conversation took place in a pub – a traditional German street-corner bar, or *Eckkneipe* – in the regional capital of Rostock. By that time Gerd hadn't been back to his home town in almost six months. Instead, ever since that awful, interminable night when he'd found himself cleaning his own vomit off his trousers under the harsh glare of the striplighting in the third-floor toilets of the Stasi building, he'd been living at a boys' boarding school in the city. This school was favoured by the government and specialised in promoting sporting excellence. Although, under other circumstances, Gerd might have responded better to the crowded, jocular rough-housing of dormitory life there, he nonetheless felt comfortable enough, if not exactly happy. He was grateful for the constant company, the benefits of which for him outweighed the lack of privacy, and the locker-room atmosphere which pervaded the school was comfortingly familiar. And of course he loved the sport he did there, heart and soul, as those who have physical talent usually do. So despite his personal circumstances it was with a certain amount of joy that he ran around the track and wrestled in the gym, and rowed like hell on the river while the sweat streamed down his face, and his heart and head hammered until they both seemed ready to burst – because that was the release his body craved, and in the doing of it his mind often found respite as well.

And then one day, after almost half a year of this, he was told by the assistant headmaster to present himself in the reception room next to the main hall at 7 p.m., showered, shaved and dressed in smart clothes, for he would have a visitor that evening. That particular room had a large fireplace, and although in Gerd's experience the fire was never lit, when he opened the door at three minutes to seven he saw to his amazement that not only was the fire blazing away, but that the granite-like figure of bald, grey Emile Koch was standing in front of it, warming himself against the bitter February cold outside, and with the same ridiculous homburg hat as before now sitting on the mantelpiece.

'Come in,' Koch said gruffly, gesturing at Gerd with one of his large, strangler's hands. 'And close the door, for fuck's sake. You're letting all the heat out.'

Gerd closed the door smartly and stepped forward into the room. The school had weekly drill practice, and as he stopped in the centre of the floor he had to resist the automatic urge to stamp his feet to attention, but he stood straight enough, with his stomach sucked in and his head held high. He was a tall lad, of course, strong and lean and very, very fit, and the granite man looked him up and down with seeming approval.

'So, Gerd,' he said now. 'Tell me. How are you finding your new home? Settling in all right? I'm glad to say we've had nothing but good reports about how you're getting on.'

Gerd was both surprised and flattered at this intimation of official interest.

'It's fine, thank you, sir,' he replied. Then he recalled himself and added hurriedly: 'In fact I'm very grateful to the State for looking after me.'

The man dismissed this with a heavy shrug.

'The State looks after everyone,' he said matter-of-factly. 'That's what's so great about the State. That's why we're all so proud to work for it – and to fight for it, if need be. Even to die for it if we must. Wouldn't you agree, Comrade Hagen?'

'Yes, sir!' Gerd barked, trying to draw himself up even straighter.

The man studied him for a moment, as if to judge whether or not this reaction was sincere. But whatever he saw seemed to satisfy him, and he stepped away from the mantelpiece, holding out a hand.

'My name is Comrade Koch, Gerd,' he said, 'but you can call me Emile. At least in private. Okay?'

Gerd hesitated for a second, unsure at the protocol of calling someone in authority – and so much older – by their first name. But he moved forward nonetheless and grasped the proffered hand, feeling his own fingers enveloped and squeezed powerfully, almost painfully. This was a novel sensation for him: it wasn't often that Gerd encountered someone with hands capable of crushing his own.

'Okay,' the boy agreed, as Koch released his grip.

'Good,' Koch said, nodding approvingly. 'That's a start. Now tell me, Gerd, do the boys at this school smoke at all?'

As he spoke he reached into his jacket pocket and pulled out a packet of cigarettes. This packet immediately caught Gerd's eye. It had an unusually glossy, garish red-and-white design, and looking at it Gerd realised with a slight shock that it didn't come from any of the Communist countries.

So he hesitated now before replying. It wasn't just that Koch appeared to be offering him Western cigarettes, it was also that smoking by pupils at the school was strictly prohibited, under threat of expulsion. But after lights out at the weekend some of the older boys made their way up onto the roof to smoke a cigarette or two, and sometimes Gerd was among them.

Yet his first instinct now was to try and cover this up.

'I'm afraid I wouldn't know, sir,' he said. 'I mean . . . Emile.'

'Better,' the grey man conceded gruffly, and this time the amusement in his voice was unmistakable. He pushed the top of the packet open with one thick thumb and slid a cigarette into his mouth, his other hand reaching into his trouser pocket and pulling out a square, silver lighter.

'You're not seriously trying to tell me that none of the boys in this school smoke?' he asked, flicking the lighter open and lowering his head to the flame. He puffed twice and straightened up, snapping the lighter shut.

'I mean,' Koch went on, gesturing with the cigarette and blowing a stream of smoke. 'It's been a while, but I can't believe that boys have changed *that* much since my day.'

Gerd didn't reply, and after a moment the grey man's eyes narrowed.

'Okay,' he said, with a heavy sigh. 'Never mind. Here, catch.'

He tossed the cigarette packet towards Gerd and the teenager caught it reflexively.

'They're American,' Koch told him. 'A lot better than the shit you boys smoke on the roof. Go on, try one.'

Gerd looked down at the packet in his hand, wondering how the man in front of him knew about what went on on the roof.

'Go on,' Koch repeated. 'Try one.'

Gerd continued to hesitate, and Koch seemed to lose his patience a little.

'Look,' he said roughly. 'Think of it as an order. Because I'll tell you now, you're going to have to learn how to smoke, although just for show, obviously. We wouldn't want your fitness to be affected – that's one of your best assets as far as we're concerned. But smoking will be a necessary skill if you want to be useful to us. So for fuck's sake go ahead and light one up, before I die of old age.'

There were too many implications in this short speech for Gerd to process them immediately. Instead he found himself doing as he was told, opening the packet and taking out a cigarette. As he put it in his mouth Koch moved forward, clicking open his lighter and holding up the flame. Gerd bent his head and puffed the tobacco into life.

'Tastes a bit better than that other crap you've been smoking, doesn't it?'

Since the other crap had been manufactured in East Germany, Gerd thought it wise to treat this as a rhetorical question. He puffed at the cigarette in his mouth and looked at the man in front of him. Koch was a few inches shorter than he was, and several decades older, but his shoulders and chest were just as broad as Gerd's, and his arms more powerful.

They smoked together in silence for a minute, each with their own thoughts.

'Good,' Koch said at last, nodding. 'You smoke fine. You should practise occasionally, but like I said don't let it become a habit. Now what about drinking? I imagine, given your father's history, that you're pretty careful when it comes to booze.'

Gerd gave a non-committal shrug. In fact he'd been drunk about ten times in his life – usually celebrating sporting victories with his friends. But he'd been left in no doubt that he liked the feeling, regardless of the occasional mild hangover.

'Well, drinking's another thing you'll need to practise,' Koch said now, clapping his hands together briskly. 'And the sooner the better, if you ask me. So what do you reckon? How about we get out of this dump and have some real fun for a change. God knows you deserve it, Gerd. And I know just the place, not far from here. And don't worry about what your teachers might think, because I've taken care of them. So what do you say?'

This attempt at chumminess was clearly forced, but Gerd found himself appreciating it nonetheless. After all, the last six months had been a very tough time for him, and the boarding school routine, although providing comfort and stability, also held its fair share of monotony. So he was more than ready now for a little excitement – for something new – and here Koch was, seemingly offering exactly that, at least for an evening.

'Great,' Gerd said simply. 'If you're sure it's all right.'

Koch slapped his thigh and smiled broadly, revealing teeth like crooked tombstones.

'Of course it's all right!' he exclaimed, giving Gerd a clap on the shoulder. Then he took the cigarette out of his mouth and flicked it into the fire, jerking his head for Gerd to follow suit.

'Don't want to stink out the hallway.' he said solemnly. 'Head-master wouldn't like it.'

Gerd did as he was told and then glanced towards the winter darkness beyond the window. It was minus fifteen outside.

'Maybe I should get a coat.'

'Nah!' Koch replied heartily. 'You don't need one – I've got a Trabi waiting, with a driver. You are the nephew of the esteemed Party Comrade Hagen, after all. We couldn't let you get snow on your fucking shoes now, could we?'

Before Gerd could think of a suitable reply, Koch put a heavy hand on his shoulder and began pushing him towards the door.

'I know just the place,' he repeated reassuringly. 'You'll love it, I promise you. The barmaid's got a great pair of tits.' He paused for a moment and then added: 'You do know about them, don't you?'

The sudden unexpectedness of this remark caught Gerd completely by surprise and he burst out laughing. And he was still laughing as he allowed himself to be shepherded out, wondering what the night would bring. He felt excited, but quite safe.

After all, he reflected, Emile Koch worked for the State, and the State certainly knew what it was doing.

Didn't it?

'Hey, didn't I tell you she had great fucking tits!'

Koch had spoken loudly, loudly enough for Gerd to hear him over the bad music, but probably not loudly enough for the barmaid who was the subject of this comment to hear it too, or so Gerd thought. But then if she had caught it, the music was loud enough for her to pretend that she hadn't. Which was probably all that mattered, Gerd thought now, although admittedly the process by which he reached this conclusion was slow and befuddled.

An *Eckkneipe* is unlikely to be a big place, as any German could tell you. In fact it's far more likely to be deliberately small, in order to promote a certain sort of atmosphere. This atmosphere is fairly intimate, at least by male standards, the kind of atmosphere likely to be generated by a well-frequented venue with just four or five tables and seven or eight bar stools – and very masculine. Indeed, usually the only female to be seen in one of these places is the one pouring drinks behind the bar. In a modern Western society such a place might possibly cater to a gay clientele, or, less happily, to the kind of lonely alcoholics who are still capable of holding down a job. In dictatorial Communist East Germany, however, where the alcoholism rate was twice that of its West German counterpart (and booze a fraction of the price) and where homosexuality would be an imprisonable offence until 1990, such an establishment was neither of these things. It was the typical destination for heterosexual East German men – married or single – who wished to get the hell out of their cramped workers' flat on any given evening. Around sixty per cent of the male population had at least one haunt like this within a ten-minute stumble of where they lived, and hundreds of thousands of men across the country could be found getting drunk in such places more nights than not, in the absence of a more productive hobby.

And it was to just such an *Eckkneipe* on a street corner in Rostock that a certain Stasi colonel who sometimes went by the name of Emile Koch took sixteen-year-old Gerd Hagen that cold February night in 1969. Perhaps he chose that particular bar because it happened to be close to the school where the teenager was living, or perhaps it was because the professionally minded colonel knew he could get the cost of the drinks refunded to him without having to go through the usual bureaucracy of submitting receipts in triplicate. But the most likely reason Gerd was taken there that night was because the bar was in fact a Stasi-run operation, which meant it was fully decked out with surveillance equipment, including a two-way wall mirror with a concealed film camera, and little vases of plastic flowers on every table containing hidden microphones, with the amplification of each receiver carefully boosted to offset the noise of the sanitised Western pop covers playing on the scratchy East German sound system.

Stasi recruitment of a low-level asset like Gerd would not normally have involved the use of such resources, but the colonel was playing a very unusual game indeed, and he was thinking a long, long way ahead.

By the time four half-litre glasses of beer had been washed down with four double shots of clear fiery vodka, young Gerd Hagen was in no doubt that he'd made the right decision in taking up Koch's unusual offer. By then he was suffused with a warm glow of satisfaction, not to mention a somewhat jubilant camaraderie, and up until this point his good friend and – well, why not? – *mentor*, Emile Koch, was proving that he could be very amiable company indeed. This, with hindsight, shouldn't have been too surprising, for it was part of the colonel's job to be a good companion when necessary. He traded in people, after all. And while, as a loyal party man, the colonel wasn't in the least bit religious, it nonetheless amused him at times to imagine that, on some level, what he was engaged in was nothing less than the buying and selling of people's souls. Certainly – and Koch would later take great pleasure in telling the teenager this – he'd known even before he sat down to study the carefully annotated psychiatrist's notes in young Gerd Hagen's file exactly what to do in *this* case. Play up to the boy's need for a father figure, be both forbidding and approachable at the same time, and of course butter him up with the occasional light touch of flattery . . .

Actually, the colonel felt, you could dress it up with any amount of fancy words, but basically he just had to offer this spoiled teenage git exactly what he wanted, emotionally. Indeed, by the colonel's estimation, such tactics would probably work with about thirty per cent of the population. Another fifty per cent could reliably be bullied or blackmailed, if necessary. And as for the remaining twenty per cent . . . Well, in the colonel's opinion – although he never said so aloud – that particular section of the population just needed to be lined up against a wall and shot, like in the glory days of the revolution, but unfortunately the political will amongst the current leadership was clearly lacking, so he and his colleagues were left to carry on the struggle as best they could.

All this was lurking at the back of the colonel's mind during the ninety minutes he spent spinning out the web of verbal silk that was the necessary preliminary to his entrapment of the boy in front of him. Long years of practice meant that he could do this sort of thing without thinking, which was fortunate, because he found it tiring to be working so late – although it wasn't unusual – and of course he was bored too, also not unusual. However he knew that alcohol would speed up the process, and he made sure the drinks kept coming.

Later the colonel would tell Gerd that he often liked to speculate on what line of work he might have gone into if he'd been born in the decadent West – he would surely have been a great success, he felt, at either pimping or PR. But at the same time Koch was

154

aware that neither of these fields would have given him what he'd always wanted so very, very badly: *real* power. Not only over those unlucky individuals with whom he came into contact, but also in general, within society as a whole. Fortunately the colonel had been brought up in East Germany, where there was a ready-made and wholly legal organisation which combined the various aspects of power that he, and a handful of others like him, sought. Against the baleful might of an organised network like the Stasi, this silly teenager he was dealing with was nothing ... less than nothing even, despite the kid's family connections.

Yet at the time, as he sat at the bar, Koch was still uneasy. For given the lad's recent background, the colonel was only too aware that he was playing a very risky game in trying to turn him to his own ends. Even so the potential rewards justified the risk, he felt. Because the colonel had a target in mind, a very definite and pretty target, and he knew that if he took good aim at this particular target and shot her down and used her for himself, it could bring the highest of rewards.

In order to do that, though, what he needed was a bullet – the right kind of bullet – and after months of searching, this callow kid in front of him, knocking back the beer and grinning like an oaf, was the best, the most likely, of all he'd examined. And so the colonel had read the boy's file one final time, and then he'd taken a good, long, and very metaphorical look around him, to make sure no one was watching, and then he'd said to himself: *Fuck it, this could cut out fifteen years of shit, climbing the greasy pole. Do it.*

So here he was.

Of course Gerd had no way of knowing any of this as he sat in the bar, but the colonel would explain it all to him – and more besides – some months later, during a deeply unpleasant and one-sided conversation in a concrete interrogation cell somewhere beneath the sprawling grey complex of Hohenshonhausen Prison in East Berlin.

All that lay in the future, though. In the bar there was simply no hint of Koch's real feelings during the hour and a half in which he conducted his courtship of the unsuspecting Gerd. Instead he managed to play the role of Jolly Host to great effect. Eventually, he finished off a joke that left the kid spluttering with laughter, then turned and with a nod of his head indicated to the barmaid that he wanted another round of beer and vodka. The girl went ahead and poured the drinks without otherwise acknowledging him, and given that she was both physically attractive and of very junior rank in his department, this casual disrespect annoyed Koch. He felt a sudden flash of irritation, and found himself making a quick mental note to call up her file the next day and take whatever small steps might be necessary in order to wreck her career and personal life. Such little things could satisfy him, at least on a day-to-day basis.

But although this prospect gave the colonel a fleeting sense of gratification, his patience with the evening as a whole was running thin, and it was probably this that caused him to go ahead and tip his hand at that particular moment. Normally he would have spent more time preparing the ground and easing the boy onto the subject gently, but tonight he simply couldn't be bothered. And who knows? Perhaps he was even a little drunk. So while the barmaid was leaning over to put the new drinks down in front of them, and the kid was still chuckling away at the bullshit story he'd just been told, the colonel took a big, long pull of his beer, then wiped the foam from his lips and gave the barmaid back his empty glass. Then, just as she turned and began moving away he opened his mouth and said loudly to Gerd, loudly enough so the barmaid would overhear:

'Hey, didn't I tell you she had great fucking tits?'

The sudden crassness of this observation sobered Gerd up a little, although not by much. Koch was already picking up the new beer glass in front of him, motioning the teenager to do the same, although Gerd hadn't finished his old one yet.

'*Prost!*' Koch prompted.

'*Prost!*'

The two glasses clinked together, slopping foam, and they both drank.

'So,' Koch said, lowering his beer and rubbing his hand across his lips again, 'what do you reckon? Good or what?'

'Huh?' Gerd asked.

'Her tits, man!' Koch exclaimed, indicating the barmaid with an expansive gesture. 'What do you think? Good or what?'

Gerd's confused gaze rested for a moment on the cleavage in question. Whether by coincidence or professional design, the barmaid had chosen that moment to lean over one of the unoccupied tables to wipe the surface down. She was wearing a low-cut blouse and her heavy breasts certainly looked good to the drunken Gerd.

'Yeah!' the boy said now. But after a moment he seemed to feel something more was necessary, and added appreciatively: 'Nice!'

Koch leaned over and slapped him on the shoulder.

'You've good taste!' he said approvingly. Then he added casually: 'So you'd fuck her then, would you?'

'Yeah!'

'Yeah?'

'Yeah,' Gerd leered drunkenly, getting into the spirit of this conversation. 'I'd fuck her!'

'Good!' Koch reached into his inside jacket pocket and pulled out a sheaf of glossy papers. Fanning these out, he laid them on the bar. Gerd looked down, puzzled, and saw with bleary surprise that they were printed with a series of photographs.

Koch pointed at the pictures, his manner suddenly serious.

'So tell me,' he asked now. 'Would you fuck *her*?'

The teenager blinked slowly, trying to follow this change of tack, and attempted to focus on the images before him. They were shots of a girl. One was a close-up of her face in three-quarter profile, and the other two were full-length shots of her wearing a skirt, heels and blouse, taken from a distance of ten or twelve feet probably, although it was hard to tell, for the pictures were somewhat blurred and there were dark shapes at the edges where other figures had apparently been cropped out. She seemed to be dancing, probably in some kind of disco, and looked pretty enough to Gerd in a hard, pinched kind of way.

'I asked would you fuck her?' Koch repeated.

Gerd glanced at him for a moment, then stared back at the photos.

'Yeah,' he said uneasily, giving a small laugh. 'Sure I would.'

'I'm serious,' Koch told him. 'I want to know if you'd be happy to fuck that girl.' And then he leaned in closer, speaking directly into Gerd's ear.

'Because we hear you're good with women, Gerd. In fact we hear that you've screwed a lot of girls for a kid your age. You seem to enjoy pussy and you certainly know how to get it. So what I'd like to know is whether you'd have anything against laying this girl here? I mean, you find her sexy, don't you, Gerd? Good body? Pretty face?'

Gerd was still looking at the pictures, but he was starting to sober up fast.

'She's sexy enough,' he admitted.

'So you wouldn't mind fucking her?' Koch persisted. 'You'd enjoy it?'

Gerd rubbed his hand slowly across the back of his neck.

'Yeah,' he said. 'I suppose.'

Koch grinned, showing his big, crooked teeth, and reached for his glass.

'Well, *prost* then!' he toasted, his grin widening even more, and he paused, waiting for Gerd to follow suit.

The teenager acknowledged the toast and took a drink, hoping that the subject had been dropped.

But instead of taking a single swallow, Koch downed his beer in large, heavy gulps.

'Drink up, kid,' he told Gerd. 'You've got a busy night ahead of you.'

Gerd looked at him, wondering what he meant. But after a second or two he followed the older man's example and tipped his head back, managing – with an effort – to drain his beer down to the dregs. Koch waited patiently for him to finish, then picked up one of the two vodka glasses and nudged the other towards Gerd. Together they knocked back the contents of those, after which the teenager couldn't help letting out a loud, rumbling belch.

'Good man!' Koch said, laughing and slapping him on the back yet again.

And then at his insistence they both got off the bar stools, Gerd a little unsteadily, and headed for the door.

*

Before Gerd really knew what was happening he was in the back of Koch's cramped chauffeured car being driven through the icy slush of Rostock's streets, while Koch filled him in on what he called 'the Background'. It took the teenager a confused minute or two to gather that they were on the way to a disco, and a minute or so more to understand that once they dropped him off there Koch expected him to try to meet up with the girl whose picture he'd just been shown. Gerd's head was spinning, and as the drinks he'd just finished began to take effect it spun even more. He was also unsettled by the fact that their driver could hear everything they talked about, but this didn't seem to bother Koch, and the driver himself might have been deaf for all the reaction he showed to the conversation.

'The girl's called Anna Schmidt,' Koch said now, raising his voice a little to be heard above the loud whine of the Trabi's engine. He avoided looking at Gerd as he talked, instead gazing forwards over the low-slung passenger seat at the road ahead. 'Her father is a professor of philosophy at the University and she's a student there.'

Concentrating as best as he could, Gerd managed to give a grunt of surprise. Somehow, looking at the photos, she hadn't struck him as a student.

'They're both involved in a club at the university,' Koch went on. 'A sort of discussion club, supposedly – politics, philosophy, that kind of crap. Outings to the countryside occasionally. Hiking and camping, and shagging under the stars too, probably. Which is all fine, but we have reason to believe that some of the members have formed a sort of club within a club, if you follow me. They seem to meet up at other times, unofficially, and we think they talk about things which . . . well, things they shouldn't be talking about, if you see what I mean.'

He stopped for a moment, perhaps waiting for a reaction from Gerd. When none was forthcoming he carried on.

'Anyway, we're not sure whether she's involved or not, although we think the father is. Nothing too serious, probably, but we like to keep tabs on these things. It's our job, after all. Fuck, it's our duty. And that's why we want you to help us, Gerd. Her parents are away in Dresden for a few days and she's got the apartment all to herself. She'll be partying at a disco down the road. Silverfish, it's called. She's twenty years old and she likes boys, especially boys who look like you. Just don't tell her your real age, whatever you do – in fact if she asks, tell her you're twenty-two.

'Anyway, about six months ago she was at a big student party given by a friend of hers called Michael and she got drunker than an Albanian whore. Some dump of a place in the Lutzow Allee. The whole party could have lined up and fucked her and she wouldn't have known the difference. But the point is it might be a good idea to pretend to remember her from that night. She'll never know any different and I'd say it's the easiest approach. When you get her into bed – but *only* if you get her into bed – find out what she knows about Gunter Lehmann or Klaus Mellisch. Can you remember those names?'

Gerd repeated them slowly. He was feeling very drunk now and slightly sick.

'Good,' Koch said, glancing at him. 'But do it casually, for fuck's sake. Best not to bring up their names until after you've banged her, she'll be at her most relaxed then. Now, when she wakes up in the morning there's a fair chance she'll go out to fetch some breakfast – she likes to feed the cocks she brings home as well as fuck them. Touching really. Assuming she *does* go out, it will take her about twenty minutes to get to the shop and back. Spend the time going through her father's desk. He's got a little study at the back of the apartment. It's the door beyond the bathroom. You're just looking for anything that strikes you as unusual. Or suspicious. But *don't* remove anything, just look, and try to remember what you see, or maybe write it down.'

Koch paused, rubbing at the fogged-up window beside him and peering out. For about a minute or so he watched the dark streets going by, and he looked like he could be thinking about anything. Tomorrow's groceries, perhaps. Eventually he seemed to rouse himself.

'So what do you think?' he asked, turning to the teenager. 'Can you do that, Gerd?'

And Gerd replied thickly:

'Sure.'

*

160

Gerd liked the disco. Under other circumstances he would have enjoyed himself, but at that moment he was doing his best to concentrate. This was the first proper nightclub he'd visited, and he'd been both surprised and gratified at the attention he'd attracted since he walked in. The place wasn't big and was obviously filled with regulars, so a good-looking newcomer was likely to get noticed. He'd been aware of quick, appraising female glances as he'd stopped at the edge of the crowd, standing a good five inches taller than most of the other males there, followed by a general round of head-tossing and increased chatter, and then much longer, bolder looks aimed up at him as he'd walked between various groups of girls to get to the bar. He'd passed through it all, enjoying the atmosphere, the music, his own easy movement, and the females all around who – it seemed to him – were competing so hard to put themselves on display. Meat in a butcher's shop, he thought, and felt smug. He moved across to the bar, ordered a drink with some of the money Koch had given him and looked around to see if he could catch sight of this girl called Anna.

It was then, as he gazed out over the 150 or so people in the crowd, that he suddenly found himself wondering what the fuck he was doing. Up until that moment he'd been trying his best to regard the whole thing as an adventure – a bit of a laugh – and perhaps also as a favour to a friend who'd helped him out. Certainly he hadn't been unduly bothered by the sexual aspect of Koch's request. Even at sixteen Gerd had slept with enough girls to be able to regard sex as something casual, mere fun. He'd never been in love – never even gone steady with a girl for longer than eight weeks – and he'd never cared much about the feelings or personalities of his sexual conquests. For him, girls were simply recreation in the same way that books might be a recreation for a different type of boy: you picked one up if it took your fancy, enjoyed it for a while, and discarded it when you were finished. Nonetheless he knew that tonight was different. For a start, at the very least, he felt required to *find* this girl, and looking around now it occurred to him that this might well prove more difficult than he'd thought. After all, that photograph of her face had been in black and white, and while the picture had seemed good enough

161

at the time, trying to spot that same face in an environment such as this, with its changing coloured lights, loud throbbing music, and the shifting crowd, wasn't going to be easy. She would probably be wearing different clothes, and her hair and makeup might well be different too. Besides, he thought, almost every girl in the place wore the same swept-up, lacquered hairstyle, and their dresses all looked similar to him as well.

Yet despite these problems it never once crossed his mind to give up. Less than twenty minutes earlier he'd agreed, after almost no consideration, to try to find this unknown girl and do his best to fornicate with her, and it never occurred to him now to renege on that agreement. Nor did he feel ashamed of the task, as if what he'd been asked to do might in any way be underhand or unpleasant. It certainly never occurred to him that he'd just agreed to whore himself.

And so he sipped at his vodka, feeling the fire of it warming his throat as he leaned against the bar, scanning the faces of the girls around him to see if any of their features matched up with the picture he'd looked at only a few minutes before. After a short time he spotted one girl who seemed to bear a definite likeness, dancing together with a friend near the left-hand corner of the dancefloor. She looked a little shorter and less stringy than the girl in the photo, and her hair was different too, but she had the same prominent cheekbones and pinched look. Gerd watched her for several minutes, long enough to convince himself that she was indeed the girl he was looking for, then he swallowed the remains of his vodka, placed the glass on the bar and pushed his way through the crowd towards her.

He would never normally have walked up to a girl who was dancing and tried to start a conversation, especially when she was dancing with only one other girlfriend, and *especially* if he'd not yet managed to establish at least some sort of eye-contact with her. There were so many better ways to approach a girl, he knew. But then he'd been given a job, and for whatever reason this job was his motivation tonight. So, numbed with drink, he made his way through the crowd until he was able to lean down to this girl and shout in her ear:

'*Anna?* It is Anna, isn't it? Anna Schmidt?'

The girl looked up at him in annoyance, then shook her head and looked back at her friend, turning her body away from him as she continued dancing.

He stood there for a second, nonplussed, then put a hand on her shoulder and shouted more loudly in her ear:

'*Anna?*' he repeated. '*Anna Schmidt?*'

This time she flinched, jerking away and shaking her head at him angrily, everything in her body language telling him to *fuck off*. He focused on her face and realised with a sudden sinking feeling that he'd made a mistake. So he put on his biggest smile, nodding and giving her a thumbs-up sign, trying to project the impression to the people around them that he'd just got the answer he'd expected. Then he moved away as smoothly as possible but his heart was hammering and his face felt hot and flushed. He was only sixteen, after all, and he was good-looking enough to be unfamiliar with rejection.

He'd just reached the edge of the dancefloor, and was glancing back to make sure there was no commotion behind him, when he knocked full-tilt into someone much smaller and slighter than himself. He reached out instinctively and caught this person by the shoulders, preventing a fall, but he was aware of a drink splashing everywhere, and he turned his face quickly to look down at the person he'd collided with.

Somehow he knew it was going to be her and it was.

'Shit!' he said, shouting over the music. 'Shit, I'm sorry! I didn't see you there.'

And then, in that moment as they both collected themselves, he at least had the presence of mind to say, as if in total surprise: '*Anna?* Is that you, Anna? Anna Schmidt!'

She looked at him with a mixture of annoyance and confusion, and in that instant Gerd realised that the photograph he'd been shown had caught her spirit perfectly.

Within thirty seconds or so he'd succeeded in soothing her annoyance, and soon after that he'd persuaded her that they knew each other from her friend's party in the Lutzow Allee. Even before he'd offered to buy her a drink to replace the one she'd spilled she was giving him that look he knew so well – the unmistakable, bright-eyed gaze of sexual interest.

163

He got her a new drink and they talked some more. She was there with a group of friends and she introduced him, and after a few minutes he asked her to dance just to get her away from them. After two dances they were kissing, and one drink later he knew she was ready to leave, although he had to wait while she made a big production out of saying goodbye to her friends. Eventually he turned the full beam of his charm onto one of her plainer girlfriends, simply in an effort to hurry her up. This tactic worked, and the poor friend didn't even get an acknowledgement as Anna finally took him by the arm and tugged him towards the cloakroom. It was still early enough for there to be no queue, and a moment later she had her coat and they were out on the street, their breath emerging as streams of mist in the clear, luminous cold.

'Shit,' Gerd said, stamping his feet on the snow. 'I didn't bring a jacket.'

'Never mind,' she said matter-of-factly. 'My place is just around the corner. I'll keep you warm until we get there.'

And so it happened that Gerd came to fuck her first up against the railings of the local park, in a patch of darkness formed by the moon-shadow of two stark oak trees, his own bare arse so numb from the cold that he didn't feel the deep scratches left by her fingernails, or worry about delaying his own pleasure for her sake, the threat of hypothermia, he felt, being a good enough reason to get it over with quickly.

Back at her parents' empty apartment they lit the stove in the kitchen and then cuddled, fully dressed, under a mound of blankets on her bed until the flat began to warm up, and once it did they fucked themselves stupid for the next five hours.

He woke the next morning to find that she was on top of him and he was inside her.

'Morning, Frosty,' she smiled down at him, her long hair forming a silken curtain around his face and her lower body rippling over him like a snake. 'I'm just trying to make sure your cock doesn't get so cold again it drops off.'

He looked up at her, blinking the sleep away from his eyes.

'Uh, morning,' he said, hoarsely, then coughed. 'So how're you doing?'

She kissed him in reply and spent some small, happy amount of time bringing him to completion. As soon as he'd finished she kissed him swiftly on the cheek and rolled off him, reaching for a robe and slipping it on. She left the room and a minute later he heard the sound of the toilet flushing in the bathroom and running water.

When she appeared in the doorway again she already had on a pair of knickers. His eyes were on her breasts as she bent over to pick up a bra from the floor and snapped it into place. Other items of clothing followed, to his regret. Eventually she stood before him, fully clothed.

'I'm just going out to get some stuff for breakfast, okay? You hungry?'

'No,' Gerd said, yawning hugely. 'Just sleepy. I think you've worn me out.'

'Hope not. Because I'll be back in twenty minutes and then I'll want some more. You're going to have to *earn* your breakfast, mister.'

'More?' Gerd groaned incredulously, lifting his head briefly from his prone position. 'What's wrong with you, woman? I'll need a week just to recover from last night.'

She laughed.

'Tough. You'll have to call the VoPos if you want to get out of here before I'm finished with you.'

Gerd groaned again and let his head drop back. He lay there with his arm over his eyes while she went downstairs and out through the front door.

A moment later he sat up. He was sore all over, and he winced at the various aches as he got out of bed. There was no heating on in the apartment and he stood for a moment, shivering and clutching himself. Naked, he limped across the landing. He couldn't see the scratches all over his back and arse, but he felt the sting of them in the cold air.

The study was where Koch had said it would be. There was a desk squeezed into one cramped corner, against the wall, with a typewriter on it that looked pre-war. Gerd tried the first drawer and it slid open smoothly to reveal nothing more than a collection of pens and pencils. He tried the other two drawers, but these were locked. For a moment he stood there, considering, then he went down on his knees and shoved his hand underneath the desk, searching with his fingertips along the surface of the wood. This was rough and splintery to the touch and revealed nothing. From this position, naked on his knees on the floor, arm extended under the desk, he looked around the room. His vision was unsteady and he realised that he was still drunk. Eventually his gaze settled on the bookcase that stood against the wall. There was a small, ornamental clay cup on one of the shelves; the sort of pointless knick-knack that might well contain paper clips, or perhaps an eraser or two. Or maybe even, he thought suddenly, a key that you wouldn't want to lose.

With no expectation of success, Gerd got slowly to his feet. He crossed over to the clay cup and picked it up, tipping the contents into the palm of his hand. A brass key fell out and lay against his skin.

He looked at it.

'Bloody hell,' he said aloud.

The key had surprised him, but he wasn't surprised to find that it unlocked the second drawer. He went through the papers quickly. Most of them seemed to be official academic stuff, but near the bottom there was a single handwritten sheet of names, the first of which immediately caught his eye: *Klaus Mellisch*.

Gerd took a pencil and a stray piece of paper and copied down the fifteen or so names on the list. Afterwards, he shut and locked the drawer. Crossing the carpet to put the key back in the jar, he involuntarily let out a long, loud fart.

Yeah, he thought to himself. *That about sums it up*.

He was back in bed and warming up under the covers by the time she opened the front door. The copied list was safely hidden inside his shoe, covered with a sock.

She ran up the stairs and into the room, letting the bag of groceries fall to the floor and leaping onto the bed with a violent abandon that made Gerd flinch. He managed to half-catch her and she lay on top of him, cradling his head as she kissed him slowly on the mouth.

'Mmmm,' she said, without really breaking off the kiss. 'This is *my* idea of breakfast.'

They didn't even bother taking off her coat. Instead Gerd helped her pull her skirt up round her waist and then she used her hands to push him inside her with the same rough eagerness she'd shown the night before.

He'd been lying there with his eyes closed for some time, grunting, when he was suddenly brought back to awareness by the shocking, deliberate sound of a man's cough coming from the foot of the bed.

Gerd sat bolt upright in panic, pushing the girl to one side and clenching his fists. His first thought was that she had a jealous boyfriend who'd followed them home, and he tensed his muscles for a fight. But he was wholly unprepared for the sight that met his eyes: the solid, grey figure of Emile Koch leaning against the chest of drawers opposite the bed, his square shoulders made even thicker by a heavy winter overcoat and his yellow tombstone smile grinning widely beneath the homburg hat. He gave every impression of having been there for some time. He also looked as if he hadn't slept, his face greyer than ever.

'Morning,' Koch rasped, lifting a gloved hand in a casual gesture. His voice was thick from too many cigarettes, and he coughed once, then leaned forward and spat a large gob of phlegm onto the carpet.

'So how're you kids doing today?'

Gerd could only stare at him, speechless. It was Anna who moved first, disentangling herself from the bedclothes and standing up. With her skirt around her waist and her knickers pulled to one side she was effectively naked from the waist down. She began to rearrange her clothing, but she did this with such a calm, unhurried practicality that Gerd couldn't help switching his shocked gaze to her. She seemed wholly unperturbed, the expression on her face one of deliberate, studied boredom.

Koch rubbed the tip of his nose with a leather-gloved hand.

Gerd finally moved, clutching at the blankets and dragging them up to cover his crotch.

'Uh, what?' he said stupidly, looking from one to the other. 'Uh ... I mean what ...'

'Shut up, Gerd,' Koch said harshly. He raised an eyebrow at the girl.

'So,' he asked. 'What's the verdict?'

Anna seemed to consider this question, looking down at Gerd with a sort of knowing contempt.

'He'll do,' she said. 'Although the first time wasn't anything to be proud of. Might even have been a real let-down for a certain type of girl.'

Gerd's mouth fell open at this and he stared accusingly at her.

'It was *cold*,' he protested. 'My bloody dick nearly froze for god's sake!'

The girl snorted, amused, then looked at Koch.

'Can I go now?' she asked.

'No,' Koch said. 'Go and wait in the study. I'm not finished with you yet.'

For a moment it seemed as if she was about to argue, but then Koch gave her a look that made even Gerd shiver, and she hunched her shoulders and left the room. Gerd listened to the noise of her footsteps as she walked the length of the landing.

'So,' Koch said finally, drumming his gloved fingers on the top of the chest of drawers. 'Tell me then. Did you manage to find anything? In the study, I mean.'

Gerd stared at him uncomprehendingly and Koch repeated himself, mouthing the words with exaggerated patience.

'I asked you if you found anything in the study.'

Gerd blinked, as if suddenly waking. 'I did . . . I mean, I found a list.'

'A list?' Koch asked. 'And what did this list say? Can you remember?'

'Well, no,' Gerd replied, his sense of unreality growing. 'No. But I made a copy of it. It's in my shoe. Fifteen names, I think.'

Koch tilted his head and seemed to consider this for a moment. Then he smiled.

'Congratulations, Gerd. Well done. I'd say you've passed the test. So you can get your things together now and leave. There's still a lot of work to be done.'

Gerd's forehead furrowed with confusion. 'Wait a minute,' he said. 'You're saying this whole thing was some kind of a *test*?'

'Yes,' Koch told him calmly. 'That's exactly what I said. What's the matter, you fucking deaf?'

'You mean this was a set-up?' Gerd went on, his voice rising. 'You're playing fucking *games* with me?'

Koch shrugged dismissively.

'Something like that. But like I said, you should be proud. You passed, and now you can serve your country. So get up and get dressed.'

'Now hold on!' Gerd exclaimed, struggling to a sitting position and pointing a finger at him. 'What kind of bullshit . . .'

But he never got a chance to finish his sentence. Koch moved quicker than Gerd thought possible. One moment the grey man was slouching against the chest of drawers, the next he was thundering across the room. Even as he registered this, Gerd realised there was nothing he could do to prevent whatever was going to happen next. He managed to turn his hands up defensively and hunch his shoulders, but even as he did so he knew it was hopeless. He felt both his wrists being grabbed in one huge hand and he was slammed backwards against the pillow with stunning force. By the time he understood what was happening he was pinned, Koch's forearm pressing down across his throat and the remainder of the grey man's body poised to bear down with whatever crushing force he might deem necessary.

Gerd froze, helpless, then let his muscles go limp in surrender. There was nothing he could do anyway.

Koch registered this and relaxed, lifting his arm slightly so that the pressure on Gerd's throat was relieved. The colonel had no intention of harming his new recruit: all he was doing was having a bit of fun after a long and boring night, stretching out the kinks in his muscles.

'Listen,' he said now, leaning forward and speaking quietly but forcefully into Gerd's ear. 'Quit while you're ahead, kid. Think about it. I can understand you're upset, but you have to realise that we needed to test you. We need to know what kind of material we're dealing with – what you're capable of. How far we can push you, you know? And I don't mind telling you, I'm impressed. I can't think of anyone else your age who would have done what we asked without questioning us. That means a lot, Gerd. And we really do have a job for you. A very *important* job, and although we wouldn't normally use someone your age, frankly we don't have a choice. What's more, we have to hurry. So I admit we're pushing you. But I wouldn't do that if I didn't think you could take it.'

He paused, looking down at Gerd's face intently.

'You *can* take it, can't you?'

Gerd remained still for a moment, getting his breath back, feeling his heart rate return to normal. Then, carefully, he nodded.

'Yeah,' he said quietly, 'I can take it.'

'I thought so. Good man.'

Koch stood up and took off his hat, rubbing his hand over his bald, shiny head. Then he grinned and stretched out an arm, offering that hand to Gerd. Gerd took it, and the colonel hauled him into a sitting position. 'There we go,' Koch said. 'No harm done, is there?'

The teenager looked down at the floor sullenly and shook his head.

'Okay. So get dressed then.'

Gerd reached for his discarded underpants. As he put them on Koch scouted around the rest of the room, gathering up the other garments and handing them to Gerd.

'All right,' he said finally, offering Gerd his shoes to complete the ensemble. 'Good as new, eh?'

Gerd nodded wordlessly. He took his shoes and fished inside the left one, removing the sock and pulling out a crumpled piece of paper.

'Here's that list you wanted,' he said.

Koch actually laughed.

'You keep it,' he told him. 'Sort of a souvenir, yes?'

Gerd scrunched the paper into a tight ball and slipped it into his pocket. Then he bent forward, putting on his shoes and tying the laces.

'Ready?' Koch asked him.

'Yeah,' he said. 'I'm ready.'

'Good,' Koch replied. 'I'm glad to hear it. Because there's a lot of work ahead of us. A *lot*.'

Gerd stood up straight, feeling a little shaky.

'I'm proud of you,' Koch said again. 'The car's waiting outside. You won't be going back to the school just yet. Horst will be driving you to a place that we have, somewhere quiet where there won't be any distractions. It's not far away and it's very comfortable. Once you're there I want you to get plenty of sleep. We'll be starting tomorrow. Okay?'

Gerd still didn't say anything. Koch leaned forward and looked questioningly into his face.

'Okay?' he asked again.

'Yeah,' Gerd said, shrugging. 'Sure.'

He began to move past Koch but when he got to the doorway he looked back.

'You're not coming?'

'Not yet.'

Gerd didn't move and his gaze held Koch's. After several seconds the grey man shrugged.

'She's a whore,' he said simply. 'She works for us.'

'I figured that,' Gerd said.

Koch reached down with one hand and began to unfasten his belt. He tugged on it sideways, sliding the length of leather out from between the loops. Holding it up, he turned his hand so that the belt wrapped once around his fist. The rest of it he left dangling, like a strap.

'You've had your fun,' he told Gerd quietly. 'Now I'll have mine.'

And then he smiled his tombstone smile.

Gerd turned and walked quickly out of the room, down the stairs, and out into the fresh, crisp newness of the winter morning. The car was waiting for him in the street. Halfway down the path, slipping a little on the compacted snow, he almost threw up. But somehow, this time, he managed to stop himself.

Perhaps he was growing up instead.

He was taken to some kind of farmhouse and once shown to a bedroom there he slept, just as he'd been told to. There didn't seem to be anything better to do and anyway he couldn't imagine that he really had a choice. In the kitchen, before being taken to his room, he'd accepted a cup of hot chocolate made by the driver,

Horst, drinking it down in the hope of settling the remnants of vodka in his stomach. Afterwards he slept so deeply and awoke so refreshed that it briefly crossed his mind to wonder if he'd been drugged, although he felt so clear-headed that he eventually decided this was impossible.

Still, he'd managed to sleep for twelve hours straight, and when he finally went downstairs he found Horst cooking him a steak-and-fried-potatoes dinner which he consumed ravenously. Later he went outside and looked at the stars, shivering in the cold, while Horst did the washing up. When he came back in the two of them slumped in armchairs in the living room to watch TV. Gerd was shocked to discover that the set was tuned illegally to a West German channel, but Horst grunted something about 'orders', so he relaxed and settled down to watch what turned out to be an American detective drama, interspersed with long minutes of brightly coloured, fast-moving and fatuous adverts featuring a mind-numbing array of goods. It was Gerd's first real exposure to Western broadcasting, and the contrast it implied with his own society made his head reel. In particular he couldn't believe that the cars being shown were really on offer to the average Western citizen. It seemed easier to accept that the whole thing was just elaborate propaganda, as he'd been taught in school. And of course there was no mention of the oppressed minorities he'd learned so much about, like the blacks being beaten in the streets (he'd seen film footage), or the hopelessness of the unemployed. At one point, during a lull in the action, he asked Horst about the cars, but received only a grunt in reply. Gerd wasn't unduly concerned by this, as it was already clear that the driver was a man of few words.

But while Horst didn't say much, he continued to be companionable in other ways, and once the programme finished he padded into the kitchen and emerged ten minutes later with two cups of hot chocolate. Shortly afterwards Gerd began to yawn again, and despite having slept for so long just a short time previously, he went upstairs and fell asleep the instant he crawled into bed. In fact he slept for another twelve hours, not waking until the clock struck eleven the next morning. Once again he felt fit, clear-headed and healthy, and he tucked into the eggs and bacon rustled up by Horst with hearty enthusiasm. Shortly after that Koch arrived and the briefings began.

So it happened that in February 1969, at the age of sixteen, Gerd Volker Hagen was successfully recruited as a Stasi informer.

The teenage boy who emerged from the farmhouse after three weeks of intensive Stasi coaching – the one turned loose to do their bidding – was very similar to the boy who'd gone in. But there was one crucial difference: the new Gerd was an informer.

Of course he hadn't planned it that way, but then, as he later pointed out to me, who the hell did? Even those children brainwashed from the cradle onwards – by the Party or the Regime or the Junta, or whatever the government of their particular benighted society happened to call itself – even those kids didn't think, daydreaming at the age of eight or nine: *when I grow up I want to be an informer*. It just didn't happen that way.

And yet. And yet.

And yet around the world tens of millions of people had somehow become exactly that. Because – and Gerd was adamant about this – anybody with a normal set of human weaknesses can be manipulated into a position where they'll be willing to sell out their friends or family, or neighbours or colleagues, to the State.

And when all was said and done, he asked now, did it really matter *why* people did such a thing? Because regardless of whether they'd succumbed to years of propaganda and convinced themselves it was the right thing to do, or whether they were simply scared, the end result was the same. Betrayal.

So no, ultimately he didn't think it mattered whether such actions had been caused by jealousy or spite (as they sometimes were), or a wish to curry favour, or the usual lust for money or advancement, or even just for the attention it brought – the feeling of being seen as useful in the eyes of those who had some measure of power. Because at the end of the day the terrible reality remained: you were selling out your friends.

As for Gerd, he felt he was unusual only to the extent that he no longer had anyone close to sell out. He was without ties, and at such a young age he was easy pickings indeed for the Secret Police. So he went along with Koch's scheme willingly enough, and while it was certainly a matter of regret to him later, he had to admit that at the time he never made any protest against what he was asked to do, or showed any sign of reluctance.

For their part, the Stasi made no secret of what it was they expected from Gerd. Right from the start the colonel was very clear about what the teenager's job was going to be: to make one particular young woman fall hopelessly in love with him.

'You're going to get to do literally what the rest of us can only dream of doing figuratively,' Koch told him once. 'You lucky bastard – you're going to get to *fuck the enemy*!'

The enemy's name was Caro Freda Schmidt and she didn't look like much of a threat to the State. Instead she looked like what she was: a twenty-one-year-old language student, and a country girl, new to the city. She'd been raised in the small lakeside town of Rewald, near the Harz mountains, where her father Otto was a labourer with the forestry service. Her mother, Elsa, had been a mechanic at the open-cast strip mine in Kassel, fifteen miles to the north – one of twenty local women trained for skilled work there during the manpower shortages of the war – and she'd carried on the job under the Soviet Occupation, not only because the shortages continued, but also because she was good at it. But in 1948, when Elsa Schmidt was twenty-six, there'd been some sort of accident at the mine, and although – much to Koch's annoyance – the official files were vague about the circumstances, what was certain was that Elsa's right leg had been crushed and she'd been left crippled for life.

Only a few weeks after this, while she lay dazed with pain in a hospital bed, Elsa Schmidt learned from doctors that she was pregnant. Eight months later she gave birth to her first and only child, a healthy baby girl whom she christened Caro, in honour of her own dead grandmother. But right from the start everybody would always call the child by her middle name: Freda.

Freda Schmidt was a reserved and withdrawn little girl who grew up into a reserved and withdrawn young woman. But by the age of seventeen she was also beautiful. Not elegant, perhaps, for she was a little too solidly built to be that, but with a full, attractive figure and strikingly pretty face, and large brown eyes and long brown hair that shone when it caught the light. There was something slightly Slavic in the angle of her cheekbones and the broad planes of her face, and a hint, too, of eastern peasant ancestry in the useful power of her legs. These were slightly squat compared to the rest of her body, and by the time she reached her teenage years she'd become self-conscious enough to hide them under thick voluminous skirts or loose flannel trousers. It was probably because of her legs that Freda was one of those girls who would never feel comfortable in a bathing suit, and the fact that men found her attractive at all was something she seemed to regard only as a burden. Her few friends – none of them close – never saw her show any interest in boys, or indeed in any of the more frivolous trappings of a teenage girl's life, and her quiet seriousness was such that it appeared at times as if she would actively welcome the chance to drop the pretence of youthful pursuits and embrace instead the cares and responsibilities of middle age; perhaps even welcome too the slow slide into heaviness that was incipient in her frame and which would surely only be hastened by her preferred diet of stodgy stews.

But at the age of twenty-one Freda Schmidt was at least a decade away from that heaviness. She was still ripening physically, and although she often attempted to play down her attractiveness, the fashions of the time usually failed to cover up the swelling fullness of her breasts or the trim slimness of her waist. She glowed with health, and as she walked in the street or the corridors of the university, men of all ages would often break off conversations to follow her with their eyes. But if any of these men tried to fall into step beside her, or start up a conversation at a bus stop or in the library, they would find themselves rebuffed quickly and coldly, and in no uncertain terms. Freda, it seemed, only talked to men she knew, and after her first six months of university even the brashest of campus seducers had given up all hope of trying to bed her, while the whispered rumours that followed her through the language labs and seminar rooms claimed that she was either a lesbian, or the plaything of one of the more prominent politicians. Some versions said she was both.

'Unfortunately for us she's neither,' Koch told Gerd during one of the early sessions at the farmhouse. 'It's a lot trickier than that. She's going to be a tough nut to crack all right, but not because she's a dyke. She isn't. We tried that, just to be sure, and it didn't fly.'

He shook his head, as if remembering, then continued. 'No, the problem with this girl is that she's sexually frigid. *Religiously* so, in fact. Her mother's Catholic, you see. A real, live genuine church-goer, even with all the clampdowns and restrictions we put on that stuff after the war. Fuck, we should've just shot them all if you ask me, but nobody had the balls to give the order. The point is that her mother's been a slave to Rome her whole life, so when poor little Freda came along she never had a chance. The Papists got their claws into her right from the start and went to work, warping her to their twisted morality.'

The colonel shook his head again.

'Who knows what mad nonsense her mamma and the church drilled into her brain, but it was enough priestly voodoo and sexual guilt to fuck her up for life.'

There was a photograph of the girl on the table between them. Koch reached out now and tapped it hard.

'So this is what we're dealing with, Gerd. A young woman who, for almost two decades, has been force-fed a bunch of superstitious, weak-minded shit dressed up as the gospel truth. Now surely she'd love a decent length of cock up her – god knows, she must be gagging for it. But she's so repressed she doesn't even know it. It's all sublimated, or whatever the fuck the psychiatrists call it. So the first hint of a tingle between her legs and she's down on her knees on the cold wooden floor for half an hour, at three o'clock in the morning in winter with the room unheated. And she's not on her knees to suck some guy's meat like any normal girl her age. No, she's down there crying to god and begging his forgiveness.'

He paused, looking at Gerd with eyebrows raised.

'I'm serious,' he said. 'Begging god's forgiveness. Just for waking up with her hand between her legs. We bugged her flat.'

Gerd blinked at this, but managed to keep his face blank, receptive. Koch leaned across the table and jabbed a finger at him.

'The point is this, Gerd. You have to seduce a girl who wants to be a *nun*.'

*

176

Three weeks later, Gerd took a train to the capital of the GDR.

At that time, in 1969, there were about four million people living in divided Berlin – spread out across the two halves of the city. At least 30,000 of them were spies.

When Gerd got off the train at Ostbahnhof in East Berlin and walked through the concrete-and-glass ugliness of the station building, nobody noticed the arrival of one more.

Gerd had been given careful instructions for what he should do as soon as he reached the capital. Although he'd been told he'd be travelling alone, he suspected Koch would have at least one 'minder' on the train keeping him under surveillance, and he was determined to do exactly as he'd been told. So the moment he stepped down from the carriage he shouldered his bag and made his way to the public toilets on the station's lower level, where he locked himself in a cubicle and sat on the seat, checking his watch impatiently until exactly six minutes had passed. Then he stood up, unlocked the door and walked out briskly, hurrying back across the echoing station concourse, passing through a sprinkling of pasty-faced civilians and the occasional pair of watchful-eyed men in uniform, before trotting down the grit-covered steps of the main entrance and onto the frozen slush of the pavement. He resisted the urge to glance over his shoulder, but he imagined that somewhere behind him Horst or another member of the colonel's team would be checking to see if anyone was showing an unusual interest in his movements – hanging around in a position where they could observe the entrance to the washroom, for example, or reacting to his sudden reappearance.

Such precautions seemed both elaborate and pointless to Gerd, but the colonel had insisted on them, and the teenager was well aware of the value Koch set on obedience.

Outside, on the pavement beside the station entrance, there was a small newspaper and tobacco shop into which Gerd now turned. The shop was empty of customers and he was served immediately. This didn't suit his purpose, so he hummed and hawed for several moments, then asked for a pack of cigarettes and some matches, delaying the transaction further by counting out the small change in his pocket, then trying to engage the shop assistant in a conversation about the weather forecast. More than two minutes had passed by the time he emerged into the chill air. As he did so he immediately caught sight of the burly figure of Horst, standing exactly where Gerd had been told to expect him, leaning against the metal post of a tram stop and hunched a little against the cold. The older man gave no indication of having noticed Gerd. Instead he was staring off into the distance with a slightly impatient expression on his face: just another tired worker waiting for a tram. He was carrying a folded-up newspaper in his gloved hand, and as Gerd approached, Horst casually let this hand drop a little so that the newspaper pointed down at the road, gripping it in such a way that three of his fingers spread across the headline. Gerd hefted his bag a little higher on his shoulder and walked past, eyes down, but from his time at the farmhouse he knew that the direction of the newspaper indicated that he was clear of hostile surveillance, while the number of Horst's spread fingers meant that he should get into the third of the vehicles parked further up the street.

All three of these vehicles were Trabants. The first two were painted a dirty cream colour and the last one light blue. Only two had drivers sitting in them – the first and the last – and Gerd walked straight to the last one. Ignoring the blurred figure behind the fogged windscreen for the moment, he opened the car's rear door on the pavement side and slung his bag onto the seat. Only then did he lower his head and speak, addressing himself to the back of the driver's neck.

'Hey,' he said. 'Thanks for waiting for me. It was good of you.'

'It's too cold to walk,' the driver replied bluntly.

This was the phrase Gerd expected. He slammed the door shut and walked around the rear of the car to the front passenger side. Even as he dropped into the seat the Trabi was already moving forward with a grinding of gears. He tugged the door closed as they pulled out into the road. Horst was still leaning against the tram stop and as they drove by Gerd craned his neck for a moment to look at him, then twisted around and stared back through the rear windscreen. The first of the Trabants, the one with a driver, had switched on its headlights and was starting up, preparing to follow.

Gerd was still looking back at this vehicle when his own driver suddenly took one hand off the wheel and punched him on the ear, hard.

'What the fuck do you think you're playing at?' he hissed. 'Turn around and face front, you prick.'

Gerd clamped his teeth in shock, bristling, but after a second or two he did as he was told. His hand went to his ear, which throbbed heavily.

'What the fuck are *you* doing?' he countered, his voice cold with anger. 'I got the all-clear from Horst, there's nobody watching – unless that car following us happens to be the opposition, in which case I think one of you might have noticed.'

The driver shook his head at this, his expression thunderous.

'You're a goddamn fucking idiot,' he swore now. 'Didn't they teach you anything? First rule of deep cover, arsehole – you always act as if you're being watched, even if you're sure you aren't. The second rule is: you can *never* be sure you aren't.'

Gerd was taken aback at the depth of the driver's fury. It appeared genuine, and he also seemed to feel a need to take it out on the vehicle, for he immediately slammed his foot down on the accelerator and hurled the Trabant into a right-hand corner, tyres screeching. The suspension of the car was so rocky that for a brief moment Gerd thought they might actually lose control and tip over. He grabbed at the handle above his window to brace himself, but it popped out of its socket and he was left holding it in his right hand.

'And try not to rip the car apart, you ape,' the driver said, as he straightened the vehicle out. 'The colonel might just decide to dock it out of your pay.'

Gerd was about to make a scathing reply when the meaning of the comment suddenly stopped him short. He realised that nobody had mentioned anything about being paid before.

His mind was still racing over the possible implications of this as they reached the monumental, mile-long boulevard of Stalin Allee. The serried ranks of workers' flats crowded along both sides, their rows of boxy balconies redundant in the Berlin winter. Along the edges of the pavements trees stood like stark, black skeletons. Each side of the road had three broad lanes for traffic, but apart from the lone Trabant still following thirty metres behind them, theirs was the only vehicle to be seen at that moment, and Gerd couldn't spot a single person on foot. Ahead, the concrete bulk of the TV tower rose up and disappeared into the low clouds, a giant grey phallus swallowed by the weather.

But Gerd wasn't interested in the view. Instead he turned and studied the man next to him, his dislike mingling with surprise when he realised that his driver wasn't much older than himself. Gerd was only sixteen, but at least he *looked* twenty-one or twenty-two. An impartial observer would have guessed that the driver was younger – nineteen perhaps, twenty at the outside. And whereas Gerd was big and broad and muscular, this young man had the lanky, slightly-emaciated frame of a long-distance runner. Yet his skinny presence vibrated with an intense, bottled-up energy, and Gerd felt an instinctive wariness.

'All I can say is you'd better be fucking important,' the driver spat, smashing his foot down on the accelerator again so that the Trabi's engine whined like a broken lawnmower. 'Koch's yanked me back over the Wall to be your fucking chauffeur. I'll be lucky not to have my cover blown sky-high for this. Fuck knows what he thinks he's playing at.'

Gerd regarded him for a second longer then turned away without replying. Instead he looked out of the window and watched the grey streets passing. It was his first time in the capital and he took the opportunity to study it all with interest.

The rest of the short journey passed in silence.

The safe house the colonel had arranged for them turned out to be a dark, low-ceilinged apartment overlooking an equally dark and gloomy courtyard near the top of a main road called Danziger Strasse. There were blotches of dampness showing through the wallpaper in Gerd's bedroom, and mould growing at the corners of the ceiling.

'Nice,' Gerd called loudly, as he dropped his bag at the foot of the bed and looked around, taking it all in. 'What happened to the cockroaches? They move out in disgust?'

The driver was rummaging in the kitchen and didn't reply, but a moment later he appeared in the doorway carrying a large metal bucket.

'Here,' he said roughly, holding out the pail. 'You'll find the place a bit nicer once it's warmed up. So get down to the cellar and fetch some fucking coal.'

Gerd stared at him.

'Tell me you're kidding.'

'What do you think?'

Gerd held his gaze for a moment, then shook his head and took the bucket, heading for the stairs.

By the time he returned five minutes later another man was standing in the kitchen, leaning against the sink while the kettle boiled. Even bundled up in layers of winter clothing this man looked tough and capable. Gerd guessed he must be the driver of the Trabant that had followed them.

'Ah!' the man exclaimed. 'There you are, Gerd! About fucking time too.'

He raised his chin and called through the doorway.

'Okay, Rudiger! The coal's here, so you can get the heating started!'

Gerd's young driver sloped in from the hallway, a filthy look on his face. He seemed ready to argue, but the man shot him a warning glance that carried the weight of authority. Rudiger bit his lip, sneering, then moved across to take the bucket from Gerd before heading back to the big tiled stove that stood against a wall in the living room.

The man chuckled.

'Don't mind Rudiger,' he said. 'I think it's his time of the month or something. He's a moody fucking tart, Rudiger is.'

He stretched out a hand.

'I'm Karl. Horst will be watching your back during the day, and I'll be the nightshift.'

'Hello, Karl,' Gerd said, reaching out a hand to take his. 'Good to meet you.'

'Want some tea?' Karl asked him. 'Horst will be here soon and then we can brief you.'

'Yeah, thanks. Tea would be great.'

By the time Horst arrived forty minutes later the apartment had started to warm up.

'Rudiger!' Horst called as he came through the door. 'I want you out on the street doing a visual sweep, and get some more milk while you're at it.'

The young man scowled, but he did as he was told. Horst led Gerd into the front room and motioned for him to sit on the sofa, before moving over to the window and closing the curtains. Then he crossed to the wall opposite. There was a very bad painting on this wall – a harbour scene somewhere – and Horst reached up with both hands to remove it, revealing a small green safe embedded into the plasterwork behind. Setting the painting on the floor, he straightened up, concealing the combination lock with his body while he spun in the numbers. As he swung the safe door open Gerd saw that the steel was a good six inches thick.

Horst pulled out a manila folder. Then he grabbed a plastic chair from beside the stove and set it down on the other side of the low table. He sat down and tossed the folder onto the table.

'Okay, Gerd,' he said. 'This is your mission we're talking about now. Are you listening?'

The teenager nodded. His mouth had suddenly gone dry and he didn't trust himself to speak.

'Good.' Horst leaned forward and removed the rubber band from around the folder and opened it.

'The first thing you need to know is something that we couldn't tell you before, for security reasons. But I've been cleared to brief you on everything now. And the main thing is that you have not yet reached your destination.'

He paused, as if expecting a reaction, but Gerd remained silent, waiting for more. Horst's gaze flicked sideways to Karl, who was leaning in the doorway with his arms folded.

'You've not yet reached your destination,' Horst repeated. 'This operation isn't going to be carried out in East Berlin. If it was, we wouldn't have to use you at all, we'd deal with it ourselves. But that's not really an option in this case, because it's not in our normal jurisdiction – you see?'

Gerd shook his head at this, bemused. He couldn't imagine a place anywhere in the country where the Stasi didn't have jurisdiction.

Horst looked down at the pages spread in front of him, then gathered up the first three and held them out.

'You should read these. They explain everything. Obviously, the contents are secret. Any discussion of them outside this room would be regarded as an act of treason and therefore subject to the full penalty of the law.'

Gerd hesitated, then reached across the table for the papers. As he took them Horst pulled out a packet of cigarettes. He lit one, then tossed the pack across the room to Karl. The two of them smoked quietly while Gerd settled back in the sofa to read.

The pages had the word 'CLASSIFIED' stamped diagonally across the top left-hand corner in red ink. The heading on the first page was also in large letters:

SUMMARY AND RECOMMENDATION FOR ACTION. CASE FILE 1759F. DEPARTMENT 5B, BERLIN.

Summary:

Subject Caro Freda Schmidt, known to acquaintances as Freda – hereafter to be referred to in these files by the appellation 'Gemstone' – fled the Democratic Republic of Germany on July 28th, 1961, some 17 days prior to the erection of the Anti-Fascist Protection Barrier. Gemstone was 11 years of age at the time and in the care of her parents (see attached files). All three subjects left DDR territory simultaneously, by vehicle, and are believed to have crossed into Fascist–Capitalist territory shortly after arriving in Berlin, probably via the Bornholmer Brucke railway bridge on the border of the Pankow/Wedding districts. Subsequently, all three remained in a rural district of the Occupied Zone. Intelligence gathered by Operatives G10 and G98, together with information received from blackmailed civilian asset 'Sandstone', shows that in addition to the overt daily lives being led by Gemstone's parents, both have also been involved for some time at an organisational level with a covert Catholic church action group, previously identified by this department (file attached) and based in the Occupied Zone. It is probable that subject Gemstone is also involved with this group in a minor capacity.

While initially confining themselves to smuggling Vatican propaganda into DDR territory and distributing it to subversives, the group's operations have expanded over the last three years to include activities of more immediate and serious concern to this department: specifically, organising and facilitating successful attempts by DDR subversives to flee to the West.

All indications suggest that this has so far been small-scale (between 3 to 5 escapees), and was accomplished by smuggling malcontents out through DDR border checkpoints in concealed compartments built into visiting West Berlin vehicles. However, information from sources also suggests that for the last 18 months members may also have been engaged in the construction of an underground tunnel, running from the Occupied Zone of West Berlin into DDR territory, and that this tunnel may now be nearing completion. Financial investigation has confirmed that a number of people with links to suspected group members appear to have been used as go-betweens, purchasing items of heavy equipment that would be necessary for tunnelling operations.

Given that our limited attempts to penetrate the inner workings of the group have failed (see attached summary) owing to the cell-like nature of the organisation, the existence of such a tunnel cannot be confirmed. But operational changes in the way that known or suspected group members meet and interact, together with evidence of a large influx of funds from Catholic charities into accounts accessible to known and probable cell members, strongly suggests that some sort of major operation is indeed underway, and furthermore is approved of and supported by the Vatican. Western government intelligence agencies may also be involved, although group members would likely remain unaware of this.

Given the propaganda damage that could be caused by the escape to the West of a significant number of DDR malcontents through such a tunnel, and given the practical difficulties of trying to locate it along the 155km length of the border area, this department has concluded that the best chance for spoiling the likely escape attempt and turning it to the DDR's own advantage would be to penetrate the project from the Western side.

Considering the inherent difficulties of trying to run a large-scale surveillance operation in the Occupied Zone of Berlin, against targets probably on the lookout for such surveillance, and considering also the high level of urgency for action in this case, we believe that the option with the best likelihood of success would be the recruitment of an active church group member to our cause.

Unfortunately there is a major drawback to this approach. Because of the strength of religious ideology motivating known group members, normal recruitment tactics including bribery, blackmail or other forms of coercion are likely to fail.

A final option remains. Following discussion with department psychologists, we believe that a successful penetration of the group might still be achieved through a classic 'Honeytrap' operation. This would stand its best chance of success if the target were to remain unaware that he or she is being used in this way.

Subject Gemstone is young and appears unusually naïve in romantic matters. In addition to her parents, she is also close to other members of the group, and as stated above is likely to be involved in some small capacity herself. Extensive psychological evaluation, based on her known behaviour and character traits, indicates that while the subject would probably evince a strong initial reluctance to engage in sexual activity, once such reluctance were overcome both Gemstone's emotions and actions would likely prove eminently manipulable.

RECOMMENDATION

Consequently we strongly recommend running a 'Honeytrap' operation against subject Gemstone, assuming that a suitable candidate for her affections can be found.

Gerd finished reading and looked up, appalled. Horst was stubbing his cigarette out in an ashtray on the table.

'Wait a minute!' he protested. 'This can't be right! I mean … fuck. This can't mean what I think it means, can it?'

Horst responded to his dismay with a curt nod.

'Oh it does,' he said. 'Believe it.'

Gerd looked down at the pages again, shaking his head. He opened his mouth to say something else, but the words died in his throat. The sheer enormity of his situation was starting to sink in.

'That's right, Gerd,' Horst confirmed. 'Congratulations. You're going to the West.'

It was half an hour later. The living room had filled with cigarette smoke, but the window hadn't been opened and the curtains were still drawn. Karl was in the kitchen boiling the kettle for another round of tea. Rudiger had returned and was in one of the bedrooms. Horst was still briefing an agitated Gerd on the plan.

'But how the hell am I meant to pass as a *Wessi*, for god's sake!' Gerd burst out now. 'I mean, there's no way!'

'You don't have to,' Horst replied calmly. 'That's part of the plan. You're not a *Wessi*.'

He leaned forward, lowering his voice as he spoke.

'Look, we've had our best people planning this for months – it's good, believe me. And this is how it works, so listen up. Three nights ago we stage-managed a successful escape attempt to the West. A young DDR male – someone fitting your physical description, naturally – made a run for it across no man's land at a section of the border near Potsdamer Platz, and managed to get over the Wall into the British Sector. In the process he was spotted by one of our foot patrols, who immediately raised the alarm and shouted a warning. When he failed to stop, shots were fired by the patrol and also by one of our sharp-shooters in the nearby guard tower. The shots missed, you understand. They were meant to. But of course they attracted plenty of attention from the Western zone, which was also deliberate.

'So the escapee wasn't hit, and he managed to get into the West. It took a British jeep about two minutes to get to the spot where he'd come over, and by the time they arrived our man was gone. The Brits will assume he was picked up by a western accomplice, or that he legged it straight into the Tiergarten Park, and then went to ground somewhere in the British sector. Either way they'll think he has western friends helping him. It isn't unusual. And so far this guy hasn't come forward to the western authorities, which is also not unusual. He's a scared rabbit, still panicked, and it's natural he'd want to keep himself hidden for a while.

'Now. Following standard procedures, all DDR border personnel involved in failing to prevent the escape have been temporarily suspended from duty and are undergoing questioning by military authorities at a secure location. Perhaps there was some dereliction of duty on their part? Some complicity with the escape? We need to check. The West expects such action on our part. But the point is that nobody else will get to talk to those guards any time soon. Meanwhile news of the escape is the subject of widespread conversation in West Berlin. There's been mention of it in three of the newspapers in the western zones, and a paragraph or two in the international press also.'

He took a drag on his cigarette and then jabbed the glowing end of it at Gerd.

'That guy who escaped, son. That was you.'

Shortly after 9 a.m. the next morning, a young Stasi agent named Rudiger Tüll – using his deep-cover identity as a West German student called Ingmar Tesche – drove a beaten-up VW Beetle into West Berlin. He crossed through the fortifications of the Berlin Wall at Checkpoint Charlie without incident. On the Communist side of the border, the major in charge had quietly been ordered to make sure his men gave Rudiger's car only the briefest of inspections, purely for form's sake. A hundred metres further on, at the American post, the vehicle was waved through after a cursory examination of the driver's identity papers. Western tourists were allowed in and out of the East at will, and Rudiger's western documents were perfectly in order.

In a cramped compartment beneath the back seat, with his shoulder blades beginning to blister from the heat of the Beetle's rear-mounted engine, Gerd Volker Hagen lay curled up on his side in the dark, concentrating all his energies on trying not to cough. But as the Volkswagen pulled away from the American checkpoint and accelerated down Friedrichstrasse, the teenager could no longer stop himself. By that time, though, the only person who could hear him was the driver of the vehicle.

Gerd had arrived in West Berlin. He was three days short of his seventeenth birthday.

Sixty-two hours later, on a Thursday evening at seven o'clock, Caro Freda Schmidt finished eating dinner in the kitchen of her little two-room student flat in Charlottenburg, rinsed her dishes and cutlery under the tap, and set them on the draining board to dry. Then she pulled on a pair of solid winter shoes, wrapped herself up in a coat, scarf, hat and gloves, and descended three flights of stairs to the courtyard where she kept her bicycle. Despite her spiritual inclinations she was a practical and vigorous girl, and even in the coldest months she preferred to cycle around the city rather than use public transport, unless the weather was especially bad. Tonight it was several degrees below freezing, her breath showing in clouds above her scarf, but the evening was crisp and clear, with frost on the ground instead of ice and only an occasional patch of stubborn crusted snow still clinging to the cobbles.

It was a half-hour cycle ride to the prayer meeting in Zehlendorf. Although she had to take care on some of the streets, most of her route took her along pavements which had been thoroughly gritted by the Western Sector's road department workers, and once she'd left the busier main roads of Charlottenburg and entered the well-to-do residential suburb that was her destination, she found a relaxing enjoyment in the quiet winter stillness that echoed among the rows of large, stolid middle-class houses. An appreciation, too, of the bright streetlighting which illuminated her way, reminding her, as it always did, of the contrast with her own upbringing in a small East German town with regular power cuts. At one point, arriving at a deserted street corner, she experienced a sudden thrill at the sight of a fox emerging sleekly from a garden hedge across the way. The animal trotted calmly over the intersection, turning its head in study of her presence as it did so. Its mouth was slightly open, its breath emerging with its lolling tongue, and its eyes reflected the light like luminous coins.

The only part of the journey that caused her any uncertainty was a short stretch near the end, along an unpaved path that ran for a hundred metres or so through one corner of a wooded park, before emerging onto the street in front of the church. There was no lighting on this path, but although it was dark it was also straight, the ground was hard, and the route saved her from making an annoying ten-minute detour. She'd never hesitated to take the shortcut on previous occasions, for she regarded the district as perfectly safe. Nor did she hesitate tonight, and once she was off the street and into the deeper darkness she found that the frost on the grass reflected the moonlight, allowing her to find her way easily enough. She emerged on the far side feeling invigorated, and a moment later she coasted into the driveway of the church and came to a halt, dismounting and bending over her bicycle to chain it to the railings.

The meeting lasted two hours. That night there was a guest speaker, so the first fifty minutes were given over to a detailed talk on the work of Mother Teresa, delivered by a female German missionary who'd just returned from three months in India, where she'd spent time with the Reverend Mother and her nuns. Freda felt moved almost to tears by the long series of photographs, and fiercely inspired by the stories of death-bed conversions. But she was given a moment's pause when the speaker mentioned, in passing, that the poor and desperate who sought care from the Order were denied any form of pain-relief medication, a strict rule laid down and enforced by the Reverend Mother herself. This, the missionary explained, was because any diminishment of a person's suffering might hinder their spiritual conversion, and thus the saving of their soul. Freda had been unaware of this fact and was unsettled by it. For hadn't Christ himself used his divine power to relieve the agonies of the sick and dying?

This was the question she put to the missionary at the end of the talk. After the lights had been switched on and the applause of the thirty or so people in the audience had died away, Freda raised her hand and spoke up with her usual mix of social diffidence and blunt intellectual confidence.

'Ah,' the woman replied with a small smile of indulgence. 'Indeed he did. But Jesus Christ was our Lord and Saviour, after all, sent by god to spread a message of Love and Salvation through the power of his Word and the gift of his miracles. And surely we, as fallible human beings, cannot presume to emulate Christ in anything but the most limited way? And surely also, if by being on hand at the bedside of the dying, we can act as the conduit of god's infinite mercy and show, through our own fallible example, the way out of the darkness of this world towards god's blessed light, bearing witness while god's great love transforms a few brief moments of earthly suffering into the everlasting bliss of eternal life ... Surely, wouldn't you agree, that is the single greatest kindness which any one person can bestow on another human being?'

A small rumble of approval and a chorus of nodding ran through the audience. Freda blushed and nodded vigorously herself, before settling back in her seat. At some level she was still unsatisfied by this answer, but she was also a girl who believed – passionately – in Christ's Passion, and the concept of suffering as a path to god and a way of atoning for sin was familiar to her. Indeed, it was something she had come to dwell on increasingly in recent years, devoting long hours of thought and prayer to the matter, to a point where it now tended to stoke her mind to a feverish intensity, so that even as she sat there she felt her heart pound and her cheeks burn.

Freda may not have been convinced that other people should be made to endure unnecessary agonies – she wasn't – but as the rest of the audience lowered their heads for prayer, she prayed too, with all her heart. And what she prayed for was that god might grant her the gift of sharing, in some small part, Christ's sufferings, that she might find the strength to bear them for the Glory of His Name.

She could not have put the fierce euphoria that accompanied these thoughts into words, but there was a part of her, a strong part, that rejoiced in the prospect of a martyr's pain. She did not know it yet, but either god, or Chance, was about to grant her wish.

The meeting ended an hour later. As usual Freda had been busy during the brief interval between prayers and announcements, going with another girl into the small kitchen attached to the meeting hall to brew up pots of cheap coffee and put slices of supermarket cake onto paper plates, which they then served from behind a wooden trestle table at the back of the hall. During this process an upsetting incident occurred. Near the tail end of the food line there was a visitor from Bonn – a publisher, she'd been told, a man who ran a small, struggling company which specialised in the production of inspirational religious books. He was a short, untidy figure in his fifties, with thinning brown hair brushed limply across his skull and a sagging face roughened by age and disappointment and probably too much drink. He wore a shabby black jacket that showed up a sprinkling of dandruff and what looked like a dried-out soup stain on the lapel.

Eventually the line shuffled forward until this man stood in front of her, and he took his plate from her with murmured thanks. As he did so she gave him a vague, harried smile, but even as she glanced towards the next person in line she felt him respond to this smile with an intense, searching look, and when she met his gaze again, surprised at this reaction, she saw in his eyes such a burning mixture of needy, sad-eyed lust and misplaced hope that she'd felt physically sick, and immediately tried to cover her reaction by busying herself with the remaining knives and forks.

But once he'd moved away she was quickly able to calm her revulsion, reminding herself as she did so that human beings, with their many weaknesses, were still all god's creatures. And by the time she was required, half an hour later, to shake the publisher's hand at the door as he left, she'd recovered sufficiently to ignore the way he clasped both his clammy palms around her knuckles and held on a fraction too long.

As usual she was one of the last to leave, staying behind to help stack the chairs and sweep the floor. Eventually she waved a farewell to her two colleagues and, leaving them to close up behind her, collected her things and emerged into the chill air. Hers was the only remaining bicycle. She unlocked it, securing the padlock chain around the stem of the saddle before mounting. Pedalling slowly through the gateway and onto the street, she picked up momentum as she rode onto the pavement and entered the park.

She was fifty metres along the dark path between the trees – halfway towards the streetlights at the far end – and remembering, with a shiver of distaste, the way the publisher had clutched her hand, when a black solid shadow came crashing out of the bushes on the right-hand side and charged straight into her, knocking her to the ground.

Freda was too stunned to emit any sort of sound. She was just opening her mouth in surprise and beginning to move when something wrapped itself violently around her neck, choking her. She flinched, twisting and reaching up with her hands, but even as she did so the grip jerked at her so forcefully that her torso was hauled half-upright and something – another human being, she realised now – began to drag her off the path towards the trees, her legs and the heels of her good winter shoes kicking uselessly in her wake.

As soon as they were off the path and into the wooded area she was hurled to the ground with a force that sent spots of white light exploding in her vision. Her chest heaved, sucking for air, but in that same instant the weight of a body slammed down on her, sprawling across her own, and a dry, tobacco-smelling hand clamped over her mouth. She wasn't aware of the small knife that slipped deftly between the folds of her coat and slit the threads of the buttons from waist to neck, but as she thrashed against the undergrowth she dimly registered the heavy material being wrenched aside, exposing her clothing underneath, and then she felt the hand of her assailant reach down and tug her loose skirt up around her waist. That was when she finally understood that she was being attacked, and the nature of it.

She hadn't known that it was possible to scream through the nose, but that was exactly what she did now, instinctively, with no thought or logic, only panic. Probably the noise emerged as some sort of squeal, but it froze her assailant for an instant and she was able to use this small hesitation to reach up her free hand – the other was trapped painfully beneath her – and claw at his face. She felt her fingernails dig into skin and dragged them downwards, unthinking in her terror and so not aiming for his eyes. Nonetheless she heard a grunt of pain, and in response to this she bucked and choked and clawed again. Then her hand was knocked to the side and she felt her arm being pinned by a bony elbow, sending shock-waves of agony up to her shoulder. The weight on her body shifted a little and a moment later a cold, razor-sharp point of metal pressed against her throat, and she went utterly still. There was no thought in her head then. No thought of god, or suffering, or rape, or shame, or an afterlife. Only the simple, terrible, animal certainty that if she moved now, she might die.

'Shut the fuck up, bitch,' a voice hissed in her face. 'Or I'll slit your fucking throat.'

The breath that washed over her smelt of cheap, chemical meat and fried onions. She winced. Then a hand thrust up between her legs and violated her.

For Freda, the next few seconds passed like minutes. Suffering from shock and pinned to the cold hard ground, she felt as if she were undergoing a terribly rough and incompetent gynaecological examination. That was all, in that moment, that her mind could compare it to. Later though, when the shock and panic had receded a little, the emotions would come crashing in and over-whelm her.

At the time, fighting for breath and trying to take control of her reactions, she only registered with surprise that the elbow which had been crushing her arm had been removed. She realised, numbly, that this was because her attacker was using that arm to work his fingers inside her. And even as she noted this, she felt those fingers withdraw in order to begin fumbling at what she assumed must be her attacker's trouser flies. And in the urgency of these fumblings, she also realised, the knife point had shifted from her throat. Her attacker was using his knife hand to prop himself up, so he could twist his body and reach his trousers, which meant that the point of the blade was no longer pressing into her neck. Instead the length of it was now several inches away, parallel to her cheek and not even touching her skin. And now the strangely calm part of herself, the detached part, realised, with a leap of hope and logic, that the knife point could no longer be used to stab into her flesh – not immediately, and not without a significant shift of posture by the man on top of her, who was currently occupied with other things.

In that moment Freda Schmidt straightened the fingers of her free hand and jabbed them as hard as she could towards where – she calculated instinctively – the eye of her attacker must be.

The shape on top of her howled in pain and shifted violently.

Almost simultaneously there was a rushing movement somewhere beyond him, and a new mass came crashing in from the direction of the path.

A third person.

She froze in fear and confusion as this dark form halted a foot or so away, and began to shout.

'What the fuck are you doing!' the voice cried in anguish. 'Leave her alone!'

Then there was a violent rush of air and the weight on top of her was suddenly and violently wrenched off.

A kick, she thought, and turned her face away.

Then the dark mass leaped over her, and there was a solid, dull thud of body slamming against body, and then a frantic, thrashing struggle that sounded almost like two elephants trying to destroy each other, and for some reason this terrified her more than anything that had happened so far. She whirled over onto her front and began to scramble away. A few seconds later she found herself emerging onto the path, registering the pain that shot through her only as an awareness, not yet personal. She turned to look behind her, but all she could see was darkness and shadows. Then there was a low cry, and a break in the noise of the fight, followed by a rustling of leaves and branches as a figure stumbled onto the path about fifteen feet away, one hand clutching the left side of its face, and immediately she knew that this was the person who had attacked her. The figure lurched into a limping, broken run, away from her, towards the road.

She couldn't move. Instead she just stood there, swaying slightly, watching the figure recede and listening to the silence. Eventually there was more movement from the bushes to her right, together with cursing, and another figure emerged holding its left shoulder with its right hand.

'Oh my god,' the figure said, in a deep voice that sounded almost like a sob. 'I'm sorry. I'm so fucking sorry. Are you okay?'

Freda drew herself up to her full height. She wasn't aware that she was trembling like a whipped dog.

'Yes,' she said, her voice dull in her ears. 'Yes thank you. I'm fine.'

*

194

They walked out of the darkness side by side and onto the street. Freda had no thought of the bicycle abandoned on the path behind her. She was very pale and shaking badly, but she remained unaware of this and believed herself to be perfectly calm. In the surreal orange glow of the streetlight she took her first opportunity to study the young man who'd come to her aid. He was big, tall and broad, with a muscular build under his cheap-looking denim jacket and dark scarf, but he was still hunched up and he continued to clutch the top of his left arm with his hand. Realising this she collected herself, feeling something akin to relief at the opportunity to concentrate on something practical. She was that kind of person.

'Let me see,' she demanded, speaking in what she thought was a firm voice and reaching up to remove his hand. As it came away she saw there was a three-inch-wide slice in his jacket, and a large patch of dark fluid had soaked through the material.

'It looks like a cut,' she said. 'A bad one. I think you've been stabbed. You need to get to a hospital.'

The young man shook his head.

'No hospital,' he said forcefully. 'Not for me. But you should see a doctor. And I think maybe you need to go to the police.'

'No,' she replied quickly, surprising herself. 'Not right now. Maybe later. Maybe. But you should definitely get to a hospital.'

The boy beside her shook his head again.

'No hospital,' he repeated. Then he turned away from her, leaning over, and a spew of vomit gushed from his mouth.

'I'm sorry,' he said again, wiping his chin and turning back. 'But what he did to you ... that shouldn't have happened. I'm so fucking sorry.'

This made no sense to Freda and she felt unaccountably irritated by his sympathy.

'I'm fine. But you need to get your wound attended to. You're being stupid.'

She was beginning to feel like she might throw up herself and resented him for it.

'No hospital,' the boy said for a third time, shaking his head. He straightened up, cursing under his breath.

'Bad language won't help,' Freda said now. 'And I don't like it. But ... Oh, I'm shivering.'

'Shaking,' the boy corrected her. 'It's the adrenaline, I think. It does that.'

She suddenly felt weak. 'I think I need to sit down.'

The boy looked back fearfully towards the park.

'Not here,' he said. 'But we could go to one of the houses. Ask for help.'

This suggestion appalled her and she shook her head.

'Then maybe we should walk,' the boy said at last. 'Get away from here. Just in case.'

Freda considered this. It occurred to her that perhaps walking would dissipate the nausea she felt, clear her head. And perhaps if she was moving she wouldn't have to think about what had just happened.

'Okay,' she said, nodding. 'Let's walk. Come on.'

They travelled in silence, quickly, their footsteps crunching on the gritted pavements.

'How's your arm?' Freda asked eventually.

The boy peered down at where his fingers still clutched his jacket.

'I think it's stopped bleeding,' he said doubtfully. 'Or at least slowed.'

'That's good.'

'*Fuck*,' the boy said savagely. 'What a mess. What a fucking mess.'

Freda stopped and turned to him. 'I told you, I don't like that kind of language.'

He paused, startled, and they looked at each other. But then, almost as if they'd reached some sort of unspoken agreement, they both turned and walked on.

At the top of the second road they turned the corner, still moving quickly. This street was deserted also, empty even of parked cars.

'Maybe we should try to find a taxi,' Freda suggested finally. She'd begun to limp a little, experiencing a pain like cramps. Her arm throbbed.

'A what?' the boy asked, confused. Then his head jerked suddenly in recognition. 'Oh, right. A taxi. But, uh ... I don't have any local currency.'

Freda was distracted and didn't notice this unusual choice of words. She was beginning to feel exposed now, panicky, and her nausea was getting worse.

'I've got money,' she said quickly. 'I'll pay.'

It took them five minutes to reach a main road and another five minutes of walking beside sporadic traffic before they finally saw a taxi coming towards them. Its roof light was illuminated and when they waved at it the vehicle swung in a tight arc and drew to a halt beside them. They tumbled in awkwardly and Freda gave her address. She'd been worried that the driver might notice something amiss, but as soon as the door closed he flipped on the meter and turned up the radio, ignoring his two passengers as he drove.

'That'll be eighteen marks sixty.'

The driver turned in his seat as he spoke. He didn't switch on the overhead light. Either it was broken or he couldn't be bothered.

The words brought Freda back to herself with a start. She hadn't been aware of the journey or the streets passing. She looked out through the window and was surprised to see the entrance to her own building. The boy beside her didn't move and it took her a moment to realise what was expected, and then a moment or two more before she located the small purse in her pocket.

'Fifty is fine,' she said, handing over a bank note. She opened the door, getting out as quickly as she could. As she straightened up her awareness of pain returned, sharp and unwelcome. The boy clambered after her. He was too tall to get out easily and was hampered by his bad arm.

'Are you sure?' the driver called behind her. 'Don't you want change?'

Freda leaned around the boy, grasping the door handle.

'Keep it,' she said in a tight voice, and slammed the door shut.

The taxi's indicator light came on and it accelerated away.

'Well,' Freda said, drawing a breath. Memories were swirling in her head and she knew, absolutely, that she didn't want them there. What she wanted instead – desperately – was something to do, a distraction.

197

'Well,' she said again. 'Come upstairs and I'll have a look at that shoulder for you.'

The boy's neck squirmed against the collar of his jacket.

'I don't . . .' he began.

But Freda was already turning away, ignoring him. She pulled out her key and inserted it in the lock of the big door.

'It's okay,' she told him. 'Honestly. And your cut does need to be looked at.'

She went into the hallway and stood there, holding the door. After a moment the boy followed, his head hanging down in a mixture of pain and shame.

She ignored the button on the wall for the timer light and they went up three flights of stairs in darkness, the wooden boards creaking. At the door to her apartment Freda found the lock by touch, fumbling for a moment with the key as she tried to slide it in. The door was pre-war and tended to stick. She leaned her weight against it and it opened with a shudder. Reaching inside with a practised movement she switched on the light. The tiny hallway beyond was fitted with a cheap, dim bulb and for once she was glad of the gloom. She tipped her head towards the interior.

'You can come in.'

He hesitated again. Even though he was big and male and a stranger, she felt no threat from him. More importantly, she wanted something to occupy herself with. She could feel the panic in her fighting to rise and the only way she knew to keep it at bay was by being busy.

'Look,' she said impatiently. 'There's no point just standing there.'

Even as she spoke there was a noise from below as another apartment door opened and somebody stepped out into the landing. The main stairwell light suddenly clicked on, harsh and merciless: awful. Instinctively she ducked inside to escape it, shielding her eyes with her hands. He followed hurriedly and she closed the door in his wake.

'Through here.'

She led the way through a door to the left. Gerd clumped after her, his damaged shoulder brushing against a jumble of coats

198

bunched on wall hooks. He followed her into a small living room. He saw a worn-looking sofa-bed against the left-hand wall, with a chest of drawers next to it. In the opposite corner, beside the window, was a high-backed armchair. A low wooden coffee table stood in the middle of the room and a few feet beyond was an old fireplace housing a three-bar electric fire. Fixed to the wall above the fireplace was a crucifix, and above that there was a large oval mirror. To the right there was a heavy bookcase filled with books. A number of fern-like plants had been placed at strategic points around the room, but she'd been judicious with these and together with the mirror the overall effect somehow made the space seem slightly bigger than it was.

Freda had switched on a lamp next to the armchair. She gestured to the seat.

'Sit down. And take your stuff off so I can look at that cut.'

Without waiting for a reply she went through an archway into the kitchen. Gerd could hear her moving about as he dragged off his jacket and dropped it on the floor. His scarf and jumper followed, more slowly, the pain making him grimace. Underneath he wore a shirt, the left arm of which was soaked with blood. He made no attempt to remove it. Instead he sat in the chair, leaning forward and supporting himself with his good arm against his knee, the bad one propped awkwardly against the arm of the chair, twisted a little so that the cut faced upwards.

'Bring scissors,' he called now, his voice emerging as a harsh croak.

He heard the sound of her rummaging in cupboards and briefly running a tap. Eventually she came back into the room. She'd taken off her jacket and was carrying a tray in front of her. On the tray was a large bowl of water, a bottle of disinfectant, a fresh sponge still in its plastic wrapping, scissors, a box of plasters and a roll of bandage. She had a clean towel draped over her shoulder.

'Always prepared,' she announced as she came in. She tried to say it lightly but the words sounded brittle. They seemed to drop from her lips and break on the floor, leaving behind a silence in which the noise of traffic could be heard on the street below.

She collected herself with an effort, moved across the room and put the tray on the table beside him, then went back into the kitchen and came out carrying a wooden chair. She put this next to his seat, facing his bad arm, and sat down, leaning over to examine the blood on his shirt.

'I think,' Gerd said slowly. 'I think you should bring a bucket too. Just in case.'

After a moment she rose without speaking and went back into the kitchen, reappearing with a red plastic bucket which she put next to his feet.

'If you're sick that's okay. Just don't forget about the bucket and kick it over or something.'

'I won't.'

She studied his ruined shirt carefully, then leaned across and picked up the scissors. She began to cut the shirt, moving up from the wound and all the way around his shoulder.

'How does it feel?' she asked as she worked.

'Sore. Almost too stiff to move.'

She finished cutting and put the scissors back. The shirt arm was no longer attached to the rest of the garment, but as she tried to pull it away she realised some of the material was still stuck to the wound. A small hiss of air emerged through Gerd's teeth and he shifted a little in discomfort.

Her hands were steady as she reached across for the sponge. She opened the plastic wrapping, then dipped one half of the sponge in the bowl of water. She squeezed a good amount onto the shirt around the wound and began dabbing at it carefully. After a few moments she picked at the material and it came free slowly, with a low sucking sound. Then she started again with the sponge, pressing it more firmly against the clotted mess of the wound, trying to remove the blood so she could see better. Eventually she straightened up.

'There's still some blood coming out but not much. I think it's mostly muscle that's damaged but I don't know about these things, and it definitely needs stitches. I can disinfect the wound, but you should go to a hospital and get it checked properly.'

Gerd took a breath through his nose and shook his head.

'I can't go to hospital.'

She seemed to accept the meaning of these words without question.

'Okay. But you'll need a doctor to put in stitches.'

Gerd made an effort to straighten his back and sit upright.

'Listen,' he said quietly, looking at her. 'I'm not sure I should be here. I'll leave right now if you want. God knows you don't have to help me, not after what you've been through.'

'I told you,' she said quickly. 'I don't want to talk about that.'

'That's fine. But if you do want to help me ... then how good's your sewing?'

She blinked at this, but appeared to consider the question carefully.

'It doesn't much matter who does it,' Gerd continued. 'You or the doctor, there's really not much difference.'

'But I don't have any anaesthetic,' she told him, frowning.

'I've been stabbed. It's not going to hurt much more than it does already.'

Freda's mouth had fallen open slightly, but it wasn't because of his request. Memories were crowding in on her again, clamouring. She shook her head and spoke firmly.

'Yes,' she said. 'I can sew. Hold on.'

She stood up and walked out into the hallway. A light went on at the far end, and a minute later she reappeared carrying a small black case.

'I don't have any sterilised thread,' she warned him.

'Just soak it in the disinfectant.'

She nodded and fetched another bowl from the kitchen.

She unscrewed the cap of the disinfectant and poured about a third of the liquid into the bowl. Unzipping the black case, she selected a needle and a spool of thread, from which she cut a good length. She sucked briefly on the end of the thread to straighten it and pushed it through the eye of the needle, tying the end off quickly with a practised movement. Then she dropped the needle and curled thread into the bowl, leaving them there. She picked up the disinfectant and sponge.

'This is going to hurt,' she told him.

'It hurts already. Just make sure you get it right in there.'

She put the sponge up tight against the top of the wound and dribbled a good amount of disinfectant down over it. Gerd flinched at the contact, gritting his teeth. She stopped pouring and, gripping the sponge tightly, moved the tip of it into the slice in his flesh, between the narrow lips of skin.

Gerd cursed, his head falling back against the chair. This time she didn't say anything about his swearing.

Freda bent down and plucked the needle and thread out of the bowl beside her. She held them up and pulled on the thread until it hung straight.

'Last chance to change your mind.'

He turned his face away.

'Go ahead. But I might have to use the bucket.'

Freda realised she was holding her breath, and this in turn reminded her of the weight of the man who'd tried to rape her just an hour-and-a-half before. She squeezed her eyes shut and breathed in and out several times, slowly, deeply. When she opened her eyes again she felt a small sense of triumph on seeing that her hand was steady, and she gripped the side of the boy's upper arm, holding it in such a way that her finger and thumb put pressure on the lips of the cut, forcing them together. Then she jabbed the needle into his flesh and began to sew as quickly as she could.

It occurred to her that she must have chosen the right size of needle, because it was easier than she'd expected. She could feel the boy's big body straining away from her, tense and hot and giving small shuddering jerks almost like shivers, but his arm stayed mostly still and she was able to finish quickly: twelve close, hard punctures that oozed small clots of dark blood. She finished by looping the needle under the last loose arc of thread and drawing it tight, then reached for the scissors and cut the thread, standing as soon as she'd done so.

'There,' she said briskly. 'If you need to be sick don't worry. The bucket's in front of you. I'm going to take a shower now. You'll need a bandage on it, but I'll do that when I come back.'

The boy nodded, wiping his forehead with his good hand. He almost told her everything then. It was only the memory of the colonel saying they'd bugged her flat that stopped him.

Instead he said thickly: 'Thanks.'

In the bathroom Freda turned on the shower. She still had enough presence of mind to close the door behind her and lock it, and to take off most of her clothes before she stepped into the bathtub. But she didn't see anything except what was in her head and she wasn't aware that she still had the scissors in her hand.

Gerd sat alone in the living room, sweating in the chair. He was very angry at what had been done to the girl, but after the events of the evening he was finally beginning to understand what the colonel and his men might really be capable of and he was also very scared.

After she'd been in the bathroom for five minutes he came to a reluctant decision.

He levered himself out of the armchair and reached with his good hand to retrieve his jacket from the floor. He held the collar between his teeth while he unzipped the inside pocket and fished out a small brown bottle. He let the jacket drop and used his teeth to unscrew the cap of the bottle until it sat loosely on the rim. He walked as quietly as he could into the hallway, holding the bottle in his good hand and moving with care. He stood there for ten or fifteen seconds, listening. The only noise from the bathroom was the sound of water falling in the shower. Satisfied, he looked around for something to put the bottle on. There was a fuse box at shoulder height on the wall beside him and he used that.

With the bottle on the fuse box he was able to use his good hand to lift off the cap. Attached to the inside of this was a short plastic stick, about the length of his thumb, with a small sponge on the end of it. The sponge was soaked with the clear fluid from the bottle and he studied it for a moment, then held the bottle to his nose and sniffed. There was no odour that he could discern. Looking at it, he was suddenly reminded of a toy his Uncle Jens had given him when he was a child, shortly after his father had walked out. Instead of a sponge, that toy had had a small plastic ring on the end of its stick, and when you dipped the ring into the contents of the bottle and then blew into it, large shimmering bubbles streamed out and floated away on the breeze.

That had been a good game while it had lasted, but it was all many years ago now and Gerd knew with a terrible certainty that this was no game. He didn't know what the liquid in this bottle was, but both the colonel and Horst had been very insistent about what he should do with it and he would have to do what they wanted until he could figure out a way not to. He wasn't sure there was a way out, but he was in the West now and he hoped that there was, for the girl's sake as well as his own.

Moving carefully – mindful that the floorboards might creak – he took a short step across the hall to where Freda's coats hung, their backs facing him. He used his elbow, clumsily, to straighten out the material of the first coat, then drew the sponge down across it in a diagonal line, in the area between where her shoulder blades would be. Moving back to the bottle, he dipped the sponge in the liquid once more, before shifting over to draw another line on the coat, diagonally bisecting the first, to complete a large invisible 'X'. He repeated this process with the other two coats, resoaking the sponge after each stroke. When he'd finished he stood back and studied the garments. The liquid didn't seem to have left any trace at all.

He was meant to do the same to the soles of her shoes but with only one good hand he was worried it would take too much time. She might finish her shower at any moment, and besides, he felt a fierce urge to rebel against at least one of the colonel's instructions. So he ignored the shoes and instead took the bottle down from the fuse box. In order to do this one-handed he had to clutch the small sponge in the crook of his thumb while he tilted the bottle. Liquid squeezed out and ran down his palm to the inside of his wrist, several drops falling on the floor. With the bottle clasped awkwardly in his fingers he screwed the cap back in, using his teeth and turning the bottle until it was tight. He moved quietly back into the living room, returning the bottle to his pocket, and placing the jacket on the floor. He sat down heavily in the chair, slouching a little and favouring his good arm. His head fell back against the chair and he closed his eyes, listening to the faint noise of the shower thrumming behind the closed door at the end of the hallway.

He was still sweating heavily and he felt very hot, and in addition to the solid pain in his arm he also had a bad headache. But his thoughts were running furiously and he soon forgot about the pain, falling instead into a deep and feverish reverie. He was so wrapped up in his worries that he barely registered the dull, shuddering thud that sounded from the bathroom a few minutes later. The vibration of it caused him to stir slightly in the chair, but he mistook the noise for someone slamming a door in the apartment below and he paid no real notice to it.

It was another half hour before he finally kicked open the bathroom door, after he'd wasted several minutes in loud knocking and increasingly sharp enquiries.

He found her curled up half-naked in the bathtub, her skin like flawed marble and the scissors hanging loose from her open fingers. There was a squashed cake of soap beside her feet, and the water pouring down on her had long since turned cold. Most of the blood in the tub had already washed away, but where it had sprayed over the white tiles above the lip of the bath there was a single smeared hand print.

Rudiger Tüll had held a knife to her throat two hours before, but hadn't stabbed her.

Somehow, by accident or design, she'd done it to herself.

Many people would be liable to panic at such a discovery. Gerd Volker Hagen was a seventeen-year-old schoolboy who'd overheard two Stasi officers discussing how his mother had died in much the same manner, and for most of the time since then he'd been so far out of his depth he hadn't even known he was drowning.

He was three streets away from the apartment and still sprinting like the athlete he was when the car finally caught up with him. It mounted the pavement in a slewing handbrake turn across his path and screeched to a halt, its bumper scraping the wall. The vehicle was so close and he was running so fast that there was no chance of avoiding it. The best he could do was try to adjust his stride and throw himself across the front of the vehicle, attempting to get his body horizontal in the air and turning as he did so. His reactions were excellent, but his left leg was too low. His thigh struck the side of the bonnet and he slid across the metal head first. He managed to roll as he came off the other side, flipping his legs underneath him and landing on his feet but he still had too much momentum and his bruised thigh gave way. He came crashing down onto his hands, the jarring impact splitting open several of the stitches in his shoulder. One of the car's doors was already gaping open and as Gerd attempted to get up he glanced back and saw the driver coming at him like vengeance. He recognised the face immediately: it was Karl, grim and viciously determined.

Gerd was almost upright again and just beginning to understand that his leg wasn't going to be much use to him when Karl hit him from behind with a crushing blow to his right kidney. The teenager's back arched and his legs gave out a second time, but before his knees could hit the ground Karl hauled him up with swift, terrifying ease, then spun him around and slammed him back against the rear door of the car, pinning him there with a forearm across his chest. Through his pain Gerd caught a glimpse of Karl's expression, coldly furious. Then the Stasi man drew his arm back a little and hit him with three straight fingers just below the breastbone.

Gerd's head seemed to explode from the inside and the breath rushed out of his body. The pain was so total he thought he was going to die, but in that same instant Karl's knee jerked up sharply into his groin, hammering his testicles, and the boy realised with an awful shock that he was still alive, and regretted the fact terribly.

He was barely aware of being thrown into the back of the vehicle, face-down on the floor, and he never felt his hands being yanked from underneath him and tied behind his back.

As the door was slammed shut the teenager's lungs finally managed to draw a breath. The horror of that was like being born all over again.

Gerd was awake the whole time but was it several minutes before he was able to comprehend that he existed as any kind of unique, separate entity: a human being. Until then he was just a writhing ball of mindless pain. But eventually the agony receded a little and he became aware of sensations outside himself: the thick, fluffy carpeting of the car against his cheek and in his mouth, and the cool, sticky sensation of his own snot and drool mingling with it. He tried to turn his head and felt resistance in the form of the metal underside of the front passenger seat. He groaned.

The car veered sharply towards the kerb and pulled to an abrupt halt.

'Right,' Karl said. 'What the fuck happened?'

Gerd's mouth was open but he couldn't speak. The noise that emerged instead was a sort of low keening. His legs moved reflexively, spasmodically, as if trying to run, but they were folded almost double in the small space and his knees knocked against something hard.

Karl waited, silent.

Eventually he repeated: 'What happened?'

'Dead,' Gerd gasped.

The atmosphere in the car suddenly went very still.

'Dead?' Karl said incredulously. 'What the fuck do you mean, dead?'

Gerd took another bubbling breath, forcing out the words through reams of snot.

'She's dead.'

There was a long silence. Eventually he felt movement above him as Karl leaned forward and reached under the driver's seat. Gerd heard a scraping sound as the Stasi man drew out some large object from beneath it. He sat up again and Gerd heard the click of a lid opening.

'Tell me.'

The teenager obeyed as best he could, the words coming out in broken staccato pairs. When he'd finished Karl sat immobile. Eventually he said: 'Are you sure about this?'

'Yes,' Gerd gasped. 'She's dead.'

Karl was quiet for about twenty seconds.

'Oh shit,' he said finally, and Gerd heard something in these words that truly chilled him: fear.

Karl leaned across and put something on the passenger seat. Then he twisted around and raised his arm above Gerd.

'You stupid little arsehole,' Karl said.

Then he swung his arm down hard, in a single swift move, and Gerd felt a piercing sting in the side of his left buttock. He opened his mouth to protest, but before any sound could come out the whole world rose up like a tidal wave, washing through his brain, and everything went dark.

He woke to the noise of screaming rage. Someone was shouting at the top of their voice, very close to him.

'... it's a *dog fuck* of a mess, for fuck's sake!' the voice roared. 'Jesus fucking Christ! Talk about a balls up! I mean, *fuck* ... look at it! The fucking target is dead, one of our deep-cover assets is about to have his left eye surgically removed, and an entire fucking operation, that I've spent a whole year planning, has just turned into a heap of stinking dog shit. And you three incompetent cunts are standing here trying to tell me it's not your fault!'

The sheer, boiling rage would have made Gerd cringe if he'd been capable of movement, but his body felt like a sandbag and he seemed to have no command over it at all. Then the ranting voice paused to gather breath and Gerd had a brief moment to register that he was sitting down, in some sort of chair, but slumped forward as though about to topple off it. His head was sagging over his chest and felt as heavy as a concrete wrecking ball. He was cold, and as far as he could tell someone had stripped off his clothes and underwear.

That was all he could grasp before the voice started screaming again.

'You fucking apes!' the voice bellowed. 'So what the fuck happened? *Answer* me, you useless fucks!'

This time there was a longer silence and Gerd became aware of several more things at once. He definitely couldn't move, not even to open his eyes. He appeared to be secured to the chair by some kind of restraints: he had the sensation of a broad, tight band binding his lower chest and biceps, and his hands were fastened tightly to the back of it. The room itself seemed incredibly close and stuffy – the air stale – and he sensed that there were several other people nearby apart from himself and the owner of the voice.

And the voice, he realised now, belonged to Colonel Koch.

It was then that he remembered: Freda was dead.

He was still absorbing this last fact when someone cleared their throat hesitantly.

'From the evidence we saw it's difficult to say, colonel. I reckon there's only three possibilities though. Either the target committed suicide, or it was some kind of accident, or the boy killed her.'

That, Gerd thought, was Karl.

There was another brief silence and then a loud thump followed by a rough clattering. Gerd thought he could picture the scene: Koch had slammed his fist down on a desk in anger.

'You're a fucking *genius*!' Koch raged. 'Two people in a flat and one of them dies and you come up with *that*. A fucking six-year-old could have figured that out!'

There was another loud curse and then a sharp intake of breath.

'Right,' Koch said at last, and this time he sounded slightly calmer. 'Let's turn to you now, doctor. Could I please have the benefit of your expert fucking medical opinion. Bearing in mind, of course, that it was you and your team of mind-fuck clowns who landed me in this fucking shit pit in the first place.'

Gerd had given up trying to move the rest of his body and was concentrating instead on his eyelids, but without success. Even his lips were slack and wouldn't move. He could feel a slick of drool running from the corner of his mouth and down his chin, pooling around his throat. Registering the course of this, he suddenly realised with shock that his head was swathed with some sort of thick hood, and that the rest of his body was indeed naked.

A third voice spoke up, one he didn't recognise.

'I would suggest,' this voice said carefully. 'That we can at least eliminate the third of those propositions, colonel. We have extensive reports and psychological evaluations pertaining to the young man here, and there is nothing to indicate any sort of violent tendency towards females. Quite the opposite, in fact. All the history we have suggests that he's very at ease with women, while at the same time remaining happily detached from the more extreme emotions arising from sexual love and intimacy. This dissociation of his almost certainly stems from identifiable incidents in his childhood – the erratic behaviour of his father, culminating in the father leaving, is likely to be the motivating factor that prevents the boy from achieving any real emotional bonding with others. He's unconsciously withholding his feelings in order to avoid the pain that would be caused by a further betrayal of love. Together with his physical attributes, it's this emotional dissociation that's key to the young man's sexual success with females. I'm certain that he's capable of the usual male-on-male violence, but as far as women are concerned he's a young man who finds sex easy to obtain, and in the absence of any long-standing sex/love bond, which he's never experienced, I'm confident that he simply doesn't place enough emotional value on females to hurt them physically, except in truly exceptional circumstances.'

The doctor paused in his speech and Koch spoke up.

'You mean he didn't slit the bitch's throat.'

The doctor hesitated fractionally.

'No, colonel, he didn't.'

'Thank you, doctor,' Koch said sarcastically. 'Go on.'

'The other two scenarios,' the doctor continued. 'Are suicide or accident – and I would have to say that both are possible. Although the female target underwent extensive religious indoc-trination at a young age, undoubtedly instilling deep-rooted beliefs that would normally mitigate against her taking her own life, it's still not possible to completely rule out suicide on her part.

'You'll recall, colonel, that while I pointed out that a sexual assault on this female would likely achieve a positive outcome, I was still reluctant to sanction it in this case. While it seemed probable that the immediate psychological effect would be to lower the value that the subject placed on her own virginity and at the same time heighten her emotional vulnerability – thus facilitating the seduction that you wished to effect – I stated that not enough was known about the subject's past life experiences or psychological profile to accurately predict her reaction. The literature regarding such cases shows that induced trauma of this kind can have profound and widely varying effects. Those subjects who already have a deep-rooted death wish, or who have previously been sexually abused in childhood and consequently retain strong feelings of guilt and worthlessness, have been known to take their own lives after being abused again.'

The voice paused for a moment, as if considering.

'Go on,' Koch ordered.

'Well, colonel. It's probably not related to the situation under discussion, but it has also been established that in a small minority of abuse cases involuntary feelings of physical pleasure can some-

210

times be aroused in the victim. This is likely to clash violently with the mental trauma caused, which in turn can lead to unresolvable psychological conflict and ultimately suicide. I should emphasise though that this is rare, and is usually related to the anal rape of male victims, when the prostate gland can be stimulated, causing involuntary erection and ejaculation.'

'Ah,' Koch said suddenly. 'You're saying maybe she liked it.'

The doctor coughed.

'It's conceivable, colonel. But highly unlikely.'

'That's fascinating, doc. Now just cut the fucking jargon and tell me what the fuck happened.'

'Certainly, colonel. I think it's safe to assume the subject was suffering from profound emotional shock. She evidently got into the shower too disturbed even to disrobe fully, and with a pair of scissors, which she'd previously been using, still in her hand. She then slipped on a bar of soap and fell heavily on the scissors, accidentally severing her carotid artery in the fall, which caused her to bleed to death in less than two minutes.'

Koch gave an exaggerated sigh.

'In other words, it wasn't your fault.'

'It was an unforeseeable accident, colonel. An Act of God, if you like.'

'Well I don't like, doctor. I don't fucking like it at all ... Now tell me, is that little cunt over there awake yet?'

Slumped over like a dead man, swathed in a black hood and drooling helplessly, Gerd felt the attention of everyone in the room suddenly fix on him.

'Probably, colonel. Given the time that's elapsed. But the paralysis won't wear off for another twenty minutes or so.'

'Give him a shot then. And get the fuck out of my sight, all of you!'

Gerd heard footsteps pass swiftly on either side, but a third set stopped next to him. A door opened somewhere to his rear and people went out. At the same time the person beside him leaned over – he could hear breathing near his ear – and something jabbed into his shoulder.

'He'll regain control of his movements in ninety seconds or so, colonel, and he'll start to feel the pain of his injuries then.'

'Doctor,' Koch said tiredly. 'That's the first welcome news you've given me today.'

The doctor left, and Gerd waited anxiously. At first he felt nothing. He remained as he'd been, a fearful mind trapped in a useless body, listening to the oppressive silence. But then, after a minute or so, he suddenly felt the life force rushing back into his limbs, and he jerked upright. His heart-rate and breathing, which had been slow and steady, accelerated violently in panic, and he gasped for air, sucking in cloth. His eyes shot open but saw only darkness. For the first time since regaining consciousness he registered fully the terrible sensation of his naked helplessness. And then the pain began.

It was so bad he wondered if they'd beaten him while he was unconscious. But after a minute or so he somehow managed to adjust to it slightly – enough to register, thankfully, that all his teeth and fingernails were still in place, and his extremities also. It wasn't much consolation.

He hadn't been aware of Koch's approach, but without warning the hood was suddenly yanked off. Light split his eyes, exploding in his head. He dropped his face forward, squeezing his eyes shut, but a hand took his chin and raised it back towards the light.

'Hello,' Koch said.

Gerd made a rough gargling noise in his throat and Koch released him.

'You're a mess,' Koch told him, stepping back. 'But this should wake you up properly.'

A second later a bucket of ice-cold water was dumped over him. Gerd snorted and shook, straining against the bonds of the chair.

'Feel better?'

Perhaps the shock of cold had numbed his pain a little, but in the moment or two that followed Gerd realised that he did indeed feel slightly better. It was as though he was himself again – naked and helpless and tied to a chair, but himself. His mind was alert and racing, desperately calculating strategies. Things were bad, he knew, but not yet hopeless.

'You're probably wondering what I want from you,' the colonel said now. 'You want to know what I want, so that you can crawl off somewhere and lick your wounds till they've healed, and then you can get on with your miserable life. That right?'

Gerd kept his face down and didn't respond.

'Well tough shit, you little fuck.'

Koch punched him then, hard, his fist slamming into the leather restraining strap near the top of the teenager's left arm, exactly over his stab wound.

Gerd screamed.

'I've got news for you,' Koch said, as the noise of Gerd's scream died away. 'You're going to give me what I want. And once I've got it, you little cock-sucker, I may or may not decide to put you out of your fucking misery ... your treacherous fucking misery, as far as I'm concerned. That's right: you're a traitor. Your fucking uncle was a traitor, your whore of a mother was a traitor, and as of this moment you're officially a fucking traitor. And you're going to sign a full confession admitting to it, right? So the question you need to ask yourself, son, is this: do you want to get it over with now, quickly, or do you want to do it the hard way?'

Gerd's head was lolling to one side. Blood was trickling down his arm, and the arm itself felt like it was made of molten lead. Eventually he managed to lift his face, squinting against the pain and the blinding overhead light. He couldn't see Koch; he couldn't see anything at all in the room. But in the shimmering glare he did see something:

He saw Freda, curled up dead in the bathtub.

The vision of her pale, marble corpse appeared to him now like an angel, outlined in the stunning glow of the light.

He swallowed thickly. He felt something course through him, something wholly unexpected, but it gave him strength.

It was anger.

'Yeah,' he slurred, 'let's do it the hard way, Koch. Go fuck yourself. You shabby, sadistic little prick.'

He expected to feel another punch, but it didn't happen.

Instead there was silence. He listened to his own breathing, his eyes squeezed shut in anticipation of further pain. But eventually he heard the noise of Koch's footsteps retreating towards where Gerd imagined the desk must be. The footsteps stopped, and then

213

there was the sound of a sharp, low buzzing. A moment later the door behind Gerd opened once more and the efficient clip of two pairs of hard-soled boots walked briskly into positions on either side of him and stamped to attention.

'Okay,' Koch said now. 'Let's give this spoiled little teenage shit something to think about.'

He paused, then added dismissively: 'Put him in the Submarine.'

The Submarine wasn't a real submarine, of course, but then Gerd hadn't expected it would be.

His restraints were unbuckled and rough hands yanked him upright, then held him under the armpits while his wrists were cuffed behind his back and someone drew the thick hood over his head again. With a guard supporting him on either side he was frogmarched, his legs buckling, out of the room and down a long corridor. At the far end they descended several flights of stairs then travelled the length of another corridor.

Gerd had the feeling he was underground now. The air seemed colder, and although he couldn't see anything through the thick material swathing his head he somehow had the impression it was darker too. Eventually his guards came to a halt, and in the sudden silence he listened again to the sound of his own breathing: too fast and loud and rasping within the confines of the hood. It felt to him as if the material was clinging to his face, clogging his nostrils and mouth, suffocating him, and he fought down a rising sense of panic.

There was a scraping of metal in front of him, followed by a low, echoing clang, and Gerd guessed that some sort of steel security gate had just been rolled back. He was pushed through the opening of this so roughly that he tripped. The harsh concrete of the floor scraped his bare toes as he tried to keep his balance, but he was grabbed before he could fall and dragged another fifteen metres or so. Again there was a short pause while one of the guards held him and the other moved forwards. This time Gerd could hear the noise of what sounded like a metal key being inserted into a lock. There was a heavy click and then the guard in front of him stepped aside. Simultaneously there was a slight rush of air against his body and the groan of poorly oiled iron hinges. Then, and to his instant relief, the hood was yanked from his head. He took several deep breaths while the man behind him fumbled with the handcuffs. There was some kind of lighting in this area, but his eyes didn't have time to adjust enough to make sense of anything.

Gerd was still squinting and blinking as his hands suddenly came free. As soon as they were released, the man to his rear shoved him violently through the doorway. He fell across the threshold and immediately smacked into a wall directly ahead of him. The shock of this made him reel, and before he could recover the door was slammed shut behind him. He barely registered the sound of it locking, but he heard the noise of footsteps as the guards walked away, and the muffled echo of the security door at the top end of the corridor clanging shut behind them. The sound of that died out, and then there was complete silence. Gerd's legs were trembling and he leaned back against the metal door to support himself.

He was alone in the Submarine.

It was too small to be a cell. For the first few minutes he tried to think of it as a sort of cupboard – albeit a tiny, cramped one, with rough concrete walls and a metal door. Standing there with his back against the door, if he inclined his head forward a few inches his nose touched the wall, and he couldn't bend his knees much more than that before the same thing happened to them. Sitting down was an impossibility, and the space was so narrow that his shoulders were jammed against the walls, with his freed hands still trapped behind him. He could probably squeeze his hands past his hips, he thought, and similarly he might just about manage to turn and face the door, but either manoeuvre would scrape his shoulders badly and worsen the bleeding from his stab wound, and he wasn't willing to try either just yet.

There was only four inches of space between his head and the ceiling, yet the air wasn't stuffy, and he could feel some kind of draught against the back of his head. He guessed that there was a slit or grille set into the top of the door to let air circulate, and he realised with an overwhelming sense of relief that there was no chance of suffocating. As his eyes slowly adjusted he began to see that this slit also let in a small amount of light from the passage outside. The light wasn't strong, but at the same time he wasn't in total darkness, and this cheered him.

Concentrate on the light, he told himself. *Take deep breaths, concentrate on the light, and breathe the fresh air.*

He'd never suffered from claustrophobia, and for that he was now profoundly grateful. But at the same time he was under no illusions: he knew that if they left him there long enough he'd go mad.

They're just softening you up. That's all. They'll be back for you in an hour or so. There's no advantage for them to take it any further than that.

He thought about this for a while and it reassured him slightly.

This is just a cupboard. All they've done is lock you in a small cupboard. It's almost funny, if you look at it that way. Juvenile, really.

Several more minutes passed. Gerd considered trying to count the seconds to keep track of time but he quickly rejected the idea. Better to concentrate on the logic of why they'd be back to fetch him soon, and hold onto that. Koch wanted something from him, and he wouldn't get it if they left him here to rot, or crumble into madness.

The side of his face was starting to swell where it had struck the wall, and his shoulder hurt badly, but he tried to forget about the pain.

If you want to you can turn round, he told himself. *If you want to you can turn and face the door. It will hurt, but you're hurting anyway and it's not so bad. So you can do it. When you can't take it in this position any more you can do it. But not yet. You can take more of this first. A lot more. But when you can't any more you can turn round, and it will be brighter. You'll be able to look up at the grille and see the light directly and breathe the air. But not yet.*

He looked at the dim light reflected on the wall in front of him and breathed the air. He felt the slight draught on the back of his head and concentrated on that for a while.

It's just a cupboard. They'll come for you soon.

Then the light went off and he was left in total darkness.

It wasn't a cupboard, he admitted to himself now, the terror rising like gorge in his throat. This was not some kind of cupboard they'd locked him into, whatever bullshit story he'd tried to tell himself.

It was an upright concrete coffin.

Time passed.

In his pain and confusion and terrible, clawing fear, Gerd lost track of time almost immediately. All he could think of – the sensation that quickly consumed him – was that he'd been buried alive. The horror of the feeling overwhelmed him. He wanted, *needed*, with every molecule of his being, to get out of there: not in twenty seconds, not in five seconds, but *now*, that instant, because he couldn't take it any more, not for anything. The walls seemed to wrap themselves around him, crushing him, and within the space of two or three minutes he'd degenerated to a point where he was no longer a man, or a boy: he was a wild creature, trapped and helpless, confined in an impossibly tight cage and by his own tortured instincts.

Probably he shouted and raved for a while, or even screamed, but if so he didn't know it, and later he could never be sure. But eventually, after some unknown period, his body and nerves exhausted themselves, and as this happened his terror began to subside a little. At last he was able to collect himself, and take slightly more rational stock of his situation.

He must have struggled in his panic, he realised now, for his hands were somehow in front of him, jammed between his crotch and the wall, and his shoulders were badly scraped as a result. His arm wound was bleeding freely again and his jaw throbbed terribly. He forced himself to take deep, slow breaths, trying to calm his racing heart, and once he'd achieved this he tried to think.

All he'd succeeded in doing by panicking, he realised now, was to tire himself out, and thus weaken both his body and his resolve. To that extent he was doing Koch's work for him, and whatever happened he knew that he wanted to resist Koch for as long as possible. He felt that he owed that much to Freda, at least, and he owed it to himself also. He'd lose in the end, no doubt, but in the meantime he still had one thing to hold onto: the fact that the colonel wanted something from him, and the bastard would surely have to open the door and let him out sometime soon. All Gerd had to do was hold himself together until then.

After all, he reminded himself, he hadn't actually been buried alive in a coffin six feet underground, and his situation wasn't hopeless. He was standing in a cell, a tiny upright compartment, at the end of a corridor in the cellar of some big building, some Stasi headquarters or prison in East Berlin (he was sure that they'd brought him back to the East) and there was a slit in the door behind him letting in air. He wasn't going to die here, and he wasn't going to go mad. They'd come for him soon. He would just have to tough it out, because there was no other choice.

The question was, how?

He thought about this for a while and eventually concluded: *Try not to think. That would be a start,* he told himself. *Try to switch off, and let the time pass. And keep your spirits up somehow.*

But how do you keep your spirits up when you're naked and cold and crammed into a concrete cell the size of a coffin?

Well, he still had his mind. And his voice.

Gerd didn't know any hymns, and he certainly wasn't about to start singing any of the patriotic Communist Party songs he'd been taught at school. But there were other sorts of music, and suddenly, from nowhere, he recalled an old drinking song that he used to sing with his friends, when they'd been celebrating sporting victories over a bottle or two of vodka behind the boathouse.

The song they'd sung was sort of a nonsense song, and it had a nonsense name. It was called, if he remembered correctly, 'Ninety-Nine Bottles of Beer'. It repeated itself over and over in a kind of repetitive, mindless countdown, but that in itself might be useful, he thought.

NINETY-NINE BOTTLES OF BEER ON THE WALL,
NINETY-NINE BOTTLES OF BEEEEEER ....
BUT IF ONE OF THOSE BOTTLES SHOULD
   HAPPEN TO FALL,
THERE'D BE NINETY-*EIGHT* BOTTLES OF
   BEEEEEER ON THE WALL:

NINETY-EIGHT BOTTLES OF BEER ON THE WALL
NINETY-EIGHT BOTTLES OF BEEEEER ...

He tried it out, tentatively. And he'd actually creaked out five or six verses of it in a half-hearted fashion when it occurred to him that the song wasn't going to be long enough. He stopped, disconcerted, then started again.

EIGHT HUNDRED BOTTLES OF BEER ON THE WALL
EIGHT HUNDRED BOTTLES OF BEEEEEER ...

His voice, rasping and low at first, was little more than a croak, but the cell was so tiny the ragged sound filled it nonetheless, reverberating off the concrete walls so that the words came back at him, washing over him almost, like choppy, sloppy waves. But he kept it up, and after a few minutes he actually found himself starting to sink into those waves a little, as if he was immersing himself, inch by inch, into the emotion of the song, and as this happened his spirits began to rally. He tried to force this small amount of newfound strength into the words of the song, and at the same time, into the sense of joyous, carefree celebration that the song embodied for him. He made a conscious effort to focus on each syllable, trying through sheer willpower to block out everything else, and also to recall better times, times of success and safety and happiness. And in the dark loneliness of the cell he grasped at these memories and drew them to him, wrapping himself in the warmth of them, until finally they ignited something deep within him, a fierce exhilaration, that burned at first with a small flickering flame but slowly grew hotter and hotter, larger and larger, until eventually it welled up and flooded through his muscles and body and finally banished his shivers.

His back straightened now and his voice gathered power, and as the cramped space filled with the sound, he sang harder, his voice deepening and bellowing, as he poured all of himself, the best of himself, all the returning strength that he had, into the lyrics and the emotion of it. And he even began to imagine, as he belted out the words, that he could hear his voice ringing down the corridor outside his cell, echoing through the building, and he pictured Koch sitting behind his desk listening to him in impotent fury.

It worked, for a while. But eventually the fierce exhilaration began to fade, the volume of his voice dwindled, and his new-found strength ebbed slowly away as the reality of his situation closed in on him again, enfolding him in its claustrophobic embrace.

He forced himself to keep singing, nonetheless. But now it was grinding, dispiriting work, and it was only a desperate determination that kept him going.

He was all the way down at 383 bottles and his voice was ragged, exhausted, when he finally stopped. He stood hunched in the all-consuming darkness, shaking miserably with cold and despair, his muscles on fire with fatigue.

And he started to sob.

He didn't know how long he'd been crying for, but it was Freda who woke him out of it.

She didn't appear to him suddenly. Instead he had a slow but growing sense that she was there: in his head, certainly, but also in front of him, as if the wall he was facing somehow wasn't real. And when he finally opened his eyes he saw that she was indeed standing there – as pale as when he'd last seen her, dead and bled-out in the bath. Yet despite her pallor she seemed to him wholly alive and calmly determined. Looking at her, fixing her with a gaze that was a mixture of shame and hope, he understood suddenly that she'd been indomitable. Unconquerable. No matter what anyone did to her, she'd had an inner strength which was unbreakable.

'*Come on*,' Freda said to him testily. '*I told you, I don't like that.*'

He made an effort to straighten his spine and stand upright.

'No,' he replied. 'I know. I'm sorry. I'm so sorry.'

'*Just pull yourself together.*'

'Yes ... yes, I will. I'm sorry.'

'*Come on then*,' she said impatiently. '*There's no point just standing there.*'

'No,' he repeated. 'I know.'

They looked at each other for a few moments, but then – almost as if they'd reached some sort of unspoken agreement – she turned and left. He thought that she'd given him the slightest trace of a smile as she did so, and he felt a lingering sensation of warmth after she'd gone. He chuckled a little, and tried to reach up to wipe the blood and snot from the lower half of his face, but there wasn't enough room to allow him to get his hand above his belly button. Instead he abandoned the attempt and drew himself as straight as he could, making an effort to gather his remaining strength and resolve.

And then he turned around.

It was a struggle for him, a painful one, but somehow he managed it. His face touched the metal of the door and the sensation was like a blessing. He raised his mouth towards the slight breath of air coming from the slit above him and drank it in, like pure water; like sunlight. A strange happiness flooded through him and tears ran down his face.

He stood like that for a long time, smiling.

Eventually, he heard the noise of the steel door at the top end of the corridor rolling back, and the light outside his cell suddenly came on again. After the long darkness that had enveloped him this light was blinding, and he closed his eyes. Nonetheless he revelled in it.

Footsteps approached, measured and purposeful. There was a slight pause, then a rough scraping sound as a panel in the door slid back. The panel was just below the height of Gerd's chin and when it opened the cell seemed to flood with light.

'Right,' Koch said roughly. 'Are you ready yet, or do you want some more?'

Gerd swallowed, trying to summon enough saliva into his mouth to speak.

'Oh yes,' he croaked, his throat sore. He could feel the smile, still on his face, spreading into a wide grin, and he fought back the urge to laugh.

'Oh I'm ready, colonel, yes, I'm ready.'

'So what's it to be, shithead?'

Gerd licked his cracked lips.

'Like I said, colonel,' he whispered. 'Go fuck yourself.'

There was a low snort of disbelief from the other side of the door. This was followed by a pause, then the panel slammed shut and Gerd listened as the footsteps receded down the corridor.

He'd half-expected the slit above his head to be closed along with the panel, and was relieved when it wasn't. Leaving it open, he thought exultantly, had been a mistake on Koch's part.

He counted carefully, wondering when the light would go out again. Roughly five minutes had passed and the light was still on, when, with no warning at all, water began pouring out of the ceiling onto his head. It streamed over him like a waterfall, freezing cold and unstoppable, and began to fill up the cell.

Within a minute it was up to his ankles; three or four minutes after that it had reached his knees. By then the light in the corridor had gone out and Gerd was back in darkness.

The water was very cold, and by the time it had almost reached his waist he was hyperventilating badly, his breath coming in and out in fast, whooping gasps. He tried to warm himself by jumping up and down, but there was only a few inches of space above his head, and he knocked his scalp on the ceiling several times. Eventually he gave up and just stood on the spot, trying to keep his circulation going by shifting his weight from one foot to the other.

It was only when the water was up to his chest that it occurred to him he might drown. Until then he'd been reassured by the existence of the grille set at the top of the door, level with his forehead. But he realised, belatedly, that in the confined space he wouldn't be able to raise his hands to grasp the grille, or use his arms to tread water, and his legs would be restricted also. So despite the fact he could swim, he realised, once the water was up to his nose it would only be a few minutes before it rose an inch or two more and he drowned.

He was seventeen years old and he was about to drown, standing upright in pitch darkness, in a concrete and metal coffin.

He stood there, shivering uncontrollably, his head bowed under the force of the water, and tried to think. But his mind was sluggish and the thoughts only came very slowly, with great effort. He had to drag himself from one conclusion to another – as if hauling himself, hand over hand, along a rope made of logic.

Koch wants something from you, he reminded himself now. *He wants you to sign some sort of confession.*

Therefore, Koch must want you alive.

Also, the Stasi built this cell, and they'll have used it on other people. And they know how long it takes people to die from hypothermia. They also know how tall you are.

And if they want you alive, they'll keep you alive.

The water felt as if it was freezing cold to Gerd, but he'd studied biology at school and was a competitive swimmer trained in life-saving. Biology wasn't his best subject, but he knew that the human body kept a constant temperature of thirty-seven degrees, and from his own experience, swimming in the sea in different seasons, he knew that a water temperature of twenty degrees felt unpleasantly cold; a water temperature of twelve degrees painfully so. A human being could survive, if moving, in twelve degree water for several hours, but Gerd was in a cell where he couldn't move, something which the Stasi would have factored into their calculations.

So, he concluded at last, the temperature of the water – almost up to his shoulders now – was probably about fifteen degrees. Which meant that, if he didn't drown, he could live for ninety minutes, maybe even two hours. And anyway, he'd heard that hypothermia was a pleasant death. Bad at first, certainly, but as the circulation slowed down and the blood retreated from the skin to the organs and then slowed even in those, supposedly you experienced a warm, drowsy sensation. Like going to sleep.

Gerd wasn't afraid of going to sleep. And he was fairly sure that Koch wasn't going to let him die. Therefore, the water would stop before he drowned. And Koch would let him out before hypothermia was too far advanced. He guessed that this would happen shortly after he stopped shivering, for that would be the sign of the hypothermia really taking hold.

By the time Gerd reached this conclusion the water was up to his chin. He'd tilted his head up towards the grille but although his lips were pressed tightly closed, the splashing of the water filled his nose and he was finding it difficult to breathe. He tried to stand on tiptoe but his trembling legs wouldn't hold him in that position for more than a second or two.

He was an inch or two away from drowning and beginning to panic again when the water gushing from the ceiling suddenly stopped. In the quiet that followed, the noise of it continued to ring in his ears.

He felt no sense of relief at having guessed right. He wasn't shivering much any more, but his skin and flesh felt like they were on fire, burning with cold, and he could barely keep his nose above the surface of the water. Standing on tiptoe, however, he discovered that if he breathed in deeply and held the air in his chest, the lubricating presence of the water loosened the grip of the walls and he actually seemed to float a little. He was even able to tilt himself slightly and lie back. Only when he exhaled did he sink and have to strain to keep his nose in the air. But after some experimentation he found a pattern of breathing – deeply held breaths followed by sharp exhalations, and then quick, deeply held breaths again – that kept him afloat. After five or six minutes he'd perfected this technique to the point where it became almost automatic, and his immediate fear of drowning subsided. Floating there, the strain on his legs was relieved, and as the cold seeped deeper into his muscles the terrible burning sensation diminished.

Time passed.

His skin was so numb that he could no longer feel the water against it. His thoughts had slowed further, and a strange sense, almost of contentment, began to spread over him. In the darkness, he started to see flashes of colour sparking in his vision, yellows and purples, splashes and whorls. He opened and closed his eyes a few times, but as far as he could tell it didn't make any difference. And he decided he should keep them open. He didn't notice when he finally stopped shivering, and didn't really register the fact that he was starting to feel warm. But he did feel the sense of peace spreading through him, seeping through his synapses like treacle, and allowed himself to surrender to the sweetness of it.

Floating there in the cramped, water-filled cell, something very strange began to happen. The walls that were trapping him, closing him in, started to dissolve around him. And his eyes, blind in the darkness, started slowly to see. The walls melted away as if they'd never existed, and at the same time the flashes in his vision began to drift upwards, stretching and diffusing, until finally they'd faded to pinpricks of light set in a deep, black firmament. Like stars.

Now the walls had gone completely. And in their place – soundlessly, seamlessly – was not the corridor outside, or the building above, or even the streets beyond the building. All that seemed to have melted away also, as if it had never been anything more than scenes painted on tissue paper: an illusion. Instead, in their place, was more water. Vast amounts of water. Oceans of water.

A sluggish wave of astonishment rolled through Gerd's consciousness, reviving him slightly. His mouth opened, and with a great effort he managed to bring his head forwards slowly until he was floating upright.

The world as he knew it had vanished utterly. Utterly. Where it had been there was nothing. Only water. An enormous, black ocean of water. And he was floating in it.

It seemed to Gerd almost as if he'd fallen back through time – aeons of time – to a point in prehistory when the surface of the planet consisted only of endless, empty ocean. Before there were continents. Before there was land. He was floating, alone, in an unimaginably large expanse of unimaginably deep water. And he could *feel* it all, somehow. His consciousness seemed to expand outwards, far beyond himself, until he could feel the entire encircling breadth of it: the gigantic, mind-defying loneliness of a huge, lifeless ocean encircling an entire world. And at the same time he could feel, too, the terrible fathoms of it yawning blackly beneath him. The knowledge of this condensed within him, solidifying like a ball of lead in his chest, and he registered it with the irrefutable certainty of truth.

He knew he was alone.

Except for the stars.

He floated there in the dark, vast reaches of water with the black sky above, and he looked at the stars. He gazed up at them in wonder. He was not afraid. He was amazed. He had no thoughts. He felt only an overwhelming rightness at the beauty of it all. He floated there, alone in the middle of an endless ocean, and was subsumed wholly with joy as he drank in the unutterable perfection of the universe.

And then, after a while, god touched him.

His mind felt god, and he was blasted – incinerated – by the awe of it.

Then, just like that, it was over.

He was hurled back into himself: banished. And he woke with shock to discover that he was lying – sprawled and coughing – on a hard concrete floor, water pouring out all around him, gurgling down a drain next to his outflung hands.

'Warm this piece of shit up until he's able to talk,' he heard Koch say. 'And bring him to me. I want to get this finished before lunch.'

They lifted him off the ground and carried him to a room some-where with a sort of bath – a deep square hole – set into the floor, filled with warm water. He was dumped into it without ceremony, and they stood watch around the edges, grabbing his hair to pull him up whenever his helpless body started to slump forwards or his face threatened to sink beneath the surface. A man came in and pushed the others aside, checking his pulse and shining a light in his eyes, before issuing clipped instructions. Then somebody held his chin and prised his mouth open while they dribbled a warm drink, thick like soup, into his mouth from a plastic beaker with a projecting mouthpiece, like a baby cup. He hadn't the strength or will to resist and his head barely moved as they poured the liquid down his gullet and his throat swallowed reflexively. The broth burned as it went down and its heat rose inside him. As the warmth began to re-enter his limbs he moaned and stirred. He was coming round towards full consciousness when they reached down and hauled him out.

They dressed Gerd roughly, pulling a pair of tracksuit trousers and a heavy jumper onto his body and wrapping a blanket around his shoulders. When they'd done that they drew a prisoner's hood back over his head.

This time they didn't bother with handcuffs. Instead they dragged him, limp and unresisting, along the corridor and up the stairs, and then down another long corridor and into a room – perhaps the same room he'd been in before. They dropped him in a chair and took off the hood, then left the room. The light was very strong and it was some time before Gerd was able to raise his head and open his eyes. When he finally did so he saw that he was sitting in front of a wooden desk and Colonel Koch was sitting on the other side of it, watching.

'You'll feel better soon,' Koch said. 'The drink you were given is strong medicine.'

Gerd stared at him, his mouth slack. Koch sat there like a slab of cement: like a bald, powerful wrestler. It occurred to Gerd that the colonel could probably just tear him to pieces if he wanted to; rip his limbs off one by one with the mindless ease of a hungry man dismembering the carcass of a roast chicken.

'I'm impressed, Gerd,' Koch said. 'You're a tough little prick, no argument there. You would have made a great soldier, if you ask me. I've got grown men working for me, real thugs, who would have been begging for mercy by now. So believe me when I say you have my respect. My full respect. Well done.'

Gerd stared at him dully.

'You've done enough,' Koch went on. 'Really. More than enough. You've proved your point. Nobody pushes you around. That's crystal fucking clear. But there's nothing to be gained by continuing like this. There's no reason for you to suffer any more than you have already. It's time to get this finished with, okay?'

The colonel looked down now, slowly and deliberately, his eyes settling on something lying on the desk in front of him. Gerd followed his gaze, and saw a thick sheaf of papers. They looked as if they were stapled together, like a manuscript. Like a book.

Koch reached forward and picked it up.

'Sign this,' he said, waggling the document at Gerd. 'That's all you have to do. Then it's over and we can all go home.'

He let the document drop back on the desk. It landed heavily, with a thud.

Gerd blinked, very slowly. His eyes closed and then opened again.

'Sign each page,' Koch said. 'And it's finished. Just like that. Ninety-eight pages. Sign them and then you can leave.'

Gerd thought about asking what the document said but he realised there was no point. Whatever it said, it was all lies.

'Just sign it,' Koch repeated.

Gerd raised his eyes from the papers and studied the colonel's face. He thought of Freda – the girl he had known briefly in life and who'd appeared to him in death. He thought too of the experience he'd had after her ghost left him in the cell: of being alone in a world full of water, alone with the stars. And yet not alone. He remembered it all and he knew it was true. He also knew then that whatever happened here, whatever happened now, everything would be all right in the end.

He had to swallow, then concentrate on pronouncing the word as he spoke.

'*Why?*' he asked.

Koch's head jerked slightly in surprise.

'Why?' the colonel repeated. 'What do you mean, why?'

Gerd had to gasp to get the words out.

'Tell me why . . . all this happened. And I'll sign it. Every page.'

The colonel's body went very still. Then he placed both huge fists on either side of the document in front of him.

'Oh you will, will you?'

Gerd gave a nod like an old puppet. His head fell forward and he had to pull his whole torso back to get it upright again.

'Yes,' he said thickly.

Koch studied the teenager's face carefully.

'Yes,' Gerd repeated. 'I swear it.'

The colonel smiled, and this time his smile looked almost genuine.

'You're something else, son. I think I need to have a word with the medics. Get them to reduce the doses they're giving.'

Gerd tried to shake his head but it just rolled loosely on his shoulders.

'Tell me,' he slurred. 'And I promise I'll sign.'

Koch leaned back in his chair and folded his thick arms behind his head.

'Okay,' he said quietly. 'I will.'

And he did.

It took a while – half an hour or so – but Koch seemed to enjoy the telling of it.

Gerd listened. He found it difficult to concentrate, but he understood the essence of what Koch was saying. Most of the time he was thinking about Freda.

When the colonel finally finished he leaned forward and put both elbows on the desk, watching his prisoner.

Gerd stared back at him balefully.

'So that's why Freda died?'

Koch shrugged dismissively.

'Her death was an accident. One that completely fucked up my operation, unfortunately. But bad luck happens. You get used to it in this line of work. Bad luck for her, bad luck for me. And bad luck for you too, of course.'

'So all this,' Gerd said, enunciating the words carefully. 'Was about your career?'

The colonel's lips twitched.

'Let's just say it's my job,' he said now. 'Sometimes I have to cut corners. Ignore some of the rules, maybe. We do have rules, believe it or not. But nobody cares about that if you get results. This isn't school any more, son. We're not playing. This is real life.'

He lifted a hand and picked up the heavy sheaf of papers again.

'And now I need to cover my arse with my superiors. Somebody's got to take the rap for this balls-up, and I've decided it's going to be you. So sign this. Because if you don't … I can promise you'll regret it.'

Gerd looked at the papers in front of him. He thought about everything Koch had said and his own part in it. He knew that he was culpable. This wasn't really about Koch, he understood now. Not really. This was about himself.

Whatever lies were written in the document, he still had a personal responsibility, a guilt that needed to be expunged.

He raised his eyes and met the colonel's hard stare.

'Okay,' he said heavily. 'Give me a pen.'

There were ninety-eight numbered pages in the confession and Gerd had to sign the bottom of every one. He did so without reading any of it. His arms were heavy and his hands trembled slightly from exhaustion. Half of his signatures were illegible but it didn't seem to matter. Koch was watching him and seemed satisfied. When he'd finally finished Gerd put down the pen and sat there, looking at his feet. He felt very, very tired.

Koch picked up the sheaf of papers, opened a drawer on his side of the desk and slid them in. He closed the drawer again and locked it.

'Very wise,' he said.

'So what happens next?' Gerd asked dully.

'Ah,' Koch said, brightening. 'Good question. Well, let's just say I think it's high time you were reunited with your dear departed mother. Let's put it that way, eh?'

Gerd sat there silently for some time, taking this in.

'It won't take long,' Koch continued. 'It'll be over before you know it.'

'Yes,' Gerd said simply. 'I know it will.'

For a brief moment Koch looked dumbfounded, then he gave a low chuckle.

'You're high as a kite, you little fuck. You don't even know what you're saying.'

Gerd lifted his head suddenly and fixed the colonel with an intense stare.

'Oh believe me,' he told Koch. 'I do.'

The colonel pushed his chair back and stood.

'Well, let's hope so, eh? For your sake. Have a good journey, shithead. I can't say it's been a pleasure working with you.'

He reached a hand beneath the desk, pressing a buzzer.

The door behind Gerd opened and the familiar noise of hard, clipped footsteps arrived on either side of him. He made no effort to resist as they hauled him to his feet, cuffed his hands and put the hood back over his head. The blanket he'd been wrapped in fell to the floor, but one of the guards picked it up and draped it over his shoulders again, tucking it under his armpits. They pulled him out of the room and the door banged closed behind him.

Gerd was taken a different route this time, along other corridors. They went around several sharp corners and he quickly lost all sense of direction. But eventually they emerged into the cold winter air and he felt a sharp wind whipping at his blanket and bare feet. He was pushed forwards and heard the rolling slide of vehicle doors being opened in front of him, and then he was grabbed roughly and bundled into the rear of what felt like a large van. He was pulled down into a sitting position on a bench, his back to the metal bodywork, and a guard sat on either side of him. The doors were slammed shut and the vehicle's engine started up with a shuddering roar.

The journey lasted about forty minutes. For the first half they seemed to be travelling through the streets of some large city or town, as the vehicle kept stopping and starting and there were occasional sharp turns at what Gerd assumed were junctions or traffic lights. But eventually the road straightened and the driving became smoother and Gerd guessed they'd reached the country-side. He thought it likely that he was being taken somewhere to be killed. The guards didn't speak and the only sound he could hear was the loud noise of the engine. His bare feet were very cold on the vibrating metal floor and he tried to warm them up by rubbing them together but it didn't make much difference.

Eventually the van slowed, then came to a halt several times in quick succession. He heard muffled voices from the front of the van and from outside, and thought they might be passing though some kind of checkpoint or guard post. After the third of these stops the van veered to the right and pulled around in a sweeping half circle. He heard footsteps outside and suddenly the double doors were rolled open, and his guards were shouting at him and hauling him up off the bench. He was pulled out, half stumbling and half carried, to stand on hard tarmac. The wind was stronger and colder here and he began to shiver. One of his guards stepped away, but he could sense more men around him and heard the muffled voices of a discussion taking place, although the words themselves were whipped away by the wind. Then footsteps approached again and the hood was lifted briefly from his face. He stood there squinting in the daylight, until a voice said briskly 'That's him,' and the hood was dropped back into place. He was grabbed under the arms once more and marched forwards ten feet or so and then another twenty. One of the guards stepped to his rear and fumbled with his handcuffs, springing them open and releasing his wrists, and at the same time the hood was pulled from his head. He felt a hard shove between his shoulder blades.

'Keep walking,' a voice ordered. 'And don't look back.'

Gerd stood there uncertainly, sightless in the cold, sharp winter daylight, until he was shoved again.

'Walk.'

He obeyed. He moved his numb feet and shuffled forwards. He tried to open his eyes and walk in a straight line but the light was blinding and he couldn't see anything except a confused blur. The wind was very strong here, rushing in from his right, cold and fresh. He had an impression of height and wide empty space and thought that he might be near the edge of a cliff or the lip of a quarry. He slowed then, almost halting, until the voice behind him shouted again with angry authority.

'Keep walking!'

He gritted his teeth and tried to tell himself that he wasn't afraid and walked forward another ten steps. He expected to plunge forwards at any moment, but it didn't happen. His eyes were starting to adjust now and he managed to open them a little more, carefully, keeping his head down, seeing his feet first of all and then the tarmac he was walking on. Then he lifted his head and saw that he was on a bridge, a narrow vehicle bridge, with green-painted metal girders on each side.

He shuffled forwards, no longer concerned about falling. Instead he expected to feel a bullet punch through his back at any moment. He was waiting for it to happen when finally he raised his head and looked out through the girders and saw a wide band of water below him, thirty feet below. Then he looked up and saw the sky – banks of white-grey clouds across a dull metallic grey – and he thought it would be the last thing he'd ever see. But then he dropped his gaze again and found that he was still walking. And straight ahead of him now was the end of the bridge, forty feet away, with the road running on beyond it and thick bare trees on either side, and a white hut beside the road with a white barrier at waist height, barring the exit. And he saw too that there were three men standing behind the barrier, watching him. Three men dressed in boots and green uniforms, with round green helmets on their heads, and he knew immediately that these weren't East German uniforms. A sudden hope surged in him then, but he tried to quash it because he assumed it was a trick: a terrible trick, and he didn't want to die a fool, although he knew he'd been a fool anyway. And although he wasn't afraid of death he was certainly afraid of dying, and he realised that in spite of everything

232

he wasn't finished with his life, and he knew also, with complete certainty and an awful regret, that he wanted so very, very badly to live.

He kept walking.

One of the men in front of him was beckoning to him now, gesturing with his arm and calling out something that Gerd couldn't hear in the wind. For a brief moment he considered trying to sprint to the side of the bridge and throwing himself off, in a desperate attempt to escape, but he knew that in his state he had no chance of moving quickly enough to avoid a bullet and he didn't want to risk the agony of dying from a wound; he wanted it to be over quickly. As far as he could tell the men in front of him weren't holding weapons, but he was still waiting to feel the bullet hit him from behind, like a horse's kick between his shoulder blades.

He was twenty feet from the white barrier now and beginning to make out the features of the men when he heard the words that the middle one was calling to him. Gerd stopped in surprise.

He couldn't speak English but he recognised the words nonetheless. The man was still gesturing at him to come forwards.

Gerd stood where he was, swaying. Then he slowly turned his head and looked back over his shoulder.

The far end of the bridge was fifty feet behind him. He could see another group of soldiers standing there, four or five of them, bunched tightly together behind a red-and-white striped barrier. They were wearing grey East German uniforms, and they were watching him.

Gerd studied them carefully. Then he turned and walked on.

As he approached the white pole, one end of it rose up until it pointed at the sky like an accusing finger. He crossed the tarmac underneath it and two of the green-clad soldiers came towards him.

'Welcome to the West,' one of them said in English.

The man put his hand on Gerd's shoulder, the other stepped to his side, and together they helped him round to the back of the hut. There was a small parking area here and three army jeeps with canvas roofs. The closest jeep had a driver in it. They helped Gerd climb into the back seat and one of the soldiers sat in front, while

233

the other clambered in beside Gerd. The driver started the jeep and pulled out onto the road.

Gerd stared out sideways as they drove, his body juddering with the movement, watching the tree trunks as they passed in a blur.

The journey only lasted two or three minutes. The vehicle suddenly slowed, then swerved to the left and rattled through the pillars of a stone gateway and up a steep, smooth drive. Through the windscreen in front of him Gerd saw a sloping, well-tended lawn emerge between the trees, and then a very large house – almost a mansion – appeared at the crest of it. They jerked to a halt in front of the doorway. The two guards got out and helped him down. The ground here was gravelled and the small sharp stones hurt the soles of Gerd's feet, but the soldiers supported him up the steps under the columned portico and the big mahogany front door swung inwards just as they reached it.

They entered a high hallway. Gerd got a brief glimpse of stuccoed ceilings and a marble staircase with a dark-oak bannister before he was shepherded into a room on the right.

The room had a big picture window and parquet flooring. It was empty save for a huge fireplace set in the far wall with a fire blazing in the middle of it, and two men standing midway between the fireplace and the door. One of these men was short and pudgy, with round wire-rimmed glasses and a pale, pasty face. The other was about Gerd's height, thin and wiry-looking. He wore a sharply pressed brown officer's uniform and had close-cropped grey hair.

'Welcome to the West, Gerd,' the latter said in German. 'My name's Colonel Beresford. I'm with the British forces. You're safe now, but there are a few formalities we have to go through that will take some time, I'm afraid. The first thing we need to do is make some checks on your health, for your own safety. So if you don't mind moving to the fireplace and taking off your clothes, we'll get on with it.'

The officer nodded to the guards, then stood aside as they escorted him across the room. Gerd registered the heat of the flames with bliss, closing his eyes and drinking it in through his pores, and he barely stirred as the guards removed his clothes for him. He stood there, soaking in the warmth, as the round-faced man approached. He was carrying the handle of a small metal box in one hand. An electric lead ran from this box to the bottom of a slim-looking microphone that he held in his other hand. Raising the microphone up to Gerd's chest he passed it slowly over the teenager's body, an inch or so from his skin. As he did so the metal box emitted a series of rapid clicks and whining sounds. The man finished and said a few sentences in English to the officer, who stepped up behind Gerd and cleared his throat.

'Ah yes,' the officer said in German. 'Unfortunately it appears that your body's been contaminated with residual levels of radiation. We've seen this before. It's nothing to be too alarmed about, though. Skin-deep only. But it means you'll have to be decontaminated, which isn't particularly pleasant. Fortunately we're set up for it here, and Jackson has a little concoction that he can give you once he's finished his check-up. Hopefully that should take the edge off it.'

Gerd didn't reply. Instead he luxuriated in the warmth of the fire while the round-faced man shone a torch into his eyes, listened to his chest through a stethoscope and strapped a cuff on his arm to check his blood pressure. Eventually the man reached towards the mantelpiece and picked up a glass syringe, pulling off the metal cap. He took the teenager's uninjured arm and jabbed the needle into his shoulder, pressing the plunger. A moment later a feeling of well-being flooded through Gerd. He swayed on his feet and his head fell back, and he was laughing quietly as they took him by the arms and led him gently upstairs to a large, white-tiled bathroom, bare except for a big showerhead in the middle of the ceiling and a drain underneath it. He stood there in the heavy rain of hot water for twenty minutes, while they scrubbed his skin raw with stiff-bristled brooms. Eventually they finished and the water was turned off. The round-faced man ran the microphone over his body again and this time the sound was more subdued and intermittent and the man seemed satisfied. Afterwards they led Gerd out along the hallway to a large, pale bedroom with a sprawling double bed and another fire blazing away in the chimneyplace. Here Jackson smeared him all over with some kind of salve and gave him a hot drink, then put him gently to bed, tucking the heavy duvet around him and wishing him good night.

And then Gerd slept.

When he finally woke three days had passed, and the pain he felt was sharp and discomforting. But it was also bearable, and his mind was clear.

And when he turned his head on the pillow and looked up, he saw his mother sitting in a chair next to his bed, smiling the smile he remembered so well – smiling through the tears running down her face.

Part Four
Wasps in the Tower

'If we should fail?' – *Macbeth*. Act 1, Scene 7.

Gerd had been talking for almost ninety minutes by the time he finally trailed to a halt, his voice choking with emotion. Holger and I sat there looking at him, stunned. For some moments nobody moved.

Eventually I managed to clear my throat and spoke.

'*You mean your mother was still alive?*'

In the silence of the tower my question sounded incredulous, and I could have kicked myself for not having taken a softer tone. Gerd's feelings, even two decades on from the events he'd described, were obviously still raw. Twice while talking he'd come close to breaking down, but had managed to struggle through and continue with his tale. In fact he'd only stopped at a few brief interruptions, caused when school kids had trotted up the path to get some piece of equipment or ask a question, or complain about some argument or perceived injustice on the beach. We'd dealt with these things briskly, and once they'd retreated back down the steps Gerd had continued his story.

Several times Holger and I had found ourselves murmuring some expression of sympathy or shock, and these Gerd had acknowledged with a nod of his head or a twist of his lips. But his last revelation had shocked me more than anything – more even than his description of the death of the girl – and I couldn't help repeating my question, although this time I made an effort to soften my tone.

'So your mother was still alive?'

Gerd reached up and massaged his brow with his fingers. Then he cleared his throat heavily, and when he spoke again his voice was rough from talking, tiredness, and an old, old anger.

'The Stasi lied,' he said simply. 'Koch lied. The whole thing was a set-up from start to finish. Every last fucking bit of it. All that

239

crap with them parking the ambulance in front of our house and telling everyone they'd found her dead, and letting me overhear Koch and the other guy in the corridor saying she'd been stabbed in the throat by my father. The fucking funeral. Even the trial. Everything. It was all staged, all planned, all bullshit.'

He shook his head in sorrow and frustration.

'They arrested her quietly on the street as she went shopping,' he said now. 'Half an hour after I left for school that morning. And they faked everything else. The colonel must have been planning it for weeks. Months.'

'But why, for god's sake?'

Gerd leaned back and sighed.

'Because my uncle had been working for the British. He was passing them information, microfilm of documents he had access to. Economic data. Production quotas that hadn't been met, that kind of thing. He'd been doing it for years. The Stasi had found out about it and used it for a while, feeding him disinformation without him knowing. And when they finally made their move they thought my mother was in on it so they pulled her in as well. They'd been watching us for months, apparently. Trailing my mother, bugging the house. They thought maybe my uncle was passing her information and she was passing it on to a British agent when she went shopping in Rostock, or took in a film at one of the cinemas there. And when Koch finally read the case files on it he decided I was perfect for this other thing he was planning, so in the end I got dragged in too.'

My mind was reeling as I struggled to grasp the implications.

'But if they arrested her, how did she get to the west?'

Gerd grunted.

'They sold her,' he said simply. 'They sold me too.'

'*Sold* her?'

'Yeah. My uncle had made some kind of deal with the British government. Remember I told you he never married? Well, turns out he was gay. Very much in the closet, of course, but somehow the Brits found out about it and blackmailed him – according to my mother he was giving them information for free.

'He did strike another kind of bargain though. And that was that if he got caught by the Stasi, the British government would

240

get me and my mother out, one way or another. And once Koch had got hold of us, there was only one way for them to do that. They paid. Two hundred thousand deutschmarks for my mum, and one hundred and fifty thousand for me.'

'Good god.'

Gerd shrugged.

'Actually it's pretty common. The Stasi do a brisk trade in political prisoners. It's an easy way to generate western currency and get rid of undesirables, trouble-makers, at the same time.'

I was shaking my head again.

'It's . . . well, it's incredible.'

Gerd grimaced.

'I only wish that it was. But unfortunately it gets worse. My uncle died from a heart attack during questioning, and my mother died of thyroid cancer eight years later. Basically the Stasi killed them both. You remember that stuff, that liquid, I was told to paint on the back of Freda's coat and the soles of her shoes? Well, that's the reason I had half my skin scrubbed off when I was sold to the West. That liquid was radioactive. Invisible to the naked eye, but the Stasi have special glasses – spectacles they can wear – and the stuff shows up through the lenses. Glows like neon, apparently. Makes it easier to follow people in crowds, that kind of thing. Only problem is, the people they target get a prolonged dose of radiation, and they'd painted that stuff all over my mother's clothes. For months before she was arrested every jacket and skirt and pair of shoes that she wore was covered with it, and eventually it killed her. I had to take daily doses of iodine tablets for months after I got to the West. Even now I get regular check-ups in hospital. I've been told I could get cancer at any time.'

'God, I'm sorry.'

'Yeah,' he said, nodding. 'Me too. But then it's no less than I deserve, I suppose, after what I did to Freda.'

I shook my head at this and reached out to grip his shoulder.

'You can't blame yourself for that,' I said earnestly. 'It's not your fault. You didn't know what would happen. And anyway, like you said, you didn't have a choice.'

'Oh, but I did have a choice,' he said bitterly. 'Of course I had

241

a choice. Deep down. Everybody has a choice, Craig, one way or another. That's the curse of being human.

'Okay,' he conceded, seeing we were about to protest, 'it's true I didn't know that bastard Rudiger was going to molest Freda, I didn't know that. And nobody knew she was going to wind up dead. But I still went along with their plan. I had the chance to tell her everything but I didn't. I kept my mouth shut, and by doing that I betrayed her. And I painted that crap on her coats, and that was betraying her too. And she died. And just because I'm sure she'd forgive me, and just because I think god forgives me ... that still doesn't mean I have the right to forgive myself.'

I drew my hand back from his shoulder and we were silent again. Eventually though, another question occurred to me and I couldn't help blurting it out.

'What about the tunnel?' I asked. 'That escape plan the group had? Did they go ahead with it?'

Gerd shrugged helplessly.

'I don't know if there ever really was a tunnel,' he replied. 'For all I know it might never have existed. Maybe the Stasi made up the whole thing to fool me, as part of some other plan. Or maybe they thought it was true but just got it wrong. Or maybe there was a tunnel, and the reason Koch told me everything and then sent me over that bridge was because he wanted to scare them off. That makes a certain amount of sense, I think. With Freda dead and me singing to any Western intelligence official who'd listen, the whole thing would've been seen as compromised. Too risky.'

He shook his head.

'There've been other tunnels over the years, but if that one ever existed it was never used. Either way, whether the tunnel was real or not, Koch came out on top. And as long as the Wall's still standing I doubt I'll ever know for sure.'

We sat in silence again, listening to the breeze beyond the doorway and the faint noise of music and chatter drifting up from the beach. I found myself thinking momentarily of East Berlin and the people who lived there; going about their lives in the drab, grey streets, looking through their apartment windows at the rounded crest of the Wall and the barbed wire and sniper's towers of the no man's land beyond.

'Do you think it will ever come down?' I asked at last.

'The Wall?' Gerd gave a bleak laugh. 'Yes, of course. You're talking to someone who thinks he's seen eternity, remember. A thousand years isn't even a blink in god's eye. Of course the Wall will crumble, sooner or later. It came from dust and it'll go back to dust, same as everything else.'

Holger shifted uncomfortably on the sea chest.

'You really believe that religious stuff?'

Gerd turned his head in surprise.

'Absolutely,' he said. 'That's what gets me through, mostly . . . that and my wife. When I wake up sweating in the middle of the night, thinking I'm back in that concrete cell or staring at Freda dead in her bathtub, and I'm lying there sick and gasping with fear. And then, after ten seconds or so, I suddenly remember. I remember everything I saw in that cell, everything I felt, and I start to calm down because I know – I *know* – that there's a reason for it all. A Purpose. A Plan. And after a while I wipe my forehead and turn over and curl up against my wife. I smell her hair and listen to her breathing, and I can feel that god's with us, in us even: in her, in me, in all of us somewhere. Even in that murdering bastard Koch. And it seems to me that whatever happens to us in this life, however bad it gets, it's all over before you know it, and then everything will be all right, for ever.'

Holger leaned forward and squinted at the bare patch of skin showing through Gerd's open-necked shirt.

'It's just I've never seen you wearing a crucifix or anything,' he said.

'Oh!' Gerd exclaimed with a small laugh. 'I'm not like Freda. I'm not a Catholic, or even a Christian. I just believe in god. I don't believe in Hell, except for the Hell we create for each other here on earth. And I'm not entirely sure I believe in any kind of Heaven either: at least not in the sense of some kind of afterlife we'll consciously experience. I just believe in a higher power . . . a Reason, if you like, and I don't need to wear a piece of jewellery around my neck to remind me of that.'

He trailed off for a moment as a thought occurred to him.

'Although,' he continued slowly, 'now you mention it I do have something, I suppose. Something I carry with me on my skin,

243

always. Not a crucifix as such, but perhaps it serves the same purpose. And any time I start to feel some sort of doubt, well, all I have to do is reach up and touch it, and the doubt goes away.'

Our confusion must have been obvious, for Gerd gave us a quick smile, then lifted his right hand and pulled back the short sleeve of his summer shirt. I looked at the exposed skin, and just above his tricep I saw a small, indented scar, about three inches in length, the white ragged tissue stark against his tan.

'That's my crucifix,' Gerd said, patting it lightly. 'Right there. The reminder, if you like, of the personal cross I have to bear.'

He let the material drop back down. The three of us sat quietly once more. There was nothing I could think of to say.

Eventually Holger cleared his throat.

'Well,' he said briskly. 'That's quite something, Gerd. One hell of a story. But I guess it's about time I got back to work. Someone should be keeping a closer eye on what's happening down on the beach.'

'Oh absolutely!' Gerd exclaimed. 'Sorry! I didn't mean to drone on for so long. I got completely carried away.'

'No problem,' Holger smiled. 'And like I said, thanks for telling us.'

He made for the doorway. As he did I started to get up, but Holger waved at me to stay where I was.

'I'll do it, Craig. Take your time. You haven't even finished your sandwich yet.'

I looked down at the tinfoil package beside me and realised he was right. I'd been so wrapped up in Gerd's story I'd forgotten all about it. As Holger headed down the steps I took a bite and chewed thoughtfully. Gerd seemed to be studying me, sizing me up.

'Do *you* believe, Craig?' he asked.

The suddenness of his question startled me.

'In god, you mean?'

He nodded.

'Um, not really,' I admitted, swallowing. 'Sometimes I wish I did though.'

'Well, just bear it in mind. That's all I'm saying. Personally I don't believe that faith, or a particular kind of faith, makes any

244

real difference in the end. But in the meantime it can be helpful. Most of us wind up in some cold, dark, lonely place sometime in our lives. Believe me. And if you can find god then ... well, it can help you get through those times. Keep you going. You know?'

I stirred in my chair. 'I'm sure you're right,' I said awkwardly.

Gerd laughed, then patted me on the arm.

'Sorry, Craig. I didn't mean to preach. Honestly. And you're still young. With any luck it'll be many, many years before you find yourself needing that sort of spiritual comfort. But when you do, just remember what I said, okay? For me.'

'Sure,' I said uneasily. 'I'll remember.'

Gerd smiled, then slapped the arms of his chair.

'And in the meantime, you've got a date with Katarina to look forward to, you lucky swine.'

My face brightened.

He laughed again, and this time I found myself joining in.

'And on that happy note, Craig,' he said, 'I'm afraid I'll have to leave you. It's high time I got back to my responsibilities as well. You've let me bore you for too long.'

He stood to go, and I immediately stood up with him.

'It wasn't boring, Gerd,' I said. 'I'm sorry you had to go through all that – but like Holger said, we're glad you took the time to tell us. Honestly.'

'Well thanks for listening, Craig. And while I'm at it, thanks for all the work you put in with the kids. We're grateful for it, even if they don't exactly show it. But everyone really appreciates what you and Holger do here.'

I felt my cheeks flush at the compliment.

'That's nice of you to say so. And I appreciate the way all of you make a foreigner like me feel a little more at home.'

Gerd grinned.

'No problem.'

He offered me his hand and shook it firmly.

'See you on the sand,' he said.

I finished what was left of my sandwich and washed it down with a mouthful of beer, then grabbed my book and went out onto the top step. I settled into the chair and propped my feet up on the railings, opening the battered copy of *Moby Dick* at the page I'd marked earlier. Pushing Gerd's story to the back of my mind for a moment, I began to read again from the point where I'd left off that morning. As usual Melville's spell cast itself quickly, and for the next twenty minutes I became immersed in the story of Ahab's obsession, barely aware of what was happening on the beach below me.

It was the children who roused me from the book. A movement caught my eye and I looked up to see a group of pupils standing at the bottom of the steps. The boldest of them, a twelve-year-old girl called Petra, spoke as soon as I lifted my head.

'Craig?' she said, smiling hopefully. 'Can we get another lesson now? You said we could. *Please!*'

The other children echoed her.

I scowled.

'What's all this "Craig" stuff?' I asked them. 'I thought I'd trained you better than that.'

'Oh!' Petra turned to her friends, giving them a look that seemed to be some sort of prearranged signal. I watched, bemused, as they organised themselves into a line, then raised their arms above their heads and bent from the waist, genuflecting before me.

'*Please, Oh Holy Master,*' they chorused, bobbing up and down. '*Please.*'

I burst out laughing.

'That's more like it,' I told them, recovering a little. 'And since you've shown the proper respect due to a Holy Master of Windsurfing Secrets, you shall be rewarded appropriately. Await my presence on the beach, Earnest Pupils.'

I stood up and raised a regal hand, dismissing them. Still bent over in mock worship, they shuffled backwards down the path, turning their heads to look at each other and giggling. Petra's face was flushed, delighted that this little show of hers had gone to plan.

Shaking my head with amusement, I leaned down and collected my empty bottle of beer, tucking it away on the floor just inside the doorway. The tower was a mess again already, I saw. Beer bottles littered the window sill and crumpled pieces of tinfoil were scattered everywhere.

I made my way down to the beach. Holger had seen me descending, and as I stepped onto the sand he fell in beside me. We crossed over to the kids, who were jumping about impatiently next to the surf rigs.

'Okay,' I said as we arrived. 'Stand back. You'll get your hands on them soon enough.'

They cleared a space. Holger and I picked up a rig each, board in one hand, sail in the other.

Petra was watching us closely, making a show of eyeing our muscles.

'Strong men,' she said approvingly.

Holger rolled his eyes, glancing at me as we waded into the water.

'Another couple of years and she'll be causing all sorts of trouble,' he said, speaking in English so the children wouldn't understand.

'Probably,' I replied. 'But at least we won't be on the receiving end, eh?'

Holger grunted.

'Maybe not. But I think I dated someone a while back who could have been her older sister.'

I laughed.

'Well then, serves you right, doesn't it?'

'Yeah.' He grinned. 'I suppose it does.'

We moved out beyond the first sandbank and laid the rigs down in the water. The kids crowded round eagerly and we returned to the beach for the other two.

'Right,' I told the children, once we'd placed all four of the boards in the water. 'You know what to do. I'm going back for my wetsuit jacket and I'll be out with you in a few minutes. Keep practising what you were doing earlier, and I'll show you some new stuff in a bit. All right?'

'All right, Craig,' one of the boys said. I glared at him and he added hurriedly, 'I mean, *Holy Master*.'

'That's more like it.'

I ruffled his hair and then watched approvingly as they took

247

hold of the rigs in the correct fashion and began moving them through the water.

'They're coming along well, your group,' Holger observed.

'Of course,' I said, affecting surprise. 'I mean, why wouldn't they? They've got the best teacher this side of Hamburg.'

Holger snorted.

'Yeah right,' he told me. 'In your dreams.'

I left him and hurried back to the tower to fetch my wetsuit jacket. By the time I'd returned to the beach more of the kids had finished their lunch and were beginning to reclaim the kayaks, towing them out beyond the first sandbank. Holger was out there as well, overseeing things. I was standing at the edge of the water, zipping up my jacket, when Gerd came up behind me and clapped an arm on my shoulder.

'Hey, Craig,' he said.

I turned round, smiling when I saw who it was.

'What's up?' I asked. 'Got a problem?'

'More of a question, actually. There's a couple of volleyball nets back at the camp and some of our people fancy a game. We were going to get somebody to drive one over, but only if you guys don't mind if we set it up here. So what do you reckon? Is that okay?'

'It should be fine,' I told him. 'Just as long as you do it over there.'

I waved my hand at a patch of sand just beyond the kayak stands.

'That way we won't interrupt your game if we have to shift equipment about.'

He smiled.

'That's great. Thanks, man.'

He turned to go, then stopped suddenly and swivelled back.

'By the way,' he said, lowering his voice and speaking in a confidential tone. 'I just heard from Katarina that you two are thinking of going out dancing tonight.'

I looked at him, suddenly wary.

'Sort of,' I said slowly. 'There's a live jazz band on at one of the clubs in Gromitz, they're supposed to be pretty good.'

'Oh really? Which place?'

'Er ... the Sound Lounge.'

248

'That's funny.' He scratched his head. 'I thought they always had sixties music there on Wednesdays.'

I shrugged at this, not trusting myself to reply.

'It's a bit of a shame though,' he went on. 'Some of us were planning a midnight party on the beach tonight. Bernward said he'd give us the keys to the tower, and we were hoping you'd like to come. So what do you say? Are you two up for it?'

'Well . . .' I said, my heart sinking at the prospect of my evening with Katarina being ruined. 'I mean, thanks for the offer and all that, Gerd, but are you really sure that's such a good idea? It gets cold here at night, remember, really cold. And you're not allowed to build fires on the beach or anything like that. I'm just not sure it would be much fun, to be honest with you. In fact, if you ask me you'd be a lot better off just staying at the camp and partying there.'

Gerd frowned.

'You really think so?'

'Oh yeah,' I said. 'Definitely. I mean if you stay at the camp at least you'll be able to build a fire, which means you can have a barbecue. And you don't have all the hassle of lugging your stuff half a mile to the beach and then lugging it all back again. Much better just to party in the camp. Way better, if you ask me.'

Gerd nodded thoughtfully, considering this. Then all of a sudden his face cracked and he burst out laughing.

'Honestly, Craig,' he said, recovering a little. 'You should have seen yourself! I mean, priceless!'

'I don't get it,' I asked. 'What's so funny?'

Gerd slapped his thigh, delighted.

'You're too honest to lie, Craig. You're not very good at it. You're coming here tonight with Katarina, aren't you?'

I glanced around in alarm.

'Keep your voice down, will you?' I urged him. 'We don't want the whole world to know.'

Gerd patted me on the shoulder. 'Don't worry,' he said. 'Your secret's safe with me. It was just a guess of mine, and I wanted to see how you'd react. So now I know, but I promise I'll keep it quiet.'

He looked at me appraisingly and shook his head.

'You're a strange fish, Craig. First of all you've walked around for the last two weeks as if you weren't interested, and then *snap*! You've hooked her up for a night in the tower.'

'It's not like that,' I protested. 'We just want a bit of time to get to know each other, away from all the gossip. Away from you and Holger, for a start.'

Gerd chuckled at this, not offended in the least.

'Good for you, man. That's all I can say. And I promise I won't tell anybody. Not even Holger.'

'Yeah,' I said grudgingly. 'We'd appreciate it, you know.'

'No problem. And don't be angry, Craig,' he added seriously. 'I know you're both adults, but she's still part of my group. It's my job to know where everybody is, just in case something unexpected happens, you know? Problems at home, that kind of thing.'

I nodded slowly.

'Okay,' I said, turning to go.

'You guys have a good time tonight,' Gerd said behind me. 'Craig?'

'Yeah?' I stopped, looking back over my shoulder.

'Use a condom,' he hissed.

Then he winked and walked off, hands stuffed casually in the pockets of his shorts and whistling loudly.

My pupils were out beyond the second sandbank, taking their turns on the rigs with an enthusiasm that seemed undiminished by the lunchbreak. They greeted me warmly as I arrived.

'Now,' I said, in response to their questions. 'Let's see how you're all doing first, and then if I think you're ready I promise I'll show you some new stuff.'

I spent the next few minutes watching them, occasionally shouting advice, as they showed off the skills that I'd taught them over the last eight days or so. When I was satisfied I called them all together and took one of the rigs myself, towing it a few metres away from their huddled group to the edge of the sandbank. The water here only came up to my lower thighs.

'Right,' I called, positioning the board so it was ninety degrees to the wind. 'This is called a Beach Start. You all watching?'

A chorus of yeses came from behind me.

With my back to the breeze and the small sail held away from my body at an oblique angle, I put my left foot on the board.

'First step. You see?'

This time there was no response, but when I looked behind me I saw they were all studying me with concentration.

'Now the second step.'

I kicked off from the sand, moving the board forwards, and brought my other foot up so I was standing entirely on the board, at the same time pulling on the boom to bring the sail in towards my body, catching the breeze. The rig sailed forward smoothly, but because the breeze was weak and the child's sail too small for me, I had to shift my stance a little, leaning forward, hoping that the kids wouldn't notice my slight wobble.

'Cool!'

'Nice one, Craig!'

'It means you can start out from shallow water,' I called over my shoulder. 'You can step straight on, rather than having to tow the rig further out and pull yourself onto the board, which might mean you get injured when there are bigger waves.'

I sailed past the group, tilting the boom towards the bow so that the rig turned into the wind. I grabbed the mast with one hand and stepped forward along the board, swinging my body around to the other side of the sail. The board turned through the wind and I grabbed the reverse side of the boom, pulling the sail towards me to complete the manoeuvre. I was now sailing back the way I'd come.

'And besides the safety aspect,' I called as I approached them, 'it also looks good, which is always important for a Holy Master.'

When I reached the group I jumped off, holding the boom above me with one hand so the sail didn't hit my head.

'Right,' I said, happy not to have made a fool of myself with the small sail. 'Who's first, then?'

There was a tumult of noise as they vied with each other for the privilege. I handed the boom to the lucky winner and watched as all four rigs were towed back to where I'd begun the demonstration. Because the children were smaller than me the water at this point came up over their waists, but it didn't stop them trying to get

251

their feet up onto the boards in the manner I'd shown them.

'Not there!' I said, laughing at their struggles. 'Do you want to hurt yourselves? Take them further back. Remember how deep the water was for me? About that level or less.'

They followed my instructions readily enough, and I watched for a while to make sure they were getting the technique right. I'd expected it to take an hour or so before anybody got the hang of it, but after a few minutes I was amazed to see Petra launching herself successfully on her third attempt, sailing her rig off the sandbank for several metres. I opened my mouth to cheer her on, but she hadn't quite got her balance and after a few unsteady moments she fell off backwards, the sail coming down heavily on top of her. She didn't surface immediately and I swam over, lifting the sail and hauling her up by the arm onto her feet. She bent over, coughing.

'You all right?' I asked.

She coughed again, almost retching this time, and I patted her on the back in sudden concern.

'Feel any better?'

She shook her head, still doubled up.

'Did you take a knock from the mast?'

She nodded, pointing to her temple.

'Your head?' I asked, worried. 'You got hit on the head?'

She didn't reply, so I reached out a hand and smoothed away her hair, looking for signs of a cut or bruising.

'It looks okay to me,' I said after a moment. 'All in one piece, as far as I can see.'

She still didn't answer, but before I could question her further a voice called out from behind us. I turned to see Katarina and her friend Anja wading out towards us.

'What's the matter?' Katarina shouted.

'Petra here took a knock on the head,' I called back. 'I don't think she's feeling too good.'

'Let's have a look.'

I moved aside and Katarina came forward, bending over the girl to examine her. Anja, a short, dark-eyed brunette, stood next to me, not looking too concerned. I smiled and said hello, and she nodded back in a friendly manner.

252

'I hope she's okay,' I said.

'Don't worry,' Anja replied casually. 'I'm sure she's fine. Isn't she, Katarina?'

'Looks like it,' Katarina agreed, finishing her examination. She addressed herself to the girl, and I was surprised at the sudden harshness I could hear in her voice.

'So what's happening, Petra?' Katarina asked sternly. 'Do you feel well enough to continue or not?'

Petra still had her head bowed and didn't reply.

'Because if you really feel ill,' Katarina went on. 'You'll have to go back to the beach and lie down in the shade for an hour or two. Understand?'

The girl finally raised her face, and I saw that her mouth was set in a sulky pout.

'Do you understand?' Katarina repeated.

'I'm better now,' the girl said petulantly, keeping her eyes on the water. 'I'll go and practise some more.'

And without waiting for a response she moved across to her rig, pushing it back towards her friends.

'Honestly,' Anja said, as the girl moved out of earshot, 'she's a real drama queen that one.'

'You're telling me,' Katarina agreed.

I looked at them both uncertainly.

'I think she really did take a knock on the head though,' I told them.

'It's nice of you to be concerned, Craig,' Katarina replied, 'but if Petra drops her toast on the floor in the morning she puts on an Oscar-winning performance. She just likes the attention. In fact, if she comes back next year I'm going to refuse to have her in my group.'

'What?' I asked, taken aback. 'Why? What's wrong with her?'

Katarina sighed.

'Oh, just about everything, really. She's always giving us problems, and she's quite manipulative towards the other kids.' She hesitated a moment, as if wondering how much she should tell me. 'In fact, do you know the girl Yvonne in my group?'

I tried to recall the name but failed.

'Sorry, don't think so.'

'Well I'm not surprised,' Katarina continued. 'Yvonne doesn't have the confidence to try windsurfing or the kayaks. She's a sweet kid, but very shy, and in the last ten days or so she's been pretty much shut out by the others in the group. And it's all Petra's fault.'

'Petra's fault?' I asked, puzzled. 'How come?'

'Because on our second day here she accused Yvonne of stealing one of her necklaces.'

'Oh.' I considered this for a moment. 'Well, I mean it happens sometimes, doesn't it? We've got five hundred kids living together in tents. It's hardly surprising if there are a few minor thefts.'

'Absolutely,' Katarina agreed. 'Except that Petra somehow seemed to know exactly where in Yvonne's possessions we would find the missing jewellery. And then, when we asked Yvonne about it, the poor girl wasn't just surprised, she was completely devastated. Which is why I'm sure she didn't do it. Because kids who get caught stealing will act guilty or resentful, but they don't break down and sob for half an hour as if their whole world's just collapsed.'

'So what are you saying?' I asked, frowning. 'That Petra planted the necklace and then claimed Yvonne had stolen it?'

'It certainly looks that way,' Katarina said, folding her arms.

I glanced across at Anja, who was nodding her head in agreement.

'I'm sure you know what you're talking about,' I said slowly. 'But I've got to say I find it hard to believe that a girl like Petra could be so wilful. I mean, she seems very bright. And popular.'

'She *is* very bright,' Katarina confirmed. 'That's one of the reasons it's so frustrating for us. And popular too. But popular girls aren't always nice girls, you know?'

'Yeah, sure.' I thought back to the little chorus-line show Petra had put on earlier, and the way she'd tried to flirt with Holger and me.

'I agree that Petra certainly likes to be the centre of attention,' I continued, 'but it's just hard for me to imagine her doing something, you know, so *bad*.'

'Take my word for it,' Katarina replied. 'But to be fair to her, it's not really her fault. It's her parents who are the problem, if you ask me. She's very spoiled. Her father has a lot of money and he gives her whatever she wants. It's turned her into a real daddy's girl. Got her own pony stabled near the park and everything.'

'Her own pony!'

Now I really was surprised. The camp had originally been set up to provide holidays for kids from poor or deprived backgrounds, and although Gerd's group didn't all fall into that category I certainly hadn't pegged any of them as horse-owners.

'Yeah,' Katarina continued. 'Her dad's loaded, and because he's away most of the time he's always giving her presents to make up for it. Whatever she asks for. Soothes his guilty conscience, I suppose. But it's not exactly good for her character.'

I rubbed my chin.

'But if he's so well off then how come Petra isn't in a private school?' I asked. 'I mean, Hamburg's not exactly short of schools for rich kids, is it?'

Katarina smiled thinly.

'Politics,' she said.

The confusion must have shown on my face, because Anja immediately chimed in.

'Ever hear of Johannes Jelkin?' she asked.

'Jelkin?' I frowned. 'Isn't he one of the top guys in the SPD? The Labour party?'

'That's right,' Anja confirmed. 'Petra's his daughter.'

My mouth fell open in astonishment. The SPD was the main left-wing party in West Germany, and I'd read somewhere that if they won the next election Jelkin was tipped to become Foreign Minister. In other words, in a year's time Petra's father might be standing on the White House lawn with Ronald Reagan.

'So you see,' Anja went on. 'Given that he's a bigwig in Germany's Labour movement, it wouldn't look good for him to send his daughter to a private school. The press would have a field day and the teaching unions would have a fit. So instead he sends her to a state school and tries to make up for it with lots of expensive presents, like the pony.'

'Right,' I said, trying to come to terms with this information. Then a thought struck me.

255

'But doesn't that complicate things for you guys a bit? Looking after her, I mean. Isn't she, um . . . a kidnap risk, or something?'

They both burst out laughing and I immediately felt foolish.

'You've been watching too many Hollywood films,' Katarina told me. 'I mean, it's not like she has bodyguards or anything. But I suppose we do watch her a bit more closely than the others. Because if there ever was some kind of a problem, well, maybe things could get . . . complicated.'

'Sure,' I said, nodding. 'I can see that.'

'But that doesn't mean we should let her get away with whatever nonsense she decides to get up to, does it?' Katarina said quickly. 'It wouldn't be good for her.'

'Absolutely,' I agreed. 'In fact I admire the way you don't pander to her. Not everyone would be so even-handed. It can't be easy.'

'It's not easy,' Anja said forcefully. 'Not with Petra.' She turned to Katarina. 'You really are doing a good job with her though, Kat. That girl needs a firm hand.'

Katarina smiled.

'Actually it's not very difficult,' she replied. 'To tell you the truth I don't like her very much. Besides, it's not like we're worried about anything happening here. With you and Holger on the beach we all know they're in good hands.'

'Thank you,' I said, grinning. 'But I think maybe she *is* in danger – of falling in love with Holger. She tried to flirt with him earlier.'

Katarina laughed.

'Actually I think she's got a bit of a crush on *you*,' she teased. She looked at her friend, eyebrows raised.

'What do you think, Anja? Am I going to have to tell Petra that he's already taken?'

Anja gave me such a long, appraising up-and-down look that I felt my face go warm.

'If you ask me, Katarina, I think you should brand him. Like beef. Right on the arse.'

Katarina laughed.

'I've told him it's fat enough,' she said. 'We've had that conversation already.'

'Don't start that again,' I protested. 'Can we leave my arse out of this? You're going to give me a complex.'

'An arse complex?' Anja said dryly. 'Didn't Freud write a paper on that?'

The two of them found this hilarious.

'You guys are as bad as Holger and Gerd,' I complained. 'Any more talk like that and I'll have to teach you a lesson.'

'Ooooh,' Anja mocked. 'He's getting all authoritarian, Katarina. I didn't know you liked the masterful type.'

'I'm serious,' I said, wagging a finger and trying not to smile.

'He's going to teach us a lesson, Anja,' Katarina said now. 'What kind of a lesson, Craig? Windsurfing or kayaking? Anja's always wanted a windsurfing lesson, haven't you, Anja?'

And as she spoke she reached down and scooped up some water, splashing me on the chest.

'Come on, Craig,' she taunted, splashing me again. 'Teach us a lesson then.'

'Yeah, Craig,' Anja said, skimming her hand across the surface so that a spray of water hit me in the face. 'Show us what you can do, tough guy.'

'If you don't stop that I will,' I told them. I was about to add something else, but another two splashes caught me full in the mouth, and before I knew where I was they'd moved forward and were drenching me in an all-out attack. I fought back, skimming my arms through the water to soak them, roaring and laughing as I did so. The conversation degenerated into a full-scale water fight that went on for several minutes – a mix of giggles, screams and choking mists of spray.

And I lost, comprehensively.

After they'd given me a thorough soaking, the girls made their way back to the beach, leaving me to recuperate. Once my nose had cleared and my eyes had stopped stinging I moved across to my pupils, checking to see how they were doing. They all appeared to be having fun and Petra seemed her usual self, unfazed either by her fall or by her run-in with Katarina. When I was sure everything was going well and that they all wanted to keep practising, I left them to it and waded back to shore. As I neared the beach I saw that Holger was lying on his back on the sand a few feet from the shoreline, propped up on his elbows, regarding the world from behind his sunglasses. He tilted his head in lazy acknowledgement as I arrived.

'Having a nice time, darling?' he drawled as I plunked myself down next to him. 'You looked like you were getting half-drowned out there. I couldn't help thinking it was a shame it was a water fight instead of mud. You could have quite a time, mud-wrestling with those two.'

'One is more than enough,' I replied, leaning forward and resting my forehead against my knees. 'Definitely more than enough.'

'You're just saying that because you got your arse kicked,' he told me.

I only grunted at this, and we sat in silence for the next minute or so. Eventually I lifted my head, squinting at the sunlight reflecting off the water.

'All the kayaks are out again,' Holger informed me. 'And two rubber tyre rings.'

I nodded. The water was almost as busy as it had been before lunch. In addition to those using the equipment there were plenty of other kids out there, playing with beach balls, doing handstands and generally messing about.

'Better keep an eye out to make sure that the rigs stay away from the swimmers,' Holger said.

'I always do,' I told him. 'Oh, and I meant to ask you. What's happening about that rowing boat you mentioned earlier? Wasn't there a bunch of people who wanted to take one out?'

'Ssshhh,' he hissed, putting a finger to his lips and jerking his head to indicate a group of teenagers about ten feet behind us. 'They seem to have forgotten about it, and frankly I can't be bothered, so don't remind them. Besides, Bernward still isn't back.'

'What? Still no sign of him?'

'Nah. I think we can forget about seeing Bernward any time soon, I've a feeling he's decided that he's going to take the day off. And you know what that means – at six o'clock we'll have to pack all this stuff away by ourselves.'

I looked over my shoulder for a moment, then shrugged.

'Yeah, well,' I said. 'It's not so bad, is it? I had to open up all by myself this morning, remember? It's no big deal.'

Holger gave me a long, hard stare.

'You've changed your tune,' he said. 'A few hours ago you were swearing your bloody head off about it. Honestly, a good grope of Katarina and a bit of French kissing and all of a sudden you're Mr Easy-Going.'

I looked back at the water, ignoring him. The dark, tanned shapes of the children stood out against the blue surface, and the shards of light dancing on it were almost hypnotic.

'Anyway,' I said at last, shifting my gaze away from the glare. 'I think we should watch out for Bernward coming back, just in case. I wouldn't put it past him to swing by for one of his spot inspections.'

'That's Bernward's style all right,' Holger agreed. 'You'd never guess he was only in the navy for two-and-a-half years. Still thinks he's Admiral fucking Donitz.'

I laughed.

'True enough. But nobody's forcing us to work for him, are they?'

Holger sniffed, unconvinced by this line of logic.

'And remember,' I went on. 'He did say that he'd be back this afternoon, to look for that wasps' nest in the dunes.'

'Well I wouldn't bet my money on it . . .' Holger broke off suddenly, sitting up.

'What?' I asked, turning to look at the worried expression on his face.

'I'm an idiot,' he said, grimacing.

'I know that, Holger. But what's the problem?'

'I'm a total idiot,' he repeated, slapping his forehead with the palm of his hand. 'I forgot about the fucking wasps.'

'The wasps?' I asked, puzzled. 'What about them?'

'I left a jam sandwich out on the sea chest,' he said slowly.

'Well so what? What's the big problem . . .'

I stopped suddenly, realisation dawning.

'Fuck, Holger. You didn't, did you? You mean you didn't wrap it up?'

'Well it was your fault!' Holger exclaimed, irritated. 'You were the one in such a big hurry to get the rigs back in the water!'

'But that's basic, Holger,' I protested. 'I mean, it's just common sense!'

'You were rushing me,' he said. 'I wasn't bloody thinking, was I?'

My heart sank as I saw he wasn't joking. I twisted my neck and looked up at the tower. The door was open as usual, but neither of us had bothered to unlatch the windows yet.

'Maybe it's not so bad,' I said hopefully. 'The windows are still closed, and there haven't been that many of them this summer. Not like last year. And how long's it been anyway? Twenty minutes?'

'Doesn't matter,' he muttered resignedly. 'Long enough.'

We sat there for a few more moments, neither of us willing to face up to this new problem.

'Right,' I said finally. 'We'd better go and see what the damage is, I suppose.'

I stood up and dusted the sand off me. Holger didn't move.

'I'm not going up there alone,' I warned him. 'You're helping me.'

'Yeah, yeah.' He reached up his hand and I took it, hauling him to his feet.

'You're getting heavier,' I told him as he brushed at his legs. 'You want to cut down on those jam sandwiches.'

Holger gave me an angry glare that reminded me of the Pit bull owner, then stalked off towards the path. I shaded my eyes and quickly scanned the water, checking for problems. After a few moments, satisfied, I followed.

The situation in the tower could have been worse, but it wasn't good either. Holger was standing at the doorway when I arrived, and he moved aside wordlessly to let me look. Taking care not to cross the threshold I craned my head past the door jamb and took in the scene, wincing slightly. Even in the gloom I could see that about thirty wasps had already managed to find their way inside, attracted by the jam. About half were crawling over the sandwich itself, and the rest were exploring the surface of the beer bottles or moving over the window sill.

I pulled my head back out and looked at Holger.

'Right,' I said, gritting my teeth. 'So how are you going to deal with it then, Holger?'

'*We*,' Holger said pointedly, prodding me on the chest, 'are going to deal with it.'

'And let me guess. There's no insecticide, right?'

Holger laughed humourlessly. 'Full marks. How did you know?'

'Because I haven't seen any. And besides, that would be too simple.'

'I've been meaning to bring some over,' Holger said, shaking his head. 'But I didn't bother today because we weren't supposed to be working.'

'I could cycle back to the camp and get some.'

'I don't know where Bernward keeps the industrial stuff,' he told me. 'And that over-the-counter shit's no good when there's this many. You might take out a few but it would just make the rest of them angry – it's like a fucking nest in here. And who knows where Bernward's got to anyway? It could take hours to track him down.'

I knew he was right, but the ridiculousness of the situation suddenly struck me and I felt a strong urge to laugh. The feeling vanished in the next instant, however, as something zipped past our heads and buzzed into the tower. We both flinched instinctively.

'Fuck,' Holger said. He ran a hand through his hair, staring at the new arrival as it joined the pulsing mass moving over the sandwich.

'I hate wasps,' he confessed. 'They've always freaked me out. I got badly stung by a swarm when I was a kid.'

We stared for a few moments longer.

'We have to do something, though,' Holger said finally. 'Otherwise there'll be a bloody army of them soon.'

'Okay.'

I waited.

'Well what then?' I asked, irritated.

He took a deep breath.

'Right,' he told me. 'How about this? We go inside and close the door, which will hopefully stop any more of the little fuckers coming in. Then we'll take out the ones on the sandwich first –

that shouldn't be too difficult. After that we'll open the windows and try to shoo the rest of them out.' He paused expectantly. 'So what do you reckon?'

'A brilliant plan,' I said dryly. 'But what happens if they just get pissed off? They tend to get upset when you start killing their friends.'

'You got a better idea?' Holger demanded.

'Nope.'

'Right then, so what are we arguing about? Better get some work gloves first though. Might come in handy.'

'Good idea.'

I ran down the steps, ducking into the work cage and rummaging around. After a moment I emerged with two pairs of heavy work gloves and Holger's wetsuit jacket.

'The neoprene should help,' I said, handing him the jacket. 'Extra protection.'

'All right,' Holger said, putting it on. 'You ready?'

'Never fear,' I told him. 'I'll be right behind you, protecting the rear.'

'I hope you get stung.'

'Probably.' I took a deep breath. 'So what do you reckon? Slow or fast?'

'Slow!' Holger exclaimed. 'Slow at first, anyway. No point in stirring them up until we have to.'

We inched our way through the door, moving softly. When Holger was well inside, I closed it gently behind us. I'd never felt claustrophobic in the tower before, but with the door shut the buzzing sounded louder and more intense, so that the space suddenly seemed very small. I was very conscious of my bare legs and face, and I began to wonder how many wasp stings it took to put a man in hospital.

'Hey, Holger,' I whispered in the gloom. 'Are you really sure about this?'

Holger was moving towards the sandwich and didn't bother to reply.

I edged towards the window sill and stopped next to it. There was a beer bottle in front of my belly. Three of the insects were crawling on it, while another two were crouched busily on the rim, their heads and feelers probing inside. The wasps were big, vividly striped, each one about the size of the first joint of my little finger. Very slowly I reached for the window latch.

Holger had almost arrived at the hairy mass of wasps crawling on the sandwich. Now he started, inch by inch, to lower himself into a crouch, and at the same time he stretched out a hand and took hold of one of the scrunched-up pieces of tinfoil on the sea chest. He smoothed it out, wincing at the noise it made as it uncrumpled. A few of the wasps sensed the movement and rose up, hovering.

Holger went completely still and I stopped too, trying not to breathe. We held our positions for what seemed an interminable time, but eventually, with a confused buzzing, the insects settled back on the sandwich. I breathed out slowly and began to move again, my hand closing around the handle of the window. But I must have disturbed something, because just as I started to turn it there was movement at the bottom of my vision and two wasps lifted in front of me, hovering and darting next to my face. I froze once more, trying not to flinch at the movements near my eyes and the intense, live buzzing that rose and fell in my ears. The wasps were so close that the air from their wing movements brushed my cheeks.

Holger had raised his piece of flattened tinfoil above the sandwich with one hand and was gesturing at me frantically with the other to open the window. I took a deep breath and was about to do so when one of the creatures came even closer and landed on my face.

Normally I'm not scared of wasps, merely wary, and at any other time I would have brushed it away, but in the close, hot atmosphere of the tower that day, and conscious of the small packets of danger in the throbbing, hairy bodies all around me, I felt absolutely paralysed. To me, this wasp seemed even bigger than its fellows, and I felt myself go rigid as it crawled across my face, its movements surprisingly ticklish and strangely deliberate. It reached my upper lip and turned in a half circle, apparently curious, until its feelers were brushing just inside my left nostril. Despite my fear an absurd comparison flashed through my mind – it felt like I was wearing a false moustache that had come suddenly and dangerously to life.

'Open the window,' Holger whispered urgently, his voice directed at the floor.

I grunted a reply, unable to move my lips. Keeping my mouth tightly shut, I began to snort air down my nose in short, sharp blasts to try to blow the wasp away. I felt it go still as my breath washed over its back.

'Is the window open yet?' Holger hissed angrily.

Squinting cross-eyed, I could just about see the dark edge of the wasp under my nose.

'N-nm,' I mumbled, moving my head slowly to one side and then the other in an exaggerated gesture. Holger was obviously fighting his own internal battle and hadn't looked round.

'I'm going to count to three,' he said now. 'And then you have to open the window. Okay?'

He lifted his head very gently and took another look at the pulsing mass on the sandwich.

'Okay?'

'Mm.'

Holger took this as an affirmative, and cautiously began to bring his arm forward.

'One.'

I saw him reach up carefully, grasping the near edge of the tinfoil. He was now holding it with both hands, stretching the silver paper as wide as it would go.

'Two.'

With the tinfoil poised about ten inches above the sandwich, he began – very, very slowly – to lower it. I twisted the handle on the window and felt it click as the latch gave. The wasp on my face had changed direction and was now crawling over my lips.

'THREE!'

In one movement he brought the sheet down over the mass on the bread, scooping the whole lot up and crushing it into a ball in his hands. I popped the window open and as I pushed it outwards he was already turning towards me. I was aware that the wasps on the bottles had sensed my movements and risen in an angry cloud around my head. Holger hurled the heavy silver mass of tinfoil past my nose. It thudded against the glass and fell down into the dunes below. At the same time, the wasp on my face zipped off and vanished into the breeze outside. We both ducked, crouching low to the floor, as the remaining insects buzzed furiously in the air above us.

'Fucking hell!' I cried in English, shielding my face with my arms. 'What are we supposed to do now?'

Holger scrabbled across to the far wall and began tugging at the towels on the hooks.

'Here!' he shouted, throwing one across. 'Use this!'

I caught it and stared at it, wondering if I should put it over my head.

Holger had pulled down a second towel and was whipping it at the wasps buzzing around him. At the same time he lunged across the floor and reached up to open the latch of the second window. I'd got the message now and quickly folded my towel in half, then began flapping it wildly in the air, trying to drive the remaining insects outside. In their angry confusion a few of the wasps left fairly quickly, but the final group of eight or so were more stubborn, and it took several minutes of panicked waving before we finally managed to force the last of them out. As they vanished into the breeze we pulled the windows shut with a slam. Holger was red-faced and panting and I could feel trickles of sweat running down my back and chest.

We stared at each other, shaking our heads in disbelief, and then we both began laughing breathlessly.

'Good grief,' I said, coughing. 'Any of them get you?'

Holger shook his head, wiping his face with his towel and then examining his legs.

'Don't think so. You?'

'No, thank god.'

Holger rubbed the back of his neck.

'Pretty lucky, if you ask me.'

'Tell me about it.'

We spent a few moments catching our breath. At last, with a wipe of his face and a relieved sigh, Holger draped the towel around his shoulder and took off his work gloves, then moved across to the sea chests. He spent several seconds studying the surface, making certain there were no remaining wasps that we might have overlooked, then reached into his mother's knapsack and rummaged at the bottom, pulling out two bottles of beer.

'Grounds for celebration, I'd say,' he told me, grinning. He reached across to hand me one and I took it gratefully. We popped them open.

'*Prost.*'

'*Prost.*'

The beer was still cold and went smoothly down my dry throat. I drank half the contents in a couple of gulps.

'Well,' Holger announced, sitting down on the sea chest. 'There's one thing we can say for sure. This beer we've *definitely* earned.'

I smiled back at him.

'For once, Holger, I have to say I'm in total agreement with you. Jesus though, I wouldn't want to do that again. Let's just stick to cheese and ham baguettes from now on, eh?'

'What's the matter, Craig?' Holger asked wryly. 'Not enjoying your day off?'

'I wouldn't say it's been particularly restful, would you?'

Holger shook his head.

'That's the problem with you student types,' he said, unzipping his wetsuit jacket and tugging it off. 'Your lives are one long holiday anyway, so you never appreciate it when you get some proper spare time.'

'Very funny,' I told him, bunching up my towel and tossing it at his head. He dodged it easily, then took another swig of beer.

'So what now?' I asked. 'Because you know those wasps will be coming back here all afternoon, looking for the stuff.'

Holger nodded thoughtfully.

'Good point. Well, I think the first thing we should do is finish off these,' he said, indicating his beer. 'And then I guess we should clean this place properly, so there's nothing to tempt them. And we should be careful to keep the door and windows closed for the rest of the day as well. I don't reckon we'll have to come in and out much now anyway.'

'Fair enough.'

'And no need to mention any of this to Bernward, if he happens to show his face again.'

'How stupid do you think I am?' I asked him.

'Do you really want me to answer that?'

'Hey,' I snapped, irritated. 'I wasn't the clown who left out a jam sandwich, was I?'

'Details, details,' Holger said. 'The point is, we've dealt with it now, and after the hassle we had this morning I can't imagine that anything else will go wrong. The world's thrown enough at us for one day, don't you think?'

'Ever heard of bad things happening in threes?' I asked darkly.

'An old wives' tale,' he said, smiling. 'But I'm glad to see you're back to your usual pessimistic self. I was beginning to worry about your happy mood. Thought you'd started using drugs or something.'

'Just this,' I said, raising my beer and taking another swallow. 'Speaking of which – how many have we had today anyway? We are supposed to be working, remember?'

Holger shrugged dismissively.

'I'm fine,' he told me. 'Not even tipsy. And you've only had about a litre and a half the whole day. Not feeling it, are you?'

'No,' I admitted. 'I'm just a bit worn out. It's been one of those days. But I think this'll be my last one, thanks.'

'Just as well,' Holger said. 'There aren't any more left.'

I twisted around and looked out the window. The shutters prevented any glare from the sun and the familiar scene below was bright with colour. Looking down, I saw that the volleyball net had arrived, and Gerd and some of the other *Betreuer* were in the process of setting it up, driving the poles into the sand and marking out lines with their feet.

'Everybody's enjoying themselves,' Holger continued behind me. 'That's the important thing, isn't it?'

I grunted at this, concentrating on counting the kayaks out between the sandbanks. When the number tallied correctly I spent a few moments scanning the water for the rubber rings, which were more difficult to spot. I located one in the middle of a group of children on the second sandbank, but the other proved more difficult. Eventually I caught sight of it out near the limit of our water, a dark shape next to the whiteness of one of the buoys. I thought I could make out two heads bobbing next to it and I leaned over and picked up the binoculars to make sure.

267

'Those two are pretty far out,' I said, staring through the eyepieces.

Behind me Holger sighed. After a moment he stood up and moved across to join me.

'One of the rings,' I told him, pointing.

He stared for a moment, then held out his hand for the binoculars. I passed them over and he watched for twenty seconds or so.

'Just mucking around with the anchor chain,' he announced at last. 'It's hardly a problem. They're all decent swimmers, and they can't hurt themselves on the buoy. But I suppose we should keep an eye on them, and if they're not back in fifteen minutes one of us should go out and check, yeah?'

'Sure,' I said, nodding and reaching for my beer. 'I'll let you know.'

He lowered the binoculars, glancing at the bottle I was lifting to my lips as he did so. Just as I was about drink from it he reached out a hand and stopped me.

'Don't!' he warned sharply, holding my wrist. 'Wrong one.'

I looked down and saw what he meant. Instead of the beer I'd just opened, I'd picked up one of the old bottles by mistake. Behind the dark transparency of the glass I could see that there were two wasps inside, floating on their backs in an inch of liquid. One of the creatures was obviously dead, but the other was still alive and struggling, its legs twitching spasmodically.

'Don't think you'd like the taste much,' Holger told me.

'No,' I said ruefully, putting it down and picking up the correct one. 'I guess you're right.'

I finished off my actual beer and began to gather the others while Holger busied himself with the litter on the sea chests. Apart from the ones we'd just finished, all the rest had dead wasps floating in the dregs. I carefully wedged the collection of glass under my arm and crossed to the door, opening it awkwardly and stepping outside. Half-closing my eyes against the sudden sunlight, I deposited the bottles on the step, then grabbed two by their necks and, straightening up, poured the contents over the bannister into the dunes below. I repeated the process until there was only one left. This was the one I'd almost drunk from by mistake, and as

268

I lifted it I paused, raising it to the sunlight and peering through the brown glass. The wasp inside was still struggling weakly, and I couldn't help but watch for a moment, fascinated despite myself at its tiny, irreducible instinct to live. Eventually, feeling a small stab of sympathy, I closed my thumb over the mouth of the bottle and swirled the liquid around inside, ending its struggle. I poured the contents into the dunes with the rest of the dregs, then gathered the empty bottles back up and took them inside, piling them all into a plastic bag.

Holger had finished with the sea chests and had picked up the broom, starting to sweep the floor. After a quick word to him I went back outside, closing the door behind me carefully to make sure no other wasps could find their way in. I trotted down the steps and made my way back to the beach.

Pausing on the sand at the bottom of the dune path, I took a few seconds to scan the water, then turned my attention to the state of the beach. Despite the mild chaos – the half-dug holes and abandoned spades and towels – I was satisfied to see that there was very little litter. Probably Edith or Gerd had detailed someone to gather up the remnants from lunch. Edith was sitting with her kitchen colleagues on the far side of the rowing boats, talking happily with a small group of *Betreuer*. She caught sight of me and raised a hand to wave, the heavy flesh of her underarm jiggling as she did so. I waved back, then turned and walked past the kayak stands, nodding a greeting to the sunburned families – strangers – I'd noticed there earlier. The parents, sprawled on inflatable mattresses, were redder than ever now, but I was relieved to see that the children were playing in the shade of the sun umbrellas, and that their skin gleamed from a newly acquired layer of cream.

I paused for a moment and addressed myself to one of the fathers, who was sipping contentedly from a can of beer.

'Better watch out for the sun,' I told him. 'It's more intense than you think, and it looks like you guys have had a fair dose already.'

The man shaded his eyes and looked up at me.

'Thanks for the warning,' he said, smiling. 'We'll move in a while, but we're fine for the moment.'

'Up to you,' I told him. 'But we've got some stuff in the tower if it really starts to hurt later.'

'That's nice of you. But I'm sure we'll be fine.'

I nodded goodbye and moved away, heading over to where Gerd and his helpers were still in the process of fixing up the volleyball net.

'Everything okay?' I asked as I came up to them.

Gerd turned from where he'd been fiddling with one of the knots on the poles.

'Just about,' he said, pushing his hair back from his forehead and puffing out his cheeks. 'Took us a while, but we're nearly ready to start.'

I nodded distractedly. My gaze had already moved past him, further up the beach, to where the Pit bull owner and his family were sitting, about twenty-five metres away. The man and woman were still sunbathing by the dune fence, I saw, and the dog was tied up next to them. But I could also see that the two boys were down by the waterline, digging a hole awkwardly in the sand with spades, and I couldn't remember if they'd brought these spades with them or not. It worried me for a moment, because if the tools were ours I wouldn't put it past the man to walk off with them at the end of the day, just to spite us.

I realised that Gerd had spoken again and was looking at me expectantly.

'Sorry, what?' I asked, turning my gaze back to him.

'Would you and Holger like to play volleyball?' Gerd repeated. 'Not at the same time, of course, but if you took turns I'm sure the kids would be pleased.'

'Us?' I asked, surprised. 'Well ... yeah, I suppose so. I mean, I'm a bit worn out today, but I suppose we could manage five or ten minutes each at some point.'

Gerd smiled at this, pleased.

'That's great. The kids will love it. So we'll give you a shout later?'

'Fine. No problem.'

With a final frowning glance up the beach, I said goodbye to Gerd and made my way down to the shoreline, walking back along the water's edge towards the tower. The lapping foam cooled my feet and I took my time, enjoying the sensation. There was a discarded kayak paddle floating in the shallows and I moved out to pick it up, depositing it on the wet sand in front of the tower before wading out to my pupils.

As I approached I could see that the number of kids practising with the rigs had shrunk. A few had obviously grown bored and moved away to play elsewhere, Petra among them. I gathered the remainder together to give some encouragement, at the same time casting a quick eye over the equipment to make sure that everything was in order. The boom of one of the rigs was lopsided, so I opened the clasp and slid it back up the mast, fixing it into place as tightly as I could. Once that was done I spent the next ten minutes watching to see how they were getting on, occasionally shouting pointers on ways to improve their technique. Finally, when it seemed there was no more I could do for them, I left them to it and made my way back to the beach. Holger had emerged from the tower now and was sitting on the plastic chair on the top step, feet propped up on the bannister and reading his newspaper. I waved to him, but he didn't appear to notice. I assumed he was engrossed in *BILD Zeitung*'s daily complement of topless girls.

I threaded my way through the sprawling groups to the dune path, starting up the slope. When I reached the crest I stopped.

'Hey, Holger!' I called up. 'Do me a favour and throw down my book for me, will you? It's on the window sill.'

Holger lowered his newspaper and looked at me from behind his sunglasses. I braced myself for a sarcastic comment, but after a moment he stood up and pushed the chair back in order to open the door. He stepped inside and a moment later my copy of *Moby Dick* came flying through the doorway and landed on the ground at my feet.

'Satisfied?' he called down.

I picked it up, shaking the sand out from between the pages.

'You're in the wrong job,' I told him. 'The way you handle books you should have been a librarian!'

'I'm only interested in books with dirty pictures,' he told me, dragging the chair back to the railings and sitting down again.

I laughed.

'Why does that not surprise me?'

'Because you know me,' he said simply, picking up his newspaper.

'Can't argue with that.'

I moved over to the bottom step and settled on it, facing the water. I opened the book and glanced at my watch. It was just after three o'clock.

I began to read happily, undisturbed by the occasional brief rustling above me as Holger lowered his newspaper every few minutes to check on the scene below.

It was just after half past three when our reading came to an end. Abruptly.

'WHAT THE HELL'S GOING ON HERE?'

I was so startled that I jerked up in fright, banging my head against the handrail and dropping my book. Holding my scalp in pain, I looked up to see Bernward standing at the crest of the path, still dressed in his jogging trousers and sweatshirt, three of our heavy work spades cradled in his arms.

'I leave you two to look after things and look at the mess I come back to!' he growled. 'Sixty kids in the water and what are you pair doing? Bloody reading!'

I stood up quickly, holding my head and leaning against the rail for support as I tried to blink away the spots swimming in my eyes. Bernward threw the spades on the ground in front of the steps, their blades clattering.

'There could be twenty people drowning out there!' Bernward raged. 'And what would you clowns be looking at? The bloody sports section!'

'Calm down, Bernward,' Holger replied irritably. 'I'm checking the water every two minutes!'

'Every two hours, more like!'

He moved forward and pointed an accusing finger at the tools he'd just thrown down.

'And why have the spades been left out where they can rust, eh?' he demanded, addressing me.

'I didn't think the kids were finished with them,' I said lamely.

'Bah! If you ask me, you didn't think at all. Get down there now and gather the rest together and store them properly, like you're supposed to.'

'But what if the kids want to use them again?'

Bernward gave me a withering look.

'Then they can come back up and bloody well ask, can't they?'

I knew there was no point in arguing, so I moved past him and headed for the beach. Behind me I could hear Bernward climbing the steps, muttering angrily as he went. I didn't turn to look, but I could imagine the expression on his face clearly enough and I didn't envy Holger.

As soon as I reached the sand I began searching for the rest of our work spades, ignoring the smaller ones – the toys – for the moment. The tools were scattered over a large area, and it took me several minutes to gather them all together. I found the final one about twenty metres down the beach, lying in the water with its blade and half the handle submerged. I knew that Bernward had been right about something at least – this one would rust if it wasn't oiled at the end of the day – and I felt a small twinge of guilt at not having collected them sooner. But at the same time I knew the others would be fine, and Bernward had just been throwing his weight about, as usual. I found myself wondering idly if he'd missed out on his lunchtime nap.

The spades were heavy and bundling them all together made them tricky to carry. I ended up cradling them awkwardly in my arms as I made my way back up the beach, feet sinking into the hot sand. As I neared the rowing boats I was concentrating on my footing so much I didn't notice I was passing Edith's group, and when she called out to me I looked up in surprise.

'I see Bernward's back then!' she said loudly, giving me a knowing wink. She nudged one of her colleagues in the ribs and was rewarded with a dutiful chuckle.

'Looks like it,' I mumbled, lowering my head to continue on my way. But she wasn't going to let me go that easily.

'Oh, Craig!' she called now.

I paused, turning round reluctantly.

'Yes?'

'Couldn't do us a favour, could you?'

'What's that then?'

'Remember that sun umbrella you mentioned earlier? If it's not too much trouble we'd be grateful if you'd fetch it down for us now. There's a good boy.'

'Sure,' I told her, then nodded at the spades. 'But I've got my hands full at the moment. Just give me a few minutes, all right?'

'That's fine,' Edith said gaily. 'Don't go digging yourself into a hole now, will you?'

By the time I'd reached the top of the dune path my arms were aching, and I laid the tools on the ground with relief, next to the ones Bernward had already brought. Judging by the sounds coming from inside the tower Holger was still getting a talking to, so I retreated back to the beach, scouring the sand for the remaining spades – the toy ones. Three of these were being used by kids to build sandcastles out on the first sandbank, but I gathered the rest and returned to the tower. By the time I got there Holger had emerged and was back sitting on the chair on the top step, glowering. Bernward was standing at the bottom of the stairs, counting the spades.

I moved past him and went to store the toys inside the cage. As I went down on one knee in the cramped entrance Bernward spoke.

'There's two missing.'

I was distracted by what I was doing and didn't reply immediately. Instead, I pushed the wetsuit barrels out of the way in order to create some room then wedged the toy spades between the wire mesh and the barrels, before carefully withdrawing from the cage. I could feel the muscles in my lower back protesting, and I put my hands on my hips and leaned back, stretching a little.

'There's two missing,' Bernward repeated. He was looking at me accusingly.

'What do you mean?'

'I mean we've got twelve work spades, Craig, and there's only ten here. So where are the other two?'

I looked down, counting for myself and frowning when I saw he was right.

'Yeah,' I said. 'I see.'

'So where are they?' he demanded.

'Well I checked the beach ...' I began, then trailed off as I suddenly remembered my earlier suspicion about the Pit bull owner's sons.

I bit my lip.

'Um, I think they're up the beach, Bernward – that guy we were telling you about earlier, the one we had the problem with. I think maybe his kids are using them.'

'Oh you think so?' Bernward said angrily.

'Well,' I looked at the ground, my heart sinking. 'I'm pretty sure.'

'I'm glad to hear it,' Bernward replied sarcastically. 'I'm glad to hear you know where our work tools are. It's a load off my mind in fact. And if I'm not mistaken, those two boys aren't guests of our camp, are they?'

'No.'

'That's what I thought. And what's our policy about non-guests using our equipment? Remind me again, Craig?'

I glanced up towards Holger. I knew he was listening in, but I could see I wasn't going to get any help from that quarter.

'Speak up!' Bernward barked.

I cast my mind back to the list of rules Bernward made us memorise at the start of every season. I had a tendency to forget the wording as soon as he'd finished testing us.

'Uh ... Non-guests aren't allowed to use any of the equipment,' I said now. 'For insurance purposes and owing to the risk of theft.'

'That's right, Craig,' Bernward said, as if encouraging a child. 'Non-guests aren't allowed to use the equipment. Any of it. So what happens next?'

I stared at my feet, concentrating as I tried to recite the formula by rote.

'Non-guests should be politely prevented from using the equip-ment,' I said. 'If they've appropriated the equipment without permission, it should be confiscated as soon as possible.'

'Very good,' Bernward told me patronisingly. 'Perhaps there's something inside your head after all.' Then he sniffed. 'But on the other hand, maybe not. Just go and get the damn spades, will you?'

The last thing I felt like was another confrontation with the Pit bull owner. I opened my mouth to explain the problem, but Bernward cut me off.

'No arguments,' he said. 'Just do it, will you?'

'Edith wants me to bring her a sun umbrella,' I replied lamely. Bernward stared at me, exasperated.

'Okay,' he told me, in the tone of a man holding onto his patience against all odds. 'Take Edith a sun umbrella and *then* go and get the spades. That clear enough for you?'

I nodded unhappily.

'And I'll go check on your pupils for you. Keep an eye on them.' He jerked his head in Holger's direction. 'I wouldn't trust him today as far as I could throw him. And I can't throw him very far.'

'Right you are, Bernward.'

'And store these away while you're at it,' he added, nodding at the spades.

'No problem.'

Bernward tucked his hands into the pockets of his jogging bottoms and strolled over to the dune path. As he disappeared towards the beach I bent down and gathered up some of the tools, carrying them over to the cage. Holger's face appeared abruptly at the railings above me.

'Hey, Craig,' he said quietly. 'Remember I told you Bernward thinks he's Admiral fucking Donitz?'

I paused, looking up at him.

'Yeah?'

'Well I got the wrong leader.' He straightened his finger and stuck it against his top lip, imitating the world's most infamous moustache.

'Fuck. Now you tell me.'

I put the rest of the spades in the cage, apart from the one that I'd found lying in the water. I left this out, propping it against the mesh of the cage as a reminder to oil it later. Finally I got down on my hands and knees and hauled out the sun umbrella, slinging it over my shoulder and carrying it down to Edith's group.

'Ah!' Edith announced as I arrived. 'Here's the butler back at last. Cucumber sandwiches, anyone?'

I ignored this, thrusting the pole into the ground and swivelling it deep into the sand.

276

'That all right for you?' I asked, opening the canopy.

'Fine,' Edith told me. 'And while you're at it give the Rolls-Royce a good wash, would you, Craig? Princess Di's invited us to a Polo match later.'

'Very funny,' I replied sourly. 'But the volleyball's just getting started, and I know how sporty you are, Edith. Can't wait to see you in action.'

'Maybe later,' she grinned. 'Now we've got some shade I'll just sit here and watch for a while.'

'Suit yourself.'

I took my leave and set off up the beach reluctantly, not looking forward to my next task. Bernward was down by the shoreline, hands in his pockets as he stared out over the water. When I neared the volleyball game I slowed my pace, squinting ahead to where the Pit bull owner was, and what I saw there made me swear under my breath. The two boys had abandoned their hole by the water and were back beside their parents now, digging awkwardly next to the dune fence. I came to a halt, hesitating, as I realised there was no way I could retrieve the spades and still avoid the man. I was already picturing myself getting into another argument with him, and my mouth felt dry at the prospect. He didn't strike me as the kind of person who'd back down a second time.

Standing there – dithering – my gaze flickered back to the volleyball players. For the first time I noticed that Katarina was part of the team on the far side of the net, and I was aware of a sudden coldness spreading in my stomach at the thought of her witnessing a probable confrontation in the next few minutes. I felt there was a chance I was about to be humiliated, perhaps painfully so, and I knew in my bones that would be something I wouldn't want her to see. Just then the point that was being played ended and she glanced up, catching sight of me. She waved happily and called something across the net to Gerd, who turned to look over his shoulder.

'Hey, Craig!' he called. 'You're right on time! We've just started. Fancy joining in?'

I shook my head dismissively, glancing back up the beach.

'Oh come on,' Gerd cajoled. He turned to appeal to the others. 'You want him to play, don't you guys?'

There was a chorus of agreement.

'Yeah, Craig!' one of the boys called. 'You be on our side!'

I shook my head again, smiling despite myself.

'What's the matter, Craig?' Katarina joined in. 'Scared of losing?'

'I'm afraid I've got stuff to do.'

'Just fifteen minutes,' Gerd said, walking towards me. 'That's all.'

'Go on!' Katarina called again. 'Play a game with us!'

I hesitated once more, taking another look up the beach, but at the same time I could feel myself weakening further. The family would probably be around until the end of the day, I reasoned now, and there would surely be an opportunity to retrieve the spades later without having an argument with the man. And what would be the point of a confrontation anyway? It was only a couple of spades, after all.

The kids were still appealing to me noisily, beckoning me to join in, and I came to a decision that was almost instinctive, a mental flipping of a coin.

'Oh all right,' I relented. 'Go on then.'

My announcement was greeted with a cheer of approval.

'Let's see if you still feel like that once you've seen me play,' I told them, relaxing a little and moving onto the makeshift court. 'I'm on this side.'

Katarina was smiling at me through the net, and when I met her gaze she winked. A sudden warmth rushed through me, displacing the coldness I'd felt a few moments before, and I found myself thinking happily of the night that we'd have together, just a few hours ahead. As I moved into position in the middle of the team I dismissed the matter of the spades, comforting myself with the fleeting reflection that Bernward was nothing more than a pedantic and grumpy old man.

Gerd had moved in next to me and was holding the ball up in one large hand.

'Ready?' he asked, raising an eyebrow.

'Absolutely.'

'Good.'

He raised his head and addressed the others loudly.

'LET'S PLAY!'

And with a neat flick of his wrist he tossed the ball up and hit it almost casually with his fist, sending it on a long, high arc over the net, and for a moment it seemed to me almost as if, perhaps, it might never come down.

It was Gerd who nailed the last point, leaping level with the net and unleashing a forehand smash that nearly flattened the skinny teenager who made the mistake of trying to return it.

'You all right?' Gerd asked the kid, as the ball landed with a splash by the waterline. 'Didn't hurt you, did I?'

The boy shook his head, clutching at the angry red blotch on his shoulder and trying hard not to show his pain.

'Good,' Gerd said. He swivelled around to address the rest of us.

'We win!' he announced happily. 'Let's mix up the teams for the next one.'

Someone went to retrieve the ball and Gerd moved in next to me, lowering his head and speaking quietly.

'Couldn't resist it,' he confided with a shame-faced grin. 'Didn't think he'd try to block the thing. Bet it stings like hell.'

I shrugged.

'He'll be fine,' I told him. 'It's probably character-building, or something.'

Gerd laughed and clapped me on the shoulder.

'You'll make a fine father someday, Craig. All your sons will grow up to be psychopaths.'

I grinned.

'In that case I'll make sure they marry your daughters,' I told him. 'Thanks for the game. I enjoyed it.'

'Thanks for playing, Craig. And tell Holger he's welcome to have a go if he wants.'

'I'll do that. I'm sure he'll be up for a game.'

Gerd turned his attention to sorting out the new teams and I raised my hand in acknowledgement to Katarina, who waved back as I turned to leave. I strolled down the beach, looking out over the water as I did so to check on my pupils. I could see that Bernward had taken out one of the racing kayaks and was floating next to them, giving instruction. But he must have been finding

279

it hot work, because he'd pushed his sweatshirt sleeves up to his elbows, a sartorial move almost unheard of for him. Bernward was a good teacher, and I knew that the kids might learn more quickly with him than they did with me, but at the same time I flattered myself that they probably wouldn't have as much fun.

I threaded past the groups of teenagers and made my way up to the tower. Holger was where I'd left him, sitting on the chair on the top step.

'How's it going?' I asked as I came up the stairs.

Holger sighed, then stretched his arms above his head and yawned.

'Boring,' he said, lifting his sunglasses and massaging the bridge of his nose. 'Boring, boring, boring. And hot.'

'I know what you mean,' I replied, smiling. 'But look on the bright side. It's better than sitting in an office all day, isn't it?'

'Yeah, I suppose so.'

'Well, tell you what – why don't you go and take a dip and cool off, and I'll take over here?'

Holger considered this for a moment.

'You know,' he said finally. 'I think that might be the best suggestion I've heard all day.'

'Oh, and you've been invited to join the volleyball afterwards, if you fancy a bit of sport.'

Holger looked down at his belly, slapping the ample brown mass with his hands and massaging it.

'I suppose I could do with some exercise,' he said ruefully. 'Maybe start working off the old beer gut a bit.'

'That might take more than a volleyball game,' I warned him.

'Ha!' He looked up at me and jabbed a finger under my chin. 'Just you wait, pal. A few more years and you'll have one too, I'm telling you. You're just young, that's all.'

'Want to bet?'

'Oh yes.'

'Well,' I said, smirking. 'We'll see. But right now I'm happy to take over if you want me to.'

'Sounds good.'

He headed for the beach and I settled back against the seat, trying to make myself comfortable. But I was suddenly aware of the cramped and heavy tiredness in my muscles, so I straightened up again, stretching out my arms and legs and arching my back, luxuriating in the sensation as the tension in my body popped and eased. After thirty seconds or so I began to feel much better, and once I'd loosened up I leaned back once more, slouching low in the chair and sighing with satisfaction.

And so I sat there for the next few minutes, eyes half-closed against the glare and breathing deeply, while the warmth of the sun gradually wrapped itself around me like a soothing blanket, perfectly offset by the coolness of the breeze. My skin felt hot and dry and smooth, faintly scented with suntan lotion, and the blood pumped slow and heavy through my limbs. The rustle of the dune grass whispered in my ears and the cries of playing children rose faintly from the water. The peace of it all washed over me, relaxing me, and at that moment I knew, on some deep level, that I was young and strong and fit, and I was wholly, mindlessly happy in my physical existence.

I propped my feet up on the railings and yawned. For that one instant, I think, I was totally content.

And then I fell asleep.

* * *

Loch Lomond is the biggest freshwater lake, by surface area, in the British Isles. Its waters are peaty and dark. Very dark. Strange and sudden currents eddy and swirl in its depths. The vast stretch of the bottom, six hundred feet down in places, is littered with natural debris: thick layers of slimy silt and algae; jagged rocks; the clutching branches of dead and submerged trees, and the occasional rotting carcass of old, sunken fishing boats.

Only a foot below the surface of the loch, in the brown light, if you hold your arm out straight and turn your open palm towards you, you won't be able to see your own fingers, and the palm itself will only be distinguishable as a pale, indistinct blob. And if, then, you lower your face a little and look down, you'll see that just below your thighs your legs seem to vanish completely, tapering away into a deep and immersive blackness; a dizzying and terrifying blackness, in fact, as you suddenly register the sheer scope and volume of the emptiness you are floating above. That realisation can hit you with a visceral force, a thumping intimation of the depths beneath you and the debris, the currents, waiting to drag you down. And you can find yourself then instinctively imagining all manner of monsters, and cold and implacable fates, as your heart starts to thud with a strong, primal fear, a sort of physical and spiritual vertigo that your mind automatically tries to choke off.

For if we allowed ourselves to think about the depths around us, that great vastness waiting to swallow us up – if we allowed ourselves to really *feel* it – the knowledge would paralyse us, utterly.

We spend our whole lives not thinking about the blackness that surrounds us, the debris waiting to drag us down. Or at least trying not to.

I found this out, at least on some level, quite suddenly at the age of five, when, and without any warning, my grandfather picked me up by the waistband of my shorts and the scruff of my neck and threw me into that loch.

Salochy Bay is on the eastern bank of Loch Lomond, about a forty-minute drive from Glasgow and a slightly shorter distance from the town of Helensburgh, where we lived at the time. A steep, winding, up-and-down single-track road from the small marina at Balmaha will take you there. These days the bay is signposted and there's a big car park under the trees with room for about forty vehicles, but back then there was a just a rutted patch of ground where you pulled in off the road.

The cove itself, a short walk beyond the parking area, is a small half-moon crescent, only about fifty feet long and ten feet wide, and consisting of large, hard stones, many the size of dinner plates. The smallness of the beach and its rocky, uncomfortable surface often act as a deterrent to visitors, and if you pulled up there on a summer day in the 1970s you usually found – during the week at any rate – that you had the place all to yourselves.

We arrived there one July afternoon for the occasion of a family picnic, although my father was absent that day, as indeed he was absent for much of my childhood. He was a soldier in the British Army and was stationed away at the time – probably in Northern

Ireland, for I know he served two tours of duty in the Province in the early 1970s, just as the Troubles there were intensifying.

My mother, however, certainly was at the lochside that day. A harried and neurotic presence even in the best of circumstances, in that period she was struggling to cope with the demands of my infant sister, Jeannie, then only three months old but already proving herself incapable of sleeping for more than forty minutes at a stretch.

And my grandparents – my father's parents – were there too. In fact the picnic had been their idea, and I suspect now that they'd organised it in the vain hope that the fresh air and sunshine of the Scottish countryside might somehow buck up my mother, an outcome which was felt to be a matter of some urgency. For although I didn't know it we had a secret in my family, an unspoken shame. My mother had been hospitalised with chronic 'nervous exhaustion' six months after my own birth, and now, half a decade on, my grandparents had begun to fear that she was showing signs of succumbing to a mental breakdown once again.

Fresh air and sunshine: the traditional Scottish remedy for depression – in a country where it often rains for most of the summer. Still, it was hot the day of the picnic, and my grandfather had just bought a new car, which probably provided an excuse for the excursion. But I imagine we must have been quite a sight as we rolled up to the bay in that new Rover 1100, its maroon paintwork sloppy with heat and all the windows rolled down to let the smoke from my grandfather's Capstan cigarettes and the howls of my baby sister stream out behind us. The torture of the journey had been such that my grandmother had her door open even before my grandfather pulled on the handbrake, and as he switched off the ignition the rest of us all tumbled out onto the grass in relief.

I left the adults to open the boot while I made my way down to the water's edge, where I quickly occupied myself by picking up some of the smaller rocks, one at a time, and throwing them in, watching in fascination as the heavy splashes rippled outwards. Behind me my grandparents were fishing out a mess of duvets and blankets and pillows, while my mother hovered anxiously some distance away, cradling my sister in her arms and trying to soothe her, with movements so tense and jerky they only seemed to disturb the baby more. I was dressed in shorts and a crumpled yellow T-shirt and sandals without any socks, and even on the beach, under the shade of the overhanging trees, it was very hot and still.

I stayed by the shoreline for the next ten minutes, while the adults arranged a comfortable nest on the rocky beach. Eventually the women settled down and my grandmother began cooing over my baby sister, who was finally and mercifully quietening.

My grandfather joined me by the water. Already in the spring of that year he'd taught me how to skim stones from the beach at Helensburgh, and for a while we hunted between the larger rocks for smaller, flat pebbles that would fit snugly between our thumbs and forefingers. Once we'd filled our pockets with these we took turns skipping them over the water. Unfortunately my talent for this fell short of my ambition, and after a while I began to grow frustrated and eventually bored.

'Tell you what, Craig,' my grandfather said, straightening up. 'How about we take a walk and leave the women to fuss over the baby? We'll come back when it's time to open the picnic hamper.'

I ran ahead while he spoke briefly to my grandmother and then followed behind me, taking care to watch his footing over the rocks.

There was no space or border between the strand and the woods. A dense mixture of low, twisted trees and high gorse bushes started the moment the beach ended. A very narrow track, probably a sheep path, wound through the thick undergrowth, about fifteen metres inland but following the line of the shore. I forged ahead, the burrs of gorse occasionally catching at my T-shirt or scratching my arms, and I had to raise my hands at times to protect my face. My grandfather followed, less troubled by the bushes, for they only came up to his waist.

After a few minutes I suddenly emerged, without warning, from the gorse-enclosed path onto a large, rugged outcrop of rock that jutted into the loch, a natural promontory of sorts. The top, on which I was standing, was some ten feet or so above the surface of the water, but in front of me I saw that there were two big dips – like giant steps, almost – in the stone leading downwards, and then there was a smooth, substantial disc of rock that actually extended out under the water itself, a hand's breadth beneath the surface. With a cry of delight I lowered myself quickly and eagerly down to it, scuffing my skin on the stone, as my grandfather followed behind me.

The air above the loch was very still, the light almost oppressive in its brightness, and as I stepped out into it the quiet, chilly water closed around my ankles in blessed relief from the heat.

There are moments – instants – in our lives which are made up of too many thoughts and emotions for us to process them fully at the time, but in the days and months that follow they shape our personalities and the course of our lives for ever.

I think my grandfather probably said something to me first, standing behind me as I splashed about in the water. Perhaps I answered him, perhaps not. But I can recall clearly enough the sudden surge as he lifted me, and then the flying forward arc of my falling, and the terrible shock of cold as I plunged beneath the surface. I remember the dark brown of the water when I opened my eyes and the gritty taste of it in my mouth, and the whiteness of the surface above my head as the bubbles rose up around me like a silver curtain.

The freezing temperature of the water was mirrored, somehow, by a freezing of my mind: because after that first instant of shock I felt, for a few moments at least, a calm, almost detached interest in the cold, wet quietness around me. And I remember too wondering – with a strangely neutral and impartial feeling – why it was that my grandfather had thrown me in.

That calmness didn't last long, however. I stirred into movement quickly enough, kicked my feet and looked down, and it was then that I saw (or, more accurately, *felt*) the great, fearful blackness of the depths below. And I understood suddenly that I couldn't breathe, and that I was sinking down into that blackness, the light receding above, and now I panicked and opened my mouth to squeal for help, and instead inhaled a mouthful of water, and then another, and I began thrashing about as my terror overtook me. I think that I would have drowned then if my grandfather hadn't plunged his arm into the water and reached down to intervene.

I felt his hand grab me by the scruff of the neck once more, but this time he yanked me upwards into sunlight. I coughed and choked and spluttered for breath as he squatted down next to my face at the edge of the rock shelf.

'Come on, Craig,' my grandfather said sternly, looking into my distressed face. 'Remember your lessons. Remember what I taught you in the pool. *Swim.*'

And with a hard but encouraging look he let me go again and stepped back.

This time – at least in memory – I sank like a stone. I hadn't been able to catch my breath properly during my few spluttering seconds on the surface, and my body and lungs were heaving with the need for air. My legs kicked and my torso and arms convulsed, my hands reaching up frantically as if trying to grab hold of the sky itself – and I realised with horror that I was descending once more. The light was fading above me and I could make out bits of twigs and leaves now, suspended in a mist of algae around me, and feel the rough rock wall as my hands scrabbled uselessly against it.

I knew then that I was going to drown, and with that realisation the fear left me as suddenly as it had come.

Perhaps it was a lack of oxygen to the brain, or perhaps it was the physical relief in my body as it gave up its frantic struggling, but for some reason my panic seemed to disappear entirely and in its place I felt a calm, a quietness. And simultaneously with this, I remembered how to swim.

I broke the surface, kicking and gasping, my hands and elbows moving in a bastardised combination of doggy paddle and breast-stroke. My eyes were wide with the urge to breathe but as soon as I sucked in a lungful of air I found myself coughing and choking on it. Somehow, though, my body managed to keep itself afloat, and as my eyes blinked and my airway cleared, I found myself, after several seconds, looking around me with a semblance of shaky control.

The loch stretched out silver and huge, the green bank on the far side almost a mile away. My ears unblocked with a pop, and behind me I could hear my grandfather clapping. I turned shakily in the water, snot running in streams from my nose.

'Good on you, son,' he said, smiling. 'Now swim around to the side here. Show me what you can do.'

Obediently, I paddled over to where he directed, and then, at his insistence, swam back again. He made me tread water for a minute, then got me to swim around in circles.

Eventually he seemed satisfied.

'See, Craig? I told you you could do it. You just needed to try. Now, come on out.'

I struggled forward to the edge of the stone shelf. He leaned down, grasped my upper arms and yanked me out, scraping my knees on the lip of the rock face as he did so. He knelt down to look me in the face. I was trembling uncontrollably.

'Good man,' he said. 'Good man. See what you can do when you make the effort, eh?'

I nodded, shivering.

'You're getting older now, son. Growing up a bit. You've got to stand on your own two feet and look after yourself. And you've proved you can do that. You should be proud of yourself. Are you?'

I nodded miserably, fighting back tears.

'So listen,' he said, his voice turning serious. 'I know your dad's away a lot, and your mum's struggling to look after your sister. So you've got to help her, yeah? You've got to help your mum while your father's away, understand? You're growing up a bit and it's time you minded your responsibilities in the house. It's time to mind and start looking out for her. What do you say to that, eh?'

'Yes,' I snivelled.

'What'll you do now?'

'I'll look after her, grampy.'

'Good boy, son. Good boy.'

He took me in his arms then and hugged me so tightly it was as though he wanted to break me.

But of course I couldn't live up to that promise. And there was nothing I could do when, six months later, my mother asked me to keep an eye on baby Jeannie for ten minutes while she went to the newsagents for a pack of cigarettes, but instead boarded the 10.25 train to Glasgow Central Station, and was never seen nor heard from again.

*

Nothing was said as we returned through the woods to the rocky beach. My grandfather acted as if nothing had happened and I took my cues from him, although I must have been subdued when we finally got back, and of course my clothes were soaking wet. Perhaps my grandmother was too busy changing Jeannie to notice, and my mother, even without the baby in her arms, merely continued rocking slightly where she sat, her dark-smudged eyes gazing out over the water at something none of the rest of us could see.

So I said nothing that day, nor did I for almost sixteen years.

It wasn't until my twenty-first birthday that I mentioned the incident to anyone, and when I finally did bring up the subject, with my own father, the reaction I got was surprising.

It was a conversation that took place sometime around 3 a.m. on that night of my birthday. I'd come home after celebrating with friends in the pub to find my father still sitting in the living room, waiting up for me, with an open bottle of whisky and two large tumblers on the table beside him. I sat on the other side of the fire and accepted the glass he offered me, and we drank and talked for several hours, about this and about that, consuming the warm, peaty liquid slowly but steadily, and at some point, to my own surprise, I found myself narrating to him what had happened on the banks of Loch Lomond all those years before.

My father listened to this story in silence, but when I finished he nodded once.

'Aye,' he said, sniffing and glancing down, swirling the whisky in his glass.

'Aye,' he repeated, with a sigh. 'Well that doesn't surprise me much. Believe it or not he did the same thing to me when I was a lad. In Kenya, it was. Although I was a year or two older then than you were. But it was the same for me as it was for you. It certainly gets your heart pumping, doesn't it?'

I said nothing, and he paused then for a long time, smoking his cigarette and savouring his drink.

'I think he did it out of love though,' he said finally. 'Your grandfather didn't want to hurt either of us, I don't think, so don't judge him too harshly. He just wanted us to be strong, you know? To be ready for all the hard fucking shite that life can throw at you. And you know well enough that shite can kill you if you let it.'

Again he paused, then slowly shook his head.

'What happened to him during the war ... it changed him, I think. I've seen it happen, to squaddies and the like. Christ, the way your mother changed, for that matter. Because things in this life can change you, boy. Slowly or suddenly. Maybe not on the surface, but deep down. Deep down, where other people can't see it.'

He lifted his glass and drained the liquid.

'Mind you,' he said, smacking his lips and sitting up straighter in the chair, his forefinger uncurling from the whisky tumbler to point at me. His eyes widened and his mouth stretched into a grin.

'You should count yourself lucky you only landed in Loch Lomond, Craig. That river he chucked me into in Kenya ... I swear to god, son, it had fucking *crocodiles* in it!'

* * *

I probably only dozed for fifteen or twenty minutes. When I came back to myself with a sudden start it seemed as though nothing had changed. I shook my head groggily and straightened uneasily in the chair. There was a stale, unpleasant taste in my mouth and a faint but annoying throbbing at the base of my skull. I lifted a hand and kneaded the muscles at the back of my neck, wondering whether the headache was caused by the sun or the beer. Glancing down, I happened to notice that Bernward or Holger had left a small bottle of mineral water next to the chair leg, and I reached for it gratefully, unscrewing the cap and draining the warm, fizzy contents in three gulps.

Irritated at myself for having nodded off, I dropped the bottle and stood up, rubbing my face and leaning out over the railings to study the beach. Everything looked the same. The groups of teenagers were still on their blankets below me, Edith was still sitting with her friends under the sun umbrella, and to my left the volleyball was continuing, with Holger joining in as an enthusiastic member of Katarina's team.

Satisfied for the moment with what was happening on the sand, I was relieved to find that the number of kayaks and surfrigs tallied correctly, and I allowed myself to relax a little, knowing that things were still under control.

Happy that everything appeared to be in order, I turned my back on the scene and pushed the chair aside in order to open the door of the tower. Inside I sifted through Edith's rucksack until I found a brightly-coloured can of lemonade. I cracked the ring pull open, peeling the metal away and swallowing the liquid greedily. When it was three-quarters empty I paused, then opened my mouth to emit a long, loud belch. After that I felt better, and I leaned against the door frame, taking occasional sips from the can and looking down absently at the sand, my head empty of thought.

Eventually I roused myself and checked my watch. It was after four o'clock now and the activity in the water was beginning to slacken off. With the sun several hours past its zenith and the offshore breeze stiffening a little, the air and water temperature had started to cool, and after all the running around the younger children had done, many of them would be beginning to tire. Most seemed to have retreated to the warmth of the sand and were now sitting, draped in towels and huddled together in small groups, chattering amongst themselves as they squirmed their feet into the soft surface of the beach or toyed idly with plastic spades.

Consequently, about half our kayaks and rubber rings – as well as two of the surf rigs – lay abandoned at the waterline, but I was pleased to note that they'd been left in a fairly orderly fashion, with the boards of the rigs upturned and the paddles for the kayaks lying across the top of each vessel. Seven kayaks and two surf rigs were still in use, however, out between the second and third sandbanks. I could see that Holger was now out there with the children, standing waist-deep in the water and close enough to give instructions if he needed to, although at that moment he appeared to be preoccupied with chatting to a young woman next to him. At that distance I couldn't be sure, but from the colour of her bikini and the shape of her figure I thought it was probably Katarina's friend Anja, and I silently wished him luck.

Katarina was with a group of *Betreuer* settled near the rowing boats, and a few metres beyond them Edith and her four colleagues were still sitting under the sun umbrella I'd fetched for them earlier. Of the twenty or so teenagers on the beach, two of the boys were playing frisbee in the shallows beyond the first sandbank, while the rest remained prone on the sand, listening to the radios in their midst and smoking cigarettes. As far as I could tell most of them hadn't moved from their positions the whole day.

Raising my gaze from the beach I took a few seconds to study the water again, fixing in my mind the number and position of the four swimmers I could see, then I leaned sharply over the railing and looked to my left. Beside our kayak stands, the two families of sunburned strangers lay sprawled, soaking up the UV rays and looking redder than ever. Even as I watched, one of the fathers – the one with the beer gut and too-tight swimming trunks – got to his feet and started packing away the group's beer bottles and rubbish. I assumed they were day-trippers from Hamburg or Kiel and would soon be heading back to their cars, eager to avoid the worst of the traffic on the journey home.

My thoughts now turned to the evening that lay ahead, only a few hours away. I couldn't help relishing the prospect of being alone with Katarina, and I smiled a little. There were a few preparations I should make, I reminded myself, like bringing over my sleeping bag to keep us warm in the tower, and maybe picking up a bottle of wine and some good-sized candles as well. And of course Gerd had been right when he'd joked with me that morning: condoms were a good idea.

I was just considering whether I would be able to borrow a second bike for Katarina to use – perhaps from Holger – when it suddenly occurred to me that I hadn't noticed Bernward anywhere.

I paused, frowning. I couldn't see how I might have overlooked him. Of course, I knew it was always possible that he might have returned to the camp, or headed off on a solitary walk along the beach, but whenever he did either of those things he invariably made the effort to warn both of us beforehand. It was a habit of his, part of his routine, and I couldn't imagine him skipping it on this occasion, any more than I could imagine him sending us a singing telegram as thanks for all our hard work.

I stepped closer to the window and looked down, checking the sand below the tower, but I couldn't see him anywhere. Holger was still in the water, talking to the girl in the bikini and keeping an eye on the kayaks and surfers. The vessels near him all seemed to be occupied by kids, but just to satisfy myself I reached for our binoculars and raised them to my eyes, then I turned the glasses on each of the four swimmers I'd noted earlier. Bernward didn't go bathing often, but it wasn't unheard of. Two swimmers were out near the buoys, while the other two were closer in, but none of them was Bernward.

Puzzled, I swept the binoculars in both directions, up and down the beach. There was no sign of him, although I couldn't help noticing, with a small flash of irritation, that the Pit bull owner, together with his wife and dog, was still lying on the sand next to the dune fence.

I lowered the binoculars again, chewing my lower lip. I was sure there must be some simple explanation for his absence, but despite myself I felt a vague, stirring unease. A chill of sorts rose up my spine and into the back of my neck, and I understood, with dismay, that the emotion I'd felt that morning, the dread that had overwhelmed me as I'd woken in the caravan, had never fully left me. For all my assumptions, despite everything that had happened since, that feeling had remained dormant within me.

Something wasn't right.

I put the binoculars on the window sill and stood thinking.

There was no reason to be worried, I told myself again, no reason at all. But at the same time there was also no harm in double-checking. Edith would know where Bernward had gone, or if not, Holger surely would. At worst I'd have to wade out into the water and interrupt Holger's chat-up routine.

This last thought almost made me smile, and I headed out the doorway and trotted down the steps, making for the beach.

I was halfway down the dune path when it suddenly occurred to me where Bernward was and I came to an abrupt standstill, exasperated at my own forgetfulness.

He's in the dunes, I realised now. *He promised earlier he'd go looking for that wasp nest in the dunes.*

My relief was instant, yet at the same time I was annoyed with myself for having grown anxious over nothing. For a moment I hesitated, unsure whether to continue on to the beach or retrace my steps.

And I was standing there, dithering, when a sudden booming shout from the bottom of the path caused me to stiffen and shade my eyes, searching for its source. A familiar, shaggy figure was on the beach below me. It raised a hairy arm in greeting and I waved back, breaking into a smile of genuine delight.

'Hey, Fred!' I called out happily. 'Come on up!'

Watching my friend as he approached, I was struck, as always, by his distinctive appearance. Perhaps it was his dark woolly beard and the wild clumps of hair on his head, chest and arms, or perhaps it was the deeply ingrained body tan he'd acquired from a decade of strolling on warm beaches, but whatever it was, he reminded me of nothing less than a small, powerful bear – an image reinforced by the barrel-like belly which protruded through the open front of his Hawaiian shirt. There was also a touch of the vagrant about him, I felt, in his heavy, shambling untidiness. For despite an expensive gold watch on his wrist and a gold chain around his neck, any impression of prosperity was immediately offset by his shaggy mane and the ragged plastic bag that invariably dangled from one large paw, and which usually contained his current reading material. I imagined that in a different environment a stranger might have mistaken Fred for a docker fallen on hard times, or a schizophrenic on skid row, but he certainly didn't look like what he was: a former librarian with an independent income, and a voracious reader of the world's great and ancient books.

'Good to see you!' I said as he arrived. 'Holger said you'd be dropping by again today.'

Fred grinned, reaching out a hand and shaking mine vigorously.

'How are you, Craig?' he asked in his American-accented English. 'Enjoying yourself?'

'Can't complain,' I told him, carefully extricating my hand from his grip. 'Or I could, but it wouldn't do much good.'

Fred barked out a rough smoker's laugh.

'Guess you didn't get the day off after all, huh? When I spoke to Holger this morning he seemed to think there wasn't going to be any work for you guys today.'

'Yeah,' I said, 'but that's the way things go sometimes, I suppose.'

We crested the top of the path and I gestured at the chairs.

'Sit down. Make yourself comfortable.'

'Thanks, Craig,' he replied. 'I've been sitting on my arse for most of my life, but another half hour won't hurt, I reckon.'

He dropped the plastic bag at his feet and squeezed his powerful bulk into the chair, its legs bowing dangerously under the strain. I sat down next to him.

'So what have you been up to?' he asked.

'Oh you know, the usual stuff. Just trying to keep the kids happy.'

Fred nodded and shifted his weight a little, reaching into the breast pocket of his shirt in order to fish out a pack of cigarettes and a gold Zippo lighter. He flicked the top of the pack back with one thick thumb and slid a cigarette between his lips, springing the Zippo open and puffing the tobacco into life. In the middle of Fred's broad and hairy face the cigarette looked faintly ridiculous, like a smouldering toothpick. It always seemed a miracle to me that he never set his beard on fire.

'Keepin' the kids happy, eh?' he repeated. 'Well, there's worse ways to make a living, if you ask me. Try twenty-five years shut away in a library.'

'But I thought it was your dream job, Fred,' I ribbed him. 'Weren't you passionately in love with the Dewey Decimal System?'

'I wouldn't call it love, exactly,' he told me. 'More like a drunken one-night stand in Vegas.'

I chuckled. 'How come?'

He drew on his cigarette.

'It's like this, Craig,' he said, flicking ash. 'You wake up one morning with a god-awful hangover, a strange blonde beside you, and a cheap wedding ring on your finger. Not to mention a portrait of Elvis tattooed on your butt. And then you spend the next three decades wondering how you got yourself into such a mess, because divorce seems like more trouble than it's worth.'

I threw back my head and laughed.

'You make it sound very glamorous,' I told him, recovering.

294

'I'm just talking it up in case you were thinking of trying it for yourself.'

'I'll pass, thanks.'

'Shame,' Fred said. 'A loss to the profession. But speaking of blondes, how's things going with yours, if you don't mind me asking? You asked her out on a date yet?'

'What blonde's that, then?' I asked, trying to keep my voice neutral.

Behind his beard, Fred's expression changed into something that may have been a small smile.

'Oh you know, Craig. That slip of a girl who's had her eye on you for the last ten days ... Katarina, or whatever her name is.'

I swore loudly.

'How the hell did you know about that?'

'I'm a trained librarian, Craig. Don't you know we have access to all the knowledge in the world?'

'Right,' I said bitterly. 'And let me guess. You read that in a periodical – *Beach Rumours Monthly.*'

'Let's just say a little bird told me.'

'That wouldn't have been a little bird with a big beer belly, would it?' I asked, scowling. 'And an even bigger mouth?'

'Sometimes even librarians have to protect their sources. But never mind that. What I want to know is what's happening with you two. Have you asked her out yet?'

'Sort of,' I said grudgingly. 'I'm meeting up with her tonight.'

Fred gave a small whoop of triumph.

'Good for you, Craig!' he exclaimed. 'I knew you had it in you!'

'Oh give it a rest, will you?' I protested. 'Christ, the way everybody's going on you'd think it was the first time anybody had ever kissed a girl.'

'I bet it's the first time you've kissed one as gorgeous as her,' he replied, giving me a wink. 'Let me tell you, I'm jealous. And I've been married a lot, as my accountant can sadly testify. So speaking as a man of experience, let me give you a bit of advice, Craig: it's never too early to bring up the subject of a pre-nuptial agreement.'

'I'll be sure to mention it tonight,' I promised.

'You do that,' Fred replied. 'Oh!' he added, raising a finger.

'Before I forget, I brought something with me today. Thought you might like it.'

'What's that then?' I asked, intrigued.

He leaned over to rummage through his bag. After a few seconds he pulled out a hardback book and held it up with a flourish.

'*Oedipus The King*,' he told me proudly. 'Best tragedy ever written, if you ask me.'

I looked at the volume curiously.

'That's the Greeks, right?'

'Sophocles, to be precise. About 2,500 years ago.'

'I'm always keen to read the latest bestseller,' I said dryly, taking it from him.

'Oh come now, Craig,' Fred chided, 'don't play the philistine with me. It doesn't suit you.'

'Hey!' I protested, hurt. 'I mean, I haven't read it or anything, but doesn't the main character murder his father, sleep with his mother, then stab his own eyes out in remorse? Bit melodramatic, wouldn't you say?'

'If you ask me it's no crazier than half the stuff you read in the newspapers every morning. And besides – strip away the good writing from most great stories and what're you left with? Pretty much all melodrama anyway, isn't it? The difference between bad soap opera and good art is the quality of the writing, not the essence of plot, wouldn't you say?'

I scratched my chin, pondering this.

'I suppose so,' I said at last.

'Course it is, Craig,' he said, slapping the arm of the chair for emphasis.

'Well thanks. I mean it. And I'll give it a go, but it might take a while. I'm still finishing *Moby Dick*.'

'Fine. There's no hurry. Just get it back to me before you fly home.'

'I will,' I promised, putting the book on the ground beside me. 'So, did you have a good walk today?'

'Oh yes,' Fred replied, stretching lazily. 'Beats working. And it's better for the digestion than playing chess.'

'What was the subject this time then? Philosophy? History? Or did you finally manage to solve the mystery of human existence?'

'No,' he admitted with a shrug. 'But I like having the time to be able to think about that kind of thing.'

'You should write it all down, Fred, publish it in a book.'

'Thanks, Craig. But I'm afraid the writer's life isn't for me. Too much like hard work. I'd rather enjoy my retirement. But what about you? You're a young man just starting out in life. Have you ever considered writing as a career?'

'Me?' I asked, surprised.

'Of course,' Fred said breezily. 'I mean, you love books, don't you? And you're studying literature. And apparently you don't want to be a librarian.'

'It's a nice idea, I suppose. But I haven't the first clue what I'd write about.'

'But what about life!' Fred exclaimed, with a look of mock horror. 'What about the world! What about the Human Condition!'

I shook my head helplessly. 'I wouldn't even know where to start.'

'Well make something up, damn it! People do it all the time.'

'I see what you're saying,' I said, shifting in my seat. 'It's just I can't imagine what, exactly. I mean, what on earth have I got to write about?'

Fred raised his hands and opened them to take in the view before us.

'What, this? The job you mean? The beach?'

'Start with what you know, they say. And take it from there.'

'But nothing ever happens here.'

Fred gave me a sceptical look.

'So nothing happened today?'

'Well, nothing worth writing about.'

'So what you're saying,' Fred persisted, jabbing his cigarette at me. 'Is that nothing – nothing at all – happened today?'

'No, I'm not saying that. Stuff happened, but it wouldn't exactly make a story. And doesn't a book have to be a story?'

'Obviously you've never read Proust,' Fred replied, exhaling a stream of smoke and leaning over to stub out the butt. 'But if you must have a story, make something up.'

'Like what?'

Fred puffed his cheeks, then pointed down at the book he'd brought.

'A tragedy, for example. Like *Oedipus* there.'

I gave a short laugh.

'You make it sound easy.'

'Well, maybe not easy, but at least you'd have a framework: the essential elements of Tragedy. You know those, don't you?'

'The essential elements of Tragedy,' I repeated blankly. 'What are they then?'

Fred gave me an incredulous look.

'Don't you learn anything at that university of yours?'

'Of course,' I said, smiling. 'I've learned how to skip classes, play pool, and drink beer from a bucket. And I'm not even in my final year yet.'

'All useful skills in life, no doubt. But perhaps I should enlighten you.' He reached into his shirt pocket for another cigarette. 'Okay,' he said, clicking his lighter shut and blowing smoke. 'The main elements in classical tragedy are as follows. Listen carefully, Craig.'

'I'll take notes.'

He ignored this, holding up a hand and ticking off the points on his fingers.

'Five things. *One*: the action revolves around a single central character. A character of average nature, neither an unusually good person nor an unusually bad one. *Two*: this action takes place over a relatively compressed period of time. *Three*: the fortunes of this main character must go from very good to very bad. *Four*: this change occurs as a result of a mistake or wrong decision by the main character – a mistake which the Greeks called the *Hermatia*. And *Five*: The character commits this mistake because of a flaw in his nature, a normal human weakness with which the audience should be able to identify, like envy, or jealousy, or rage. Or – in the case of *Hamlet* – indecision ...'

'Yes,' I interrupted eagerly, 'Hamlet can't make up his mind, and it's through his hesitation that he loses his kingdom.'

'Exactly,' Fred acknowledged. 'He thinks too much. Not a good quality in someone with a responsibility to act. But the opposite can be true too, of course. Decisiveness can be tragic, if the decision taken is impulsive or flawed.'

'And you think I should write about that?'

'It's an option.'

I considered this, and as I did so Gerd's story rose to the surface of my mind once more. It was a story of betrayal, certainly, the betrayal of a girl who was a stranger, and the way his own State had betrayed him.

But was it a tragedy? I wondered now.

I didn't know the answer to that, and anyway, it wasn't my story to tell.

'Listen, Fred,' I said. 'Do you believe in god?'

'Whoa! Where did that come from?'

'I was talking to someone earlier, and he told me he believes in god – or a higher power, anyway. He called it a Purpose. A purpose to the universe. To life. To existence.'

'Who knows?' Fred replied, releasing a cloud of smoke. 'If you ask me we *can't* know. Trying to understand either the purpose, or the entirety, of the universe … shit, it's like an ant trying to comprehend New York City.'

'But what do you *think*?'

He pursed his lips.

'I think, in essence, that it's up to each of us to find our own purpose in life. Whether that purpose is religious belief, or something else, is up to the individual.'

'So what's your purpose?'

'To make the most of life, and do as little harm as possible.'

'So you're an atheist?'

'To the extent that I don't believe in organised religion, yes. But as to the existence of a god – or gods plural, for that matter – you should call me an agnostic.'

'This guy I was talking to,' I said at last. 'He didn't believe in organised religion either, as such. But he believed in god. Some-thing he called god, anyway. He said he found forgiveness in god. Strength as well.'

'That's one of the main reasons people embrace belief,' Fred told me. 'Of course another is fear.'

Gerd's story had been uppermost in my mind, but as Fred said this my thoughts shifted slightly, away from Gerd and towards my grandfather. I recalled again the old family tale of how his ship had gone down, and the long and awful night that followed: a night spent clinging to the charred body of a shipmate, my grandfather half-mad with horror at the thought of the depths waiting below.

And at the same time as I remembered this, I remembered too the line from *Moby Dick* that had stopped me dead that morning. The words appeared in my mind's eye, starkly outlined as if on the page:

> *The sea had jeeringly kept his finite body up, but drowned the infinite of his soul ... He saw God's foot upon the treadle of the loom, and spoke it; and therefore his shipmates called him mad. So man's insanity is heaven's sense.*

My grandfather's shipmates had sung hymns in the water, their voices carrying up to the stars. Had my grandfather prayed that night? Had he prayed to god – some higher power – to save him?

Yes, I thought. Surely he had. Wouldn't anybody?

'So what happens,' I asked Fred now, my brow furrowing as I tried to unravel the confusion of my thoughts. 'If you can't find god? If it turns out that belief is beyond you, under any circumstances. What happens if you just *can't* believe?'

'Well,' Fred said, leaning back in his chair and sighing heavily. 'I suppose you'd be left struggling with what you might call the classic existential burden, and all the dread and angst that comes with it.'

'Which is?'

He shrugged.

'That there is no higher power. And no overarching, god-given morality to guide us in our lives. We have to choose our own purpose and morality. We exist in the world only through the choices that we make, and we can never disclaim those choices, nor the consequences that follow from them.'

I closed my eyes in concentration and tried, with painful effort, to follow my thoughts clearly

'And what happens,' I asked now, 'if you embrace that responsibility, if you do accept it and create a purpose for yourself, and struggle to live up to that purpose. But then, after all that – after you've invested everything you have into that purpose you've created for yourself – what happens then ... What happens if ...'

I trailed off, unable to get the words out – unable to face up to the conclusion they were leading to.

'Go on,' Fred prompted.

I looked at him, feeling my face redden and twist as I did so.

'Well!' I burst out. 'I mean, after all that ... Fucking hell, what happens if you *fail*!'

Fred didn't reply at first, waiting until the brief cry of my last word was carried away on the wind. He studied me calmly, then to my surprise he suddenly grinned and reached over to clap me on the knee.

'Honestly, Craig. You remind me of myself at your age. You take life a little too seriously. And the only piece of advice I can give you, son, is that it's good to think, but it's bad to take life too seriously.

'After all, whatever happens, at least you'll have something to write about!'

Fred didn't stay much longer after that. He took his leave, saying he had to meet up with a friend for dinner. I walked a little way down the path with him, shaking his hand and thanking him again for the book.

'My pleasure,' he said, grinning. 'Hope you enjoy it.'

'I'm sure I will.'

'Oh,' he said, stopping abruptly. 'And I'm supposed to give you a message from Bernward. I bumped into him on the dyke and he told me to tell you that he'd be back soon.'

'You mean you saw him just now?'

'About half an hour ago, maybe,' Fred said nodding. 'He was heading to the shop. Going to buy some sailing magazine or something.'

'I thought he was sorting out a problem in the dunes,' I said slowly. 'But I guess not.'

'You have a good time with that girl of yours. I'll swing by tomorrow.'

'Great. See you then.'

I waved as he headed off, then returned to the tower. It was getting late and I knew that the plastic chairs wouldn't be needed any more, so I took them inside, piling one on top of the other against the far wall. I emerged into the sunlight once more and stood at the railing to check the beach. All the kayaks were back on shore now, pulled up in a ragged row at the waterline, although two of my surf rigs were still in use beyond the second sandbank. I made a mental note to call them in soon, but decided to get the rubber tyres and other paraphernalia stored away first.

Holger was back on the beach too, talking to his mother and her friends as they made their preparations to leave. The sun umbrella I'd given them earlier had been folded up and was lying on the ground, and I watched as Holger tucked it neatly under his arm. Then he grabbed the two chairs they'd been using, one in each hand, and began crossing the sand with them.

'Hey,' I said, as he broached the crest. 'You have any luck with that girl in the bikini?'

'Early days,' he replied, panting a little from exertion. 'But you never know. There's always hope.'

'No problems this afternoon?' I asked.

'Nah. The usual stuff. Some of your surfers are pretty keen, though.'

'I saw. I'll call them in soon. But they're doing all right, don't you think?'

'They're having fun.'

'Good. I'll get the tyres back up, and the kayak paddles.'

'Okay. I'll speak to Gerd about getting the volleyball net cleared away.'

We descended the path together and parted at the bottom. I crossed to the kayaks and began gathering up the paddles, as many as I could carry at once. I saw that my remaining pupils had begun towing their rigs back to shore, so I crossed to the water's edge, waiting for them to reach the first sandbank.

I was just about to start moving through the shallows to help lift the rigs when a heavy, stinging blow struck me across the back of my head. I twisted round, angry and ready to shout, and almost knocked into Bernward. He'd come up behind me and was standing there, glaring, with a tightly rolled up magazine in one hand.

'Ow,' I said, reaching up to rub my scalp. 'That bloody hurt, Bernward.'

'Serves you right,' he replied bluntly. 'Why the hell haven't you got this stuff cleared away yet?'

I glanced at my watch, defensively. It was only quarter to five.

'Christ Bernward,' I protested. 'We've still got half an hour.'

He sniffed, unimpressed at this argument.

'And in the meantime our stuff could get damaged or lost. Not to mention the fact that it looks unprofessional. If the equipment's not being used it should be tidied away. You know that, Craig. Sort it out.'

'I was about to, Bernward,' I said fiercely. 'That's why I'm down here.'

He gave me another meaningful glare and walked off, heading for the tower.

'Hey!' I called at his back, still angry. 'Did you check for that wasps' nest in the dunes, Bernward? Like you promised?'

'Too busy,' he said dismissively, over his shoulder. 'I'll do it tomorrow.'

I stood there, grinding my teeth as he walked away.

'Fucking great,' I muttered. He'd only spent about two hours on the beach the whole day, and now he was giving me shit again.

The children were struggling with the rigs so I splashed through the shallows to help.

By the time we had the second board on the sand, Holger had rounded up Gerd and some of the teenagers to help with the kayaks. Together they began carrying them over to the stands and hoisting them up to store them.

I turned my attention to my pupils.

'Well done,' I told them. 'You all did well today. You should be proud of yourselves. Take off your wetsuit jackets and hang them on the fence, and then get dried off. I'll take care of the equipment, okay?'

They scampered away and I turned my attention to the rigs for the next ten minutes.

I dumped the last load of equipment next to the cage entrance and paused, reaching up to wipe a film of sweat from my forehead.

I'd had enough for the day. All I wanted now was a hot dinner, a long scalding shower and a few hours of sleep before meeting up with Katarina. A nap would give me some energy, I hoped, and the massage that she'd promised me earlier, which I'd assumed was just an excuse for meeting up, was seeming more and more attractive.

I was about to count the spades when my attention was caught by agitated voices coming from the dune path. I turned in time to see Bernward, flanked by Anja and another female *Betreuer*, appearing at the crest. The girls were appealing to him in distressed tones, and the old man was trying to calm them.

'I'm telling you,' Anja was saying. 'They're missing! Nobody's seen them for an hour or more. And the last time anybody did spot them they were way out in the water!'

Bernward was shaking his head.

'You're getting worked up over nothing,' he replied in an irritated tone. 'They've wandered away up the beach and no one's realised, that's all. They'll be back before you know it. Happens all the time. You can't keep track of everyone. It's not your fault. They'll turn up soon enough.'

I straightened up, wiping sand from my hands, and started towards them.

'I'm telling you!' Anja repeated. 'They're missing! And the last time anyone saw them they were out in the water!'

'What's up?' I asked, joining them.

Anja turned to me immediately, sensing an ally.

'Petra's missing,' she said quickly. 'And another girl too. One of her friends. They were out in the water, but it looks like no one's seen them for an hour or more.'

'Petra?' I asked. 'You mean the politician's daughter? The one who hurt her head when the mast fell on her?'

Anja's eyes went wide and her hand shot to her mouth.

'Oh my god!' she exclaimed, horrified. 'That's right! She might have had concussion or something! And we let her stay out there!'

'Calm down!' Bernward looked alarmed at the turn the conversation was taking. 'Nobody's drowned, for god's sake. They've just wandered off somewhere. They'll be back soon, you'll see.'

Both girls began to protest again and after a moment he raised his hands in partial surrender.

'Look, if it'll make you feel better, we'll check, okay? It's a waste of time, but we'll have a look. Craig,' he added, turning to me and for once speaking politely, 'do me a favour and get the binoculars, will you?'

I took the steps two at a time, grabbed the binoculars from the window sill and brought them down to him. He raised the glasses to his eyes, studying the water. After a minute or so he lowered them again.

'Nothing,' he said, shrugging. 'Even if they were out there, under the surface, it's shallow enough that we'd see something. But there's nothing. They're not in the water.'

'Mind if I check?' I asked, reaching for the binoculars. He yielded them reluctantly and I focused on the water below. I knew that Bernward was right, of course – we probably would be able see them. Even if they were on the bottom they'd show up as shadows.

But not if the bodies were tangled up in the lines of seagrass, I thought. *We might not see them then. And not if they were in the depths beyond the swimming area either.*

I was staring hard through the lenses, and it took me a moment to register what Anja was telling Bernward.

'They got bored with the surfing practice this afternoon,' she was saying. 'So they started playing with one of the tyres. They were quite far out. And that was the last time anybody remembers seeing them.'

These words clicked belatedly into place in my head, and as they did so my mouth fell open and my arm dropped a little, as if the weight of the binoculars was suddenly too much. I turned towards Anja.

'They had one of the tyre rings?'

'That's right.'

A horrible suspicion was unfolding within me. I crossed hurriedly to the cage, ducking inside. The inflated inner tubes that I'd brought up from the beach were wedged together on one side, but I hadn't bothered to count them before putting them away, and I saw immediately that there were only three – one less than

305

there should have been. I yanked the rings apart, checking behind them, then crawled further into the cage and bundled aside the plastic tubs containing the wetsuits, hoping to find the fourth.

It wasn't there.

I swore quietly, backing out of the cage and running up the steps of the tower again. At the top I leaned over the railings and raised the binoculars once more, training them on the line of buoys at the edge of our water.

Bernward came up the steps behind me. The two girls hovered uncertainly at the bottom, trading worried glances.

'What is it?' Bernward asked.

'I saw them earlier,' I said tersely. 'Out with the rubber tyre ring near the buoys. I pointed them out to Holger, and he said I should keep an eye on them. But with all the other stuff I had to do today I just forgot, damn it.'

Bernward ran a hand through his hair.

'Ach, it's nothing,' he repeated, but there was suddenly less conviction in his voice.

I was still studying the water, working at the focus on the binoculars to get the image as sharp as I could. Eventually my gaze settled on something next to the boundary buoy that lay directly in front of the tower, a small, dark shape about two feet long, flat in the water and difficult to see clearly, but it seemed too dark to be a shadow.

'There!' I said, pointing and handing Bernward the binoculars. I was already heading down the steps as he raised them to his face. Passing the girls, I reached down and grabbed one of the kayak paddles.

'If they got into difficulties they're dead already,' Bernward called. 'There's no point panicking.'

I saw the girls' faces whiten in shock as they took this in. For my own part I knew he was right and I felt a leaden sensation spread through my stomach. Something must have shown in my expression, because Bernward's tone immediately softened and he turned to address the girls.

'Listen,' he said calmly. 'Don't worry. Our water's safe enough. If there'd been any trouble somebody would've noticed or heard something. It's easy to lose track of a couple of kids when there's so many on the beach. I'm sure they just wandered off. But I know you're concerned, so to be on the safe side Craig will go out and check the water, just to make sure. In the meantime you should get some of your colleagues together and have a look for them, okay? I'm quite sure they'll turn up safe and sound.'

The girls nodded uncertainly and at a signal from Bernward I left them and ran down the beach. Our two racing kayaks were still on the shoreline and I sprinted to the nearest one, grabbing it by the prow and towing it into the water. As soon as I'd dragged it across the first sandbank I held it steady and hopped in, dropping into the seat with a slight wobble and settling myself. I used the paddle to push off from the sandbank, then swung it around in front of me and leaned into the first strokes, attacking the water with the blades.

Behind me I was aware of a small commotion on the beach, as the girls began calling together the other *Betreuer* to begin a land search and curious teenagers gathered at the shoreline.

It took me about a minute and a half to reach the buoy, and I was sweating with effort and fear the whole time.

As I came closer I saw that the shadow I'd spotted from the tower was indeed our missing rubber tyre, deflated now and floating forlornly on the right side of the white plastic ball. I aimed the prow of the kayak at the left side, and as I drew level with it I leaned over and plunged my arm into the water, grabbing the anchor chain in order to come to a halt. I steadied the kayak, then clutched at the black rubber tubing, lifting it up. Part of it was caught in the chain and my fingers fumbled for a moment as I tried to untangle it.

When it came free I swung the kayak to put myself in profile to the beach and held the loose rubber strip up in front of me, jiggling it in my hand. I could see the small dark form of Bernward on the tower's top step, silhouetted against the blue sky, and knew he'd be watching through the binoculars. Once I was sure he'd seen it I threw down the rubber ring and my kayak paddle and, taking two deep breaths, I heaved my body sideways and rolled the vessel over, plunging beneath the surface.

As soon as I was fully submerged I slid free of the kayak and grabbed the buoy's anchor chain, pulling myself a few feet lower and looking around. Without goggles my vision was blurry, but I was familiar with the sensation and knew I'd be able to see well enough.

The first things I noted were the jellyfish. There were five or six of them, floating at different levels, the bell-curves of their bodies billowing like animate flowers. The sea bed, fifteen feet down, was mostly sand, scattered with pebbles and a few clumps of large stones, but to my left there was a large, ragged patch of seagrass growing on the bottom. This took up an area about thirty feet long and twelve feet wide, the thick green fronds bending and rippling in the slight current. Something in the midst of these fronds caught my eye, but my heart was still pounding from the effort of paddling the kayak and already I had to breathe.

I arched my back and kicked upwards, breaking the surface with a gasp. I filled my lungs quickly and ducked under again, swimming down towards the seagrass as fast as I could, the light seeping away above me as I descended.

The waving fronds formed a dark mass, but I could see something protruding from them that was darker still. I kicked my way over to this and reached down, dragging it out from between the weeds. It came free with a slow tug of resistance and I held it up, raising it towards the shafts of light spearing down through the gloom.

It was a wetsuit jacket – child's size – and a mass of bubbles escaped from my mouth as I cried out in fright.

This time I broke the surface in a panic, reaching my free arm to grab the overturned hull of the kayak. But the hull was an awkward shape and I slid off, knocking my chin painfully as I did so. The best I could do was tread water and try to raise the jacket above me for a few seconds, before slinging it over the kayak in the hope that Bernward would see it there. Then I heaved in another few breaths and doubled over, heading down again.

Now as I descended I was looking for something pale: something light or marbled floating among the fronds, and hoping desperately as I did so that I wouldn't find it. I could see nothing unusual as I approached, so I steeled myself and kicked down towards the mass of vegetation. The seagrass was about five feet

308

high and as I moved into it the tendrils parted around my body and closed over me again, swallowing me whole.

It was dark among the weeds, the light barely penetrated, and my movement caused swirls of sediment and algae to stir from the bottom and rise up around me like a mist. I grasped the fronds, slick against my palms, and pulled myself forward, my head darting frantically right and left. I moved blindly ahead, small bubbles escaping from my mouth and brushing my cheeks.

I'd covered about half of the patch, perhaps, zigzagging from right to left and back again – terrified the whole time of what I was expecting to bump into – when something large and long suddenly thrashed against my right arm with wild energy and shot along the underside of my body. Even as it broke contact I was already heading up in mindless panic. I was halfway to the surface before I understood it must have been an eel, a big one, but by then it was too late to go back.

I could see the shadow of the kayak above me as I rose, the sunlight fragmenting around it, and I burst through into the air about ten feet away from it. The glare was too much after the darkness below, and I squeezed my eyes shut momentarily, choking for breath as I struggled to keep my head above the surface. I already knew I would have to go down again and I dreaded it. But I was steeling myself, about to do so, when a piercing shout broke through the fog in my head.

'CRAIG!'

I managed to raise a hand to shade my eyes, squinting against the water and the sun.

The dark form of another kayak was sloughing through the water towards me, about twenty metres away. A familiar, bulky form protruded from the cockpit, and I realised it was Holger just as he yelled across the water again.

'CRAIG!'

'Over here!' I called, my voice small and sputtering. Then a low swell slapped into the back of my head and my face dipped under the surface. I struggled up again, coughing and spitting water.

'I found a wetsuit jacket!' I gasped. 'They're down there, man!'

Holger was almost upon me, the kayak surging forwards and sending up a small spray from under the prow. Just when I thought it was going to collide with my head he lifted his paddle and jabbed a blade down to the left, slowing the craft and swinging it sideways. His timing was expert and the kayak came to a halt at a point where I was able to grab the side of the cockpit. He reached for my arm and gripped it tightly, leaning over. I looked up, ready to pull him into the water to continue the search with me. But then I saw the expression on his face and I halted in dismay.

For a second I thought he was choking, but then the noise coming from his mouth penetrated the water in my ears and I realised that he was laughing.

'No they're not,' he said at last, his shoulders shaking. 'They're on the beach, mate. They're fine. Honestly, they're fine.'

I looked up at him with dumb incomprehension.

'They're fine,' he managed again. 'They were hiding in the dunes . . . It was a prank.'

'A prank?'

He nodded, trying to get his laughter under control.

'A joke, Craig . . . They were playing a joke . . . And fuck . . . they got you good.'

Holger watched as the expression changed on my face and then he collapsed back against his seat, guffawing.

'You think this is funny?' I demanded, flushed with anger. 'I thought they were dead, for fuck's sake! I thought they'd fucking *drowned*!'

Holger let go of my arm to wipe away the tears at the corners of his eyes.

'Oh priceless,' he said. 'Brilliant . . . We'll be talking about this one for years.'

I lifted my fist and punched the hull of the kayak, hard.

'You'll be talking about how I strangled the little fuckers,' I said fiercely. 'How I beat them to death with a shovel.'

That was too much for Holger. He was laughing so much he couldn't speak.

'And screw you too, Fatso.'

Holger shook his head. 'Okay,' he said at last, wiping his eyes again and calming a little. 'All right . . . So how do you want to do this? Do you want to try getting back into your kayak?'

I bit my lip. It would be a very difficult manoeuvre and I realised it wasn't worth it. I turned my face away and spat in the water.

'No point,' I said. 'Too much hassle.'

'So what then? Want me to tow it?'

For a moment I considered dragging him into the water anyway, but it would just mean that we'd both have to swim our crafts back to shore.

'Okay,' I said, reluctantly. 'I'll hook it on your stern.'

I swam over to my kayak and grasped hold of the small loop of rope projecting from the top of the prow as Holger backpaddled his vessel towards me. There was a similar loop through the stern of his, and I tied the two together awkwardly. The loops weren't long, and when I'd finished my kayak was tilted sideways, but at least Holger would be able to tow it back to the beach.

I pulled the child's wetsuit jacket from the hull of my craft and tossed it to him. He caught it and placed it in his lap.

'Race you?' he teased.

'Right.' I waved at him dismissively. 'On you go. I'll catch you up.'

'Whatever you say, hero.'

I watched as he started off, then lay back in the water and spread my limbs, staring up into the blue of the sky and swearing under my breath.

I floated there for several minutes. At last my anger started to fade, replaced by an all-consuming tiredness in my body and mind.

I knew that I'd have to swim back eventually, and I tried to cheer myself a little by thinking about Katarina. But it was the fact that I was starting to feel cold that finally prodded me into action. With a small groan I rolled over onto my front and began to swim a slow, heavy breaststroke. The movement warmed me a little and gave me heart, and after twenty metres or so I'd roused myself enough to break into a more respectable front crawl.

I was expecting a small crowd to be waiting on the beach, all ready to enjoy the joke at my expense, but as I hauled myself from the water and trudged onto the first sandbank I saw with relief that everybody had dispersed. The kids were packing up their belongings under the direction of the *Betrauer* leaders, while the family of sunburned strangers had already departed, leaving behind only scuff marks where they'd spent the afternoon between our stands. Edith and her colleagues had gone as well, and the volleyball net had been dismantled and removed. The beach looked clean enough, free of litter apart from a couple of damp, unclaimed towels.

I was surprised that Bernward wasn't there to gloat, but as I walked onto the beach I saw that he was helping Holger with the task of storing away our two racing kayaks. I ignored them both and made my way up to the tower, keeping my head down and my gaze fixed on the ground in front of me.

The surf masts were still propped against the fence, where I'd left them, so I decided to deal with them first. The sails were dry now, so I picked up each mast in turn, flapping the sails out a few times to remove the remaining sand, then rolled them tightly around the masts. I used the dangling boom cords to tie the sails in place before sliding each mast into the plastic pipes in the stand and replacing the lids.

I secured the stand and started up the steps, picking up the skegs and fins on the way and dumping them in the sea chests. Pausing, I took a moment to look at my watch. It was twenty past five – only a few minutes after our locking up time. I fished out a tin of oil and an old rag from the sea chest, then emerged from the tower. I could see Katarina at the top of the dune path, coming towards me. I stopped and looked at her in surprise as she smiled uncertainly.

'Hi,' she said now.

'Hi.'

'How you doing?'

'Me?' I shrugged. 'Fine? How are you?'

'I wanted to apologise,' she said. 'For that stupid little stunt Petra just pulled on you.'

'Oh that.' I sighed. 'Don't worry about it. It's no big deal. I'm just glad they're okay. For a moment there I thought they weren't. Besides, I needed the exercise.'

'Well it's not okay,' Katarina said firmly, pursing her lips. 'As far as we're concerned, it's the last straw with that girl. She had Anja worried to death. I think she really thought the little brat had drowned. And to top it all I just tried to get Petra up here to apologise to you, and she refused point blank. So that's it. As soon as we get back to camp we're going to phone her mother and ask her to come and pick her up. Petra's finished here. We're not putting up with her spoiled little princess act any more.'

I nodded slowly, taking this in.

'You mean tonight?' I asked carefully, trying to keep the note of disappointment from my voice. 'Does that mean you'll have to stay at the camp to talk to her mother?'

Katarina studied me for a moment, and as she did so her face opened into a broad smile. She reached out a hand and placed it flat on my chest, just over my heart.

'No, silly,' she said, shaking her head. 'First thing in the morning. We're still on for tonight, if you want. I've spoken to Anja and she's okay covering for me, although I won't be free until eleven or so. That's all right, isn't it?'

I returned her gaze, aware of the warmth of her hand on my skin and feeling my tiredness slough off me.

'Sure,' I said. 'Definitely.'

A faint colour came to her cheeks and she dropped her eyes. Then she stood on tiptoe, glancing down towards the beach, before putting her arm around my neck and kissing me on the lips. I reached for her, but she pulled away, stepping back.

She raised her palm and kissed it, blowing the kiss towards me, then turned and walked away. I stood there, staring after her as she vanished down the path, with no more sense in my head than a plank of wood. But after a few seconds I collected myself, reaching for the spade that I'd found lying in the water earlier. I sat down awkwardly on the steps, the spade across my knees. Making an effort to focus my thoughts, I pulled the lid off the spout of the tin and poured a goodly amount of liquid onto the rag. I placed the tin on the step beside me and set to work oiling the metal blade, whistling softly through my teeth and smiling to myself as I did so.

When I'd finished the job to my satisfaction I set the rag down, raising the spade in front of me to admire the way it gleamed smoothly in the sun. I plugged the lid back on the tin's spout and hopped off the steps. I was still whistling as I approached the pile of spades dumped near the cage entrance. I chucked the one I was holding into the cage and began sliding the others in after it, counting them absentmindedly in my head as I did so. I finished the task and stood up, about to turn away, but then stopped suddenly and trailed off into silence, frowning slightly.

I was two spades short.

Surprised – sure I'd miscounted – I crouched back down and counted them quickly a second time, touching each with my finger as I did so. There were ten spades, just as I'd thought. But there should have been twelve.

I straightened and swept my eyes over the ground around me in case I'd missed any. But the sand was bare, so I stepped to the rear of the tower and checked the space there. It was empty. Which meant that the spades must still be on the beach somewhere, and I'd have to go down again to get them.

Irritated at this final nuisance, I turned and moved past the steps to the wire fence beyond, and from that vantage point let my gaze run over the strand to see where they might be lying.

The kids were all gathered in a single large group now, about ten metres to the right of our upturned rowing boats, while the *Betreuer*, including Katarina, were double-counting heads to make sure everyone was there. Holger and Bernward were nearby, beside the waterline, chatting to Gerd and reaching out to shake his hand as he took his leave.

Otherwise though, the beach was empty. It was churned from the activity of the day and dotted with holes, but empty. I couldn't see the spades anywhere. I stood there, my mind blank and heavy with tiredness, trying to think where they might be.

A memory was just beginning to glimmer within me – rising up in the back of my mind – when I heard the first, piercing scream. It came from a point somewhere further up the beach, far to my left and out of sight behind the tower. And it was followed immediately by two more.

It was a woman screaming – shrieking as if she was being stabbed. I stood stiff with shock, then fell forwards against the fence, stretching my body across the wire as far as I could, almost toppling over, looking in the direction of the noise. As I did so the figure of the Pit bull owner's wife suddenly appeared, still

314

naked apart from her thong. She was rushing panic-stricken down the beach, waving her arms helplessly before her as she stumbled, almost drunkenly, across the sand. I watched her for an instant in disbelief. I was just straightening up and taking a step backwards when she screamed again.

And everything that happened next, in the following twenty seconds, seemed to happen very slowly. I looked away from the woman, towards the waterline, and realised that Holger and Bernward were shouting at me, yelling at the tops of their voices, their hands cupped around their mouths and urgency straining their limbs. Gerd was moving over the sand, heading for the tower in great leaping strides, but at the same time the horror of knowledge was rising within me, paralysing me, and I was both aware and yet not aware of what was happening. I could hear the shouts quite plainly, Bernward's words were perfectly clear, but something – something in my head or in my chest – somehow blocked the message. I looked to my left, and as my neck turned it felt as if I was moving underwater. I could see the woman running down the beach, I could see her trip and fall heavily and then get up again, still screaming, and all I noted in that moment was the ridiculous bouncing of her breasts. And I saw too that Holger was moving now, running flat out towards her in slow motion. Then I blinked and Gerd was halfway up the path towards me, but I still hadn't moved although Holger was closing on the woman and sprinting like a fat Apollo for the dunes. The woman was on her knees again, clawing at her neck and screaming hysterically at the sky. Bernward was still shouting, but it seemed as though I couldn't hear him, I couldn't hear the words because of the pounding of my heart, but it didn't matter because I already knew what he was yelling. I knew everything then, in that instant, and I think I'd known it even before he and Holger had raised their hands to shout at me. I'd known it from the moment I'd heard the woman's first scream. And maybe I'd known it even before that.

Bernward was shouting: 'BRING THE SPADES! FOR CHRIST'S SAKE BRING THE SPADES!'

And then Gerd was over the crest of the path and his body slammed past me, knocking my shoulder with his own. I was still staggering back with the force of it as he ducked down at the cage entrance, then suddenly he had two spades in each big hand and was pushing past me again, pelting down the dune path with his arms outflung, trying to keep his balance, slip-sliding onto the sand as he tore after Holger, with Bernward staggering behind in their wake.

And then – at last – I began to run. Fifty thousand volts of terror blasted through me and I shot forward, flying down the path, grabbing the wooden post at the bottom to check my momentum and swing myself round to the left. The speed of my arc and the force of my grip pulled the post from its root and left it sagging, ripping a broad flap of skin from my palm as it did so, but I sped on unheeding, my fingernails digging into the bloody pulp as I narrowed the gap on the others ahead.

I tore past Bernward just beyond our stands, registering him only as a vague presence. As my vision blurred and my legs and arms pumped like pistons, I lengthened my stride even further, clinging to the desperate hope that there might still be time. The beach seemed to elongate and recede in front of me, falling away down a darkening tunnel, and everything was silent, as if I'd gone deaf. I dropped my face, staring blindly at the sand, trying to wring every last bit of effort from myself. Just as I thought my body was about to burst my head shot back and I gasped in great sucking lungfuls of air.

My sight cleared, and a few metres in front of me I saw Gerd, struggling to duck through the wire strands of the dune fence, dragging the spades behind him, while the tethered Pit bull strained and leapt and barked against the tautness of its leash. Holger was already halfway up the face of the slope, straining against the incline.

I hurled myself at the fence, slapping my torn hand down on the nearest post and shooting my legs sideways, clearing the wire with ten inches to spare. But I landed off balance and stumbled to my right, knocking against Gerd as he straightened up. For a moment I grabbed his upper arm and clutched it, steadying us both; then, as he regained his balance, I reached down and grabbed the two spades from his left hand, and started up the slope in front of me.

It was steeper than it looked. My feet sank into the surface, sending rivulets of sand cascading down behind me. There wasn't much scrub, and with a spade in each hand I couldn't use the grass to pull myself forwards. I was almost on my knees as I caught up with Holger at the summit and looked over.

The far side of the dune sloped away at a sharp angle. There was a narrow gully at the bottom, about five feet wide, before the next row of dunes began. These were higher than the ridge I was on, and in turn rose up towards yet a third row behind them and the elevated dyke beyond. There was a lot more scrub in this area and I could see paper wrappings and other litter trapped amongst it, and the dull glint of broken glass and weathered aluminium cans poking from the sand. A little to the left in the gully I saw the charred remnants of a fire, and beside it a single spade lay inverted on the ground, dropped or abandoned, and I realised with horror it was one of ours.

All this I understood in an instant. At the same time I took in the scuffed marks of recent tracks – footprints – all around the area, ending at the base of the dune opposite, and as I raised my gaze to this dune I saw two things: that the sandy surface wasn't smooth and flat like the others, but darker and heavily churned, for the whole front of it had recently shifted, collapsing down on itself in a small, localised landside. And I saw also that three new holes had been dug near the base, straggling diagonally one above the other, while a little above these the Pit bull owner – the man I'd argued with that morning – was frantically digging a fourth, sand flying behind him even as more tumbled down the slope to hamper his progress. Despite the hammering of my pulse in my ears I could hear his choking sobs carried to me on the breeze.

I wanted to call out to him, to let him know that help was coming, but my body was heaving for breath. Holger was slithering down the slope in front of me and I jumped after him, losing my balance, and landing in a jumbled heap in the gulley.

Holger grabbed a spade from my hand, charging forwards towards the Pit bull owner. I was trying to stand up when I heard Gerd shout from above me:

'WHERE ARE THEY?'

The man didn't look round, or break off from his frantic digging. 'I don't *know*!' he cried back in an anguished voice.

I turned my head in time to see Gerd leap the last three feet into the gully and sprint past me, dropping one of the spades he was carrying and attacking the slope with the other. He plunged the blade of it deep into the sand and pulled out a great slab of the stuff, dumping it to one side. But even as he did so the lip of the hole collapsed. I struggled upright, staring dumbly at the dune, overwhelmed by my own guilt and the hopelessness of the task. My head dropped and my shoulders sagged, and I couldn't do anything but stare at the ground as the others dug frantically above me.

I was standing there, helpless, when the footprints in the gully suddenly revealed their truth. Holger and Gerd had passed me heading straight at the dune, and I could see their tracks distinctly, while the other set of large footprints had surely been left by the father – the Pit bull owner. But there was a mess of smaller tracks, scrambled in widening circles around the remains of the fire, and I saw clearly where those traces broke off and straightened out and headed towards the dune in front of me. I swept my gaze along these tracks and looked upwards, studying the slope, and saw a patch of surface that looked slightly lighter and looser than the rest.

I raised my hand and cried hoarsely: 'THERE!'

I sprinted up the slope and fell to my knees to dig. The other three had broken off at my shout, and now they hurried awkwardly – stumbling and slipping across the incline – towards me. Holger was the first to arrive and started to dig beside me, but when the sand shifted down to hamper our progress he plunged his spade in above my own to prop up the hole. The others arrived a few moments later and did the same.

I'd hollowed out ten or fifteen spadefuls when I saw the younger boy's bare foot and ankle emerge from the sand. For a brief instant hope surged in me once more, until I reached out and grabbed his ankle to pull.

It was then that I knew, once and for all, that we were too late.

*

With hindsight, I think even at that moment I could see the vicious irony of it all, the joke that Life had played on us:

My grandfather had endured a horror of being burned alive, but wound up lost and terrified in the middle of the ocean, wishing he'd died in a fire.

Gerd had feared betraying his duty to the State, even as the State blithely tricked him into betraying himself and others.

And as for me . . .

I'd been watching the water – as always – while those children drowned in sand.

The whole time, as we dug their bodies out and the helicopter arrived, clattering above us, I knew that, unlike my grandfather, I would never be able to find some purpose in my tragedy by teaching others to survive it; nor like Gerd find relief and solace by surrendering myself up to some other, higher purpose. Because for me, at the end of that last day, there was simply nothing left to find.

And once the parents had been led away and the doctor had gone grimly through the formalities – and the police had finished steadying the two stretchers, one at a time, as they were winched into the air – I made my way slowly, numbly, back over the dunes and down to the water's edge, where I sat huddled, the waves lapping my feet, and ignored Gerd and Holger and Bernward, and Katarina too, as each of them came to me in turn and tried to console me. I'm sure I replied with words and reassurances, promises even. I must have done, for after a while they left me alone. And although I cannot remember it clearly, I think it must have been Katarina who put the blanket round my shoulders and bandaged my hand, whispering gently in my ear as she did so, while more and more people gathered near the dunes to blurt out shocked but excited comments – their muted, self-conscious hum rising inexorably to a more unseemly chatter. And as evening approached and the sun sank, a fire was built and lit; for there is no better excuse than mortality to prompt a breaking of the rules. And alcohol was drunk, perhaps medicinal at first, while food was brought and eaten. Until eventually – hours after the last school children had been hurried, questioning, back to the camp – the beach turned into the site of a wake and the wake turned into a party, although no one called it such.

All that time I sat looking out over the water, the endless empty water, watching as the stars slowly appeared and brightened in the deepening, darkening sky. Until at last, after a long, long while, I tore my gaze from the moonlight shimmering on the sea and rose stiffly, wearily, to trudge back up to the tower, where I dried myself and dressed.

I was not alone on the journey back to the camp, and I was not alone the next day, for it was Bernward who drove me first to the police station to formalise my statement, and then to the airport and the plane that took me home.

But I never saw any of them again.

The lead article from page five of a British tabloid newspaper, dated 10th April 1988:

Krauts Blame Brit for Kiddie Deaths

Two children died because a British student was drinking beer and flirting with girls instead of doing his job.

That was the finding of an official inquest in the German city of Hamburg yesterday.

British citizen Craig McInnes, 20, from Helensburgh, near Glasgow, was slammed by justice officials investigating the deaths of two young children on a German beach nine months ago.

They found him to be 'largely responsible' for events leading up to a horrific accident in August of last year.

Seven-year-old Oliver Schmidt and his brother Maximilian, 11, suffocated to death after crawling into a tunnel they'd dug in sand dunes on a beach near the northern town of Gromitz, a popular holiday resort on Germany's Baltic coast.

The roof of the tunnel collapsed on top of them, and despite frantic efforts by rescuers – including McInnes himself – both children died before they could be pulled out.

Now the inquest has laid much of the blame squarely on the shoulders of the Glasgow University student, who was working on the beach at the time as a lifeguard. It did so after hearing witnesses testify that he'd deliberately ignored an order from his employer to confiscate spades from the children prior to the accident.

He'd also been told to make sure they stayed away from the sand dunes – closed to the public – but again failed to do so.

The inquest had already established that McInnes had been drinking heavily the night before the accident, and had consumed a 'significant' amount of alcohol on the beach while on duty that day.

He'd also been spotted 'kissing and fondling' a girl he was having a holiday romance with, at a time when he should have been monitoring windsurfing pupils.

Other staff at the children's watersports centre where the tragedy happened were criticised for their lax attitude in following safety procedures on the beach.

The inquest's findings pave the way for possible criminal proceedings against McInnes and Hamburg City Council, who fund the centre.

A spokesman for the public prosecutor's office, Andreas Mann, said yesterday that some of the people involved could face charges of manslaughter arising from negligence.

He added: 'Clearly something went terribly wrong that day, and although the criminal investigation is still ongoing, I can assure people that if a crime was committed the perpetrators will be brought to trial.'

Meanwhile the dead boys' father, Wolfgang Schmidt, 37, immediately vowed that he wouldn't rest until those responsible are behind bars.

He said: 'Ever since my sons died on that beach people have been trying to claim it was just a simple accident. But there was criminal negligence involved and the people responsible should be in jail.'

McInnes himself was not available to give evidence at the inquest. He's currently receiving psychiatric treatment following a nervous breakdown he apparently suffered in the wake of the incident.

The student's grandfather, 74-year-old Gordon McInnes – the only member of the family to attend the two-day inquest – refused to comment on the verdict yesterday.

Epilogue

It's been five years since I left, but even now when I close my eyes I can see the tower as it looked from the beach at the end of each day: a black form rearing up from the dunes; its windows, lidded by propped-open shutters, gazing blindly out over the darkening sea. At such moments I don't need to hold a shell to my ear in order to hear the low sloshing of the surf or the sound of the breeze swishing through the dune grass, and if I draw in my breath I can still smell the great, clean, living smell of the sea and taste the salt of it in the air.

It brings it all back. Everything:

The sound of wailing behind us. The sweat that ran slick as we dug. The feeling of my spade hitting that first small, still body.

These have been my memories, the wasps that stung me. The wasps in the tower.

But nothing lasts for ever. Nothing. And as I found out when my grandfather threw me into Loch Lomond all those years ago, it's only once you stop struggling that you remember how to swim. It's one of our deepest instincts, after all: just watch those babies in the birthing pools.

And I think that maybe, in recent months, I've finally begun rising upwards, floating up, rushing up ... so that I can see the lighter shades above me now, although I'm not quite there yet.

Perhaps though, one day soon, I'll burst up through the surface and take a deep, sharp, shuddering gasp at life.

Until then, I'm still holding my breath.

Author's Note

The World War Two section of this novel is overwhelmingly fiction, although my own grandfather's merchant ship was torpedoed and sunk off the coast of Africa during that war. I know little more about his story than that he survived without serious injury, but I trust he didn't suffer events like those depicted in this book. Some of the historical, technical and geographical details presented in this section are inaccurate or wholly invented, in some cases having been deliberately changed from actual facts to fit my convenience. The most glaring example – but by no means the only one – is that Germany actually lost control of all its African colonies, including the territory now known as Namibia, at the end of World War One.

It is, however, historically accurate that the British government built prison camps in Kenya in the 1950s. According to independent academic estimates, up to 320,000 native Kenyans may have been imprisoned in these camps, but only 200,000 may have been released alive. Successive British governments have disputed these figures and vigorously denied that any crimes against humanity were committed in the camps.

In 2010, after almost six decades of campaigning, a handful of survivors were given leave by the High Court in London to bring a test case against the British government seeking compensation for torture. Two male plaintiffs in the case have no genitals, and maintain that their sexual organs were cut off by white guards who were in the pay of the British government. Other plaintiffs say that they saw male friends and relatives tied to chairs, doused with petrol and burned alive. Significant numbers of other eyewitness accounts also allege that the immolation of live inmates occurred with some frequency.

The case is ongoing, but if the plaintiffs' claims are upheld legal experts expect it will open the floodgates for tens of thousands more compensation cases to be brought against the British government, either by former prisoners of the camps or the relatives of those alleged to have died there.

The Cold War story is overwhelmingly invention also, although most of the things that Stasi members are depicted doing in that story have a counterpart somewhere in historical fact. Part of the inspiration for this section originally came from something that happened to an East German friend of mine in 1987. He planned an escape attempt over the Berlin Wall, but was betrayed to the Stasi by a friend, and subsequently arrested and interrogated for three days and nights without sleep. I am grateful to him for relating his experiences – to my utter surprise and shock – one sunny day in Berlin over several beers. I'm equally grateful to him for paying for the beers.

The fact that there were approximately 30,000 spies in Berlin at any given time during the Cold War is correct according to the sources that I've read and the specialist tour guides whom I've talked to, although the terms 'Ossie' and 'Wessie' didn't come into general usage in Germany until after the Wall fell.

During Mother Teresa's lifetime she and the organisations she founded were heavily criticised by both the British Medical Association and the British *Lancet* medical journal for poor standards of treatment of patients in their care. The Reverend Mother's openly-stated policy of withholding pain relief from the terminally ill was particularly condemned. One nun who resigned from the Order published a book in which she called Mother Teresa's 'Theology of Suffering' for dying patients unacceptable.

The Stasi prison of Hohenschönhausen in Berlin has been preserved, and visitors can take official guided tours. If you take such a tour you will see the claustrophobia cell in the basement complex, although the walls of that cell are white-tile rather than rough concrete. It may be that the Stasi never filled that particular cell with water. They probably never had to. But they did use various

325

forms of water torture in other cells at Hohenschönhausen.

The radioactive liquid that Gerd paints on Freda's coat is a real substance and was sometimes used by the Stasi in surveillance operations. Some of the victims abused in this way later died of rare cancers thought to have been caused by exposure to the liquid.

The holiday camp, the beach and the lifeguard tower all exist, although certain details have been changed.

Most of the rest is fiction.

Kenneth Macleod
December 2010

Acknowledgements

The following people gave me great practical help or encouragement, or both, during the process of writing and publishing this novel.

In the UK:
My parents Rona and Norman Macleod and my sister Heather; Christine Brooks; Joyce Devenny and family; Andrew Proctor; David Lewis; Doug Cowie; David Brooks and family; Martin Brooks; John McFarlane; Neil Motion; Andrew Motion; Graeme and Ally Bell; James Sumner; Mike Simlett; my agent Peter Straus, Jen Hewson and all the staff at the RCW literary agency; my editor Kirsty Dunseath, Sophie Buchan and all the staff at Orion Books.

In Germany:
Rolf and Alexandra Hilke; Volker Jelken; Jamie Sewell and Claudia Mellisch; Mark and Vanessa Peschel; Kitty Socia; Simon Wilson; Corinne Hundleby; Matt and Corinna Slater; the wonderful Sparks family; the wonderful Scraton family.

Also the staff and owners of the excellent *Circus Hostel* and *Circus Hotel* in Berlin, who made me feel at home and gave me half-price beer and free internet to boot.

And the staff and owners of the outstanding Insider Tours company in Berlin, whose exhaustive knowledge of the city's history is so impressive and whose warm friendship was always much appreciated.

Thank you all for your help, friendship and forbearance.

With special thanks to Victoria Gosling, my best and first-choice reader, whose great enthusiasm for the book kept me going when things got most difficult.

The Incident

Reading Group Notes

About the Author

Kenneth Macleod was born in Glasgow in 1972 and began working as a newspaper reporter at the age of seventeen. He worked in the Scottish media for twelve years before completing a Masters Degree in Creative Writing at the University of East Anglia. He divided his time between Glasgow and Berlin, where he worked as a tour guide, until a year ago when he returned to Scotland to study for a PhD in Philosophy and Creative Writing.

For Discussion

- How does the author use the opening of *The Incident* to set the tone?

- 'I couldn't help reflecting that their daily labour, in attempting to impose a human order on the beach, was ultimately a waste of effort.' Did it strike you in the same way? What does the thought say about Craig?

- '"You know what your problem is?" Holger said from behind me.

  "Go on then," I said, "enlighten me."

  "Two things. First, you think too much. And second," there was the sound of clinking glass. "You don't drink enough."' Do you agree with Holger?

- What is the significance of the wasps?

- 'The problem with this world, I found myself thinking irritably, is other people.' How has Craig come to feel like this at such a young age, do you think?

- 'The intense concentration of self in the middle of such heartless immensity.' How does this quote from *Moby Dick* sit at the heart of *The Incident*?

5

- 'Everybody has a choice, Craig, one way or another. That's the curse of being human.' Is it?

- 'We spend our whole lives not thinking about the blackness that surrounds us, the debris waiting to drag us down. Or at least trying not to.' Do you?

- 'Because things in this life can change you, boy. Slowly or suddenly. Maybe not on the surface, but deep down. Deep down, where other people can't see it.' Is this what *The Incident* is about?

- 'It's only when you stop struggling that you remember how to swim.' Is this a good philosophy for life?

In Conversation with Kenneth Macleod

Q Is Craig you?

A No. He's several inches taller than me, for a start. However he is doing a summer job that I used to do and it's fair to say that some of his thoughts and concerns are similar to things I thought about at that age, and indeed still think about.

Q How did you physically write *The Incident*, and why?

A I wrote most of it electronically, first of all on an old laptop that a friend of mine was kind enough to give me and later on a PC. Because I had a day job I wrote mostly in the evenings or late at night. The reason that I wrote the book was firstly because I've wanted to be a novelist since I was nine years old – it's been my main ambition since the sad day I realised that becoming Zorro wasn't a viable career option – and secondly I thought that Craig's story would allow me to address certain philosophical themes that I was preoccupied with, in particular by using the landscape of that story as metaphor. The Second World War and Cold War stories actually came later, but I felt that, amongst other things, they allowed me to amplify those themes.

Q 'In such curious ways does our past determine our future, and those who are spared to their later years always find something to marvel at in the course their lives have taken.' Have you something to marvel at yet, or are you still too young?

A I generally think that there's lots to marvel at in life, and real life is often at least as strange as fiction. As for an example that I've experienced personally . . . well, in 1992 I walked into a small shop in Berlin to ask for directions, and as a direct consequence of that rather random act the entire course of my life changed.

Q Silence or music while you write? If music, who do you listen to?

A Silence, most definitely. In fact, I usually wear earplugs while I'm writing.

Q 'Anybody with a normal set of human weaknesses can be manipulated into a position where they'll be willing to sell out their friends or family, or neighbours or colleagues, to the State.' Do you agree with Gerd?

A To an extent. But in addition to personal weaknesses, all human beings are endowed with personal strengths, and individuals with certain combinations of moral or mental strengths cannot be manipulated in that way. A very extreme example, but an instructive one, can be found in the torture of Jehovah's Witnesses in Nazi con-

8

centration camps. Not only did most of those victims refuse to renounce their religious faith, they actually requested more torture, because they believed that their suffering was glorifying God and securing their place in heaven. Those people couldn't be intimidated – Himmler openly admired their 'fanaticism', a term he meant as a compliment – and in a similar way not everybody subjected to pressure by the Stasi to inform on their friends and family in communist East Germany actually succumbed to that pressure.

Q Which authors do you admire and why?

A If I were to give you a list of the authors that I admire, it would be a very long list indeed, but the reason for my admiration is simple in each case: they've all written terrific books. There's so many out there.

Q 'Personally I don't believe that faith, or a particular kind of faith, makes any real difference in the end.' Do you agree with Gerd here?

A Yes.

Q What single thing about you would surprise us the most?

A Although I hope that readers see some instances of humour in my book, I'm aware that much of *The Incident* is pretty intense and grim, so you might be surprised to find out that I'm someone who laughs a lot, often to the point of helplessness. Laughter is by far my favourite drug, not least because it's free.

Q Does *The Incident* have all the main elements of Classical tragedy?

A The beach story in the novel is certainly meant to conform very much to the template of Classical tragedy – to be a modern version of it – and I would like to think that it does. Really, though, I think that has to be a question for other people to decide.

Q What's your most vivid memory?

A I have many very vivid memories, and to be honest it's impossible to pick a particular one out as more vivid than all the others.

Q 'It's good to think, but it's bad to take life too seriously.' Do you agree with Fred?

A Not necessarily, although I do think that taking life very seriously – in a philosophical sense – increases the chances of an individual being unhappy for long stretches of time or even permanently. But then I also think that there are more worthy goals in life than just being happy.

Q Any clues about your next book – any snippets for us?

A The main story in the next novel is set in Scotland in the 1980s, but the book will also include an extensive Second World War flashback story. Here's hoping people like it.

Suggested Further Reading

Moby Dick
by Herman Melville

The Alchemist
by Paulo Coelho

Oedipus Rex
by Sophocles

East of Eden
by John Steinbeck

Stasiland
by Anna Funder

The Rime of the Ancient Mariner
by Samuel Taylor Coleridge

W&N
blog and newsletter

For exclusive short stories, poems, extracts, essays, articles, interviews, trailers, competitions and much more visit the Weidenfeld & Nicolson blog and sign up for the newsletter at:

www.wnblog.co.uk

Follow us on

 facebook and twitter

Or scan the code to access the website*

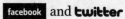